FOX DEN
BOOKS
Oregon

The Seed of Winden

Fox Den Books may be ordered through booksellers or by contacting

Fox Den Books
PO Box 39
Brightwood, OR 97011

Fox Den Books rev. date 4/4/2019

The Seed of Winden

A fantasy by

Miranda Mayer

The Seed of Winden

Miranda Mayer

www.mirandamayer.com

Model:

Hayley Stavenger

www.hayleystavenger.com

Instagram: @hayleystavenger

Editing:

Sunwalker Press

Photography and Cover Art

Feffie's Cottage

Dedications

To all the bleeding-hearts and nature-lovers, fighting the good fight.

And to Wendy Pamay, to whom *all* of my books are dedicated, stated or not. May all children have at least one teacher like Wendy Pamay in their lives.

1. Halenwood

Tammin Halenwood wiped the blood from his lip with the back of his hand, and his fiery green eyes narrowed. A sly smile formed on his mouth as his fists fell to his side, still clenched.

"Why are you smiling? I struck you!" Raynes Bellworth snarled in confusion—his fingers balling up again and rising in front of his chest. His nose was flecked with blood and his right knuckles were throbbing red from fresh gouges on the joints.

Tammin did not lift his hands. He merely grimaced at Raynes with an expression of amusement which served only to further agitate his opponent. Both of the other boys, Clemon and Hareth were terse and expectant, watching the scuffle unfold from a safe distance.

"What is there *not* to smile about? I'm about to trounce you yet again. I have the upper hand, as usual, and you will again be laughed at by everyone. You are weak. You have always been weak, and I have only proven that again and again. What I don't understand, and what everyone finds so remarkably curious about you, is that you keep coming back. Is it that you enjoy defeat and humiliation?" Tammin guffawed.

Raynes roared and threw himself at Tammin. The sixteen-year-old eastern boy with green eyes and hair as black as raven's feathers laughed merrily and sidestepped the assault with a dancing grace. The two onlookers were now snickering in amusement as well.

"I mean, you at least managed a hit in this time, so that's progress, is it not?" Tammin raffishly chided the boy, whose rage now flowed freely, making him even clumsier and slower. Tammin ducked and swerved from the fresh onslaught of lunges and swings with a flashing white smile and a twinkle in his eye. The more he joked and evaded the flying fists and inept kicks, the angrier Raynes became. His pale brow, blue eyes, and nearly white hair were a stark contrast to the younger boy. Raynes was slightly taller, a little rangier, but infinitely less agile and dexterous as the shorter, denser young fellow that Tammin was. Raynes was a full year older than his opponent. But he had yet to best him.

As if Tammin had suddenly gotten bored of this little dance, his cheery demeanor suddenly melted into open malice, but still with a haunting grin. He swept his leg at Raynes's feet as he ran at him once again, and the assemblage of long, gangly limbs crumpled to the ground. As the young man tried to regain his footing, he was met with a solid smack of a hard fist right on the cheekbone. The sound of the knuckles connecting with the boy's face was flat and staccato, and it stunned Raynes. The young man rolled onto his back, hands covering his face.

Tammin shook his hand out and blew on his knuckles, his jaunty smile now painted with a wash of odium. He straightened and reached up, his fingers tugging away the intricate folds of his cravat, yanking it out from beneath the collars of his waistcoat and shirt. Once freed, he bundled the long, white, starched fabric into a ball and used it to clean his lip and his hand, which was red with Raynes's blood.

"I imagine that settles it," he said through gritted teeth.

"I don't think so," Raynes said weakly from underneath his hands.

"No, the matter's settled," Tammin insisted. "I warn you not to contest it again." He threw the cravat onto Raynes and then glided across the grass in just a few liquid strides to where a sleek, leggy bay mare was tied to a tree along with two other horses.

"She's mine! I paid for her!" Raynes tried to clamber to his feet but failed and stumbled.

Tammin knew what it felt like to have the cheekbone struck with such force. There were most certainly stars to be seen, and a ringing, lingering agony still ebbing in Raynes's skull.

"I bought her first, Raynes. If you have issue with Vanacken taking your money for a horse that was already sold, you take it up with *him*. I'll see to it that your tack is returned to your man by the end of the day." Tammin threw himself up into the saddle after untying her lead and affixing it around her neck. He took up the reins and with a click of the tongue, he rode away.

The matter, however, was not settled as cleanly as it ought to be. It never was when it came to Tammin's father. The man found him before supper. Tammin was in the stable, admiring the horse, when his father moved on silent feet behind him, and before Tammin knew it, it was his turn to be rolling on the ground favoring his jaw.

"You fool!" Viscount Halenwood hissed. "Why must you persist in this aimless rivalry with Bellworth? Why? Idiot! You were the best of friends!" he barked, throwing back his foot and landing it with efficacy into his son's side. "Now your rivalry only serves to humiliate me at every turn. Give him the bloody horse!"

"No..." Tammin croaked through his pain, managing to roll onto his feet and stagger back from the looming figure of the Viscount. His father's blows packed a greater punch than Raynes's ever could. He imagined that this conditioning to his father's abuse was what made him so resilient against Raynes's attacks. "I paid for her. I bought her," he growled. "That snake tried to buy her from under me, bidding up her price after I'd already exchanged the money with the seller. I had already shaken Vanacken's hand. She is *mine*."

Fenwick Halenwood was an intimidating man. He loomed tall with broad shoulders and the hard face of a man who'd served with distinction as a Major General in the Hetta army during the Atlian War. He had not been coddled or protected as most of the nobility were during the Edgeland Wars. He had seen the savagery of combat, willfully so, many times. He now lived in a perpetual state of barely-contained rage. Few did not fear the Viscount. His third wife,

Tammin's stepmother, was one of the few who dared to confront him. But Lord Halenwood disliked her greatly, and treated her as if she had no consequence at all. They argued a great deal, and the mood in the house was unpleasant enough as it was without Lady Halenwood provoking the surly man further.

Bellworth, Raynes's father, was also a rugged man in gentleman's clothes—a Baron, but only by appointment by the Hettan King for his service to the throne. The ruggedness was grown from the roots of a commoner—an enterprising, charismatic one— who managed to claw his way up from the gentry as a land and slave owner to governance, and eventually the condescension of the King himself, after making his mark during the wars. The conflicts over the greenlands had elevated many an enterprising commoner or middle class man to the elite.

The Viscount and the Baron shared many interests in business and enterprise—it was a tenuous partnership, where two prideful, barely stable men cooperated. Their sons, having mostly grown up together, began as inseparable friends from a very young age. The pair, as a team, terrorized and bullied everyone they could, and drew great amusement from it. But something had driven a wedge between them in the past year, Raynes had gone sour on Tammin after an inducement over a girl, and their dislike for one another seemed almost to mirror their affection they once had for the other with equal intensity and zeal. Their newfound rivalry had caused no end of trouble in turn.

"Straighten yourself up," Fenwick growled.

Tammin complied, brushing bits of straw from his clothes.

"You look like a savage," the Viscount snarled. "Where are your cravat and your frock coat? How can you ride across the countryside in such a disheveled state?"

Tammin did not reply. He merely bent to sweep up his bridle which he had been holding when his father assailed him.

"I'll have Vanacken come and explain himself, and you will stand beside me, do you understand?" the Viscount shouted, spittle flying out of his mouth.

Oddly, in spite of Tammin's frequent conflicts with the Bellworth boy and the inevitable beatings and censures, Fenwick never allowed his son to lose the upper hand in his dealings with

Raynes. Tammin would suffer a beating, but ultimately he would keep the horse. The beatings were rarely measured to change what had happened.

Whatever the aggression was for, it was inevitable. If Tammin did something rebellious or publicly embarrassing to his father—which was fairly often these days—or whenever he bested the Bellworth boy, his father would invariably appear and knock him flat. If it was to appease the witnesses and victims, Tammin did not know. What he suspected was that it was merely an act to ensure that Tammin was not growing strong enough to best his father—and was still marginally controllable. He had an idea that his father, in all his brutish hostility, feared that the cruelty he burdened his son with would come back upon him one day.

"Get in the house and clean yourself up. We are to dine at Emmensdale tonight. You are not fit to be seen, but you will have to endure the scrutiny. I will not excuse you from your obligations!" He pivoted on his heel and stalked away, leaving Tammin in the stable with his new horse.

The boy exhaled and let out a wavering breath of air, bending forward and resting his hands on his knees, his head still spinning from the blow to the head. He walked to the water pump and churned up a few gushes to splash on his face, shaking his head and spraying droplets everywhere. He straightened, squared his shoulders, took a deep breath, hung up his bridle, and walked towards the great house.

Tammin was scrappy and toughened because of his upbringing. He fought his way through his childhood, and upon entering Avenpaige College, he'd already squared up with several young men to establish a pecking order. He had ensured a rather serene existence when away from home, having set the bullies into their place. Alongside all the soft and squashy blue-bloods, it wasn't too difficult. He had come to enjoy his schooling for the peace of it. He had come to dread returning home to the cold, indifferent air, his embittered stepmother, and the father who loomed like a great shadow.

Tammin was by no means pleased with the string of obligations and social responsibilities that accompanied his home life. There was nobody he cared about anymore. Now that he and Raynes had ended their camaraderie—and because Tammin was now largely absent at school, their shared friends had chosen to keep Raynes' society, and there was nobody left of interest to speak to. There was nobody left but the dull society that his family kept. He could only look forward to mind-numbing tedium. Just reward, he thought bitterly, after his father's beating. He longed for his return to school.

2. *Nieve*

Nieve let the tadpoles slip away between her fingers, and then dried her hands on her skirts, sitting cross-legged on the grass banks of Narroway Pond on the very edge of the water. It was afternoon, and the sun's golden light washed over her tiny form as if painted there by an artist's hand, the glow of her fly-aways like a corona around her sweet face. She watched the squiggly creatures wend about through the water between the flotillas of duckweed. They had legs already, splayed out on each side of their shrinking tails. She'd never seen tadpoles before. She was fascinated. Water spiders skated along the surface and dragonflies skimmed the water's edge. She could not help but gawp in amazement at everything.

Nieve's once neat coif had fallen mostly loose, strands of which hung down her temples and her back. The braided bun had unraveled a little and several of the pins were lost. The curls that had been so carefully set in rags the night before were now flat and gone. Her pale blue muslin gown and white petticoat had grass stains on them, and the hem had been dragged through some deep, dark, old muddy humus. Her slippers were beside her with her stockings wadded up in them.

She had decided this very afternoon that Narroway Grange was a suitable place to live. She very much liked and approved of it. She had spent the whole of the day exploring while her aunt Landie was seeing to the placement of the furniture and the unpacking of things. The hall itself was rather nice, and the farm buildings attached were at present empty of livestock, but clean and well maintained.

Landie was only just married. She had inherited her niece after Nieve's mother and father disappeared along with the sand-ship they were on, crossing the Neddum straits towards Sableston. Nieve was thirteen years old. A quiet girl who had lived two years with her aunt and now was forced to share her with a rather brusque man whom she now addressed as Uncle, whom she did not know well, and was afraid of. He would have arrived sometime around lunch time, and Nieve was diligently avoiding him at all costs, exploring the new home and its acres.

Narroway was less pasture and more grove, with plenty of shaded, bluebell-rich wooded paths. It had a pond, a brook, and the acreage butted up against a lake on the other side of which was a beautiful great-house which looked like a wedding cake with all its buttresses and galleries. The small pastures were overgrown with thick, lush grass, evidence of which stained her gown. They were cut through with stone walls, and looked like they needed a horse, a cow, and some sheep to keep them trimmed. She had waded through these green seas already, leaving wakes as if someone had run their hand against the pile of velvet.

She sighed, blowing some hairs from her face, glancing up at the pink and orange sky, reluctant to obey its silent command to head back to her new home. But with a groan she got to her feet, and bent down to pick up her shoes.

Nieve squealed out in astonishment as the slick grass and thick muck at the bank gave way. Her waify body keeled backwards, falling feet first into the pond. There was little there as a gradual shore—but a bank of mud and then the grass, both slippery. She was engulfed by water every time she slid back in. She flailed, her skirts tangling around her legs. She swallowed water, unable to scream or shout for help. She could only fight against the pull of the greedy water, and try to grapple something to help her ashore. She could taste the turbidity her movements caused in her mouth; the loamy soil and algae mixed in with the water.

Seemingly out of nowhere, something powerful grabbed hold of her upper arm and hoisted her up into the air. She was lifted out of the water coughing and retching, blinded by her own hair, and flopped unceremoniously onto the bank. She lay there hacking, desperate for a full gulp of air that wasn't interfered with by the water she'd aspirated. She could hear someone breathing heavily during her struggle to breathe herself. Someone whacked her back a few times while she fought for air. It came. At length—one retching cough after the next, until she was gulping air in great big wet wheezes, coughing out water. She then rolled onto her back and took deep, cleansing breaths, occasionally coughing, but now not so desperately.

When she had regained her wherewithal, she reached up and pushed her hair away, twisting her head to look at her savior.

Reclining in the grass, soaked from head to toe, was a young man. His black hair was slick and washed over his forehead, dripping glistening, golden drops into his eyes. He was propped up on his elbows. He wore only his sopping shirt and breeches. His top boots were soaked and covered in duckweed and mud. Seeing her calmed and stirring, he turned to peer at her with the most brilliant green eyes she'd ever seen, and his brow furrowed with overt disapproving annoyance.

"Can't you swim? Why would you venture so close to water if you can't swim?" he asked with clear scorn; all said in the strong Plateau accent.

Having moved from Rethros, she found the accent here rather off-putting. She coughed again and forced herself to sit up, pushing back her hair. She frowned, wiping her face with her arm.

"I had no idea it would be so deep right there at the bank," she snapped with equal irritation. "And the bank was slippery. I didn't know!" She glanced at him from the corner of her eye and glowered. "Where did *you* come from anyway?"

"I was riding through when I heard a shout and then a splash," he replied, glancing at her awkwardly. He got to his feet and bent down to scoop up the garments he had shed. He stalked to a horse which had, upon being hastily disembarked, taken to grazing calmly on the grass. He led the horse close, and then knelt, grasping Nieve under her arms and lifting her up.

She squealed in surprise, but let him do it. He plopped her, sopping wet, onto the saddle sideways, and then gave her his frock coat to put on her shoulders. He took the reins close to the bit, and began to lead the horse, striding with a slight squelching noise in his boots, next to the horse.

Without the horns of a sidesaddle, sitting on a man's saddle was tricky, especially in a slippery wet gown. So she angled herself a bit, lifting one leg to rest on the pommel and gripped the horse's thick mane. Without asking, he led the animal towards Narroway Grange.

He said nothing. Nieve gazed at his back as he walked. He loosened his grip a bit on the reins, and let the horse come abreast, so that he strode beside her. Nieve studied him as they slowly made their way towards her new home, silent except for the occasional cough or sniffle. He was probably about sixteen years old, she guessed. He moved with an easy grace. His shoulders were broad and his back triangular. His hair was true black. He had a bruise on his cheekbone and a cut on his lip, but despite these marks one would expect on a street thug, he was adorned in the clothes of a gentleman. At least he had been. *She* wore some of them now.

He glanced up at her, his face still a mask of annoyance; his eyes narrow with soft folded lids under which the vivid emerald of his eyes glinted in the last light of afternoon. But there was kindness in his glance. Nieve could only offer him a sheepish purse of the lips and an embarrassed roll of the eyes, turning her gaze away for a moment.

"What's your name?" the dark-haired boy asked, his eyes flashing over onto her shy face.

"Nieve. Nieve DenTrynne," she replied timidly.

"You may call me Tammin," he offered in return. "I am the son of the Viscount Halenwood."

Nieve merely nodded once, her eyes wide and glancing furtively at his face as he addressed her.

"I was on my way to meet your family," he said. "My father said the new tenants at the grange had arrived. You're from Rethros, from what I understand."

"Yes," Nieve murmured quietly.

"That explains why you can't swim. That's a long journey," he said absently. For some reason he kept looking at her hands, tangled in the horse's shining black mane.

"Two and a half weeks," she replied. "Mostly by sand-ship."

The mare's hoofbeats fell softly on what had become a mat of mossy ground. They crossed the patch as if walking on carpet, the pillowy earth slowing her pace a bit.

"What's it like in Rethros?"

"Not cool like this," she exclaimed. "Every day here has been like a winter's night there since we crossed the mountains. And it's almost summer! The desert lands are nothing like this."

"Yes. Outside of this great plateau, it is all like Rethros, is it not? Hot and disagreeable," he added.

"And stormy in winter. Not green. Just brown everywhere. Fawn and brown. The air does not smell as nice as it does here," Nieve offered. "This countryside, it's so alive. I can smell the water in the air." He watched her attentively as she spoke, taking in her golden hazel eyes which were alight with pleasure when she spoke of this new place. "It's so lovely. You must feel so fortunate to have been born to such a beautiful land."

"I suppose," the boy sighed heavily.

"You do not like your home?" Nieve asked. She found that almost offensive, considering how many people struggled to live comfortably in the arid lands. He had grown up in a paradise, and he had the gall to scowl at it. Her brightness faded, and she frowned darkly.

The boy shrugged. She supposed, by looking at his wounded, dejected demeanor, that he would be unhappy anywhere right now. She gave him a glance and then turned her attention to her hands which were fidgeting with the mare's mane.

"Why are you so beat up? You've got bruises and cuts all over your face and hands," she observed. There were several paces that were taken in silence.

"I sparred with someone," he finally replied. "An idiot."

Nieve's snort of derision brought his eyes to her in a snap, and she pursed her lips in disgusted disapproval and disappointment. "You oughtn't fight."

He twisted to give her an unconvinced look and opened his mouth as if to snap at her. She interrupted. "It's not gentlemanly. You are a Viscount's son, not a ruffian. Why are you behaving as such? You should have more pride and dignity than to resort to violence to settle your differences."

She shifted in the saddle, and stared at him for a while. "I imagine you must be quite unhappy by your bearing. Whatever it is that is burdening you, you should not let it lead you to things you will regret later on. Fighting and scrapping with people... that accomplishes nothing and will only hurt *you* most in the end."

"Who do you think you are, little girl, to be telling me how to comport myself?" Tammin grumbled.

"I'm nobody," she said lightly. "But I have eyes. I can see you are unhappy with something. You should try to do better for yourself, and you will be happier for it. And if something is making you unhappy, you must not yield to it or let it win."

"I am not unhappy," he mumbled.

"Oh, please, don't lie to me, let alone yourself. There are lots of things that can make one miserable. My mother used to say that it was fine to be miserable when the situation calls for it, but one must never allow it to become the very essence of who you are. It will eat you up. Just be miserable for a bit, and then don't."

Tammin suppressed an amused smirk and said instead, "I think one oughtn't presume to tell me what to do." He threw a glare at her.

She was immediately contrite as she realized she was lecturing a senior. He surprised her with a flashing grin.

Nieve's thirteen-year-old heart exploded into flutters. She blushed and hid her face behind her stringy, still-damp hair. When he turned his face back towards the path, she peeked at him through her locks. The late afternoon light was about to disappear behind the horizon, and those final strokes of color washed across his face. He looked striking and radiant, if not a little sullen in the eyes.

As soon as they came into view of the grange, Nieve's aunt appeared in full cry, clutching her shawl to her breast as she loped through the small field between the bee-baskets to meet them. Insects rose up all around her as she ran, like a wake of will-o-the-wisps, their wings and legs cast golden in the halo of late afternoon light.

"Oh, oh, dear Nieve, what happened? Goodness, bring her this way, please," she gasped, breathless as she neared. Like Nieve, she had mahogany colored hair and hazel-brown eyes. She was an elegant creature, even when possessed by alarm as she was at the moment. Her voluminous hair was tied up into a loose bun on her head, and then tucked into a sheer cap of organdy edged in delicate ruffles.

The boy followed the stricken aunt, with Nieve in tow, her fingers still laced tightly through the mare's mane. The boy helped her down when they reached the little courtyard.

"Thank you," she whispered as he lowered her to her feet. She alighted onto the cobbles and stepped back, dipping into a graceful little curtsey before blushing again. Tammin bowed to the aunt and then to the uncle, who seemed to manifest himself out of nowhere and offered a brief bow of introduction to the young fellow. Uncle then scooped Nieve up and carried her inside to her room.

Enna, the ladies' chamber-maid, was there waiting for her with towels and a fresh nightgown and dressing gown. Nieve only heard the sound of the mare moving away, carrying her new friend along with her. She didn't see anything more of her rescuer that night. He was thanked profusely by her aunt and uncle and sent to venture home to the great house by the lake.

Nieve was given a stern dressing-down for wandering off for so long, and for inconveniencing the Viscount's son and ruining his clothes which were most certainly costly. After having been dried off and changed out of her ruined clothes, she endured a lecture from her uncle about the cost of the shoes she had lost and the silk stockings, and another half hour of worried what-ifs from her aunt, who vacillated between anger and tears.

"I could not bear to lose you, too, Nieve. Not you, too. You are all the family I have left," she blubbered. Her husband stood behind her, his hand on her shoulder, glaring at Nieve in displeasure. "Thank goodness for that young man," Landie declared, dabbing her eyes with a kerchief. "Thank goodness."

3. *Andenswegg*

The day was bleak and blustery and grey, but that was not reason enough to sway Nieve from escaping into it. It was too tempting, all this free water, falling so liberally from the sky. It was nothing an umbrella could not keep at bay, and it would only guarantee her solitude on a walk. So, while Aunt Landie was taking a late morning nap after a hearty breakfast and Uncle Bohan was out at the stock market, seeking to populate his fields, Nieve changed out of her old tea-stained morning gown into a warm linen petticoat and frock, drew her evergreen hooded cape over her shoulders, and grabbed an umbrella. She slipped out into the rain in her old brown boots, and took her explorations eastwards, towards a place called Andenswegg. She'd heard of it from Enna, who was the girl that saw to both her and her aunt's personal care.

"Take the old cobbled road all the way to the river. And then go left and follow the river to its fall. Andenswegg is below. There is a path with steps, but it is slick and steep, so you must proceed with great caution. But you will not regret it. It is lovely as any sight," the girl told her.

Nieve could not stop thinking about it and would not allow a delightfully rainy day to stop her from seeing it.

She skipped happily down the cobbled road from the town as instructed, leaving behind Narroway, and passing—nearly half an hour later—the entrance to the great house where her rescuer Tammin lived. She wondered about him in passing, smiling to herself as the image of him entered her mind again.

She could scarce keep herself from picturing him every moment she had nothing else to occupy her mind. Lying on the grass, his knee bent, resting on his elbows, the afternoon light turning the droplets in his hair gold before they let go and fell onto his pleasant face. This guardian, this champion. Her protector.

She'd scarce taken a moment to think about what happened. Not after Uncle Bohan had been so harsh and angry with her. Not after her actions had caused her aunt such suffering. But her own feelings on the matter were unbearable. The idea of falling in water again imbued her with such dread, and here she was advancing on another place of watery coffins.

She'd never felt so powerless in her life than when she was drowning. She was almost about to give up the struggle before Tammin came. It felt like it was an impossible feat to escape the water. Her gown, her weight, all seemed to drag her down. And then there she was, lying on the grass next to this beautiful boy. He'd saved her. Rescued her, like some knight of ancient times. He picked her up and threw her into his saddle with so little effort. He'd walked beside her and smiled up at her. And from his lofty height, when she stood beside him, he gazed down at her with kindness and respect.

He saw her. Truly *saw* her. This dark, hooligan of a boy. She felt her heart skip a beat as she pictured him again, that black hair washed over his forehead, over his fine profile, and she frowned, unsure what to make of these feelings.

Around her the rain fell in an incessant hiss, the thick, heavy drops splashing back up from the worn cobbles and soaking her hems. The dampness that bled into her stockings and wicked up her skirts did not bother her. The birds still sang in spite of the rain. The trees bowed and swayed to the blustery wind, branches waving like graceful dancers. Nieve had never felt so invigorated and happy in all her life as she did since she had come to the greenlands. She felt as if she belonged here all along.

The din of the rainfall was so great that she did not hear the gig approaching behind her until the horse was nearly upon her. She heard the animal snort, shying from her umbrella, and she turned, squealing in startlement and further spooking the animal. She staggered backwards out of its path.

Only when the horse had stopped, and the gig drew to a halt behind it did she realize it was Tammin driving the thing. Huddled comfortably beneath the broad calash with his legs covered by a wide leather curtain from which the rain slid in rivulets, he looked irritated to see that it was Nieve. "I would ask you why you were out in this weather, but you seem to have a habit of making bad decisions. Where could you *possibly* be going on a day like this?"

"Is that any of your business?" she retorted over the rain, glowering at him.

"It is my business when you nearly end up trod into pudding by my horse," Tammin blurted angrily. "Get in!"

Nieve was by no means willing to brook a bullying from this young man, no matter how much he set her breast aflutter. She had a mission to find this mysterious Andenswegg.

She turned and continued on instead. Tammin clucked his tongue and his horse lunged forward, bringing the body of his gig abreast of Nieve.

"Where are you going?" he insisted. The wheels of his gig rattled beside her.

"To Andenswegg," she replied. She saw his eyes widen and his brows arch in surprise and alarm.

"Oh, no you are not. That is a grave accident waiting to happen, and I can't rescue you from that. If you slip, you'll tumble down countless mossy stairs into a heap of broken bone. No," he barked, "get in. I'm taking you home! If you do not obey, I will turn this gig around, go and fetch your Uncle and Aunt, and have them collect you."

Nieve stopped short, her ears growing red with frustration. She wished he would simply leave her be. He reined in his horse and halted the gig again. Once he was within view, she shouted: "I'm not a walking tragedy. Just because I slipped once doesn't mean I will again!"

"You don't understand. And until you *see* the old keep, you won't. Get in, *now*," he commanded her. He gave her a stern look when she challenged him with a glare. "Now," he said slowly and firmly. He put the reins in one hand, opened up the leather boot, and reached out his right glove to hand her in.

Exasperated and angry, Nieve stamped her foot and threw her fists down, umbrella and all. She could plainly see him suppressing a smirk at her childish temper tantrum, which made her even angrier and embarrassed. But she obeyed, grasping his proffered hand, using it to pull herself up into the gig. She plopped down beside him defiantly, and closed her umbrella, her face a mask of anger. He fastened the leather cover over their legs, and redistributed the reins and whip in his hands.

"I was told that Andenswegg was a true sight to be seen," she whined ruefully. "I've been looking forward to it all morning!"
Tammin took a quick sideways look at her and chuffed through his nose. "Stop behaving like an infant." Urging the horse forward, he followed the main road, and then veered off to the left onto a smaller one that dipped down. The rain hammered the calash around them and pummeled the leather boot that was stretched across their legs, protecting them from the downpour. She wasn't sure where he was going, but it wasn't back towards Narroway or Halenwood Hall.

Instead, the road led them deeper down into a valley that was dense with growth. The cobbled pavement leveled out and came to a riotous, whitewater river which roared with the addition of the rainfall. The road led upstream into a veritable theater of greenery, complete with a great canopy of leaves and draping mosses. The river beside them made its presence known by overpowering the song of the rain and rumbling its dominant noise at them. The road rose a little, and then turned abruptly with the river, which was now tumbling down an incline of boulders smoothened by ages of water wear. And then what Nieve knew to be Andenswegg by description alone appeared in view.

An old stone keep, ancient and impervious to time, sat against a precipitous hillside, all rock and moss with wild growth springing out from the steep walls. The keep was a great big drum tower with two parapets coming off its sides in wings to become wide box turrets. All of these were crenelated, flat-topped constructs; all dripping in vines and moss, surrounded by blooming shrubs and a narrow garden edged by a short garden wall. The old-fashioned, narrow balistraria holes had been replaced by modern window casements, all in stone with fancy chiseled stone mullions and tracery with glinting glass within. This ancient building was still well-used and loved by its owner. There were even lace curtains to be seen behind the windows.

But the most astonishing thing was the sight of the broad waterfall behind the keep from the hillside, cascading down a jumble of tiered rocks into an unseen riverbed, and then washing in another violent churn from the foundation of the drum tower, its box turrets, and garden, then sluicing from the a gallery of arched stone culverts, pouring into the river that now roiled wildly past them. Tammin drew the coach to a stop so she could see for herself what he had warned her against.

And see it she did. For beginning at the edge of the waterfall's crest descended a narrow, terrifyingly steep stairway. With steps no broader than the length of her foot—hundreds of them cut from the stone of the cliff-side—winding down without railings to hold, between boulders and along pathways where small sprays of smaller, deviated courses of the waterfall splashed down. The hillside, too, was dripping in thick, slippery-looking mosses and the steepness of the incline did not relent until near the bottom where the talus of rocks spread out to the side of the castle-keep and turned into a narrow path that disappeared into the trees.

Even through the rain and mist, she could not mistake the perilous nature of that path. She grew pale underneath the calash of the gig. Tammin turned to look at her with the most "I told you so" expression he could muster. She merely swallowed hard and gazed again at the beauty that was Andenswegg, determined to at least see it all anyway.

"I understand," she finally uttered, her eyes returning to the death-defying stack of stone steps she'd thought she'd conquer today. How glad she was Tammin was there to stop her. Indeed, a dangerous venture. She was struck cold by the idea of stumbling and losing her purchase on that frightening descent. She would surely have died. She would reproach Enna for telling her to visit it, and to do so from the top of the falls.

As if reading her thoughts, Tammin leaned forward a bit. "Every year, someone is terribly hurt or killed scaling the Andenswegg stairs. Whoever told you about this without proper warning ought to be whipped. Who told you to come here?" he asked her suddenly, anger in his tone.

"My chamber-maid," she confessed, her face a mask of humiliation for being gullible enough to listen to the girl.

"Well, your chamber maid is a blithering idiot! She endangered you terribly! I ought to speak to your aunt about her," he snarled.

"Surely she did not mean to endanger me," Nieve said in the girl's defense. "Perhaps she did not think I would climb down the stairs, but thought I would merely admire it all from above."

"I will speak to your aunt, regardless," he grumbled. "Her suggestion could have been disastrous."

Nieve did not like to see Tammin so angry. So she distracted him with her commentary on the keep. "This is the most beautiful house I've ever seen."

Tammin had persisted in his questioning glare, but relented at the sight of her relieved and amazed expression. He exhaled as if in defeat and shook his head in resignation. "You'll see the place first-hand I'm quite certain. Soon enough. The Bevvins family is interminably and intolerably social, and once they discover your family, they will pester you ceaselessly to visit their home. They bought it only in the last eight years and they are very proud of owning this great pile. They invite everyone all the time. They have assemblies and balls, parties and plays, performances, shows, games, and gatherings throughout the year. You'll be sick and tired of Andenswegg within three months. I promise you." With grumpy sigh, he pivoted the gig on the narrow road, and cracked the whip.

"Now it's time to take you home, Miss Nieve. You are more trouble than you are worth, I think. But at least you delayed my obligatory social visitation to our neighbors at Hedshall. There's one good thing," he rationalized, twisting his lips. "I shall deliver you home safely yet again."

"Master Tammin," she began, causing him to look square at her as the coach rolled along. "Thank you for bringing me to see the place anyway." She offered him a smile.

Tammin nodded once, with an awkward expression on his face. "I only brought you here to teach you a lesson," he replied sternly. "I know you would have defied my warning if I hadn't shown you the danger first."

"All the same, thank you," she insisted, gaze fixed upon him.

Nieve leaned back in the coach, sheepishly turning her face away when he returned her look. How could someone be both so annoying and yet so darling at the same time? She wondered to herself. She toyed with the ivory handle of the umbrella and watched the greenery pass by, both delighted and deflated to be once again at the mercy of the ruffian she now thought of as a friend.

4. *Winden*

Tammin sat on his rock. It projected out of the edge of Liar's Hill. The hill itself was covered in brush and trees, tucked deep in a wood, but it offered a surprisingly open prospect down into the hollow from the same height as the canopy. He would sometimes sit quietly and observe a host of wild creatures such as deer and wild fowl, two bears, many foxes and wolves. Today he saw a wild little thing indeed—wee Miss Nieve, out and about again, in a pristine gown. He'd seen her a few times in the past few days as the weather had cleared, unbeknownst to her, traipsing unchecked around the countryside.

Today she was in a scant muslin gown of pale white with no spencer or redingote, not even a wrap or shawl. Her boots were a deep wine red, and she had a ribbon in her hair the same color. It was wrapped around her skull like a diadem with the ribbons falling free with the rest of her locks that cascaded down her shoulders and onto her back.

It had rained most of the morning and was suffocating in the great house. He was feeling particularly tortured these past few days, after finding Nieve on her way to Andenswegg. The event had brought back a rather burdensome sense of guilt Tammin had struggled to forget. He had not shared with Nieve that he had persuaded several people in his days as a bully, to scale those dangerous stairs, and two had been severely injured for it. He was overcome with a sense of shame after saving Nieve from that possible fate, and it had made being alone with his thoughts, locked in his house unbearable. Tammin sought escape these oppressive feelings as soon as the clouds parted. At present, he sat with his arms wrapped around one knee; the other leg was hanging over the edge of the rock.

He watched the girl move down one of the many paths that wound through the tall trees. The canopies were high, most of the trunks limbless for at least thirty feet before they reached out for the sun. The hollow was particularly gloomy and dark because of the dense trees, the forest floor mostly free of wild growth, but thick with a fragrant humus of needles and leaves. The white barked, strangely pale-leafed shade-witch trees were the only kind of prolific greenery to be found besides the tree trunks. That and moss.

In her white gown, Nieve looked like a lily against the dark backdrop. Assuming nobody was about, she began to dance. Taking long, elegant strides and casting her arms out, she twirled around a shade-witch tree and skipped prettily along, humming something in a soft voice.

He muffled a soft laugh through his nose at the sight of the girl. A whimsical smile crossed his lips. She was a graceful little thing—adorable little Nieve, with her sweet blushes and flashing eyes. She evidently liked to be out of doors like he did. He wondered why she was not schooling with a governess or with her aunt.

He picked up a pine cone, of which there was a pile he had collected to scare off animals if he needed to. He had seen too many wild turkeys and foul caught and killed by a predator not to try and save one or two. With careful aim, he slung one out into the hollow. It tumbled between trunks of trees and landed with a thud at Nieve's feet. She stopped short and knelt to pick it up, looking straight up at the canopy. He landed another one, this time hitting her in the leg. Her face turned immediately towards the source and she glowered at him when she saw his face high up on the sheer hillside, laughing down at her. She picked up a pinecone and tried to lob it back, but it fell hilariously short. Red-faced, and clearly realizing he'd seen her dancing about like a fool, she dashed away in humiliation.

Tammin got to his feet and jumped down from the rock onto the narrow deer path down the steep slope. He skidded down gingerly, grasping tree trunks as he descended, and came barreling to the floor of the hollow just in time to see the white skirts vanish 'round the side of an outcropping on the path towards the old quarry. The large steps cut from the limestone were not hugely deep, but he worried she could still hurt herself. He broke into a run after her.

He found Nieve navigating what was known locally as the giant's stairway—her little form dropping down a second level just as he appeared at its edge. The tiers had long worn down and grown mossy. In the center of this quarry was the quarry pond, which was a body of green, algae-filled water shaped into a large rectangle. It was quite deep in this coliseum-like space, at least deep twelve levels down, surrounded by the stepped walls from which myriad blocks of stone had been cut to build the many great houses and landmarks of the region.

He skipped down two layers, and then jogged to catch up with Nieve, who attempted to climb back up. Because she was still rather small, she had great difficulty. Failing to get up, she turned to glare at Tammin. There was a dark stain of dirt on the front of her gown.

"It's all your fault," she snapped.

He slowed and stopped a good measure away from her and crossed his arms. "What exactly?" he asked, one of his brows rising sardonically.

"I'm stuck," she replied with exasperation.

"I didn't *make* you jump down these steps, did I?" he retorted, tilting his head.

She snorted and turned her back again, clutching the edge of the step and trying to jump up high enough to fold her chest onto the top of it. She was too short.

Tammin approached and grasped her by the waist and hoisted her. She protested with a squeal, and scrambled to her feet. Her brows slanted downwards, and her mouth in a straight determined line, she glared at him, turning to advance on the top step. She tried with a running start, and failed again, emitting a little "ouf" when she collided with the stone.

Tammin vaulted up with ease, and stood behind her, arms crossed again, a smug look on his face. "Why do you keep doing stupid things? Do you have a death wish? You are awfully young for that."

She paused in her effort to climb to turn and shot him some daggers. The sight of his amusement made her grumpier. "Oh, shut that mouth."

"That's rude, after all the help I've given you. I saved your life, if you recall," he reminded her. "Twice, if I'm honest. You would have surely died at Andenswegg had I not been out that day."

"You don't know that," she said defiantly, but clearly not as confident in her own words as she wanted to sound. She shot him a dark glower and stepped back to have another run at it.

He watched her fall short again and snorted. "Apologize."

"I will not," she retorted stubbornly. "What business do you have spying on people anyway? Why are you lurking around all the time? Don't you have anything better to do?"

"Well, you're not getting out of here if you don't apologize," he sighed. With liquid grace, he skipped up the wall, straightened, turned, and then crouched at the edge of the quarry, his forearms resting on his knees, the tails of his frock coat draping down behind him like the tail of a big awkward bird. He gazed down at her with smiling eyes.

She began to walk along the step, looking for a lower spot. He unfolded himself and followed along on the top step.

"Three words. I. Am. Sorry." Tammin counted on his fingers. "Not complicated. You can add Tammin, if you like, as that is my name. But I'll accept the apology with or without it." He clutched his hands behind his back and swaggered alongside Nieve.

She glanced up and caught the flare of his frock coat tails, taking in the fawn-colored breeches and his top boots, which appeared to have been restored to their original luster and polish. He wore a periwinkle blue waistcoat with fine stripes, and his frock coat was deep burgundy wool. His black hair, which had a bluish shine to it, was teased into handsome tendrils and combed forward onto his temples and his brow. The bruises had gone a little yellow on his face, but there was still scabbing on the corner of his lip. It had been less than a week since the day at the pond. But he still looked quite handsome despite the marks of his scuffle. Nieve's heart quickened when his green eyes caught hers.

She kept her obstinate silence. He stopped and looked at her expectantly. Nieve crossed her arms and turned away, moving quickly along the wall.

"Oh, well. Rot in this great big pit if you'd like then." And with a swish of his tails, he disappeared from view.

Nieve felt the sting of tears in her eyes as she made the circuit of this broad hole in the earth, finding no stray rocks upon which to climb. She searched another twenty minutes, made the full perimeter twice, and then, angry with herself, she plunked hopelessly down on the ground with her back against the step and began to cry.

Her day had an unpleasant start. Her aunt and uncle had argued about her that morning over breakfast and were cross at one another and at her. Uncle had suggested she attend a ladies' school, and her aunt had disagreed. That is what started it all.

"Only the classless, common folk use those schools," she argued. "The desire to prepare their daughters to marry higher, to teach them airs they are not born with is what drives someone to school their daughters in such places. Girls from these schools can be spotted a mile away when the season opens. Hangers-on, social climbers with no dignity. There is nothing formative offered there. What will she gain by learning the harp or making samplers?"

"Do you not think she should be prepared for marriage? She's half-wild, roaming the land like a hermit all day. She ought to be turned into a young lady." Uncle raked his fingers through his long, sandy-colored hair which had not yet been styled into his customary queue or set into the double side-curls he normally sported.

"She's *only just turned thirteen*, my dear," Aunt Landie argued, reaching for a little mustard for her ham. "She's still but a child. Let her enjoy some freedom before we begin imposing such responsibilities as marriage upon her. I could not bear to be parted from her." Aunt's voice cracked.

Nieve recognized that her aunt's sorrow cut particularly sharply into her uncle's heart. She could see him swallow his frustration every time she resorted to tears when it came to Nieve.

The loss of her sister had been a great blow to Landie. Nieve's mother was eight years older than Landie. They had been exceedingly close—more like a mother and child than sisters. Landie had been resident of her sister's married home as a girl after their father had died and their mother had remarried to a man who desired no step-children. Landie was twelve years old when Nieve was born and was present for the occasion.

After the disappearance of Nieve's parents and the sale of their home and possessions, she and Nieve had taken up residence in a small cottage paid for by the inheritance Landie received from her father's estate, which was a small amount, but kept them comfortable enough. She held onto Nieve with a desperation that might not be understood by all. But Nieve was all that remained of her beloved sister. For a long time, it was only the two of them and the Spinster Mrs. Brave, who was hired to keep their home.

Uncle Bohan had come along only in the past year, a chance encounter with Landie and Nieve one day when they were out in the town, walking. A sudden sand-storm resulted in a dash into the doorway of the nearest shop, where the tall, rugged man was shopping for a broad-brimmed hat.

He was a sight older than Landie. Entering his forties, he was still very much handsome and desirable—a longtime bachelor who many believed would always remain so. His proposal to Landie was a great shock to those within his circle, and many of the unmarried and widowed ladies of his age who were holding out for his attentions were much-disappointed and they treated Landie very ill for her usurpation of this eligible man. It became immediately unbearable for Landie to mix with any company that had been friends of Bohan prior to their engagement.

Uncle Bohan *adored* Landie. His attraction to her was immediate and insistent. His courting of her was fervent. When she consented to the unexpected proposal, the marriage was arranged post-haste, and they took their vows only a few months after meeting for the first time.

It was Uncle Bohan that decided that they ought to leave Rethros to help Landie escape the spiteful behavior of the women of their circle. To begin afresh in the sacred land of the Plateau—where he'd been granted entry, a rare opportunity—and to break away the remnants of the molds that shaped their pasts. They left their home so the couple could start anew without scrutiny or judgment.

He was a stoic character with a hard way about him. He seemed from the beginning quietly perturbed by the presence of the child. Landie's gentle airs softened him a bit, but he never quite let go of his discomfort with Nieve, as if perhaps she represented an obstacle in his having the marriage he had hoped for. He was unnecessarily brusque and sometimes rough with Nieve. Although they had only been married some months, the longer they were a family, the more liberties he seemed to take in disciplining Nieve.

The argument that he felt Nieve caused between he and his beloved wife left him bristling. But when he caught Nieve in his library shortly after, he'd cuffed her across the face with the back of his hand and sent her to the floor. She had only wished to help unpack the many books they had brought, but he had deemed the space off-limits to her.

She slunk away weeping, vanishing out of doors until the beauty of this verdant land had whisked away her tears and restored her ease. How she had reveled in the peace and quiet, and the solitude. She was still feeling fragile.

And now *this*, she thought, looking at the walls that surrounded her—imprisoned her. *That Tammin,* she fumed. How embarrassing that he had seen her dancing like a lunatic. How stupid she must look to him. She covered her flushed, embarrassed face with her hands and wept afresh. Her sobs were soft and breathy. Her narrow shoulders shook.

There was a sound of pebbles being crushed under boots beside her, and her *bane* alighted as gracefully as a cat next to her, falling into a crouch. He hugged his knees; his feet flat, and rested the side of his face on his kneecaps, looking at her. "Now, now, don't cry," he said slightly mockingly.

Nieve turned her face away from him and wiped her eyes with the heels of her fists.

"I would not leave you to fend for yourself. I'm not *that* cruel," he assured her. "It would be inadvisable to stay here. With the bears and wolves and the vultures—not to mention the rumored quarry monster that lives in the depths of that pond. Inadvisable indeed." His tone was teasing. Nieve continued to sniffle and sob. "How stubborn must you be to choose to die in a pit, than apologize to me?"

"Stop," Nieve croaked through her tears. "I don't want to play games today," her sobs deepening. She turned and looked at him, and Tammin's usual jaunty air vanished.

Her large hazel eyes, rimmed in dark lashes, clumped by tears struck him silent.

He gaped at her, and she at him, through her sniffles and hiccups. It was then he noticed the red mark on her cheekbone. Her shyness had made her hide her face from him almost perfectly, and even when he did glimpse her face, her blushes had hidden it until that moment. Something dark washed over him.

"What's that?" he asked in a quiet, chilling voice.

Nieve furrowed her brow. His hand slid across the space between them, and his finger touched her cheekbone. Now, in her pale, waxen state, it stood out. She winced at his touch.

"Leave it," she whispered, turning her face away.

"I don't suppose it was a tree branch or a doorknob. Or let's see... I fell and struck my face. Oh... was it a horse that inadvertently hurt you when rubbing its head on you? I used that one once," he rambled coolly.

Nieve turned her head back and looked at him with unreadable eyes. "My uncle struck me. I entered the library without his permission."

"Does he do that a great deal?" Tammin inquired.

"Strike me? No. Only a few times since they've been married," she told him.

He mulled it over a while, propping his chin on his knees and looking down into the depths of the quarry below. "Once a hitter, always a hitter. Your aunt, she will suffer too, eventually. Perhaps when you are no longer around to receive it."

"He wouldn't harm a hair on *her* head. He positively worships her. I, *I* am the one he dislikes. I am an interloper. I was never part of his plan." She then stopped and emitted a tremulous sigh. She remained quietly still, and studied Tammin's profile. "I *am* a nuisance. I think he expected me to go to another relative when they married. I know he resents my presence. My aunt, she needs me. She clings to me. And that bothers him because he can refuse her nothing. If it was in his power, he would refuse having me in his household, but he risks angering her by proposing to send me away. He still tries. He always tries."

"There is never an acceptable reason for a grown man to lay his hand upon a defenseless child or a woman. Even if the person isn't wanted," Tammin muttered bitterly.

"I know," she conceded. "But it sometimes simply makes some kind of absurd sense. Like it belongs with the whole experience of being unwanted." She buried her face in her arms for a moment and fought back tears.

They remained in thoughtful silence. Nieve's tears subsided and she collected herself. It was only then that Tammin straightened himself, and without warning, picked up the girl and propped her on the top step before climbing up behind her. "Come, I'll walk you home."

He took her hand and led her along, almost dragging her. Nieve felt so childlike and small next to this strapping teenage boy. She barely reached the middle of his upper arm in height. And next to his bulk, she was just a waify little thing.

"Slow down!" she gasped, stumbling behind him.

Tammin complied and let her come up alongside him. They fell into a slower, contemplative walk. It gave Nieve the opportunity to take in the beauty around her. He took her down the horse path, which was mostly overgrown with grasses and weeds. Nieve reclaimed her hand and stopped to pick some daisies and buttercups, which she began to weave into a crown as they walked. Tammin watched her cheekbones occasionally come into view as the curtain of her hair shielded her face from his. She walked without looking, her hands working on the bundle of flowers, one blossom at a time.

"Do you like it here?" he asked.

"Oh, yes," Nieve replied effusively. "Although I'm uncertain as to how long I will continue to live here. Uncle Bohan seems intent on sending me away. I've never liked a place better. I've never felt so much like I belonged somewhere. As if I was born to live here. So many trees and so much water."

"That's why you don't know how to swim. Not a great deal of water around growing up," Tammin ventured.

"No. Not at all. The largest amount I'd seen before was the small pond at the Sableston Oasis. Or maybe it was the water pools at the bath house. And that's not the freshest water. They clean it using weirs and plants, and then flush it back into the pools. But now that I feel this water, I realize that the bathhouse and oasis waters were not fresh. Not like the water here. Seems such a waste that they simply dump the bathtubs when we're finished bathing here. To just let it go into the ground like that." She shook her head, incredulous, her fingers plying and plaiting the little flower stems together using strong blades of grass gone to seed. She worked fast.

Tammin watched, slightly fascinated by how dexterous her fingers were, and how lovely her creation was. "There's no shortage of water here. Wait until autumn and the rains and flooding comes. Then winter, the heaps of snow and snow-melt. Then you'll feel very little guilt about a bath's worth."

Nieve, having completed her creation, lifted her little circlet of flowers to her head and stopped to pose with her new crown for Tammin. He snorted with a half-smile. He became suddenly thoughtful as he looked at her.

She was easy to please. It was not hard to make her smile, and he liked her smiles. Seeing her with such sorrow had made his heart ache a little. He thought of something that would make her grin, and would surely impress her.

He quickened the pace a little and half-dragged her up a hill, taking a long horse path along a switchback off the lands of Narroway Grange and the park of the great house. Up and up they went, poor Nieve gasping for breath. Steadily Tammin led her along until they rose up above the trees to a rocky hilltop where he took her to the edge of a great jutting outcropping that overlooked the forestlands.

It took Nieve a moment to regain her breath and her senses, and to take in the prospect. Her companion was barely winded, and he had a smile on his face when he looked at her. He pointed out over the tree tops and the receding swells of hills and farmland. In the distance, far on the horizon, was a tiny figure against the early afternoon sky. Tiny perhaps from their perspective, but they both knew its colossal scale to be seen from so far away.

The Titan, one of the many great guardians of the edgeland gates of Mennan greenlands, stood with one foot on each side of the Tralmin Mountain pass. He, and a small platoon of similar colossuses, had been built by the first peoples to guard the plateau lands against the encroaching deserts. This land, known as simply the greenlands to most, was called Mennan, after the original people; the stewards of nature, the Mennin.

Long gone now, their legacy remained in the form of these colossi. They were positioned along the ridges of both mountain ranges and the edges of the raised lands that contained the greenlands. The deserts were stopped only by these walls of mountain and the cliffs of the plateau on the northern and southern ends.

"Goodness…" Nieve exclaimed, squinting to see it better. She lifted her hand up to shield herself from the light. "I secretly believed that they really didn't exist. Where we came through at Nehelsands, there was no such colossus."

Tammin peered down at her little form, and the look of awe on her face. "Perhaps one day you'll see one up close. They are immense by any definition." He puffed out his chest a little.

The wind was astonishingly strong in this place, and the treetops looked like a field of wheat in its sway, the tops bowing and waving to its whims. It was almost unbearable for the two people that now stood against it.

Nieve's attention was not long held by the titan or the swaying forest. Instead, she turned and took in the hilltop. It was a strange, surprising place, hidden by the forests and hills all around Narroway which was somewhere below. The spires and coppery hip roof of the great house could be seen rising up to the east.

It was the hilltop that caught most of her attention. A great flat was carved from the rock, as if a giant had sliced the crest of the hilltop off with a cake knife. There was a large circular platform in the center, and pillars made of the same rock rose up, studding the perimeter of the circle. There were eleven, all wind-worn and covered in a calico of lichen. There were also eleven colossus guardians encircling the green lands.

"What is this place?" The wind whipped her skirts around her legs. With nothing to stop it or slow it, the gusts were powerful. She moved towards the circle, drawn there.

"This is Winden Hill," Tammin offered. He followed a few steps behind, intrigued by her curiosity. "It is an old ritual site. Hasn't been used in a hundreds of years, I'm sure."

"Used by whom?" Nieve asked, glancing back at her companion. A gust blew the crown of flowers from her head, which Tammin dexterously caught before they were absconded by the wind.

"The Mennin, of course. The original people of Mennan. The same people who built the titans. We've eschewed those old religions now. This is naught but a remnant of a past that is no more," he said over the sound of wildly blowing air.

To Nieve, his voice sounded as if it was someplace remote and far away. For in her ears she could only hear the howling of the wind whistling through the pillars, which was almost sounded like voices, too. As she neared them, she saw that they were riddled with etchings that were nearly worn away. Spirals and lines, stylized creatures, trees and shapes. She put her hand on a delicate-looking tree, whose roots were a mirror of its branches. She stepped up onto the circle and wandered to the center. Tammin followed, the wind making his coattails fly madly.

"What is that?" she heard him say, his voice still miles away.

The whispering voices crafted by the wind were forming words.

Come child, where horned princes be,
With gifted eyes, thee cannot see,
Come the child, where winged paupers dwell,
With a blessed voice that never tells.

The wind stopped. Silence fell upon them like a great stone. Not a bird chirped. Not a blade of grass stirred. Nieve turned to face Tammin who stared at her with confusion, his fingers delicately gripping the little crown of flowers.

"Did you hear that?" His voice was almost deafening in the silence. Blunted, as if they were in a small room.

"Yes," Nieve replied, tilting her head. "You heard it too," she whispered in puzzlement.

From all around them, a din the like of which neither could ever imagine exploded. It was the sound of a thousand-thousand voices screaming, wailing, keening, and crying. Laughter, mad cackles, desperate cries, weeping. The voices of men, women, and tiny babies.

The sky darkened to midnight, and then brightened again in but a few moments, the orb of the sun setting and rising in a smooth arc going beneath them and emerging again. Nieve screamed and threw herself into Tammin's arms, burying her face against his chest. She had never been so frightened in all of her life. He could feel her trembling like a leaf. Then the commotion ceased. And the wind returned, along with the whispering voices.

Come dear child, come unto us.
Ever shall thee remain thus.
Come my child, no thing shall break
The bind that we now do make.
Blessed child, no harm will fall.
Thine undying ardor, save us all.

The wind then abruptly softened, and the birds sang once more. Tammin clutched Nieve to his body and turned, ushering her out of the circle. He led her down the hill, slowing only when they were back in the valley where the trees caught the winds, and there was warmth and familiarity again. It felt cooler than before. Wordlessly, they fell into a stride towards Narroway. Neither spoke for a long spell. But then he stopped.

With a look of wonder, he drew up his hand to offer her the garland he'd caught, and she took it, her eyes wide in shock. The flowers were dried and brittle.

It fell apart when she took it from him, the stems and grass floating away on the breeze.

"What do you suppose made that happen?" Nieve asked Tammin.

"The wind dried them?" he offered.

Her eyes dropped in confusion, looking at her empty hand.

When they arrived at the gates of the grange, he took her hand and stopped her before she could leave him outside, peering down at her pale face with its red mark now turned slightly blue. "I want you to tell me if he hits you again," he said. Her heart-shaped face was so endearing to him suddenly. She offered him only a faint nod, as if unsure of it all.

"What would you do if he did?" she suddenly asked.

"I don't know. But he should never lift a hand against you. Ever," he said with conviction.

"Why do you care?" She wasn't sure why she responded so defensively to his concern. It came out before she realized it, and it was accompanied by a demeanor of anger and resentment.

"Don't ask me," he laughed, his devastating smile disarming her. She gave him a quick glance, a nod, and then disappeared into the courtyard, leaving him to his own devices.

When Nieve stepped into the house, she was met with a violent slap across the face and another for good measure by a red-faced, livid uncle. She was reprimanded and disgraced and shouted at. She was called shameless and thoughtless, stupid and inconsiderate and sent to her room. At first, she had no idea why. Two hours later, when she was sitting on the edge of her bed, contemplating what she could have done wrong, and her aunt entered, carrying several small, crustless tomato and salmon sandwiches and some tea. She looked pained and frightened and upset. A maid entered with her, carrying a pitcher of hot water for Nieve to use.

"What would possess you do disappear for a whole day and night, Nieve?" she asked.

"I beg your pardon?" Nieve asked. "I've only been gone since this morning."

"Don't lie to me!" Landie snapped, her face a mask of anger. "You've been gone since yesterday morning! There were twenty riders out looking for you. Were you with that boy from the great house? Where did you go?"

Nieve was without words. Her face was a mask of bewilderment.

"Landie, I promise you, I was only away from this morning. I left only after tidying the work table in the drawing room. Then I went to walk the forest," she replied in shock.

Her aunt only looked angrier. "That was yesterday, Nieve!"

Nieve frowned darkly, her eyes filling with tears of frustration. She wasn't mad. She was sure of what she had done. Her searching gaze seemed to convince her aunt that perhaps she might have some seed of truth in her words, for there was no insincerity in her. Landie appeared to be giving her some benefit of the doubt, but without an explanation she could not pardon her.

"I don't understand," Nieve muttered, reaching up to touch the burning skin where her uncle had hit her twice. "I went to valley forest, and the quarry, and then to the temple on the hilltop to see the colossus. Then I came straight home." She looked at her aunt, a tear falling onto her cheekbone. "I promise you, that is what I did."

The new maid that had replaced Enna after she had been sent away for her reckless suggestion, placed the decanter on the wash table, drew out two towels to place beside the washbowl, and turned to peer at Nieve. "Do you mean the pillared temple?" she asked, her voice markedly filled with dread.

"The one on top of the hill. At Winden. The stand of pillars," Nieve affirmed. "We saw the Titan from there."

"Oh, dear," the girl said, clutching her hands nervously.

Landie's brow slanted into a glower and she put her hands on her hips. "What 'oh dear?'" she exclaimed angrily. "What does *that* mean?"

"The Winden temple … The circle of eleven," the maid replied, her voice shaking. "And *you* lost time there, Miss Nieve?"

Nieve did not understand what she meant by lost time. Nieve did not have an answer.

The servant only lowered her eyes and shook her head once. "You lost time," she repeated. Then she curtsied suddenly to Nieve and swallowed what seemed like a sob. Not one of fear or sadness, but one of joy. She blinked out a tear and then darted out of the room.

Nieve looked at her aunt questioningly and received only a mirrored expression of bafflement in return.

5. Ruffians

Several days later, Nieve was permitted out of the house only to embark upon an errand. Her long absence that fateful day, knowing or not, had earned her this punishment. The servant girl had not returned for further explanation of the Circle of Eleven, but Uncle Bohan had heard some whisperings among the staff about the cursed place, and that the child had likely been possessed by magical things.

Uncle Bohan was from Emraith originally, and there was much of magic in that place where such things were revered and respected. In turn, his furor over the matter was quickly quashed by a sense that perhaps Nieve had stumbled into something dangerous and had indeed *lost time*, whatever that actually meant. After she described the hilltop in detail, and what happened to her and to Tammin, her uncle seemed suddenly a little cowed. He did not lift the punishment, for she had still been thoughtless, as far as he was concerned. And she had again stained a perfectly good dress. But from the moment he understood Nieve might have been touched by something magical, his whole demeanor around her and her aunt changed. Both of the ladies were befuddled by it, but also pleased, for his bullish nature had been eradicated for the time being by the respect and fear of anything magic-related.

Nieve was delighted to be sent on this errand now, and was walking to the town to purchase some paper and a bottle of ink for her uncle, who had asked her kindly to do so. She had promised to keep her gown clean and to not stray.

The idea of being out and about filled her with joy. She skipped to her room and prepared with zeal. She put on her best silver-grey silk spencer and her favorite walking gown of delphinium blue. She even donned a smart ruby bonnet. She carefully oversaw Dreya's work on her hair, as she was the newest chambermaid to come into their employ after the departure of the first two, and she was young and fairly new to assisting ladies with their daily preparations. Nieve then put the coins her uncle had given her into her little reticule and set out on a bright morning.

The road was dry, and the sun was shining. She had a little yen to see her friend Tammin again, and had made herself especially pretty for the possibility that she might chance upon him on her errand. But before encountering Tammin, she found herself blundering right into a gathering of young fellows.

She was scarce a quarter mile from town, and the three young men were sitting on their horses, idly moving towards her, laughing and talking loudly. They gave her a bad feeling, and she wanted nothing to do with them. She lowered her eyes and shaded her gaze from them with the brim of her bonnet as she passed.

"Good day, Miss," one of them called out.

She gave a polite nod and stopped to curtsy as they clippety-clopped by, and as soon as they did, she resumed her stride, glad she was rid of them. To her extreme delight, not another half moment later, Tammin trotted up on his fine mare, looking all the gentleman that he was. He glanced down at her as he was about to ride by and did a double-take when he realized it was Nieve. He leaned back in his saddle, and his mare fell into a halt. He wheeled her around and rode back.

Nieve glanced up the road at the boys riding away from town, saw them observing this interaction, and was curious why they would at all. Meanwhile, Tammin peered at his friend as if in a new light.

"Good morning, Miss Nieve," he said formally, tipping his hat at her.

She blushed. Her heart fluttered and her belly filled with the sensation of a thousand spiders dancing around. She was indeed only thirteen, and such feelings were mostly unfamiliar to her.

"What brings you out today? I haven't seen you about at all," he added.

"I've been under house arrest," she said, peering up at him, her eyes bright. "The fact that we were gone *so* long on the day of the hilltop… and that I ruined another gown. A week's worth of prison, I'm afraid. Possibly more, as I am only allowed out today to perform an errand."

"Yes, we *were* gone a long time," he said with a strange smirk. His horse shifted on her hooves, and he rocked a bit in his saddle. His reached out and patted her smooth, shiny neck with his gloved hand.

"Longer than we ever knew," she added tentatively, unsure of how to bring up the matter of lost time.

He frowned, looking at her earnestly. "We were weren't we? Gone for longer than we thought."

She nodded.

"I thought so. I'm not a lunatic then…" He exhaled in relief, tilting his head, lifting his reins a bit to calm his restless mount.

"Did you not know either? When you got home?" she asked. "I was cuffed the moment I came in, and punished severely for being gone all day before and the night, too!"

"Nobody was home when I got there. Nothing *seemed* amiss. When my parents came home that afternoon, I was told it was time to play at cards with the Wenrights. In my mind that was still a full day away. It is one of our weekly activities that I most detest, so I would not forget it easily. My stepmother and I argued what day it was when I protested. I could not make heads or tails of it. I had forgotten an entire day." He shook his head. "I thought I was a little mad, in honesty. To have returned home a full day from when I thought it was. I had a notion that it was only me, that I had somehow lost track of the days."

"You parents would not have noticed you gone the night before?" she asked.

"I sometimes go days without seeing either of them," Tammin replied with a shrug.

"Goodness," she whispered in reply, the shock evident on her sweet face. She might not have the most ideal of family situations, but at least her family would notice if she was missing for any length of time.

"My *man* was concerned for my whereabouts when I went to change for the evening, of course. But by then, I was already aware of the problem. And he didn't alert my family because I've been known to jaunt off now and again to the city without notifying anyone." He shifted in his saddle, his face all puzzlement. "How do you think it happened? To lose memory of an entire day and night?"

"The servant girl, she said that I lost time. I think we simply bypassed the day when we were in the temple. When the clamor of voices and wind and madness encircled us, the sky darkened and then brightened again. I think we somehow watched it happen from outside of our own world..." she said, her eyes locking onto something faraway.

Tammin watched her in bewilderment. "The whole thing seems absurd. I've lived all my whole life here, and never once did I ever have an experience like that. I've heard rumors about the hilltop. I thought they were nonsense. But one time with you, and it happens, and you have some untold understanding of it all..."

"I understand nothing," Nieve retorted defiantly. "I've only thought about what happened at that moment, and then what happened when I got home. It's the only explanation I can think of. That and the servant girl who became fearful of me and ran away when I spoke of going to the hilltop and ostensibly losing time."

Tammin sighed and shook his head as if it was simply too much to wrap his mind around. He scratched behind his ear with the handle of his crop.

"In truth, Miss Nieve, I am just relieved to find out I'm not harebrained." Tammin laughed merrily, his flashing smile and dashing air making Nieve all the more weak-kneed.

"I think we should speak nothing further of it," she said, offering him an equally relieved grin.

He nodded decisively and peered at her with curiosity. "And you are free now?"

"I'm afraid I've been tasked with some shopping at the stationers," she told him. "I am to go straight home when I am finished."

"Well then, I shall accompany you," he said cheerfully and he dismounted, his boots crunching onto the dry pebbles of the road. He swept off his topper and grasped his mare's reins as he walked with her toward town.

"And what have *you* been up to these past days?" she asked him.

"Nothing as astonishing as our last time together; or as tedious as being locked in the house," he said with a laugh. There was an odd, pregnant silence for a moment as they each recalled how strange the event at Winden was. But neither expounded further upon the subject.

"No. When I'm home from college, I spend most of my time out of my father's way," he told her.

She nodded, relating well to that sentiment.

"I was, however, on my way Narroway, for my stepmother has learned that we are friends, and has decided that she simply *must* meet you, and your aunt and uncle of course. Customarily, you all should have already come to dine at the great house, but my father is not always sensitive to these things. I was issued an order to make an invitation today. I shall have to accompany you home."

"I see," she said, not hiding her intimidation well.

He offered her a soft, conciliatory smile. "Fear not, Miss Nieve. Your aunt will entertain my stepmother greatly, for she delights in nothing more than having a subordinate companion to lord over, and condescend to. And my father will cast his withering stare upon your uncle, and we shall entertain ourselves with cards or whatnot. You can always hide behind me if anything seems too much to bear."

From her diminutive place beside him, he seemed like a pillar. "Very well, then," she conceded. She gave him a sheepish smile, and blushed when he returned it.

His wild thick, shaggy hair had fallen into his eyes. He flipped it back with but a shake of the head. They walked mostly in silence into the square, and he patiently waited for her while she was inside the stationers making her purchases.

When she emerged carrying her paper-wrapped package, she found Tammin had gained company. It was the three young men she'd seen leaving town earlier. They'd returned and were talking to Tammin. They all bowed and tipped their hats to her as she made her way toward them. She nodded shyly in greeting and curtsied. Tammin did not make any introductions.

"Well, Miss Nieve, shall we?" Tammin asked.

"Miss Nieve, pleased to meet you. I am Raynes. This here is Clemens, and that ugly fellow there is Hareth," the tall, fair-haired young man said, pointing at them with his topper. He watched Tammin closely as he spoke. "New faces are rare about these parts." He smiled crookedly, revealing white, flawless teeth, and a soft, rather disarming air about him.

"Pleasure," she replied diffidently. He looked positively charming, this tall fellow. But she suspected he was quite good at being so when he needed to. Nieve could not help but notice the bruising and cuts on this person's face. She looked upon him and saw both sides of the coin easily enough. Even at thirteen, she could tell what kind of person he was.

She was unsure what else to say in return to his exclamation. She merely smiled. "I must be on my way," she told them. "I will be punished if I deviate from my task. Master Halenwood, shall we go?"

He nodded. He'd been leaning on the edge of a bollard with a tie ring on it, holding his mare's reins with his arms crossed and his hat in the other hand. He plunked it onto his head and straightened.

"Tammin will catch up. We need a word with him, if you don't mind Miss," Raynes told her, his pale eyes boring into hers. She chewed her inner cheek, curtsying again before scuttling away.

"So, Halenwood… shall we reprise the conversation we so recently shared about the ownership of that mare?" Raynes spat.

"I've been told that I ought not fight—that it's ungentlemanly. So I will spare you a beating today, Raynes, as much as you seem to desire one. Now, if you don't mind, I have tasks of my own to complete, and invitations to make on behalf of my mother." Tammin fixed the angle of his topper and prepared to mount his horse.

Raynes laughed raucously at this and slapped his knee at the joke. "You ought not fight? You?" He roared again and the companions joined the mirth. "All you *do* is fight. Why the sudden penchant for passivity?" Tammin put his foot back down and turned to look at the boys. "I have my reasons." He crossed his arms, glancing back to see if Miss Nieve had gotten far ahead. He watched Raynes's gaze following the retreating form of the girl.

He burst into riotous laughter again and pointed at Nieve just as she disappeared around the side of the millinery shop. "That *child* is your reason?"

Tammin did not say a word. He merely gazed at his old friend, now enemy, with an arched brow.

"Did that child admonish you for fighting? Did she tell you not to? Is that what you are up to these days? Capitulating to the demands of a *little girl.*" Raynes laughed. "How pathetic." He narrowed his eyes and tilted his head when Tammin gave no reaction.

"You deflower her yet? She's a bit tender, but pretty enough for what she is."

A shadow passed over Tammin, darkening his demeanor. His warm, laughing eyes grew icy. "I'd watch myself if I were you," he warned Raynes in a chilling voice. He turned and started to mount.

"I didn't take you for that kind. Rather disgusting, as far as I'm concerned," Raynes taunted. "But I suppose if the little trollop is willing enough..."

Tammin had managed to get his foot in the stirrup after his warning, but he lowered it and turned slowly. Heat crept up his neck from underneath his cravat.

"What? Have I spoken ill of your little *woman?*" Raynes laughed obnoxiously.

He got out two good guffaws before his face was punched into another direction. His top hat flew off and he staggered back, roaring and running at Tammin. The two collided, and fell in a tangle of struggling limbs, rolling in the dirt in front of the stores, fists flying. Tammin landed several good punches and kneed his opponent soundly in the groin. He stood up when Raynes was incapacitated and reached out to grab Raynes's topper.

"If I catch you even *looking* at her the wrong way, I will gouge your eyes out. If I catch you speaking to her with even the slightest ounce of disrespect, I will rip your tongue out. If you touch her, I will break your hands," he warned through gritted teeth. He crushed Raynes's topper flat and threw it on him. "Now you've made me fight and act in an ungentlemanly way, haven't you? What should be the consequence for this, I wonder?" He paused and stared down at Raynes, who was still rolling around in the dirt as he always ended up. "I will have to think on it, I suppose. But I'll deliver you the decision once it's made. Now, I have to go and apologize to my friend for disobeying her wishes."

He brushed off his hat and put it back on, mounting his horse. With a nod to the other two boys, he rode after Nieve. He was glad these feckless idiots that followed Raynes around were too cowardly to firmly take anyone's side since their parting as friends. They merely stood by and watched their enmity unravel. He did not have any inclination to include those two in his regular distribution of beatings.

Tammin spent much of the ride to Narroway brushing the dust from his clothes and mumbling angrily to himself, embarrassed by his state. Nieve glowered at the sight of him when he rode up, and walked on in silence for a good measure of the trip. She only spoke when he dismounted and began to walk alongside her.

"You have been brawling again," she said with a curl of her lip.

"I had good reason," he replied defensively.

She gave him the side-eye and frowned. She did not respond to that. Instead she clutched the ream of paper to her chest, and her delicate hand around the bottle of ink, and soldiered on.

"If you see any of those boys, you walk the other way, do you understand?" he told her firmly.

She arched her brow and looked at him dubiously. "I think you ought to follow that advice yourself."

"I mean it. They are the *worst* people. They will torment you. More so now that they know we are friends, do you understand? You do not go near them. At all," he instructed her in a brotherly tone.

Nieve studied his serious expression of concern and found his brotherly behavior to be simultaneously infuriating *and* charming. She nodded once in concession. They did not say anything until they reached the grange, where they came upon Uncle Bohan who was in exiting one of the barns where there was a great thrashing sound of hoofs in hay and the baying of sheep. He closed the gate and looked at Nieve, and then Tammin.

"Good morning," he said politely, bowing to the boy who returned the greeting. "Where did you find her this time, Master Halenwood?"

"On an errand," Tammin replied brightly. "I was issued an order to make an invitation to your family, and I asked if I might accompany the young Miss home from town."

Uncle Bohan nodded stiffly, and gestured towards the house. "Go on in. I'm seeing to the new stock."

Nieve was incurious about the noisy sheep. She could smell the lanolin in their wool from where she stood. She wrinkled her nose and wordlessly moved towards the house. Tammin tipped his hat to Uncle, and followed.

They found her aunt at work in the drawing room, carefully stitching together some little fabric diamonds to make a quilt made from old gowns and clothing. They were all mostly made of the light, airy fabrics needed for life in the arid countries. She'd layered them in different colors, and it made for a lovely effect on the swatch of quilt that was already completed. She glanced up when Nieve entered and smiled twinklingly at Tammin.

"Oh la! What a delightful surprise!" she exclaimed, rising to her feet.

Tammin bowed deeply and took off his hat. She invited him to sit and ordered tea. Nieve went to put her purchases in the library, and removed her spencer and bonnet, returning to the drawing room only after she'd inspected herself thoroughly in the mirror. She gazed at herself for a moment, frowning at what she saw.

She was anything but pretty in her appearance, she mused. She still had a rounded face of a little girl. She thought her lips were too large and her nose too small. Girding herself for the visit, she pinched some color into her cheeks and squared her shoulders. In her most ladylike walk, she moved to the drawing room to join her company.

Tammin was seated on the edge of one of the blue silk wingbacks, as if fearful of getting dirt on them from his breeches, which were marginally clean but still marked with dust from his fight. They were discussing this as Nieve entered.

"It was not a fall from my horse, ma'am," he insisted. "I had a brief tousle with a young man who was extremely disrespectful towards the Miss."

Nieve froze, surprised by this news.

"Indeed? How impertinent of him. He doesn't even know my little niece to speak of her with contempt," Aunt Landie exclaimed.

"They are not good people. I'm ashamed to say that I was friends with them once, and that I, too, was disposed to cause suffering to others as these boys do. But I have stepped away from all that. I fear Miss Nieve might be exposed to it for being my friend," he said with a sigh.

"I am glad you are no more a thug that would predate upon a helpless girl. I am proud of you that you were able to rise above those things to be a better person. Am I impudent to ask what it was that caused this falling out, that made you such a better young man?"

Nieve watched Tammin, curious herself. And she only saw him squirm.

Tammin had to ruminate on the question posed by Mrs. Marielle. Mostly because he didn't have any definitive answers. The core reason why Raynes now disliked him was never truly clear. It had started over a young woman whom Raynes had chosen to court, and Tammin did not approve of but that was nothing the two of them could have worked out together. Something else happened that Tammin was unsure of. They had a row one day, and broke into a terrible fight over something trite and useless. And from that day on, neither of the boys were willing to see sense when it came to the other. Raynes in fact, became hell bent on hating Tammin.

As for Tammin becoming the better man, that was another mystery. His habit of treating those with disdain... he wasn't sure where that went. He thought of Nieve, and his brow knit up. He realized, that day, when she fell into the water, it was the first time he'd ever extended himself for anyone. Before that, he might have been angry with Raynes, but he was still the privileged, entitled snot he had always been.

Tammin's discomfort apparently had been quite overt, for Mrs. Marielle simply veered the conversation away from necessitating a reply, for she was so considerate a person. "Nieve might risk encounters with those boys, but you will mind after her then," Landie declared. "For she cannot be without her friend now, Master Tammin. You must always be Nieve's friend. I hope you gave him a good throttling for speaking ill of my niece," she said sweetly, in a conspiratory whisper.

He laughed softly and said with a wry grin, "I did. And there's more where that came from if they try it again. And I've warned the Miss that she ought to stay away from them, for I cannot be here to watch over her when I am at college. But they'll know what will happen to them if I hear of anything happening to Miss Nieve."

"Well, good on you, Master Tammin," Landie exclaimed with conviction. "I shall never forget that you put yourself in harm's way for Nieve's sake." Her eyes misted up.

They both then glanced up and noticed Nieve, and Tammin looked down and away, a bit embarrassed. Nieve closed the door where she had been standing while eavesdropping and curtsied to them both.

"I did not mean to do that," she whispered.

Tammin's eyes subtly took in her appearance and Nieve blushed. She had taken such pains that morning, wearing a nice dress, arranging her hair carefully with braids swagged prettily on each side of her face, and wound into a tidy bun. She assumed a demure pose with her hands clutched against her ribs, her little elbows, fringed in tidy, narrow ruffles of lace and organdy, pointing out on each side.

She moved around his chair and sat on the one next to his, only a small oval table between them.

"I hope what that boy said did not hurt your feelings, my dear Nieve," her aunt told her.

"I was not present when he said it," Nieve ascertained. Her gaze then fell onto Tammin, who was fiddling with the brim of his hat, which he clutched still in his hands.

"Might I ask…" Aunt Landie began.

"I'm afraid it was something that cannot be repeated," Tammin said quickly. "I am glad you will be joining us tomorrow to dine at the great house. My mother insists on sending the coach so that you do not have to walk. She told me she would send it at a quarter to six. Is that acceptable?"

"Of course, Master Halenwood, of course. We are so honored and delighted," Landie exclaimed, clasping her hands together. "We will be ready at a quarter to six."

Tammin nodded in affirmation, his demeanor grave and stiff. He stood, bowing deeply to Nieve's aunt, and then to Nieve. He put on his hat and stalked out of the room. By the sound of it, he encountered Uncle Bohan on the way, and there were final farewells and formalities shared before they heard the sound of his mare's hooves retreating from the courtyard.

"Well," Landie blurted, flopping down into her chair. "He didn't even stay long enough for the tea to arrive." She laughed merrily.

"He doesn't seem to be the sort to linger," Nieve retorted absentmindedly.

"It's odd that he is so different from the accounts I've heard of him. He's been nothing but pleasant and kind to us. But hear tell, he is thought of as rather a bully in the neighborhood. I heard the tale of his driving a young fellow away to live with another relative in the sand-countries, the bullying was so severe. There are people who have told me that the sight of him will send most young people running, except for a few girls who think him to be the epitome of attractiveness. But here he is, as sweet as can be," Aunt Landie said in wonder.

Nieve pursed her lips and her brow wrinkled. Tammin? A bully? A ruffian, perhaps. A scrapper, but a bully? That was absurd. "Master Tammin is many things, but he's not a bully," she opined.

"It's likely he simply hides his true colors from you in particular," Uncle Bohan said as he strode into the room and shut the door. "The nobility and the rich, they are quite apt at playing whatever role benefits them the most. He's a fine enough boy, I imagine, but likely as duplicitous as the sky is blue."

"Uncle," Nieve pleaded. "You oughtn't make such assumptions about him. He saved my life and has been very kind to me." She clutched her hands tightly in her lap.

"Perhaps there's truth to the gossip, but perhaps he has changed," Landie offered. "Maturity often brings such alterations to peoples' habits. A view of the real world, perhaps, sobered the arrogance out of him."

Uncle Bohan's view of most peerage was low to begin with, but he was mercenary enough to know he should respect and capitulate to them for his own benefit. It was such a thing that had earned him his place in the greenlands, for he had assisted a greenlander noble with some dire business matters, and had won his place at Narroway for it. But in private, he spent a good deal of his time criticizing and disparaging the wealthy, titled folk upon whose coattails he rode.

He gave his wife a dubious arch of the brow, and a sardonic snort before serving himself of some port from the sideboard.

Nieve merely frowned and shook her head. She could not imagine that any of it was true of Tammin. She wasn't sure how disappointed she would be if she did find out all these assertions were indeed accurate. Or should she be proud of him for changing for the better? Or was he merely playing a game with her, intending to do something cruel later on after he'd earned her trust? She tilted her head and gazed off into the fire while she ruminated upon these thoughts. Why *was* he being kind to her?

"So the boy brought an invitation from the big house, eh?" Uncle Bohan said with a rare smile on his face. Again, he delighted in the acceptance, but it would do little to change his private opinion of the family.

Landie nodded happily. "We can thank our Nieve for the invitation. For, had she not fallen into the pond, she would not have made friends with the young master."

"The Halenwoods seem a polite enough people that they would have issued an invitation eventually," Uncle grumbled dismissively. "However, if it means that there is a prospective match, I don't want to get ahead of myself, but it would be advantageous for us. She's young yet, but one cannot foster those kinds of connections early enough." He lifted the goblet of dark, viscous sherry, and drained it.

"You speak so ill of the family, and now you promote a match between the two?" Landie asked, her eyes falling upon him critically.

"The girl doesn't seem to have any objections to the boy, does my opinion truly matter, if it provides for her future?" he asked, refilling his glass.

Landie seemed to process the idea of a match between Nieve and Tammin, and she nodded. "Indeed. I hadn't thought of that. *I* would be concerned about the validity of the rumors about him if that is the case." She shifted in her seat. Even in this little gesture, she was graceful and lovely. Landie peered at Nieve, and her eyes softened. "Nieve is still, in my eyes, a little child. But you are moving quickly towards that age, aren't you? It would save the both of us a great deal of concern if you found someone like Master Tammin before we had to send you to the Capitol for the season, or outfit you with coming out gowns and all that fuss, now wouldn't it?"

Nieve did not answer. She sat still, her hands folded daintily in her lap, and her eyes cast onto the floor. She did not have any objections to the idea of Tammin. She liked him. Even if he was a bit of a hooligan by nature. She was still very young. A girl could not marry until she was sixteen, and even then, that was considered very young to wed. Most girls didn't even come out until they were eighteen. Tammin was also still in college, and likely would be until he was eighteen. He had informed Nieve on their walk before the incident on the hilltop that he was sixteen years old.

She mulled this in her head, and then realized how stupid all this speculation was. Tammin had not in any way indicated he had that sort of interest in her. She was younger than he by three years, and she was certainly not the kind of girl any family of their status would envision their first son marrying. He would marry from a titled or rich family. She was not impoverished or without pedigree, but she was not high-bred.

He either was simply a kind boy who had taken Nieve under his wing, or he had other motives. He surely would only see Nieve as a child, and nothing else. She hid her frown. She stood up and left, climbing the steps to her room, overcome suddenly with sadness.

Miranda Mayer

6. *Covetousness*

Raynes Bellworth flung himself into a deep, squashy chair in his father's office and library so brusquely that slips of hair fell over his forehead and into his eyes. He raked the pale, almost snowy locks back with his long fingers, and then proceeded to gnaw on the cuticle of his thumb, his eyes cast somewhere faraway.

He had a hard, bitter look on his face. He hated it when Tammin was back in town. It rankled him miserably to see him, or even hear of him. Luckily, this brief interval would end, and the Viscount's son would be returning to his college where he could rot. Raynes threw his foot out and kicked the edge of an oaken tea table in the center of the seating arrangement, shoving it away by a few inches and upsetting a small pile of books that had been stacked there.

"What in the name of the Titans are you doing to the furniture, you confounded hooligan?" a voice barked from behind him.

Raynes twisted to see his older brother entering the room, balancing an open book on the tips of his fingers. He had his back arched in his usual priggish way, with his chest pushed out and his calves flexed as if there were five lovely ladies around the corner he was wanting to impress. He was dressed faultlessly, as usual, down to the perfectly set collars and the careful pleats and folds of his voluminous cravat. The dandy irritated Raynes to no end. But still not half as much as Tammin did.

"I take it you've been scrapping with your former friend again. You know father will have your hide for it," Alderny snapped. As he circled the chairs, he tugged down the front of his layered blue and green waistcoats with his free hand. He threw out the tails of his frock coat and sank down with deliberate slowness—as if he were sitting on a heap of whipped cream—into a chair across from his brother. He then primly crossed his legs, his breeches tight on his knees, his sage-green stockings with fancy clocking on the ankles stretched over his legs. He was wearing a pair of slippers so scant, they barely covered his toes.

He had the same pale hair as his younger brother, but he had a sharper face and a larger, rather hooked nose, which took after their mother. She had not been a raving beauty, to speak the least of it, but she had been a good mother; a kind mother. The thought of his mother made Raynes's glower darken, and angry thoughts of Tammin filled his mind.

"I do wish the two of you would put away whatever grudge it is that you've mustered up between you and bury the hatchet. Life was greatly better when the two of you were the best of friends," Alderny muttered, throwing out his fingers and tidily turning the page of his book, peering snootily down his nose at it. He then seemed to process some thought, and lowered the book, rolling his glassy blue eyes up at his sullen brother, a brow forming into an arch. "Now we mention it, what is it that turned two friends into fighting enemies?"

"Mind your business, popinjay," Raynes spat.

"Now, now, no need to throw invective about like that. I was merely curious. One has the impression you expend a great deal of your person in hating someone who used to be closer to you than I," Alderny retorted with a sneer. He lifted the book and ran his fingers down the text to find his place again. "Seems to me Tammin is a decent sort of young fellow. A bit shaggy for a Viscount's first son, but decent, nonetheless. I can't imagine he has it in him to do something so vile as to deserve your hatred, especially after all the time you two spent together as boys. It is utterly incomprehensible to me why you hate him so."

"You don't know anything," Raynes hissed.

He heaved himself onto his feet and stalked out, leaving his older brother to the library. He walked instead to the garden. It had begun to rain a little, but he found shelter under the ugly folly his father had insisted on installing underneath the twin oaks, and he flopped down onto the stone bench within, watching the rain fall and soak this verdant, green countryside. He thought back to the day when he and Tammin had their falling out.

The fight they had was one so filled with anger and violence; there were broken bones and broken spirits in the end. Raynes's face had been a muddle of blood and furious tears, Tammin also bloodied and battered, with a stricken expression of shock and bewilderment. They never told anyone what had caused it. But there had been a flurry of things to happen at that time, the worst of which was the Bellworths' matriarch, Raynes's mother, abandoning her family, leaving only an approved bill of divorce on her husband's desk—something rarely dispensed by the council, or obtained by plaintiffs. It must have taken quite a bit of planning to do it how she had. It took everyone by surprise.

Many within the circle, including the fathers, believed that Raynes was acting out in anger over that event, somehow placing blame or resentment upon his friend for his mother leaving. But that was only a shred of the whole truth. And Raynes could not let his rage over this mysterious crime go. He wished only to inflict as much pain and misery on Tammin as he believed he had done to him. He glared at the rolling hills of his father's estate, something he had earned with his own grit and wherewithal. Unlike Tammin's father, who merely had the privilege of inheriting his riches. Raynes sneered at the thought of it, crossing his arms.

Now Tammin was acting all high and mighty over a stupid child, he snorted to himself. His train of thought then veered from Tammin to the little girl he'd been treating so kindly that morning. It was astonishing that Tammin would lavish a little girl with such attentions. No more than twelve or thirteen. Pretty? She had the potential of it. But she still looked like a child, with rounded cheeks and great big eyes and a wholly uninteresting, boyish figure. He could not see why Tammin would take an interest in her. But he was seen about town and the countryside with the little slip of a thing several times already, and people were whispering about the sweetness of the Viscount's son, to be so protective and kind to the new child from the arid lands. They all spoke of his reformed ways, and how the introduction of this little girl must be the reason for it.

There were tales of heroism being passed along, of how Tammin had saved her life, and now seemed to have some sort of sense of obligation towards her. But Tammin wasn't acting as if he were merely obliged. He was obeying the child's demand that he not fight, and he was standing up for her honor. Raynes shook his head in bewilderment. This was not the Tammin he knew.

He thought again about her fresh little face, shaded by the broad brim of her bonnet. Her gloved hands gripping the packages, her eyes downcast and bashful when he had so warmly greeted her. Did Tammin deserve even the attentions of this little thing?

At first, the whole idea seemed laughable—that his peer was finding something to gain by traipsing about with a chit like that. But now, it started to irk Raynes. Another year or two, and she would start to round out into what would surely be a fine young lass. Tammin already had the unyielding attentions of the few, most eligible grown girls in town. Miss Vaye, Miss Urdlin, Miss Ellow, and Miss Pine—all of them had eyes only for Tammin. Getting any of those girls to even consent to a dance at assemblies was a challenge, for they all refused to accept anyone until they were sure Tammin was not going to ask one of them. And they were the top tier of choices in this small berg. What was left after those were middling choices? It started to make sense now, why Tammin might glom himself onto a new face, one still years from coming out, if he truly had no interest in the older girls available to him. But he also lived in the city most of the year, and he would surely find a fine array of young women to choose from. Why this child, this little Miss Nieve? It was inexplicable.

Raynes resolved at that moment to find out what exactly made her so interesting to his rival. He was not sure why he decided to do this. He just wanted to know. Maybe he could machinate some way to get in between them. If Tammin found the little thing so endearing, maybe he could connive some way to make her hate him as much as Raynes did. That would be a delight. He smirked to himself. He decided he would seek her out soon, and begin to assess the situation in earnest.

Raynes and Tammin grew up under the shadow of bullying fathers and permissive or indifferent mothers. They were both shaped by lives of great privilege and entitlement, and they treated everyone below them as exactly that—below them.

Reflections of their fathers, they tormented the passive and held no remorse for it. They had been the bane of the region to any young person, and even the occasional adult of lower status. They were not discriminating and disrespected anyone they could get away with. But even if they did not respect anyone else, they had held one another in great respect and were inseparable. Bound by hatred for their fathers, they had a great deal in common to draw their bond from, and they had confided all their woes to one another and trusted the other unflinchingly.

In private, they were contemplative and thoughtful. Kind to one another, in a chiding, boyish way. Understanding and always present when the other needed. In public, however, they were intolerable bastards.

The fall of this friendship in part drew a hatred of the worst kind from the boys—a hatred that was fed from a place of love. For both boys dearly longed for the companionship they once shared, and the ire that it was impossible to restore. Both boys had allowed too much to pass, too much to be said, too much pain shared to ever have the friendship they once had again. And the resentment of this manifested itself a desire to hurt the other in every way they could. Raised with violence, they only knew how to express themselves in violence.

But the sad truth was, Raynes missed Tammin—the Tammin he knew. The one who'd sat beside him on the bridge, with their feet dangling over the water, his hand on Raynes's back, heads hanging low, while Raynes blubbered like a child after his father had beaten him and his mother and then killed Raynes's favorite hunting dog in front of him. He missed the Tammin who gave the irrepressible social-climber, Miss Avela Tine, hope of an engagement by his advances, and then broke her heart the same way she had done to Raynes when she jilted him for being from common stock.

Instead, he had a Tammin who he could no longer look at without wanting to wrap his fingers around his throat and to strangle the life from him. Tammin who had suddenly grown a conscience, who no longer tormented people for fun, and who was being praised for it by everyone, including Raynes's own father and brother. Tammin who saved the lives of little girls and who doted upon them for whatever reason. He had to be up to something, because otherwise it made no sense at all. How could Tammin find friendship in someone so young and guileless?

7. Confessions

Landie was, without a doubt, overcome with joy as the coach drew away from Narroway and took the lane that would circle the lake and bring them to Halenwood Hall. Nieve sat quietly next to her aunt in the direct line of scrutiny of her uncle. He watched her closely, with that strange, expectant, wary regard that had come to possess him the moment he heard about the Winden Temple and the lost day.

The ride was a short one. Ten minutes had them at the doorstep of the great house just as the clock knelled the sixth hour. They were met by Lady Halenwood. A tiny thing, with long, dark hair that was styled in a slightly old-fashioned way, with a weft of hair resting in a carefully buffed curl on her right shoulder. The rest was curled into a great pouf around her head. Her jewelry was heavy and a little too much for guests of so little consequence. She wore a short-sleeved gown of light, sumptuous taffeta the color of a steely grey sky, with teal gloves wrapping her long, thin arms.

She was pretty. A lady of perhaps twenty-six years or so. Her face still had a youthful plumpness and skin without a single blemish. She spoke in soft words, so quietly at times; one had to strain to hear her. She stood beside her towering husband who looked very much like Tammin, Nieve concluded. He had the same thick head of black hair, save his had some silver dusting at the temples. He had eyes of the same vivid emerald green. But she detected something in his eye, something murky that Tammin did not possess. It was reserved, this murk, for the members of his family alone. Especially his wife, for whenever they met eyes, there was a noticeable dislike between them. He was tall, and also broad—with wide shoulders, like his son, and thick arms. He moved with the same predator-like liquidity as Tammin. His hard eyes examined Nieve closely, which made her shrink and blush. There was no malice in his gaze when it was set upon Nieve. In fact, she saw something quite warm inside his intimidating air when he bowed to her and took her hand.

"Welcome young lady," he said to her with a strange, almost clumsy smile. "We are delighted to welcome your family into our home. It is high time we had a young lady like you to visit."

The family was greeted with a polite warmth from Lady Halenwood, especially towards Landie who was only two years her junior. Lady Halenwood, upon seeing how lovely and well-mannered Landie was, puffed up a little, and her keen, sharp eye fell with a calculating scrutiny upon her. She claimed Landie at once, and made a grandiose display parading them towards the parlor, taking Landie's arm, and going on about the improvements she'd made to the hall.

"My wife was very close to her friend, Mrs. Bellwood," the Viscount whispered to Nieve as they followed. "However, sadly the lady moved away, and my wife was devastated by her abrupt departure. I am certain she will come to value your aunt as her confidante, for she has been lacking such a friend for some time."

Nieve observed that there was indeed a latent glee in the Lady's bearing at having an audience in Landie. It was pressing against the measure of her words and shining behind the steady, condescending gaze that rested on Landie's face when she responded the Lady's questions.

They were led to the parlor, and then filed into an intimate seating arrangement inside a circle of chairs and sofas around an oval, black-lacquered and gilded tea-table.

"My dearest Mrs. Marielle, I understand you have come all the way from Rethros. Is this true?" the Lady asked. "It is rare to see new faces from the arid lands these days. The congress of selection seems to have become too strict in their choices these past years."

"They have been particularly stringent for the past decade," Uncle Bohan said. "I understand that there are several newly elected members who have extremely conservative views on the matter of immigration into the greenlands, and one must meet exceedingly high standards to qualify for residency these days. I was fortunate to have the patronage of the Earl of Halleks, for it is the only reason we are here today."

The Viscount cast a strange regard upon Uncle Bohan for a moment, but it passed. Nieve could not quite make out what the man was about.

Landie, on the other hand, did not pass up the opportunity to wax poetic about the hot, dry, featureless home she sprang from, unused to it being spoken of as something undesirable. The way she painted it, even Nieve would have missed it if she herself didn't remember what it was really like.

"Some might describe the desert lands as empty, unchanging and barren, but for those of us who were raised in the dunes, it is anything but those things. They are as varying as the lands here. Red sands, gold sands. High dunes, ribbed dunes, the flats and the heights. Mountains rising up, canyons gouged from the earth. Oases and valleys. Broad rivers, spiny forests. There are so many things to see in the desert countries. And to me, there is such beauty.

"You must yourself experience a dune-rise, when the sunlight touches the sands and it sparkles like myriad diamonds, to understand my love for it. Or when dusk falls, and the flats look like lakes of gold. The bone-trees are so majestic."

"They look like skeletal hands of giants clawing their way out of the sand," Nieve murmured. "I would *hardly* call them majestic."

Landie shot her niece a bit of a withering glare, and continued. "What makes them beautiful is not their appearance alone, but the broad leaves that spread from them during the short rain seasons, like great big fans. And the clouds of bird-lizards that they attract to feast on the dried growth once the rains have passed. Their wings are the color of sapphires.

Nieve did not bring up the accompanying fleets of spear hawks that banded together during this short period and feasted themselves on the lizard birds, to leave their mangled dried wings behind like so many autumn leaves. Far be it for Nieve to throw more mud on Landie's idyllic nostalgia. She merely smirked at her aunt.

Personally, Nieve was happy that she didn't have to exist under the shade of a parasol every time she ventured out of doors or to be besieged by sand and grit in her eyes and ears all the time, not to mention her clothes and shoes. She had almost forgotten what it was like to feel as parched as paper after only a short outing, or to be so hot, she thought she was going to die.

Nieve's eyes instead took in the spacious parlor with its tall fireplace and pale green paneled walls. The adult ladies were seated side by side, the men across from them on a dainty sofa. Nieve was on a backless saber chair between them, and Tammin was across from her on the chair's twin.

Landie's open, effusive nature appeared to intrigue the Lady in spite of being a complete contrast to her own. Her eyes however, seemed a bit hard as they took in Landie's bubbly laughter and her graceful gestures as she described Rethros and her childhood home as if it were the land of a fairy tale. The Lady was surprised to learn that the ladies of Narroway Grange came from good, well-bred stock. The mention of Grandfather's title of Baronet, albeit lower than their own, made Lady Halenwood's eyes shine even more. As the girls' family was mostly dead and gone, this represented very little, as they did not inherit the title. But it signified at least a respectable upbringing to Lady Halenwood, who put a great deal of importance on breeding.

Nieve began to notice that Lord Halenwood too seemed intrigued by Landie as well—but in a different way, which was not unnoticeable to the others in the room. He watched her unceasingly with his piercing green eyes. Nieve saw how the couple drank in her aunt's very essence, and she peered at the familiar face as if to see for herself what they found so fascinating. She often took for granted how lovely her aunt was. But she *was* lovely. It was her beauty that had captured Uncle Bohan's eye that day. And it was her beauty and her charm that turned a hardened bachelor into a married man.

There was no doubt of her beauty. Perhaps Nieve needed to be reminded of it. Like her niece, Landie had dark, shining, wavy hair which she had styled in such a fashionable coif, with coils dangling down against her smooth, flushed, elegant neck. Her eyes, the same golden-hazel as her niece, were bright and full of life and joy. Her skin, flawless and flush with health and vitality. Her cheeks rosy, her lips a bright, vivid pink. Her brows were graceful and expressive, her teeth white and dazzling. She wore a gown of fuchsia pink with little pearls stitched into a delicate embroidered design on the front of the bodice. It was a cross-over, the diagonal lines sweeping from her shoulder to meet the cleave of her breast. The neckline was edged in a barely visible ruffle of pale silk gauze.

She wore the lovely parure gifted to her by Nieve's mother: A necklace of sparkling baguettes of rare Ametrine with a matching set of earrings, and a bracelet on her mustard-gold gloves, as well. The lavender and gold stones sparkled almost as brightly as Landie did.

Nieve's gaze then moved with curiosity onto her uncle who seemed to be back to his state of perpetual simmering rage. The reason, it seemed, was because his eyes were locked with on Lord Halenwood, unnoticed by the gentleman who was so entranced by Nieve's aunt, he didn't see anything else.

In fact, the adults were so absorbed in Landie, that nobody noticed when Tammin moved out of his seat, and circled the company. He slid his hand around Nieve's wrist and drew her away from them. "Come away. Let us engage in something. Cards or music perhaps. Something that will keep them from interrupting us until dinner," he whispered.

Nieve's brow furrowed and she glanced back. The adults were too enraptured indeed. A part of Nieve wanted to stay, and to further witness this strange dynamic developing between the three grow-ups in the room. But Tammin took her away in haste, a wry smile on his handsome face. With a bit of a disappointed frown, she followed Tammin.

Tammin led Nieve towards a small table by one of the towering windows and helped her to sit in one of the fragile chairs. Before her was a little wooden box filled with ivory sticks.

"Oh, Spillikins!" she exclaimed, reaching for the box.

Her exuberance might have revealed how childlike she still was, but she was comfortable with Tammin and did not try to act differently. Tammin watched her open the box, dump out the little bundle of sticks onto the table, and remove the hook. She slid off her gloves and threw them onto the table. She gathered the game sticks up and tamped them even, then arranged them into a little standing cone shape, dexterously leaning one against the other. His gaze never left her as she concentrated on this delicate task.

She looked so happy, he thought to himself. Her hair, all tidy and neat, seemed strange to him that way. He liked it when she was wild. But he liked it when she was pretty, too, he chided himself, observing her dainty braids, the string of pearls wrapped around the crown of her head, her small, sparkling pendant, her earrings all so carefully appointed for the evening. Her gown was white silk with a sash the color of her pale pink cheeks. Her slippers were red. She swung her feet thoughtlessly as she worked.

She glanced up when her task was done and caught his eye. She gave him an awkward smile. It made Tammin realize he was staring. He startled out of his reverie, and she merely grinned broadly at him.

"It has been a bit strange and lonely these past days, Tammin," she told him. "I realize that I've come to like adventures with you."

Tammin smiled softly. "Indeed, we do have adventures, don't we? I like them, too."

"*Your* company is my favorite," she said absently, tilting her head as she adjusted the sticks and then picked up the hook.

She then froze and her face took on a faraway sort of expression. She seemed to be mulling something over in her head, as if trying to understand her own thoughts. Then she lowered her hand with the hook in it and peered at him guilelessly. "You are going back to your college soon?"

"Yes," Tammin said with a hint of regret in his tone. It was the first time he lamented the departure. He'd come to enjoy his times with Nieve, brief and eccentric as they were. He'd grown attached to her.

Nieve's face fell a little and she tilted her head. "It is not going to be pleasant to have you absent," she confessed. "I've gotten used to you being around in a place where everyone else is a stranger to me. And these past days I've thought I'd rather be out with you, and the want of your friendship made me ache a little bit in here." She tapped her stomach. "I didn't like it very much. And now you'll be gone for months on end, and I'll have nobody to talk to. The aching will be interminable and unbearable."

Tammin bowed his head and hid the soft smile that formed on his lips. When he looked up again, she was gazing past him into some other place.

"I shall miss you," she said. Then she seemed to snap to, shrugged, and turned her attention back to the table. They proceeded with the game, each taking turns prying out little sticks as carefully as possible.

"It will only be until the end of Autumn. A few months," he assured her. "I'm certain you will have made loads of friends by then, and have forgotten all about me."

"Doubtful," she exhaled dejectedly, taking her turn and almost immediately causing the jackstraws to shift.

She pouted as she handed the hook to Tammin. He took it and assessed the heap of sticks to find one he could extricate without moving the others. He pulled one out and two fell. He handed her the hook.

"Well, Nieve, I shall miss you, too. But I shall come to call at Narroway the moment I return from college. And I shall expect you to have a list of at least three adventures we shall have to embark upon during my visitation," Tammin told her.

She smiled and nodded. Then she went pale again, looking up at him with stricken eyes. "Tammin, what if my uncle succeeds in sending me away, and we are parted? What shall I do if I can no longer see my dearest new friend?"

"I shall come find you then," he told her, the idea of it happening striking him more deeply than he had expected. He, too, suddenly felt an ache in his stomach at the idea of never seeing her again, she who had so understood him, and who he so understood. He studied her sweet face, those caring eyes. The girl who had worried for his dignity, his gentlemanliness, and his happiness, when nobody worried about him at all.

"Promise. If we are *ever* parted, I shall come and find you," Tammin reassured her, feeling that he was reassuring himself, too. She was the only thing he could think of that made him look forward to the next break in schooling. There was nothing else here but Nieve.

At dinner, the goodwill seemed to shift into something a little unpleasant. Lady Halenwood, whose overt welcome of a new friend had been so noticeable, now seemed to have a change of heart. She finally saw how rapt her husband's attention was upon this newcomer, and her gentle, passive, but superior comportment became something much bristlier. But she dared not say anything, even in passing, for her wariness of her appearance was evident.

His Lordship casually invited Landie to visit with his wife once a week. He then offered to show her the whole of the house while she visited, and also suggested they go for a country drive when the weather was good. Landie, seemingly oblivious to the nature of his regard, only agreed with great alacrity, and exclaimed her joy at having a lady friend with which to spend time at last.

"It has been an age since I had a friend and confidante," she told Lady Halenwood, whose glower seemed to go unnoticed by Landie. "And your company is so kindly and welcoming. I have so many ideas of things we can do and share together. How kind and generous you are, My Lord and Lady."

Meanwhile, Uncle Bohan was staring daggers at Lord Halenwood, who made a bit of a show of ignoring this challenging gaze, and put his energy into devouring his meal, heartily helping himself to more from the veritable feast that had been laid out in the center of the long table. From tall, gleaming flummeries to glistening, glazed roast pheasant decorated with its beautiful plumage and a great salmon set in jelly with elegant little flowers made of vegetables decorating it, everything was as sumptuous and delicious as it was presented. Nieve had eaten well before, but never quite so stylishly. Even the white soup sat in an ornate tureen of an earthy blue with white ceramic cameos and swags of laurel leaves decorating its sides.

Nieve and Tammin looked on over this feast of delights at the scene unfolding with the adults, both entertained and slightly horrified by this display. It was only after dinner that the true nature of this interaction made itself fully known. As the Nieve and her family departed, Lord Halenwood walked them to the door, leaving her Ladyship in the parlor by herself. He took Landie's arm, and led her along, with her husband in tow. When they bade one another goodbye, he took her hand and placed a kiss upon it, declaring her to be the loveliest of neighbors. His mannerisms were suggestive—even blatant.

Uncle Bohan stepped in between them with a dark glower on his brow. Lord Halenwood stepped back and smiled almost smugly.

"A good evening to you, sir," Uncle Bohan snarled. He gripped Landie's arm and nearly yanked her out the door, shouting after Nieve once he was outside. Nieve curtsied to the Viscount and then Tammin, scurrying out the door after her aunt and uncle.

The Seed of Winden

8. *Turmoil*

As soon as the coach departed, the Viscount returned to the parlor to tell his wife he was to retire for the night. Tammin followed but stopped when his father went into the door where he was met by his wife's ire.

"You made such a spectacle of that woman's visit, it mortifies me!" she hissed. "And that girl, hovering about Tammin like a... like a...."

"You mean that child? A child has no such intentions. She is only kindness to Tammin," Lord Halenwood said in Nieve's defense. He gave her a withering, dismissive glance.

"Oh, you mustn't have any illusions that little girl isn't perfectly trained to seek out an advantageous match, and Tammin would surely be marrying low if he were to attach himself to *such* a creature. They are Arid-landers. Why not further burrow their roots into the protected lands by securing a marriage to a natal resident Viscount's son?"

"They are not commoners, and they have already been granted residency by the congress of selection, *my dear*," he replied. The last two words were uttered through gritted teeth, in a deep, growling voice.

"No, they are not commoners, but they are neither anything of note, since they are all that remain of their family. And what does well-bred mean when one refers to Rethros? I have no idea. Do you?" Lady Halenwood sailed from the chair to the sideboard where she poured herself some port. "They could be gypsies for all we know. There's no way to verify who they claim to be." She drank bitterly, before spitting out, "I do not like them."

"I do," the Viscount replied. "Miss Landie is all-affability and kindness. Unlike you. You should take her example, instead of acting like a dour old cow." He sneered at his wife.

"That child should not be close to Tammin. I am relieved that Tammin will return to school in two days. And I shall be going to Derenath at endweek. I will find him suitable matches there. You will accompany me," she told her husband.

"I will do no such thing!" he shouted in reply.

"I will *not* have you alone here with that woman!" his wife shrieked.

"You will not tell me what to do!" he barked loudly in reply.

There was a pall, and the couple stared each other down. Tammin remained rooted in his spot in the darkened hall. He knew that this would escalate into a clash soon if someone did not intervene. She might throw something at his father and instigate a fight. It was how it was.

They had hated one another almost from the day of their wedding, it seemed. Tammin could scarce stomach the woman, and it seemed the Viscount felt the same. Why he chose her, was still a mystery. The Viscount was scarcely an easy man to live with, but Lady Halenwood made it all the harder, for in sometimes even in close company, she was a harpy. She hit and spat and threw things. She shrieked and wailed. And she found things to enrage her every day, and instigated disagreements that almost always escalated into violent outbursts that the Viscount would have to squash. Once even, when pushed to the edge of his vast bank of rage, with the back of his hand—a mistake she used against him at every turn now.

In this case, she had been justified in her jealousy, but Tammin could scarce blame his father for being attracted to someone warm and kind and lovely, when he had no such qualities in his wife.

He could not believe he was justifying his father's behavior, but he could understand why Landie was like a breath of fresh air next to the harridan his stepmother was. She was so quiet and calculating when she wanted to be, but when she became angry, she could be relied upon to goad her husband. It certainly made Tammin angry. It was as if she delighted in provoking his father, who would likely take it out on Tammin. He would have to intercede again to prevent a second event that would end with his stepmother being harmed, and that would mean a yet another beating for him, which inevitably happened if he got involved.

"You may go wherever you wish, but you will not tell me where I shall go. I will remain here, and do as I please," Halenwood told her with a tone that implied that no argument would be borne.

"I will then. I will take to the city house," she said defiantly. "You are free to do whatever it is you please with that woman, but be assured you will have nothing more from me. *Ever.* And," she added as if the thought only just occurred to her, "…you shall have no say in what *I* do, nor what I speak of to our friends, in regards to your actions." She stated the last few words as if they were a threat.

"I have no concern what others think, or say about me, woman. In the end they will come crawling to me anyway, because it is the title they want to be connected to. Not an unwanted wife of a Viscount," he spat.

Lady Halenwood looked startled by this acid declaration, and for the first time in many arguments was left speechless.

Tammin was surprised when his father turned on his heel and burst through the secondary door into the adjoining room, curtailing the inevitable scuffle that would have followed if the argument had escalated. It was almost too strange to believe. His father would never, ever back down or walk away when there was a chance for conflict. Tammin stood in shock.

When the moment passed, he sauntered into the room. His stepmother scarcely acknowledged him at first. Then she drank more port and twisted her head to look at him as he threw out his tails and sat down by the fire.

"You are to stay away from that girl," she snapped at him.

"I am not your son," he replied quietly. "I will choose my own company."

"You are to stay at school, and you are not to return to Halenwood Hall, do you understand? I will do whatever I can in my power to keep that girl and her vile aunt away from you. I will not have that woman attached to our family in any way. Mark my words," she hissed. "Now get out. I want to be alone."

At Narroway, things weren't any better. Bohan was irate from the moment they left the great house, all the way home, and his irritation was at last acknowledged by Landie. She was sure she had done nothing to earn such rage from her husband. She did not see her behavior as flirtatious or forward, but instead believed she was merely being gregarious.

The reprieve from her uncle's anger ended that night when Nieve stepped into the house. She was met by a flying hand as he smacked her square in the face for some unspoken offense. Landie shouted that he should not take his anger out on the girl, and then she too was hit violently. He then set to beating them both until they retreated to their rooms in sobs, both sporting throbbing, smarting cheekbones, a scattering of new bruises, and—in Nieve's case—a burst vein in her eye.

The next morning, Tammin came by to tell Nieve that he was to return to school, and found her in the state that her uncle had left her, with a bruise the color of mustard forming on her cheekbone and a bloodied eyeball. The boy's anger was insurmountable, and he got up from the chair in the parlor and burst through every door downstairs until he found Uncle Bohan at his desk in his private office.

Without the slightest hesitation he threw himself at the larger man, fists balled up and aloft. The noise of it was astonishing, and Landie took her niece's hand and led her out of the house. They ran towards the great house, leaving the sound of crashing and breaking things behind them.

"We can't go there, Landie, don't. Tammin will suffer for this," she told her aunt fearfully.

"He must be stopped. Someone has to intervene, or Bohan will kill him!" Landie replied desperately.

They encountered Lord Halenwood just ten minutes into the flight, riding his horse down the main road towards the great house. He looked greatly concerned when she saw both Landie and Nieve bruised and frightened.

He did not linger. The sight of Landie's face and listening only briefly to her words, and he kicked his horse into a gallop and raced towards Narroway.

The Viscount not only thrashed Uncle Bohan to the edge of death. As the chief constable and magistrate of his county, he convicted Bohan Marielle of being a *Criminal of Barbarity* for his crimes against the girls and Tammin, and his residency permit was immediately revoked. That very night, he was put in a box carriage back to the gates to be sent by sand-ship to Rethros accompanied by two guards to ensure he left the greenlands as he should. Landie and Nieve were granted asylum by the Viscount and allowed to remain.

Lord Halenwood then declared that he would hire a land manager to see to the day-to-day workings of Narroway. Landie and the girl would stay at the grange on their own, and their rent and manager's pay would be provided by the returns from the farm. He would see to it all.

There was a satisfied look on his face when he explained this to them over breakfast in the low-ceilinged dining room of Narroway Grange. He took on an air of a benevolent provider, with his eye mostly on the stricken and wounded Landie. The ladies were still in a state of shock that Uncle Bohan was sent away so quickly and efficiently, and they were presented with the strange void of his absence. Nieve was relieved. Landie was a muddle of confused feelings, amongst them anger and fear.

"How can they just send him away like that? That cannot be allowed, can it? He is my husband. These are *his* possessions amid mine. Lord Halenwood cannot make him leave everything behind just like that... can he?" she rambled after the Viscount left them. They watched him from the window as he rode away, following the box cart containing Uncle Bohan.

Without answers, and shaken by the event, the ladies were left to a strained, silent evening, and a fitful night of sleep.

The Viscount's bulk filled the doorway early the next morning. He arrived with a footman, carrying a hamper of produce, some exotic fruit from his hothouse, and some fresh and cured meats from the estate.

Landie felt obliged to ask him if he had had breakfast and invited him to sit with them. He joined them to dine on the cold ham, boiled eggs, toasted bread, and jam that comprised the ladies' simple, rustic breakfast while their housekeeper ferreted away the new spoils for later on. Neither of the ladies had much of an appetite. Landie seemed like she'd been crushed by the doldrums until the Viscount arrived that morning. She was driven to bouts of weeping, she was so divided and bewildered by how to feel about her husband being exiled. Nieve, on the other hand, was ambivalent about the situation concerning her uncle, and was instead made miserable because her only friend was to soon abandon her for school.

Tammin had borne some wounds from his confrontation, including a broken bone in his hand. When they arrived back at the house, he was in such pain, and Nieve could not bear to see him so. She knelt beside the battered boy, tears sliding down her cheeks, wishing for the doctor to make haste. She had gingerly gathered up his left hand with both of hers, and cradled it against her chest, trembling and sniffling until the doctor arrived.

"Pay no mind to me, Doctor. He is in great discomfort!" she told the elder, silver-haired, somber physician as he stooped to look at her bloodshot eye.

Tammin did not speak. Not a word. He only gave her hands a soft squeeze with his good hand before being hoisted to his feet by his father and another man and loaded into the family's coach to return him to the great house for the Viscount's personal physician to attend to him there. Landie submitted to an examination of her bruises, and then it was finally Nieve's turn.

Bohan's office was a shambles, utterly destroyed by the confrontation that occurred within its walls.

"I can only offer my sincere apologies for the destruction that befell your home, dearest Mrs. Marielle. I will see to it that everything is restored and repaired to the condition it was before the events of yesterday occurred," the Viscount told Landie.

She bowed her head and nodded mutely, her lips tight and her shoulders stiff.

"You must not lament the departure of your husband, dear Mrs. Marielle, for no man should ever lift his hand against a woman, much less a little girl," he continued. He reached out and took Nieve's chin in his hand, turning her face toward his, leaning close to look at her bruises and the splash of red marring the white of her right eye.

Nieve studied his face while he did this. There was so much of Tammin in his features. But he was not like Tammin. There was a darkness—a shadow—that dwelled inside his gaze. She shivered at it, for he frightened her. Nieve understood that Tammin's concern towards her mistreatment stemmed from his experience with his own. This man had hurt Tammin. And here he was, gently cupping her chin and patting down the flyaways on the sides of her face.

"This is a travesty," he whispered, his large hand falling away from Nieve's waxen face. He turned to Landie. "I understand you cared deeply for your husband, and you were a dutiful wife to him, Mrs. Marielle, but we cannot abide by men who beat their wives and daughters in this land. Our place here is not to be taken for granted. We are privileged to live here, the only place where life thrives and grows abundant, and we must abide by the laws of the congress to remain here. To treat those who are powerless with respect and compassion."

Nieve wanted to scoff at him, for he most definitely beat his son. But she restrained herself from her urge. She let her gaze lock onto the untouched food on her plate, and she glared at it, her eyes stinging with tears.

"How is Master Tammin, my Lord?" Nieve croaked.

Lord Halenwood reached across the table for the butter and shook his head. "Broken hand, for certain. He hit your uncle very hard. My boy might be misguided about many things, but I could not be prouder of him than I am right now. He acted as any conscionable man ought to have. And for a boy of only sixteen, he did a right good job of it against the grown fellow." He clucked his tongue and swung his head, his face suddenly beaming with pride.

Landie all this while stared too at her untouched breakfast. The man stuck 'round for another hour, idling in the small parlor, smoking a pipe and watching Landie as she listlessly stitched at her quilt, her face still a mask of uncertainty. Nieve stood and excused herself. She felt as if the Viscount was claiming his place as head of their household.

Nieve pulled on her redingote against the cool morning and huffed out a puff of steam. How could it be summer and yet be so cold? The greenlands were high on the plateaus, but still, it was incomprehensible to her. This was as cold as an autumn night in the arid lands. She buttoned the three large buttons on the short bodice of her coat as she walked, and then wrapped the long, knitted scarf her aunt had bought her upon crossing into the greenlands around her neck another time for good measure. She set out amid the mists of morning towards Liar's Hill.

She walked through the quiet town towards the wild wood. Most people had only risen at the knell of the second morning bell from the temple, and were still breakfasting. The Viscount had arrived just after dawn, and the ladies, because they had not slept much, were thankfully up early and already in their morning gowns when he arrived.

As she passed the last of the small town's inner buildings, she came across the young man that Tammin had sparred with. She had forgotten his name from their quick introduction the other day. He was out walking a large, scraggly looking hound, tall as a pony and the color of rust, with a beard and shaggy brows and wiry fur all around its lanky frame. Both boy and dog appeared forlorn. It seemed as if bad feelings were contagious in this berg.

He saw Nieve and waved at her, breaking out another of his charming, and disarming, smiles. He bowed and removed the broad-brimmed felt hat from his tousled head and bowed again. "Good morning, Miss... I'm sorry." Apparently, he couldn't remember either.

"Nieve, you may call me Miss Nieve," she replied, approaching. When she did, she saw his eyes fix on her bruises and her eye, and a curious arch rose up in his left brow.

He did not, however, ask her about it. "And I," he said instead, "am Raynes, if you recall." He gave her a patronizing smile, which she returned with equal insincerity, and then reached out to pet the dog's shaggy head. It sniffed her arm and licked her fingers. "Are you by chance seeking out your friend Master Halenwood?" Raynes asked.

She shook her head, but that was a lie. She pursed her lips, her fingers scratching behind the dog's ears. "Just getting a bit of air this morning. I was feeling stifled in the house."

He nodded as if he understood this all too well.

"And who is this," she asked, her eyes moving down to the canine companion he walked on its short lead.

"This is Parsnip," he replied.

Nieve could not help but giggle at the name.

"Shall we walk together then, you, me, and old Snip?" he asked.

Nieve was too polite to say no to someone who was her senior. Instead she asked where he was going.

"Nowhere in particular. Just like you, I needed air. I was heading in the direction of the hills." He gestured towards Liar's Hill.

With a suppressed frown, she nodded, and joined him as he and the dog proceeded. She could see him taking surreptitious glances at her from the side of his eye. She was suddenly conscious of her hatless head, the scarf wrapped around her neck so that it covered her chin, and the redingote with the dewy hems. She did not have her hair arranged in any way, so it hung free, partly wrapped in the scarf and partly flying against her shoulders and back. She had not brushed or combed it, so it was rather unruly. She sank her chin and mouth deeper into the scarf.

They did not speak for a long spell. They simply walked. Finally, Raynes said, "Your friend is supposed to depart to matriculate soon, is he not?"

Nieve only nodded. Raynes reached down and ruffled his dog's shaggy head.

"He and I were once the best of friends," he told her.

Nieve's eyes widened with interest, and she gave him a direct look, as if to demand more information. He was not especially prolific with it.

"Now, we are not so much friends anymore," he continued.

"That is too bad," she offered. "My father told me that true friends are rare. That one can be surrounded by many people one calls friends and not have a single true friend among them. Was he a true friend to you?"

"I thought so," Raynes admitted.

"Then that is a great shame indeed," Nieve commiserated. "You have been fighting with him?"

"Yes. From what I understand, you think the whole idea of fighting to be less than gentlemanly," he said with a bit of a sneer.

"I do. I believe physical violence to be a crass way to try and resolve differences, and it rarely accomplishes that, if anything at all, except to create more rancor," she concluded.

"What does a little girl like you know of the world?" he admonished, stopping in his tracks and glaring at her. "You are a presumptuous little thing!"

"I know that problems are rarely solved with aggression," she replied flippantly, returning his glare as an equal.

He was surprised by the strength of her resolve and her confidence for such a young girl. But he swallowed it, angry that she'd hit the nail so squarely on the head. "Who said we are trying to solve anything?" The words came out in a derisive snort.

"Then what purpose does it serve to hold such anger and a grudge and to confront one another again and again over something that has long passed?" she retorted in a louder voice, her words clipped and angry, her wide, bright hazel eyes alight with fire. "Please, indulge me and explain.? Why not ignore one another altogether? Why not agree to disagree and never speak again? Why fight, unless you want something from it? What is it you want to happen by resorting to fists every time? Is it because you simply want to hurt one another? Cause the other pain?"

Raynes suddenly realized with crystal-clear clarity, what it was about this child that might make Tammin so intrigued. She was sharp and bright, perceptive and empathetic. But she was also filled with a beautiful strength and a depth of understanding he never would have imagined in a little girl.

"Maybe. But maybe you should ask *him*," he said in a calmer voice.

"You provoke him, too, of that I'm sure," she muttered accusingly.

"Did he tell you that?"

"He only spoke of you once. When I asked him if he got into a fight, he said he had—with an idiot. He never uttered a single word about you after that. *I* draw my *own* conclusions from what I *see*," she scolded him. "And you seem to be the kind of person who creates situations that will instigate conflict."

"Do I now?" He laughed.

Nieve said nothing but crossed her arms and gave him an expectant look, as if she was waiting for an admission. Raynes did not dignify her with one. Instead, he tilted his head and studied her with his pale eyes.

"I think I like you, Miss Nieve, even if you are but a little girl," he declared.

She chuffed at that admission and started to laugh. "Indeed." She seemed to find it all quite funny.

"You're astute. And well, rather endearing. I think I might have to spend some time with you. After your friend Tammin is gone, that is," he said with a wicked little smile. "We can become fast friends. And Halenwood will have to live with that."

"And there it is," she exclaimed, as if she'd discovered a pot of gold. "The instigation of conflict. Tammin won't want you bothering me, of that I'm sure. So you are quick to do exactly that. I won't have it."

"Oh, Little Miss Nieve, you think my interest is insincere," he said mockingly, putting his hand to his heart. "Will you do only as Tammin wishes? What if you find that you *want* to reciprocate my attentions, and become *my* friend? Will you not have the courage to do as you please? Or is Tammin's will paramount?"

"You may needle Tammin all you wish and he will respond in turn. But you will *not* use *me* to get to Tammin. I won't let you," she told him, her fists clenched. She threw up a finger back towards the town. "Now you go that way… I'll go this way." And she stalked off towards the forest in a flare of skirts.

Raynes watched her storm away, and he stared after her, his heart racing and his eyes wide. Just who *was* this little creature? He marveled at her. Parsnip whimpered after her and tried to follow. With an obstinate tug at the leash, Raynes pulled the dog back towards town, still a little stunned.

Nieve found Tammin pouting on his rock. He, too, had bruises, but he also had cuts on his face, fingers, and hands. His injured hand was in a splint and wrapped tightly in white cotton. His demeanor was downcast.

Nieve brushed aside the heap of pinecones he had collected and sat there beside him. They brooded together in silence for a while. Just before he got to his feet, he looked down at his little companion and his angry face softened. "I shall miss you, Nieve."

"I shall miss you, Tammin," she replied, her voice cracking. "I'm worried about you." She reached up and wiped away her tears with the edge of her sleeve.

"I'll heal up fine. I'll see you in a few months," he assured her. "Go home, brush that rat's nest of hair you have. Stop weeping." And with that, he pushed through the dense growth behind the rock and disappeared.

Nieve picked her way along the path homewards to Narroway, awash with misery. The idea that she would have to exist with this hollow, aching emptiness inside her for months to come now seemed unbearable. With Raynes possibly bent on tormenting her—and the Viscount looming over her aunt like a desert carrion-bird waiting for its prey to die before descending upon it—she felt like this new world, as beautiful and lush and green as it was, was about to suffocate her. Home she went, in a roiling cloud of sorrow, feeling a heaviness in her heart she was too young to fully understand.

9. Bully

Tammin sank back into the seat of the coach and glared at his stepmother. She sat, oblivious, her gaze locked on the passing buildings and people as the coach navigated the busy streets of the city of Derenath.

"I will be sending for you on the endweeks. You will come and dine at the townhouse, and meet some proper young ladies," the Lady Halenwood declared.

Tammin's eyes flashed and he frowned. "I will be doing no such thing. I am here for schooling, and I will concentrate on that. I will not be meeting any such young ladies, proper or not."

"I will not brook any..." she began.

"You are not my mother. I've said it before, and I will say it again. I have been respectful of your wishes up until now. But I am finished capitulating to you to make my father happy. Your separation from him is a separation from me as well. You best forget any notions of controlling anything I do, or who I meet," he snapped.

"That girl is not worthy of you, and you cannot see her," the woman did not give up. It was profoundly irritating to Tammin.

"I will decide who is worthy of me. Not you. Now if you please, I wish to no longer discuss anything further with you. I will go to my school, and that will be the end of it." He crossed his arms and swept his angry gaze to the street, where the city's residents bustled about, slowing their progress.

Lady Halenwood set him out of the coach at the gates of his college. Neither spoke a word. His trunk was unloaded and hoisted away by a pair of footmen that worked for the school; and the coach rumbled away. That would be the last time Tammin would ever see the Lady Halenwood.

Instead, the young man followed them across the main green—a meticulously kept quadrangle of the college—through the path between the tall, old brick buildings, to the main paths where two of the nicest resident buildings were, nearest to the huddle of academic buildings.

The one he lived in was one of the oldest buildings which still had the original gallery of cloisters and its own private yard with an ancient tree—which could be seen from his second-floor rooms— occupying its center.. He, like most of the nobility, occupied the finer of the available dormitories, and each student had their own small set of apartments which included a bedchamber, a bath chamber, a cozy room with a with a nook for a desk, and a little sitting area around the undersized fireplace. As he made his way to his rooms, he was welcomed by other young men who had already returned or who had remained there through the summer break.

"Halenwood, glad you're back," a young man emerged from the large common room and greeted Tammin.

He stopped to greet Effrid Finn. He was already an Earl at eighteen—having inherited the title after his father passed away of dry fever when Effrid was nine. He was an easy-going fellow with jaunty brown hair and gleaming blue eyes. He was wearing a banyan and a pair of frayed jacquard slippers.

"I've been waiting for you. I've a question to ask you," Effrid said, patting the younger man on the back.

"I've barely arrived and you're assailing me with requests already?" Tammin grumbled with a half-smirk. He moved to the door of his rooms and pushed it open. The older boy followed him in.

"Goodness, what happened to your face… and what's this? Your hand?"

"I broke it on someone's skull," Tammin replied, stopping in the center of the small sitting room by the wall to pull the summoning cord.

"Ah. Fighting with that fellow you talk about then?"

"Not this time. It's a long story."

"I was going to ask you if you wanted to represent the college the season's first boxing match, but I suppose you cannot now."

"I might have to wait for the next season, I'm afraid. And I think boxing might no longer serve as a suitable pursuit for me," he added.

"Why the blazes not?" Effrid demanded, astonished.

"I have, in essence, promised someone to no longer pursue acts of aggression."

"Oh, good gracious. Boxing is not an act of aggression, it is a sport. Both opponents are choosing to participate honorably," Effrid rationalized.

Tammin stared into nowhere as he mulled this. The door opened after a soft knock, and a young boy of ten or eleven entered carrying a pail of firewood and kindling and a lighting box. He set to lighting the fire while the older boys conversed.

"I suppose you're right." Tammin tilted his head thoughtfully. "I will have to see if the young lady accepts the distinction."

"Young lady, eh?" Effrid smirked, raising a brow suggestively.

"It's not like that. She's a friend," Tammin blurted, raising his hand. "She's barely older than the boy there. But she was the one bright spot of the summer break. For once, it was not entirely horrible at home, because she was there."

Effrid's nod was one of deep understanding, as he was one of the few young fellows at college who knew Tammin's whole story, and to whom Tammin confided most of his secrets. He was his only true close friend. The rest of the young men he was acquainted with remained safely distant.

"What of your former friend, now enemy?" Effrid inquired, flopping down into one of the two leather chairs that flanked the fireplace.

"I had a scuffle or two before the young creature appeared. Nothing of note," Tammin reported.

"I take it there continues to be no dialogue?"

"None," Tammin replied.

Effrid could only shake his head and purse his lips in a regretful manner as he crossed his legs. "Well, I suppose I should say welcome back, friend. Anything else of note happen while you were away?"

"Nothing really, except one oddity. I thought I'd ask *you* about it, since you have extensive knowledge of the history of the Mennin," Tammin said.

The mention of Effrid's favorite subject perked him up, and he straightened himself in his seat.

"There's a ring of eleven in a place called Winden Hill, near where I live," Tammin began.

"I've heard of that one. It's the center circle, isn't it? Did you visit it?" Effrid asked, intrigued.

"Yes. I think it is the center-circle. It isn't the first time I've been there, but something unusual happened while I was there, and I thought perhaps your knowledge of the mythologies and the religion of the Mennin would perhaps elucidate what might have occurred, as I am unable to make out what truly arise that day."

"Do tell," Effrid insisted.

"I was there with the young lady I mentioned earlier, and it was quite blustery. The hill is named for the fact that it is nearly always unbearably windy there. But as the wind whistled through the stones, it began to sound as if there were voices," Tammin explained.

Effrid's brows rose in astonished delight.

"And when the young woman, her name is Miss Nieve, stepped into the circle and I followed, there was first an unnatural hush, more words spoken by the wind, and then the sky darkened and then lightened again. We discovered only after leaving the place that we had been gone an entire day. I thought at first it was some sort of misunderstanding or miscalculation on my part, but it was not. We returned a full day later, and we did not experience the passage of that time. It seemed to have been lost to the circle of eleven," he rambled.

Effrid looked as if he was about to leap from his chair in excitement. "The consecration," he whispered, his hands shaking. "Do you recall the words, what they said?"

"Not entirely. It spoke of an unbreakable bond, and ardor."

"Love," Effrid said. "It spoke of love, and a bond. With both of you standing inside the circle?"

Tammin had not thought that hard upon it. But he nodded, because what Effrid said was essentially true.

"You received a consecration of binding from the stones," Effrid declared with awe. "I am not entirely sure of what this means, but we can find out more. There are some who know a great deal more about Mennan's oldest religion than I, and I will take you tomorrow to meet one." He stood. "In the meantime, tell me more about the girl. Who is she? Is she of Mennin descent perhaps?"

Effrid began to list an innumerable amount of questions Tammin could not even begin to answer. All he could dwell upon was what Effrid had just thoughtlessly rattled off before leaping into his inquisition—a consecration of binding.

* * *

Only three weeks had passed since Tammin had left in the company of his stepmother, and the Viscount was now as present in Nieve's life as Uncle Bohan had been. He had already taken both she and her aunt on a long tour of the countryside in his coach. He had invited them to join him to dine nearly every night, and to remain afterwards to play cards at leisure and converse with whichever guests happened to be present, or amongst themselves if they were only just the three of them. The Viscount seemed to like Nieve a great deal more than Bohan had, and he was particularly kind to her—even doting, on some occasions. His gruff persona seemed to vanish when it was in their company alone. He was calm and pleasant to be around, which was a shock to Nieve. Even more shocking was that the darkness that Nieve had seen so clearly in his gaze was ebbing away into sincerity.

It was just such an evening where the Viscount had invited them to dine again, and they remained quietly together after dinner in the private parlor, a place the Viscount only brought his very closest friends. The Viscount was reading a periodical and Landie was contentedly working on her quilt, which she'd brought with her in anticipation of the quiet, introspective company they kept when with him. Landie and Lord Halenwood seemed quite suited to one another in this respect. They were happy to spend inordinate amounts of time in company, without feeling burdened with conversation or pleasantries, contentedly pursuing peaceful tasks, with the occasional mutter or exchange of smiles. Nieve had to admit to herself that this was an improvement, in spite of her initial dislike and distrust of the Viscount.

Landie had been won over by the Viscount in respect to Uncle Bohan. Her shock had waned to resignation and acceptance, then to contentment. Lord Halenwood had sufficiently vilified her husband enough that she now agreed that it was best he had been removed from the greenlands, and from their lives. Nieve, on the other hand, was still divided in her thoughts on the matter—for although relieved to no longer suffer the abuses of a man who did not want her; she still thought it was a manipulative and deliberate act on the married Viscount's part to take possession of a woman he clearly admired. So much so, he sent his present wife away so that Landie could replace her beside him on the saber-chair by the fire.

There was little that could harm a man of his status by doing so rash a thing as exchanging one woman for another. The sad part of it all, was that in spite of the current Lady Halenwood's bad character, of which both Landie and Nieve were learning about via the society the Halenwoods kept—the poor woman would be the one who would be shamed and ridiculed in the end, in spite of her having been the one to be expulsed from the family by the Viscount, and replaced so brazenly.

Society was a cruel thing, Nieve mulled as she reflected upon all that had happened, and how much their daily lives had changed since the day of the incident and Uncle Bohan's eviction. She frowned over her work, and tried to concentrate on it.

Nieve had taken to knitting and was making a scarf for Tammin. The summer would soon give way to autumn, and the Viscount had been quite explicit about how cold autumn and winter would be here. "You have experienced frost, or snow?" he had asked them a week before when they were eating dinner.

"Never snow," Landie replied, her eyes twinkling pleasantly at the idea of it. "I'm most excited to see it for the first time."

"But frost yes?"

"There have been the occasional nights in the deserts where the cold was so strong that it edged the well water with ice, and inside the windows have been known to frost as well. But rarely." She dipped her spoon into the soup and drank delicately.

"I suggest you visit Mrs. Prestin at first chance. You may have her send the bill to me and see to it that she supplies you both with warmer garments and woolen things for the winter. You will need them. Also, you should acquire a fur-lined cloak, a muffler, and some fur-lined boots," he told them between forkfuls of venison and potatoes.

Landie nodded and thanked him with a shy smile. He seemed to melt at the sight of it. He daubed his mouth with the corner of the tablecloth, and his eyes roved over to Nieve. He took her in for a moment, a soft smile on his mouth. "You should also think about taking riding lessons, young lady. All young ladies of means should be accomplished in the saddle."

"I can ride," Nieve replied quickly. "I had my own sand-dancer before I came here. I had to leave her behind."

"Well, a sand-dancer is a delicate little horse for this climate. She would have been very unhappy here. And they don't grow winter coats of the like greenland horses do. I'll see to finding a suitable mount for you that is as spry and graceful as any sand-dancer," he told Nieve, who gaped at him in shock.

"You should commission a habit and some boots for that, as well. Hats, you will both need hats. I think perhaps you two ought to consider coming to stay here as guests at Halenwood for the cold months at least. Narroway is old and does not stay very warm. It will be difficult for ladies who have grown up knowing very little of the cold."

"We could not hope to impose upon you, my Lord. And what will people say? And your wife would not be comfortable with that arrangement," Landie protested.

"My wife and I will be divorcing soon. I have sent my petition to the council, and it will surely be ratified. What *she* thinks about anything is irrelevant," he told them. "As for what others think, my dearest Miss Landie, I have never given much import to what those so very below me have to say about anything."

Later on that week, Nieve had gone out to wander as she usually did, and she encountered the Viscount riding towards Narroway on his elegant black horse. When he saw Nieve, he halted his mount and stared down at her.

"You have a bit of a wanderlust, don't you, little lady?" he said, his eyes smiling.

"I suppose I do," she replied.

"It is no surprise you and Tammin get along so well. He, too, is a wanderer," he sighed thoughtfully. "I have wished for him to be home these days. I find the company of you and your aunt to be most soothing to my soul. I had always wanted a daughter to dote upon, and now, I sort of have one. And your aunt, she is a scintillating, pleasant, wonderful person. I find you both to be everything a man could desire in domestic contentment. I think Tammin would much enjoy the agreeable atmosphere you two have brought to Halenwood."

Nieve wanted to speak of why he was cruel to his son, why he beat him, but she did not. She held back the words. She saw him as a different man these days. Changed by the absence of his acrimonious wife and the end of an unhappy match, perhaps. She did not truly know what changed him, but she wondered now if he would be kind to Tammin as well, or if Tammin could ever truly trust him to be someone other than he had always been.

Instead she offered the man a timid smile and she curtsied a farewell to him. He called out that they would be joining him for the evening again, and then he rode off towards Narroway to see Landie.

That same night, he continued his campaign to convince them to remove themselves to Halenwood to winter, to which Landie finally conceded. And after dinner, he brought up another proposal.

"I am safe to assume you ladies have never been to Lake Adaskus?" the Viscount suddenly blurted from behind his nightly periodical after a good half-hour of comfortable silence.

Landie started at the abrupt, loud words, and laughed gaily at the shock. "No, we have not. But it is impossible not to have heard of it. It is a recurrent setting for many a novel."

"Indeed. It is the place to be during the social season. Even off-season it is a cultural center. There is always something going on there. Even in the height of winter, you will find operas and plays, dances and assemblies to be attended. I will furnish you both with subscriptions to myriad events, if you wish it. And Miss Nieve, there is a circulating library there with an untold number of titles, with editions that go back a *thousand* years. I know you like to read. I thought perhaps I might take both of you in a month or so, and we can winter there, as it is done. How does that sound?"

Landie's expressive, lovely eyes shone with delight, and Nieve could not help but feel excitement herself at this suggestion. Even in her sorrow to be parted from Tammin, she could not help but revel in the idea of visiting this famous city by the lake. The Viscount drank in the happiness he had just created in his newest wards, and nodded.

"Well, that about answers that, doesn't it?" he chuckled. "I shall make the arrangements. If you haven't got to the modiste yet, I suggest you do it very soon. The lake can be even colder than here."

They both nodded enthusiastically and returned to their quiet tasks, Nieve's needles clicking, Landie's needle stitching, and the Lord's paper crinkling along with the fire's snaps and pops.

Nieve was walking from town in the afternoon two days later. She first stopped at the stationers to buy a new journal, and then she visited the post, to have the brown-paper-wrapped scarf she knitted, along with a cheerful letter sent to Tammin at school. She was busy imagining him wearing the thing, with its uneven stripes of silvery grey and midnight blue, and was feeling rather jolly about it; when she came across Raynes, who was out again with Parsnip. She was planning to go past him without acknowledgement but was thwarted.

Raynes made his way straight towards her and bowed, removing his hat. "Miss Nieve. I've been hoping to run into you." Parsnip was quite glad to see her, and nuzzled her hand for attention.

Nieve frowned, and glared at Raynes, her hand unconsciously responding to Parsnip's demand for ear scratches. She looked away, and refused to speak to him.

"May we call a truce for a short while at least?" he asked.

Nieve remained silent, but she did not move away. Raynes was about to speak when a voice called out his name, and they turned to see Clemon, Hareth, and two more boys rounding the corner of Mill Street on foot. They looked like a horde of genteelly dressed thugs, their smiles wicked, and their mannerisms brash as they rambled toward Nieve and Raynes.

"Isn't this Tammin's little pet?" Hareth asked jovially, looking at Nieve with a bit of a leer as they came near. He reached out and flicked the brim of her bonnet. She shied away.

"Yes, it is. I don't recall her name. What was it again, chit?" Clemon asked her, getting right up into her face.

Nieve's gaze went from one to the other, but she remained tight-lipped. She was chewing her inner cheek, and her hands were balled up inside the deep pockets of her plain woolen redingote. Her heart was hammering in her chest, for she could not help but glean a bad feeling from this moment.

"Halenwood has a little pet?" one of the strangers asked, his voice filled with glee. He inspected her like she was a sheep at auction, circling her, gaze washing over her being. "Well, well, well, isn't the little thing precious? What shall we call her, since she will not give us her name?" He reached out and grasped one of the carefully shaped curls from the side of her temple, which her aunt had so meticulously curled on a rag the night before, and pulled it hard.

Nieve yelped and smacked his hand away. "Don't touch me!"

"My goodness, she's got a temper. Angry little mite." He laughed uproariously, dancing away as if she was a barking lap dog.

"She is a mighty mite," the other boy said. They all laughed again.

"What's she carrying here? A journaling booklet. Shall I have a look to see if she's written anything in it?" Clemon yanked the brand-new book from her hand, making the other supplies she'd bought for the trip to the lake fly out of her hands and onto the ground.

She protested with a shout and knelt to pick up the quills and the ink and the sheets of expensive paper she'd treated herself to. All the while Raynes looked on with a detached look on his face.

One of the boys put his foot on her behind when she was leaning and kicked her over. She fell onto her knees into the dirt with her white linen and cotton skirts, dropping all the things she had collected again. She felt the burn of tears rushing into her eyes, and she fought them with defiance. She did not want to dignify these beasts with them. Her lower lip was shaking as she tried to gather herself after every onslaught.

That was when Raynes finally acted. But it was not in the way one would expect a gentleman to act. He strode forward and grabbed her arm, yanking her with ease to her feet. He put his arm around her shoulder, knocking her hat forward into her face.

She reached up to put it back in place, shaking from anger and frustration.

"I know what to call her," he said with a smug expression, hugging her to his side. "Mine. This one is mine. Tammin's little mite will be mine to own now."

The other boys, knowing their place in the bullies' pecking order, relented. He then stooped to gather up her things, and proceeded to pile them into her arms, snatching the book back from Clemon and putting it there, too.

"Go. Flee little one. I'll find you later." He dismissed her condescendingly with the flick of the hand.

Nieve wiped her eyes with the back of her hand and moved away when Raynes stuck out his foot and tripped her with it. She fell flat on the ground, her bonnet flying off and rolling away, and her items scattering out before her yet again. The boys broke into uproarious laughter, and Raynes gestured for them to move on. He yanked his dog's lead and they paraded away, taking up the rear of the group. He glanced back once, and through her tears as she gathered her things, she saw him frown.

Nieve could tell the Viscount about it, she thought, but she would not. She scurried up to her rooms at Narroway, and put her crinkled, dirt-stained paper, scuffed book, little bags of wax pastilles, and frayed quills into her writing slope and then threw herself onto her bed. She sniffled miserably. She was so confused by Raynes. One moment, marginally kind, the next, evil. She sat up and looked at the dirt embedded in her skirts and the flecks of blood that had seeped through from her knees which had been scraped by the gravel and pebbles when she fell. Her stockings were ruined.

She undressed, still crying, and changed for supper at Halenwood. She could not wait to leave for the lake. How she wished Tammin were there. But he would have fought with them. She shook her head and glowered as she put new stockings over her raw, scraped knees, and put the knee garters back on. A new gown of a teal blue and a sleeveless spencer of stormy grey silk over that, and she felt human again. Her hair was beyond salvaging at this point. The hat pin had pulled out her coif from the morning. So she merely pulled it all down and then drew it back again tightly into a bun with a single part down the top of her head.

The Viscount must have been aware of her subdued mood that night, for he doted upon her even more than usual. He made sure she was offered the best portions of the roast mutton and the sweetest of the desserts. He took her arm and walked with her to the parlor, and he brought her a blanket for her knees when she shivered a little.

"You are unhappy, Nieve. What is it?" he asked her when they were settled into the parlor.

She shook her head and offered him a forced smile. "I'm just tired," she lied.

The Viscount looked unconvinced. He shook out his paper, but it did not rise up to cover his face. Instead, he stared at her over it. "I don't believe you. Miss Landie, do you know what is affecting our poor little Nieve? She's so quiet and sullen."

Landie tilted her head and she furrowed her brow. "Isn't she always quiet?"

"I suppose. But she's not knitting or reading, and she has been walking about as if there is a dark cloud hanging over her head."

"She misses Tammin," Landie suggested.

"Is that it?" the Viscount asked. "You miss the boy? He was your only friend here, wasn't he?"

"I do miss him," Nieve admitted.

The man still would not look at his paper, but studied her while she affectedly set to casting a new project onto her needles, pretending that everything was fine. Finally, as if he could bear it no longer, "What happened? Something happened today, and you're not telling us about it. It can be the only reason why you are so low. This is not like you, for you have missed Tammin for all this time and have still been you. This is not you."

"Nothing…" she began.

"Miss Nieve I am going to be very clear here, for if you are to become part of this household I will brook no secrets or falsehoods, and I am an expert at rooting such things out. You can continue to try to deflect me from what I want to know, or you can just tell me now and save yourself from my intervening. Trust me when I say that I will until I get the truth from you."

Nieve contemplated his words, and the stern, reproachful look on his face. She frowned, bowed her head, and sighed tremulously. Through a tight throat she said, "Some of Tammin's old *friends* were a bit bullish to me today. He was not here to keep me from them or to keep them at bay, and they were rather cruel."

Landie's eyes widened and she glowered at the Viscount and then at Nieve. "It was that boy that Tammin throttled for speaking disrespectfully to you, wasn't it?"

"It was not him that started it. But he ended it," she replied. "He told the others that I was his to torment only, and when I thought I was safe, he tripped me."

"Who was that?" The Viscount looked livid.

"His name is Raynes. That is all I know about him," Landie replied in Nieve's stead.

"It's not him that started it. That was the other four boys…" Nieve added.

"I know exactly who they are. The Ostin brothers, and the two idiots, Clemens and whatever the other one is called. Tammin used to run with them, the troublesome boy. Oh, the stupidities he was responsible for when he was trying to impress those idiots." He crushed his periodical onto his knees and threw one leg over the other, his face a dour, baleful glower. "I've had quite enough of the reign of terror those little bastards have been inflicting on this town.

It was bad enough when my son was part of it... now they're tormenting Nieve. Why?"

"Because Tammin was my friend, and he protected me while he was here..." she whispered.

The Lord looked like he was about to explode, and when she said the last words, he became deflated. He looked—guilty. "I don't know what's worse–having my son part of a horde of ruffians upsetting our small society, or having a son that has become the enemy of the ruffians." He rubbed his temple. He then dropped his hand and looked at Nieve, eyes soft and concerned.

"We will be leaving for the lake soon enough. But in the meantime, I'll have a word with the fathers of those boys. I won't have anyone harming you for amusement," he growled.

Landie's eyes were fixed upon this frustrated man with outright affection for his reaction to all this. She reached out and patted his arm, startling him.

"Thank you for watching over my niece. She is so very dear to me," she said in soft voice.

The Viscount peered at her and his demeanor melted even more. "You are both become dear to me as well," he said in a hoarse voice. "I will protect Nieve as if she was my own daughter."

10. Service

Nieve was awoken by the most horrendous noise she'd ever heard in all her days. There was no sound in her experience that would compare to it. It was like a hundred-thousand howls of a thousand-thousand hounds all at once, long and unending and sonorous. She sat up in her bed in a cold sweat. Below, doors opened and closed, voices called out, and feet stomped on the wooden floors. She slid out from under her blankets and grasped a dressing gown, drawing it over her arms as she exited her room to find her aunt.

They were at Adaskus. It was only the second night. The first night, they'd arrived just after midnight and had fallen into their beds from exhaustion, as the journey took four days by coach. The next day was spent idling about the tall townhouse, recuperating, resting ,and reading the local periodical to make a list of all the activities they might wish to partake in when they were feeling up to it.

Now this noise had roused them from their slumber, and the whole house was in a dudgeon. Servants and the housekeeper were scuttling about, running down the stairs from their quarters in the attics. None stopped to speak to Nieve. They ran past and clattered down the narrow servants' stairways, taking the glow of their candles with them.

Nieve found the Viscount bleary-eyed and ruffled in a night gown and banyan, his slippers on his large feet. He was going to Landie's room to see if she as well.

"What is that?" she shouted over the noise at her host.

The man glanced down at her as if he'd only just noticed her, and he put his hand on her shoulder. "Don't mind it too much. It is only the breach siren," he said.

Landie's door opened and she stepped out in only a nightgown and her long, luxurious hair tumbling down onto her shoulders. The Viscount's candle rose up to cast its light upon her, and his gaze took in her bare feet and ankles.

"What is all this noise, it's unbearable!?" she gasped, pressing a hand against her breast.

"The breach siren," he told her, too. "It will stop soon. You should go back to bed. Some of the young men in service will be leaving us. The siren is meant to summon them. Go back to bed. You, too, Nieve. All is well. See? It has stopped.".

The siren had indeed stopped, the sound of it suddenly becoming lower and lower in tone until it was inaudible. It was haunting and horrifying to anyone who'd never heard such a din before.

"What does it signify?" Landie asked.

"You don't know?" He seemed astonished that she did not. "Then again, you certainly never had to worry about the greenlands spreading into your deserts. When the living sands have been discovered to breach the plateaus, the alarm is sounded. The young men will be conscripted to dig them out, and stop the advance of the deserts. I served once at a breach at Mulladain. It took four full years to restore the lands from the desertification, and to fight back the invasive sands. The colossus also needed repair and restoration."

The ladies looked upon him in mystification. He peered at them in all-seriousness.

"It is the price we must all pay to live in this sacred, blessed place," he explained. "Rich or poor, prince or pauper, every eligible young man must submit to service when he is called." He paused and reflected a moment. "Tammin is sixteen. That means he will be on his way to the breach as we speak. He will remain in service until the breach has been pushed back and contained. That means we will likely not see him for a long while."

Nieve felt the immediate burn of tears in her eyes.

As if sensing her sadness, the Viscount placed his hand upon her shoulder again to reassure her. "He will be back, my dear. He is not going to war. It is just Breach Service. He will be fine. We will write him when we find out more of where the breach is, and where he will be staying."

Nieve nodded sullenly and let the Viscount nudge her back towards her rooms. He took Landie's hand and patted it gently, and then guided her back through her door.

* * *

The Fohomok, or the Earth-Masters as they were sometimes called, shouted unintelligibly at a distance, guiding the hordes of young men towards the line of drays, box carts, and other vehicles containing the countless portable circular structures that would house them while they engaging in this newest skirmish against the living sands.

These men were always a bit of a shock for newcomers to see. Tall, pale and gaunt, their rickety bodies a testament to the price they paid for their magical abilities. They fought the living sands, and in many respects, were the only things holding the invasive tendrils back from taking root in the fecund soil. There was a pair of them at the breach itself, doing some kind of magic there, where the arms of sand were trying to reach out and find purchase in the land's edges.

The structures that were being erected were old and well-used. The system was well-organized and familiar to the small legion of Fohomok that orchestrated the armies of young men conscripted to the fight.

This would not be a battle of arms. This would be a battle of nature. The weapons were already beginning to arrive along with the housing and supplies that would help sustain the hordes that would be working to contain the breach. Wagons of trees, their root balls tightly wound in canvass, oxen carts filled with heavy, loamy soil, more vehicles containing digging materials to draw water from the earth to bog down the soil and to keep the living sands and the dry desert winds from carrying it away.

Tammin studied the breach. A landslide had taken a great bite out of the plateau, and the slide had broken off the cliff-like upswelling and washed like water into the sandy deserts below. The wind was now pushing the sands up the low incline, and he could see tendrils of the living sands worming their way up like fingers creeping towards the lush greenery that teetered over the slide's edge. There, the Fohomok were working to suppress them, and restore the magical barriers that had been broken by the slide. It would take a great deal of work to wall in the gap created by the massive slide and to stop the living sands from penetrating the plateau. Effrid, Madrick, and Aul were with him, sitting on the edge of a large, flat-bed dray with a group of other fellows.

Tammin had almost been excused duty for his broken hand. But the breacher conscription officer said they needed many hands, and he had him sent to a knitter—a costly endeavor for anyone, let alone the breachers—to have his bones knit by a healing spellbinder. Tammin would not have spent that kind of gold to do it for himself, in spite of being well-off. The breachers must have been desperate to engage such an expensive service for him.

"You're officer material," the conscription man told Tammin. "And we're short of that kind of leadership. We'll get you all sorted with your hand, you do a few months of regular duties as a breacher, and then we'll start you with some more responsibility. We will need good organized leadership at this breach. It's a big one, and will require a lot of time and effort."

Tammin and his friends exchanged their school robes for the dress of breachers. Scratchy trouser breeches of fawn-colored linen, black and white vertically striped stockings, old fashioned buckle shoes, a waistcoat of pale green, and a short-tailed frock coat with a broad cutaway of evergreen, white button panels, and a tall collar that brushed the tops of their ears. This could be closed over the face to protect the breachers' mouths and noses from the blowing sand. The hats were low, felt hats with broad brims.

A loud, barked order startled the fellows from their gaping reverie. "Off the carts, men. Get to the dray and start unpackin' your house, or you'll be sleeping under the stars tonight!" a tall, hollow-cheeked Fohomok in white robes commanded them.

The Fohomok were the last vestiges of the Mennin religion. They were there to battle the living sands while the Breachers worked to wall them out and restore life to the soil that had been tainted by the deserts and the tainted magic of the living sands. The Fohomok were pale of skin and shorn clean of hair. Those born with the abilities of a Fohomok always had the same pale, glassy, near-white colored eyes and elongated bodies, hands, and faces. They were haunting to look at.

Tammin slid off the edge of the cart. His friends followed, and they made their way to the dray nearest them. The horses were being detached from the harnessing and led away as they approached. The Fohomok drew a roll of paper out from one of the smaller crates, unfurled it, and pinned the corners down with some rocks on the cart's footboard.

"There're your instructions. I'm confident at least one of you fancy-boys knows how to read. Figure it out," he snapped. He sailed away in his white robes and left the twenty-two men from Tammin's breacher group to assemble their own housing.

The platform was the first thing to be built. They set to work, dragging the pre-assembled pieces from the carts, toiling well into the afternoon until the large, circular cottage had been assembled on its wooden platform, and all the cots and trunks and supplies had been set up inside, along with the small iron stove for heat that was set in the center of the space with its labyrinthine flue finally shooting up through the hole in the conical roof.

Tammin was the one to attach the flashing to the pipe and the small cone that would keep rain from it. He was on the roof with another young man of twenty by the name of Tebrin, laying down the two layers of waxed canvas that was then tied to the walls below to prevent it flying away in the winds.

"*Sand-ship!*" someone shouted.

Tammin and Tebrin from their prospect on the roof peered out towards the noise, down the long, slow incline of the landslide to the sand where to Tammin's astonishment was a Rethrian sand-galleon with its cloud of sails—their pristine white painted orange by the setting sun—crossing the ocean of sand towards the breach. The Rethrian colors fluttered brightly on the mast flag.

Its bright white keel cut through the sand as if it were water, leaving a stunningly patterned wake behind it. The stabilizers reached out from each side, their own pontoons of sorts painted the same bright, blinding white, the wash comprised of the material called darash, which was what allowed these vessels to sail on sand propelled by the power of the wind.

The sails were dropped, and ship was slowed by the fork brakes that were engaged on the ship's aft. The sailors descended, along with the colorfully garbed captain, and they walked across the sand towards the rubble of the slide.

Two senior Fohomok and a greenlandian army general went out to greet them, raising their hands in a friendly way as they approached. Goodwill aside, the militia moved quietly towards the breach and took their places along the edge of the slide—for it was forbidden for anyone to enter the plateaus without approval of the congress. Even though the Rethrian vessel seemed merely curious about the breach and in possession of only good intentions, someone had deemed it necessary to take precautions and station men at the breach in case there was an attempt to cross.

"Good skies, they're just saying hello," Tebrin muttered in awe.

Tammin nodded, kneeling on the rooftop, one hand draped over his raised knee. He took off his hat, raked back his dark locks, and then put it back on.

"The land can only sustain so many people. If we are not careful, it will become overrun, and it, too, will be wasted like the rest of the world," Tammin concluded.

He gazed at the sands at the slide, shifting and moving, fingers of grains inching forward. He didn't comprehend why the people of this world did not make a greater effort to understand the ways of the past, and how they kept the sands at bay everywhere. But as the old religion waned, the arid lands grew. All that remained now was the greenland plateau, the colossi, the walls of upsurged earth, and the mountain range that kept the greedy living-sands at bay. That and efforts like these, which would keep him and many young men working for at least two or three years, to make yet another patch to prevent what Tammin and many others felt was the inevitable from happening.

A few hours later, the Rethrian vessel had sailed out further into the desert before anchoring down for the night. It was rather peaceful out here, Tammin thought. He had taken a meal with his cottage mates, and then moved out to look over the desert below the slide, listening to the hissing living-sands still moving below. Inching, inching. Further out, he saw the telltale signs of desert bison moving along the horizon, a cloud of dust in their wake. All he could see were tiny black dots against the navy sky.

He turned his thoughts inward as he watched the world outside of his small green one, wondering what Nieve was doing. He wondered if she missed him. If she was safe. It would be a long while before he'd see her again. There were no spring or summer breaks for breachers.

He leaned back on the rock he sat against and tilted his hat so he could see the stars. He would have to write, he decided. He'd received the parcel she sent just as the breacher summons occurred. The scarf, along with her latest letter was packed away in his trunk at the foot of his cot. He dropped his chin and frowned in thought. When he had the chance. He had so much to tell her after Effrid had taken him to see the old druid, and what he had told Tammin about the experience at Winden Hill. Nieve would be greatly amused by what the old man said about her. And about Tammin. She would laugh, and then blush. He smiled at the thought of Nieve's sweet face. He took in a deep breath of air, and shook his head.

He missed her more than he'd missed anyone ever. A silly girl, who made him want to be a better person. To be more gentlemanly. He didn't really understand exactly how much he had come to like this girl; the true the extent of his feelings, until he was here—understanding that he would not see her in a few months now. It would be years before he would set eyes on the girl again. His chest ached at that notion. Why did it do so? He emitted a shaky sigh. I will write. So she will not forget me, he mused. He feared she would grow up and end up becoming fond of someone else. He could not bear to think of her being fond of anyone but him. Their adventures, they must continue, no matter how long he was mired here.

"Halenwood! You out here?" Effrid called out.

Tammin twisted to see his friend standing by the cottage, his left side painted yellow by the light of the fire.

"I am," he replied, getting to his feet, sore from the work of the day.

"Come back in. One of the boys has dice. Let's make a game."

* * *

It was evening and it was very cold. There was a festival in progress along the promenade. Nieve's gripped her lantern with gloved hands as she gazed in confusion at the old woman that had approached her. Her aunt and the Viscount were walking ahead. All of the participants in the promenade were carrying lanterns and circling the common. It was a beautiful sight to see, hundreds of lanterns sparkling in the night.

All of the many commons parks through the city were doing the same, and the walkers would soon diverge from the circular march to the street, and merge with the throngs of others. All of them would join at the royal parkway towards the palace, where there would be music, performers and dancers, and lots of celebratory activities for them to see and do. It would end with fireworks to celebrate the advent of winter, and the end of harvest. There were many pavilions that had been opened up to the cold air for dancing, and music would surround them. Nieve was extremely excited to experience this event.

Landie looked radiant, aglow in the light of her lamp, her face encircled by white fur lining her hood. The Viscount was dressed in an elegant black greatcoat with several capelets on his shoulders, and a broad bicorn that was edged in gold with a silver cockade and feathers billowing from the top. He wore a graceful wig with side-curls and a queue.

Nieve was sporting a new cloak of vermillion with a dappled grey fur edging along the front and bottom of its hood, and a little puff on the tip of the pointed top of her hood that hung down low on her back. Underneath she wore a woolen gown of red, with rich walnut brown gloves that were lined in natural wool and delightfully warm.

She was happily larking along behind her guardians when an elderly woman slid up beside her. She was garbed in a redingote of black wool with a modest train that dragged behind her, a black lace ruff around her neck, a voluminous, ruffled cap of black organdy with an inner ruffle all around her face made of creamy-white lace. The cap also had two long lace lappets that hung down the sides of her head and over the front of her shoulders. She had black gloves. Her cuffs were also edged in white lace. She was tall and lean, with a drawn, wrinkled face, and wide blue eyes that fell upon Nieve searchingly.

"Greetings, lovely, lovely," she said to Nieve, her cane tapping as she walked beside Nieve.

"Ma'am." Nieve curtsied quickly and then kept walking, her eyes locked on her aunt and the Viscount as they strolled ahead.

"I'm *moved* to see you, my dear, dear child. Moved to my very soul. I thank you for returning. I thank you from the very bottom of my heart." She reached out and put her hand on Nieve's arm.

The girl stopped short. "I believe you must mistake me for someone you know. I am sorry Madame. I am not who you think I am."

"Oh, sweet thing, I know a *Saed* when I see one. I might have never known one in all my life, but I was born to recognize what you are," she said laughingly, pointing a long finger at Nieve. "There's another, too, over there," the old woman gestured to her aunt, "but she is not fecund. Not as you are. I can see it glowing from you. And I can see by your light that you are bonded with your counterpart already. How joyous an occasion this is! Where is your bond-mate? I wish to congratulate him, too... There will be growth!"

"My what?" Nieve asked, confused. Her aunt and the Viscount were well-ahead now. Nieve wanted to find a way to kindly cast this mad old bat aside and catch up before she lost them to the throngs.

The old woman began to walk again, gesturing for her to follow. "No need to worry. You cannot lose those you come close to. Come, I will walk with you. I see them. The lady's glow is hard to miss," she blathered. "Such a pity she is not viable. There would be two, and that would be a marvel! And she is of age, too. True pity." She waved her lacy hand at Nieve. "Come child."

Nieve sighed and fell into step beside her. She gazed ahead at the Viscount's feathery bicorn blowing in the chilly wind.

"Your bond-mate is not here? Shame, shame. You must be together. You must. Your bond can never break, that will not happen, but nothing else will happen if you are parted. You must be with your mate," she prattled. "Find him immediately. You should never have parted after your bonding within the circle of stones. Yes, you are young, and there cannot be much to happen now."

Nieve's eyes widened in shock.

"Mother!" a voice called out.

A pair of little heels clattered on the cobbles and a lovely, plump, freckle-faced creature with glistening dark eyes and pale golden hair in perfect ringlets circling her pretty face appeared in a flurry of wool and silk and flouncing hat, lantern waving, cheeks flushed, short of breath. She curtsied clumsily to Nieve and then took the old woman's arm.

"Mother, come. You cannot simply go drifting off like that. Yev's brought the litter. You should get into it and let the men do the walking for you," the girl puffed.

"I can walk perfectly well, you tiresome girl. Now leave me be. I've found a true Saed, and I will not lose sight of her ever again!" she declared stubbornly. "We must reunite her with her bond-mate, or we are all lost!" She waved her cane threateningly at her daughter.

The girl looked at Nieve with an embarrassed smirk and lowered her eyes. The fuss had caught the attention of Nieve's aunt and the Viscount, and they had stopped and were retracing their steps to Nieve. The Viscount bowed low to the old woman when they arrived, and greeted her with a warm, knowing smile.

"Well, if it isn't the indefatigable Lady Parendil. My goodness, you become more beautiful every time I see you," he bellowed.

The old woman gave him a once over from hat to boots and then frowned at him. "Halenwood, you big fool. I see you found yourself yet *another* woman. At least *this* one will stay," she said. "Saeds make *bad* Greenlander men better. You best marry this one and keep her close. She will bear you children, but they will not be Saed. Not like this one." she gestured towards Nieve.

Landie blushed and looked at her feet.

"I like this girl. I aim to keep her," Lady Parendil informed the Viscount.

"I'm afraid not. If I do indeed marry this woman, the girl becomes *my* responsibility," he told her.

"The daughter you never deserved, eh? And what luck for such an unworthy man, to have two such rarities under your roof. They have made you worthy now. I will visit you. I must remain close to this one," she insisted, her gloved hand gripping Nieve's wrist. "She's special in a way you're too stupid to understand."

Two panting men in fine livery tottered up to the curb carrying a sedan chair. They knelt in their yokes and plunked it down. The plump daughter then insisted the old woman release Nieve and sit down inside the litter. The old woman gave Nieve one last look and patted her cheek sweetly.

"Good girl. You find that mate of yours, and do not part from him again, do you understand? You must save us all." She then climbed up onto the sedan chair and sat down. The little door was closed and the footmen hoisted her up with their yokes, and the lady and her mother moved away from the Halenwood party.

"Good heavens, that woman was quite touched in the head, poor dear," Landie laughed merrily.

At first, Nieve had thought so, too. But doubt niggled at her mind. She gripped her lamp and numbly followed, her mind reeling. How did the old woman know about the standing stones? And was she talking about Tammin? Surely she was. Nieve furrowed her brow and walked on. Neither the dancers, performers, musicians, the scents of food, the warm toddies, nor the elegant show of fireworks afterwards could distract her from her thoughts now.

Part Two

The Seed of Winden

11. Better Men

Nieve was glad for the white veil draped over her bonnet. It hid the dismay in her eyes when she entered the tea-house with her aunt to see Raynes amid a party of lively young people at a large table just inside the conservatory attached to the broad room. She exhaled and girded herself.

Raynes had somehow circumvented the summon of breachers back when it occurred four winters before and took Tammin away—and he did not go when the five other breach summons occurred since. She had encountered him shortly after that festival at an assembly on Timber Street, and he had been as awful to her as he had been before, once more claiming her as "his" and establishing himself as her primary tormentor.

She had endured that winter, and the next three, chancing upon his unwanted company. And when she was back at Halenwood, although he was less overt with his torture and enacted it with more subtlety in order to avoid censure from the Viscount and his father, she still did her best to ignore him. The more she did so, the more he worked to needle and provoke her.

She had not seen him this whole past year after their return from Adaskus to Halenwood Hall last winter. He had remained at the lake for the duration, and it allowed for Nieve to enjoy some peace from his constant persecution through spring and summer. And because he had claimed her of sorts, the other boys left her alone even in his absence, so for that, she was grateful. She did not enjoy much society for it, for if Raynes had marked her as worthy of only his torment, then all below him acted accordingly and deliberately left her out of all their invitations and activities. She had only been invited to Andenswegg by the resident family; the Bevvinses, which true to Tammin's claim, were relentlessly social. Otherwise, the only other recourse for Nieve was to walk her walks in the familiar forests and paths around Halenwood and the town. It was enough for her. She was content as long as Raynes was out of sight.

Coming into her eighteenth year, Nieve had changed quite a bit. Her shape finally had filled out, and it was not unpleasing. She had grown from a slightly gawky, boyish figure to a sweet, elegant young lady with a nicely developed bust, a narrow waist, and pleasingly curved thighs and posterior, all of which were subtly displayed in the movement of the skirts of her high-waisted gowns, and the neckline of her tiny, delicately seamed bodices. Sheer tuckers, chemisettes, and fichus may have been meant to hide away her newly grown assets, but instead they only enhanced her loveliness and served to frame her ladylike figure.

Now fully established as a member of the Halenwood family—her aunt was wed to the Viscount the summer after Tammin departed, and was now upon their fifth year together, was swelling with child—Nieve was dressed in all modishness and grace in the finest of silks and muslins, the loveliest of cuts and shapes, the most stylish of hats and gloves and accessories. She reflected well, the status of her patron, the Viscount, who doted upon her almost as much as he did upon his wife.

Although Raynes Bellworth had influenced her society back home, here at Adaskus, Raynes was nobody special except to his immediate circle, and here she had some friends. She was eager to see them, for she had not since last winter. Aunt Landie was certain they would not recognize her, for she had so changed and grown over the past year.

Nieve had also one more thing to look forward to as well as dread, and that was the return of Tammin, who had written to his father that the Norcliffs breach, which was the one Tammin had been assigned to, was nearly finished. After five long years. They would be releasing the men from service back to their homes. All the land was ecstatic for this, for society was suffering a shocking lack of young men to attend assemblies and balls as this record number of breaches in so short a span seemed to have drained the land of its young fellows. Nieve did not care about those things. She just wanted to see Tammin, in spite of her divided feelings.

She was angry at Tammin. And tempted to forget all about her feelings for him.

He had stopped writing her not long after he had gone. She wrote almost once a week, and only received a few replies at first. And after some months, his letters dried up altogether, and she was resigned to learn of his situation through his very rare letters to his father. She continued to write for some time before finally giving up in desolation.

She was harshly disappointed that he had written so little. He asked after her when he wrote his father, and learned that her aunt was to become his stepmother in that way. But there was never anything addressed directly to her. She tried to hide her wretchedness about it and not to burden her family with her disillusionment.

Nieve only wished only to see Tammin's face again, and to walk with him in the forests. She missed him terribly. She wanted nothing more than to sit with him and relate every detail of the past four, almost five years—and to express how dearly she missed him, in person. She wished that he, too, had missed her as much as she did him, even though he had stopped writing her. She feared he might have indeed forgotten her, or found affection for someone else. She worried that this might be true, but she swallowed her sorrow and soldiered on. She knew he would come home eventually. She would manage her hurt when he returned.

Tammin informed his father that he would be home before the end of winter and that he would meet the family at Adaskus—that he would be traveling with one of his superior officers. When, specifically, he did not know yet, as breacher Officers were needed to the very end of the project to coordinate the releases of the breacher forces and to finalize the build itself.

Nieve had read a great deal in the newspapers about that breach, and the architecture of the wall, and how it had restored the shelf of land that had been swallowed by a great landslide. She learned how the men toiled to build it and push back the advancing hands of living sands which had several times almost trounced the efforts of the earth-masters and the builders. She had learned all about the irrigation ditches that were meant to act as barriers as they pushed back the sands to restore the platform of land, and the pump and aqueducts built to carry water where the living sands had crept up and parched the plateau. She had learned about the great cemetery where all the land's dead for three years were sent to be buried in the soil as they backfilled the great retaining wall to make the soil fertile again after the dark magic of the living sands had sucked the fruitfulness away from it. She had prepared herself to talk with Tammin about all of this if there was nothing else to discuss between them.

Nieve had resolved to look at her infatuation with Tammin as a product of her immaturity, and that perhaps she had fabricated a greater affection on his part than truly existed. It was the only way she could survive the hurt of his silence; to take the blame onto herself.

The Viscount, who had become a tempered, happy man with his new wife and soon-to-be-born baby, was eager for his son to come home, too. How changed Tammin would find everyone, Nieve thought.

It was only their first full day at Adaskus since they'd arrived, and Aunt Landie would not miss a moment or a chance to take tea at the grand tearoom. So, with her lump of a belly draped beneath a dark, ferny-green redingote and a large shako bonnet of epic proportions, she herded her niece out of the townhouse to tea.

With child, Landie was even more radiant than ever, and she drew every eye as she entered the vaulted space in all her splendor. Raynes's eye was amongst those that turned to look. At first he looked away, but then, a strange expression formed on his face, and he looked again. His brow rose, and he tried to see through the delicate lace of Nieve's veil. She looked away and ignored him, and she and her aunt found a pair of seats at a small square table not twenty paces from Raynes. Nieve sat with her back to him, and lifted her veil aside, removing her gloves and placing them delicately on her lap.

Landie now knew Raynes from the occasional gathering at Halenwood, and she made a little face when she saw him weaving around the tables to greet them. "Oh dear," she said quietly.

He was hindered by a server who had come to take their order. Landie placed it at leisure, pretending not to see Raynes. However, his joining them was inevitable, and he materialized before them no sooner did the server step away. He first looked at Landie and bowed elegantly, removing his steel grey beau hat, and then faced Nieve in turn.

He was unable to hide his astonishment at how changed and grown she was. His eyes widened and he stammered for a moment when he endeavored to greet her. "Miss Nieve, it's… it's… it's been a sp… spell," he said, his brows rising at the sight of her pretty face. "Y… you've certainly g… g… grown." He gave an awkward laugh, straightening from his bow and sweeping his pale hair back.

Nieve smiled wanly. "I have, as it often happens to girls my age," she replied coolly.

"I have not seen you in a year," he said inanely. "How are you? Are you ladies well?"

"We are indeed well," Landie replied politely. "And you?"

"Ah, yes, I am well indeed. I have been enjoying the fruits of Adaskus through the high-season," he rambled, putting his hat against his chest. "You are here for the winter as before?"

"We are," Landie replied.

A pot of steaming tea was brought, along with a plate of assorted sweet and savory items, including some small sandwiches. The servants arranged the cups and filled them, leaving the pot for the ladies to drink from as needed. Nieve occupied herself by disbursing a few lumps of sugar chiseled from the cone and furnishing both of them with sweetness for their tea.

As usual, Raynes was visibly irritated that Nieve was largely ignoring him. "I'm certain my father will be pleased that the Viscount is come to Adaskus. We will most certainly see one another in myriad parlors through the winter season. And surely we will come to call as well."

The ladies both nodded in agreement and turned their attention their refreshments. He bowed again. Before he was about to take his leave, a waify little blonde thing came sailing up to his side, sliding her hand around the trunk of his arm, her eyes taking in Nieve with a critical, arched brow.

"Raynes, dear, are you not going to introduce us to your friends?" she inquired with a whimsical smile.

Nieve knew Raynes did not dare do or say anything untoward or teasing with Landie present. Instead he made introductions all 'round. The girl was named Miss Morrie Lands-Tremmen, and she was a snooty little thing in spite of being nothing more than the daughter of a knight.

She gave Nieve several admonishing sweeps of her eye, and then as if bored by the whole interaction, she directed her attention to Raynes and said, "Well, shall we rejoin our party?"

"Oh," Raynes muttered hesitantly. "Only after I extend an invitation to Miss Nieve to join us this evening for our schedule of activities. We are to go to hear the incomparable Lady Unila sing three arias, with the infamous Geord Weake as her accompanist. Then we are to go to the rooms at Eckerly, for there is an evening of carding hosted by the Marchioness of Namay. You are more than welcome to take a place amongst our party." He was almost too eager.

Miss Lands-Tremmen took on a look of exasperation at this invitation and she turned her head away to not-so-subtly roll her eyes.

Nieve, having not bothered to even look in his direction or at Miss Lands-Tremmen, merely shook her head once, and lifted her teacup to her lips, sipping before providing her brief reply. "I thank you for your thoughtfulness to invite me, but no. I have other plans."

"Other plans? A shame? If I might ask…" Raynes started.

"Raynes, dear, clearly she has no interest in what we are doing. Why must you insist on imposing upon her to ask her what she is doing?" the girl groaned in annoyance.

Landie's eyes flashed, and she lowered her head to keep her countenance. "Master Bellworth, we are to attend the opera this evening. Damsel of Spells, to be specific. We have been told it is a masterpiece. We thank you kindly for your offer, however the Viscount has secured us seats in a box and we have been much anticipating the performance." Landie spoke with deliberate slowness, as to keep Raynes at their table longer, simply to further provoke the impatient, rude girl.

"Viscount?" Miss Lands-Tremmen murmured, her brows rising. It was too late, however, to recover any semblance of class or decorum after she had so been so uncouth.

Nieve merely took another mute sip of her tea, measured herself. This new face was really nothing new to Nieve. She was the same sort of girl that followed Raynes and his minions about during the social seasons every year. They were all invariably snobs. They were jealous and catty little things, with great airs and little class. All cast from the same ugly mold, time and time again.

"Ah, well, I see," Raynes murmured. "Well then, perhaps we can find another event soon that we can join together. Ladies." He bowed and put his hat on. They moved away at last, Miss Morrie Lands-Tremmen latched securely on his arm.

"Ugh," Nieve said after they'd gone, "if he isn't repulsive enough, he surrounds himself people who make him appear kind." She reached for a sandwich and bit into it.

"We *will* have to accommodate him as Bellworth is Fenwick's peer and close partner in so many of his business endeavors," Landie said cautiously. "We cannot spurn Raynes for the whole winter like we did these past two. There have been mutterings about it from Mr. Bellworth and Fenwick has said something to me about it."

"Oh, Landie, really?" Nieve exclaimed, sighing intolerantly and sagging her shoulders. "Can we not explain to his Lordship what suffering I must endure to appease Mr. Bellworth?"

"I have tried," Landie insisted. "He knows that Raynes has been unkind to you. I have truly tried. But it is the nature of our place in society, Nieve. We must endure things we don't like at all for the sake of peace. At least you may comfort yourself that in the company of his parent, he will not dare to be so cruel." She ate a sandwich, too, popping it indelicately into her mouth. She had been devouring almost everything of late, with this baby soon to arrive.

"Can we at least postpone it until Tammin arrives, so I am not the lone deer surrounded by wolves?" Nieve asked.

"Tammin will likely arrive midwinter. I am unsure if we can delay it that long, but we can *try*," Landie exclaimed.

They both refilled their cups and drank in silence after that.

There was no luck in postponing anything, for Raynes had his own methods of getting his way, and as the small Halenwood party entered the opera hall and climbed the steps to the boxes, they found themselves face-to-face with Mr. Bellworth and his sons. The dandy Alderny was primping at his cuffs but stopped short at the sight of Nieve who was looking particularly lovely for the opera.

Enrobed in a trained gown of silk taffeta the color of the summer sky, she was resplendent. Plied with gold embroidery down the center-front, along the hem and on the bodice, it was a rich and graceful vision. The broad neckline with only the tiniest little gold-lace tucker edging it exposed the sweeping line of her neck and décolletage, as well as the sapphire-studded necklace of her new parure gifted by the Viscount for her eighteenth birthday. Her earlobes were hung in matching stones, and her goldenrod gloves and shoes made for the perfect accent to the ensemble. Her hair was swept up, and dripping in ringlets around the back of her head and on the sides of her face.

Alderny bowed elegantly and took her hand during the introduction, for it was the first time he had accompanied the Bellworths to Adaskus. Raynes's look was one of frustration and disgust as Alderny exercised his seniority and dominated Miss Nieve's attention at once. Nieve was only too happy to lavish her attention on him and ignore the younger brother.

Bellworth bowed in greeting to Viscount Halenwood.

"Well this is unexpected," the Viscount exclaimed.

"I heard you were in town. Thought I'd share a box with you," Mr. Bellworth replied loudly. "Haven't had a chance sit down and enjoy some of the pleasantries in life with you in some time, old fellow. So I did a little surreptitious maneuvering. Hope you don't mind."

"Not at all, Endres. Not at all," the Viscount replied with a jovial smile.

"Shall we go in?" Mr. Bellworth, who had taken to Landie very much from the first moment he met her, claimed her arm and led her into the box before her husband, and helped her sit. She sank down with difficulty, her belly protruding quite a ways.

"I'm amazed you're out and about so much, Lady Halenwood," Bellworth exclaimed. "Most ladies go into confinement so close to their time."

"Indeed they do, but that would mean I would have to stay in bed all day and I cannot abide by that. My legs still work, and until the child is born, I intend to make the most of my freedom. For I am told by many a mother that I will not have time to sleep, let alone take company, for months with a new child. Not without a wet-nurse," she explained.

"Then you should engage one," he suggested.

"No, no, no. Rethrian women do not let anyone other than themselves raise their children if it is within their power," she said firmly.

The younger people sat down around them, Raynes taking a place beside Nieve and moving his chair closer. Nieve continued to behave as if he did not exist.

"Do tell, Lovely Miss Nieve, how do you like Adaskus?" Alderny asked in a haughty voice.

"I enjoy our winters here very much," she replied, flicking her fan open and airing her rosy cheeks. It was close and warm in the theatre from the sheer volume of people crammed into the broad space; and the heat rose right up to the boxes. She was already uncomfortable for the situation and the warmth seemed only to enhance the unpleasantness. "It took some months for me to become used to the depth of cold that we experience here on the plateau, but I am now acclimated and I find winter to be my favorite season after autumn."

"I thought it slightly tiresome until this evening," he told her, a soft smile crossing his lips. "I am used to the broader society of the city, and although Lake Adaskus is lovely and abounding with activities and events, it is still limited in comparison to the great city. So much more to do there, so many more faces to meet." He fidgeted with his waistcoat buttons and tugged on the cuffs of his shirt this whole while so that they were perfectly even, protruding from beneath those of his blue frock coat.

"Shall I fetch you some port, dear Miss Nieve?" he asked politely, then added, "I am thirsty myself."

"That is very kind, Mr. Bellworth," she replied elegantly. She then put her fan between herself and Raynes as his brother unfolded himself from the little chair and vanished through the curtains.

"Are you still holding a grudge against me, Miss Nieve?" Raynes asked, pressing her fan aside so he could see her face. She did not look at him; she merely pursed her lips and snapped her fan closed. "I suppose it is well-deserved. I did treat you notoriously these past years," he confessed. "However, it is partly your fault."

Nieve's eyes widened and she twisted her head to glare at him. "I beg your pardon?"

"The only way I can get your attention is to demand it in an inimical, adverse way," he said with affectation. "If you would respond with even a little kindness, I would not have to torment you."

"Master Raynes, if we were not sitting in a box at the opera, I would smack your face," Nieve hissed. "How dare you blame me for your injurious behavior towards me! The gall!"

"I have only wished to be your friend," he pled.

"I've never heard such falsehood in all my life!" her whisper was nearly edging on loud, and she had to contain her anger, and swallow it down, for the grown-ups were glancing over at them in curiosity. She composed herself and took a deep breath.

"You have endeavored only to make your company as odious to me as possible. Every winter, you have found ways to humiliate and make a mockery of me with your revolting friends. You have tripped me, spilled things on me, left me alone after inviting me, you have provoked me, laughed at me, and delighted in my tears," she murmured under her breath, all the while trying to keep a straight face. "That is not the behavior of someone who wishes to be friends," she concluded. She snapped her fan open, and she waved it frenetically in front of her face, feeling the burn of tears in her eyes.

Raynes leaned back in his chair and contemplated in silence for a moment, while Miss Nieve bristled in her chair, her fan moving at a blur.

"Then I should venture to apologize for being a boor," he said at length.

"Too late," she hissed in a whisper, smiling at the senior Mr. Bellworth who was looking over at them, made curious by Nieve's pale face.

"I will not distinguish that answer," Raynes said, crossing one long leg over the other. They watched the orchestra as they ceased their tuning and noise, and began to prepare their sheets for the overture.

"All I can do is attempt to regain your trust and your admiration," he decided.

"You never had my trust, nor my admiration," Nieve retorted.

"Then I shall work to earn it."

Nieve rolled her eyes and lowered her fan. "Why?" she asked him squarely.

"Because I like you," he replied earnestly.

The words cut hard, and put her into a shock. She could not believe he had the audacity to say such a thing. Who in their right mind would say they like the person they relentlessly tortured? She felt as if she was going to scream at this mad assertion. Her hands shook. She took a measured breath, and swelled her rage.

"You certainly have a strange way of showing it," she said stiffly. She wanted a glass of chilled water. *No. Something stronger.* And an escape from this conversation.

"If you want to gain a lady's regard, shoving, tripping, or laughing at her usually won't accomplish what you think it will," she hissed angrily.

Raynes did not reply. His face tightened and his jaw rippled as he looked out at the people below in the general seats shifting about and settling in. At a glance, his eyes were glassy and he actually appeared upset. The orchestra began the first strains of the overture, and the ushers exited with their lamps.

Alderny reappeared carrying two tiny little glasses of port, delicately handing one to Miss Nieve before sitting down on her other side.

She drained it all in one gulp, and held the empty goblet in her trembling, gloved hand. The overture ended and the curtains parted to reveal a large woman in an old-fashioned pannier gown and towering wig. She put her right hand on her silver-embroidered stomacher, and the other in the air, and belted out into song. It was so loud and surprising, Nieve jumped a little. Alderny reached into his pocket and extricated a pair of opera glasses which he flipped over on the handle and thoughtfully handed to Nieve.

She accepted them with a polite smile, and put them to her eyes. The glasses served perfectly to hide her anger. She wanted nothing more than to storm out of the box and to leave the detestable Master Raynes behind.

12. Even a little chance

Bellworth had set his heart on Nieve as a daughter-in-law, but to Raynes's ire, it was for Alderny who was the chosen groom. Bellworth was overcome by the whole idea, for Alderny was an infamous dandy and rake and had shown little interest in settling on one particular girl at all. But his fascination with Nieve was sparked from that very evening, and the father was beside himself about it.

"We shall have to arrange for more occasions where the two of you might meet. She is young and is not out yet, but the earlier you create an impression, the sooner you win her over and the surer you will be that you will make a wife of her," Mr. Bellworth explained in the coach on the way home from the opera.

Alderny was pensive and waxing romantic. "She's the prettiest, sweetest thing I ever beheld," Unlike Raynes, Alderny had not suffered too much by his father's hand. He was a compliant, rather weak-willed creature compared to his younger, willful, and rebellious brother.

Raynes scowled in the darkness of the coach, unnoticed by his father and brother. He fumed. "She's already all but engaged to the Halenwood boy. For all we know they already have an understanding between them."

"There is nothing official," Mr. Bellworth interjected, waving his hand dismissively at Raynes. "Not to mention that the boy has been serving as a breacher for the past how many years. Hearts change. People change. There are plenty of gatherings held for the young breacher officers to keep morale up. There's no saying another pretty face from the edgelands hasn't already led him astray from the girl. She was much younger when he left. Faced with grown ladies, there's a good chance he's all but forgotten his attachment to her."

Raynes never put much stock in his father's words, but he truly wanted to believe him this time. He *had* to trust that this was the case—now that he held the full realization of the innumerable chances he had wasted—and how ineptly he had tried to protect her from the others, all of whom would have delighted in doing harm to the traitor Tammin's favorite ward. Raynes could only dwell on how bumbling his efforts to connect with her had been. How could he know? When everything he'd known in his life was communicated through insult and meanness?

Perhaps he'd started out with the intent on sabotaging whatever there was between her and Tammin. But the more time he spent doing what he knew best, tormenting and vexing this girl, the more he realized that it was her attention he wanted. And now. Now that she had grown into such a beauty, the desire for her was even greater. But she hated him. Her dislike and anger, it had once been enough. But now it was not. And she did not see how what began as a game, only became their prison. For he had no choice but to be mean to her. This unforgiving circle of friends, he was forced to establish himself as top dog, or they would have torn him to shreds as they most certainly would have her. If he had not interceded and claimed eminent domain, she would have been eviscerated. Did Nieve not see this? That he was doing it all *for* her?

* * *

Miss Morrie Lands-Tremmen's eyes were narrow and resting with a burning gaze on Nieve. She made no effort to hide her dislike of the quiet girl. She tapped her fan on her wrist, and leaned slightly away from Nieve, who was quietly ensconced in the velveteen sofa. The young people were in the parlor of a Lady Rample-Of-Shea, who had organized a concert for the young people to attend, followed by a light repast of finger foods and then some quadrilles. Nieve had been obliged to attend at her aunt's behest as a gesture of goodwill towards the Bellworths who had been particularly insistent that Nieve accompany the sons on social visitations.

Raynes was at present engaged with the other men in the billiards room, leaving the ladies to interact without their company. There were eleven other girls scattered about the spacious room. Nieve had already made the circuit to admire all the paintings hanging on the wall. With that finished, she had taken a seat. A girl by the name of Gillian, whom she had befriended two seasons before, had come to talk to her, and along with her came the odious Miss Morrie Lands-Tremmen.

"You uncle is so generous and thoughtful. I begged and begged and begged my father for a dale horse. And you received one without even asking. I am utterly beset with envy," Gillian sighed. "And he got you that simply perfect little dapple pony two years before."

"I outgrew dearest little Kata for the saddle last summer. I was very gloomy for it, but we've kept her as she is such a good driver, and she is so reliable with my little gig," Nieve told her friend.

Miss Lands-Tremmen looked on in silence, with the air of barely tolerating the banality of their conversation. But there was a definite look of jealousy when Gillian mentioned Nieve's new Dale horse.

"Onyx is miles from any kind of horse I've ever had. He's taken some getting used to. His trot is like a box-cart on cobbles." Nieve giggled timidly. "But I've learned to move with it well enough. He is also a great deal hotter than any horse I've ever had; a different experience entirely keeping him in hand."

"Oh, I'm sure a dale horse is vastly different and better than the desert breeds. Those are spindly little things. They're almost goats," Morrie interjected laughingly, waving her fan in front of her face.

"Hardly," Nieve replied archly. "Have you ever ridden a sand-dancer, let alone seen one?" She made a point of not laughing or showing any amusement at all, finding the observation to be vapid and a bit cutting. Miss Gillian also remained tightlipped and serious, clearly feeling the same.

"I've seen linotypes of them. They are odd looking little things."

"They're not little. They're tall. Long-legged. Broad hoofs for the sands. They are also willful and single-minded. Not the easiest horse to ride. Kata was a dream to ride after growing up on the back of a sand-dancer. Compliant, maybe a bit stubborn, but nothing compared to the constant defiance of a sand-dancer." Nieve directed this to Miss Gillian. She then turned to look at Miss Morrie and said, "They have finer lines than highland horses, for certain, but they are not in the slightest way goat-like. They are quite beautiful and graceful."

"But too frail to live happily in the highlands," Miss Morrie argued.

"They are perfectly suited to navigate the deep sands of the deserts, where they belong. As the dale would not do well at all in their environment, I imagine. Probably sweat itself to death in the heat of the summers and in the effort to pull its weight through the shifting sand. But I shall not begrudge Onyx for that weakness. He is where he belongs," Nieve replied coolly.

"But *you* must not feel like you are where *you* belong," Miss Morrie ventured.

Both of the other girls arched their brows at her in both shock and puzzlement at the curious direction she'd taken the conversation.

"I don't follow," Nieve said.

"You are of the desert countries. You surely must feel out of place here. Well outside of what you are used to."

"No. In all honesty, when I first arrived at Narroway, I felt as if I'd finally returned to where I was truly meant to be," Nieve said with a whimsical smile.

Miss Gillian made a sweet little coo, and tilted her head. "How lovely."

"I imagine any common person from the deserts would think that way, given the great advantage of being permitted to enter these sacred lands," Miss Morrie dismissed. "But in all reality, you are not of here."

"I am now," Nieve insisted, her ears growing red.

"You don't fit in quite perfectly with the rest of us, now do you? You are timid and meek in company, I think. I…"

"That would be because she is kind and polite and thoughtful. It is not a detriment," Miss Gillian interrupted Miss Morrie with a defiant slant of her brow. "I do believe you are being a bit rude, do you not think, Miss Lands-Tremmen? To imply that Miss Nieve does not belong here."

"I imply nothing. I am plainly saying that she is a foreigner, and a much-blessed one, to be permitted to live here among us," Morrie said outright. "She is lucky in many ways. From her presence in the greenlands to her wardship with the Viscount. I am merely ensuring that she understands her good fortune and does not take it for granted or is unappreciative of the generosity that has been visited upon her and her aunt." She had been sitting so listlessly and indifferently, bored at first, but now sat upright, her back rod-straight, with her chin jutted out defiantly.

"Where is this acrimony coming from?" Nieve asked plainly. "What have I ever done to you to earn your resentment?"

"You do not have my resentment. I feel nothing at all towards you," the haughty creature laughed.

Both of the girls looked at her in astonishment.

"I think perhaps Miss Morrie might be jealous of the attentions that Raynes showers upon you when you are in his company. She was quite put out when he spurned her to meet you at the opera," Miss Gillian said pointedly.

Miss Lands-Tremmen's eyes widened and her neck grew hot. "Nonsense," she hissed angrily. "Raynes sees only someone to mock and tease in this girl. He treats her infamously, anyone can see it."

"I do, don't I?" A voice startled the three. Raynes and another young man had somehow stealthily approached the scene. None of them were certain how much of the interchange had been heard, but Raynes looked angry for what he did hear.

"Yes, you do," Miss Morrie replied smugly, laughing, bolstered by the affirmation of her assertions by Raynes.

"But *you* may not." His face melted into a hard, almost frightening darkness, and he glared at Miss Morrie whose laugh halted abruptly, and she winced.

"I've been clear in my circle that Miss Nieve is to be treated with civility. I might tease her, but that does not give you permission to do so. And if you step even further and are intentionally and unnecessarily cruel to someone who has done nothing to you, that is all I need to know that I wish nothing more to do with you," he added.

Miss Lands-Tremmen's eyes became glassy as she stared up at Raynes. Her chin began to tremble, and she flicked open her fan and hid a sniff behind it. She shot to her feet and flounced away in sobs.

Raynes glowered at everyone who had witnessed this interchange, then sank down next to Nieve and crossed his legs.

"You see what kind of trouble you stir up, sand-girl?" he said.

Nieve gave him a baleful glare and looked away. She was divided in her feelings. There was a triumph to see someone like Miss Lands-Tremmen being put in her place so well. But also, there was the idea that Raynes could dictate how people interacted with her and controlled how they treated her. He seemed to have some sort of air of ownership of her when his brother was not present. Just as she thought this, his arm slid along the back of the sofa behind her. She shrank into herself a little.

"I don't know why everyone likes to be cruel to you," he wondered airily, watching the group of people return to their conversations, their games of cards. The girl who had been sitting at the harp returned to plucking at it.

"Because *you* are," Nieve told him. "Your teasing invites disrespect and disregard as they interpret your treatment of me as exactly that on your part."

Raynes mulled this over, and again, seemed perplexed by this observation.

"I don't know how this is so difficult for you to understand. You manage to treat all these other ladies with modicum and civility."

"I don't *like* any of those ladies," he said with an air of frustration. "I don't like them enough to treat them with anything more than just politeness."

"So you think that you must be mean and unkind to the person you think you like?" Nieve asked, appalled. She glared at him in mystification.

Raynes seemed to be divided on his own opinion on the matter, and seemed unable to rationalize his thoughts in any way that could help him, or more importantly, Miss Nieve, understand why he was like this. He exhaled with defeat and shook his head. "Just know that my opinion of you is greater than any that I hold for any one of these vapid creatures in this room. I clearly lack the capacity to express it in a reasonable way, apparently, but it is the truth."

Nieve turned to look at him. He turned peer at her with a pair of sad, blue eyes. She had to concede that he had done something kind for her today. He looked so conflicted and confused. So was she.

"I thank you, Raynes, for sending her packing. I don't know how much I could have borne of her nastiness without becoming angry. And these days, I cannot be angry without tears, and to dignify her with my tears would have been mortifying."

Raynes's eyes lit up at the expression of gratitude and he smiled a little. His eyes warmed, and his gaze softened as it took in her face. "She will no longer be a problem. Nobody will, I promise you that."

Nieve felt the tenderness of his gaze, and the ardor hidden within it, and she blushed. She was overcome suddenly with uncertainty. She bent her head to peer at her hands, which were folded in her lap.

The two of them remained quietly side by side the remainder of the evening, oddly comfortable with the silence. Nieve realized that from this moment, she neither felt awkward in Raynes's presence; nor did she feel completely repulsed by him anymore. He was so changeable, only time would tell what motivated Raynes. At least, with this act, he had earned the benefit of her doubt.

* * *

Tammin moved with purpose through the assembly hall toward Effrid and Andin, the fellows he'd grown closest to for the duration of his service to the breach. He was handsome and stoic in his officer's uniform, the colors the same as the slops they'd all started in—except these were tailored, clean, and of quality. He had learned the value of starting with all of the breachers as equals, to be put to work, and then to lift those with advantages of education, acumen for leadership, or good breeding up only after they'd tasted what it was to be among the laborers. He had learned equity and empathy. He had learned the value of hard work, and more importantly, the worth of hard workers. He had grown into a respectable, honorable young man in those five years away.

The officers had been released at last, and sent to Amredian, one of the wealthiest cities on the plateau. This was where the upper crust of the plateau's highest society owned large estates and city homes, all parceled out with enough space for gardens and topiary, follies and fripperies, with stately avenues and parks between them, and centers of culture for the residents to congregate. There were some enclaves of diminished affluence to house the many servants and tradesmen that were required to manage the great houses, estates, legal offices, municipal services, banks, and whatnot.

Tammin thought it was the most pretentious, horrifying place he'd ever been. But he and all the officers were stationed there temporarily until they received their full releases and their medals of service that would excuse them from future breaches if they desired.

Effrid had been promoted to Lieutenant Colonel and was overseeing the discharge of all those in his brigade. Tammin, nearly 21 years of age, had achieved Major in ranking and was tasked to assist. Neither wished to continue on in service and was each quite glad to leave with their respective rankings.

Brigadier General Glass's family lived at Amredian, and he had in part arranged for a variety of events for the officers to participate in while they finished their service for the crown council breacher army. His wife, a woman of irascible social appetite, orchestrated with the assistance of her many friends an endless array of obligations for the Fohomok and the officers that were at present mired at Amredian. The social requirements were inescapable, as the higher officers expected all to attend as long as they were still in service to the crown council and the congress.

Tammin was included amongst these obligated fellows and forced to endure assemblies and gatherings, carding evenings, and shrill performances by countless daughters that relatives and friends of the Brigadier General hoped would benefit from the influx of young officers from all over the greenlands and edgelands. The whole thing reminded him of the sand-hags. He learned about them early on as he was warned not to bleed onto the living or the passive sands. The brigade's Fohomok had produced a piece of pork, and he flung it out a good way into the slide where the sands had been encroaching. It fell and rolled a bit. Within a few seconds, a slithering mass of hideous, black, wrinkled leech-like creatures had churned to the surface and tore apart the piece of flesh. As quickly as they'd appeared, they were gone, leaving no trace of the meat.

"They'll eat you alive if you shed even a drop of blood. If you are standing in sand, always be wary," the Fohomok had warned. "We will strive to keep the sands at bay while you work, but it is inevitable that it will encroach during the build. It is your responsibility to keep from drawing the dangers the sand carries with it, understood?"

Tammin felt like every officer in the room was that piece of pork, and the daughters of Amredian were the slithering sand-hags.

Tammin found refuge from the throng of ladies by Effrid's side. He had learned by the frenzied whispers of the ladies that Effrid was devastatingly handsome and the most eligible of all the officers. However, his airs were even more unwelcoming than Tammin's. The only difference was, unlike Tammin, Effrid did not have someone he already preferred. He was simply a surly, discriminating snob who wanted nothing of the gold-seeking girls of Amredian. He acted in outright disgust, and the only reason why he got away with this overt and unforgivably rude behavior was because he was a titled peer. The Brigadier General might outrank him as a breacher, but not as a man with a mere knighthood.

"They are tantamount to prostitutes," Effrid mumbled under his breath to Tammin as he slid up beside him and took a deep, intolerant breath. Effrid's prickly countenance alone kept the women at bay.

He was the Fohomok of women, thought Tammin. His dour demeanor and sneering glare kept the waves of ladies from encroaching on his corner of the room. The ladies were at present gathered 'round the demi-lune pianoforte as yet another nameless girl in white a muslin gown and coral necklace sang and played very ill upon the poor, besieged instrument.

"Any idea when we will be permitted to flee this place?" Tammin asked Effrid.

"I believe it'll be another two or three days, from what I understand. The weather is not getting any better. I'm hoping for relief soon," Effrid replied. He reached out his arm, the gold-bullion-trimmed sleeve catching the candlelight; and picked up a wide snifter of apple brandy the region was known for.

"Back to school for you?" Tammin asked.

Effrid wagged his head from side to side. "What about you?" he inquired, swallowing back the brandy. His glass was now empty save for the viscous coating left behind.

Tammin wagged *his* head side to side. Effrid snorted through his nose, and gestured to the footman for a refill. Tammin indicated he wished one of his own.

"I will go to Adaskus first. To see my family," Tammin finally said. "After that, I am unsure. I would prefer to have completed my schooling, but I will have to begin where I left off, and I don't half want to sit in a lecture hall full of unworldly sixteen-year-olds anymore."

"Speak to the Chancellor," Effrid suggested. "I'm sure something can be worked out so that you can matriculate with your peers and not with juniors anymore. This isn't the first draft. I'm quite certain there's a procedure that is available for the returning students."

"Major Halenwood," a singsong voice interrupted, "I was hoping to find you here."

Effrid turned to the source of these words and held up his glass. "Congratulations. You deduced the Major would be where *all* of the other offers are. Cheers for your ingenuity, Miss Glass," he said in a level, mocking tone.

The girl, an attractive redhead with wide blue-green eyes and an alluring smile burst into musical laughter, as if truly amused by Effrid's cutting tone. He sneered at her and turned his shoulder to her, facing Tammin.

"I'll leave you to the wolves," he said to Tammin in a low voice. "Or the red wolf, at least."

Tammin was not happy to watch his friend drain his brandy and then stalk from the room to abandon him. Effrid gave Tammin a wry smirk before he ducked through the doorway, bicorne and all.

Tammin was now at Miss Glass's mercy. She had been a difficult inconvenience to bear from the first year when she arrived at her uncle's residence and met the aspiring officers. Her gaze had fallen upon Tammin and never deviated. Wherever Tammin was, when he was not performing his duties, she inevitably appeared. She was persistent and unrelenting, refusing to take no for an answer.

She did provide the advantage of chasing other ladies off, but she was probably the worst of them all. Tammin had lived his entire youth inflicting selfish cruelty on people. His newfound decency, which had been both precipitated by his falling out with Raynes and the boys, and the influence of a certain Miss Nieve, made it difficult for him to step back into that old persona and drive Miss Glass away as surely as Effrid drove everyone else away.

Tammin was without ideas, and the Brigadier General was the girl's uncle, so his options were limited even if he could be cruel and awful again. Instead, he quietly stood by and tolerated her attentions, giving her nothing in return. Still, even with a stoic, unresponsive beau, she seemed quite content to hang onto him and pretend there was something to hope for. He had on numerous occasions explained that he had someone he cared about that he was waiting to reunite with, but she was adamant that she would not accept this truth until he had reunited with the girl. She was sure they would have changed so that they would not recognize the person they had become fond of years before.

"I am desolate," she exclaimed sorrowfully, throwing herself into a chair near Tammin. He stood rigidly, sipping his drink, gazing off into the room filled with green frock coats, tall bicorns, and girls in white muslin. When Tammin did not flinch at her complaint, she sighed loudly. "You will be released soon. I have begged my uncle—begged and begged him—to find a reason to keep you close to us, so that I would not be lost to you, but he said that there is nothing to be done. You have earned your release from the breacher army."

Again, Tammin remained silent and indifferent to her suffering.

"Where are you to go now, Major Halenwood? Where are you going so that I might follow?"

"To seek out and find the lady that I love," he said bluntly. He drained his brandy, bowed curtly to Miss Glass, and then to the Brigadier, who toasted him as he left.

Two days, he repeated to himself. Two more days.

13. The Dance

It had become nearly impossible to do anything, go anywhere, or even remain at home without a Bellworth materializing beside Nieve like a specter of some unpleasant future. Alderny was persistent, and attentive to the point of suffocation. It never would have occurred to Nieve that she would someday view Raynes' attentions as a welcome relief. But Raynes had become a shelter from his brothers' notice, even if it meant it was accompanied by Raynes' rude and misguided behavior. In spite of his revelation that he had developed a romantic interest in Miss Nieve, he had yet to find a way to express it in a way that was not negative in one fashion or another.

At this particular assembly, organized by a Lady Ellancourt, a twice-monthly event to which Nieve had subscribed access to for three full months, Raynes had succeeded in distracting his brother by introducing him to an acquaintance who was as great aerostat enthusiast as Alderny. The fellow was named Tareyn Rilkes, and he had even bought a share in a massive balloon that was being assembled by the Duke of Edanshayne with the notion of flying it over the Arven Sandsea to Rietchtan and ultimately to Rethros. When Alderny heard of this, he could scarce contain himself, and

Raynes was only too happy to make the introduction before he ducked away to seek out Miss Nieve.

He found her in the supper room, partaking of the plentitude of refreshments to be had. The center of the room featured a table of mountainous proportions, tiered so high with dishes and platters, tureens and towering constructs of fruit and flummeries that it looked as if the table might give way from the weight of it all. To top it off, a bronze statue of the god of Lednus was perched over the lot of it like an ornament atop a tower. As the god of plenty, his placement overseeing a mountain of food was appropriate.

Nieve was standing at the foot of this great berg, hand poised over a tray of small and fragile-looking petit-four cakes. They were intricate little things of forget-me-not blue, with white royal icing lace piped all around the edges, and a little marzipan cameo on the top of the palest pink and white. She plucked one up and put it into her mouth, rather than onto her plate, moving down with wide, roving eyes while she chewed and took in the panoply of delicious goodness laid out before her in a soaring spread.

"There you are," Raynes called out. "I've set him on the aeronauts, you shall see neither hide nor hair of him now," he grinned victoriously. "I almost feel sorry for them," he laughed. "And if we're lucky," he added, "we shall have the promise of an unwise investment in a great balloon, and the inevitable inferno that will ensue on the part of my father when that happens!" he chortled.

Nieve's eyes rolled up at him with the predictable look of trepidation, and the customary frown he received. She swallowed her mouthful of cake, and blinked her large eyes. His heart fell yet again. But he girded himself up, and took to her side, regardless, snatching up a pretty plate and eyeing the fare.

"What looks most delectable to you, Miss Nieve?" he asked as brightly as he could manage, peering at her beautiful face. She had applied a little color to her cheeks and lips for the assembly. Her gown was a sumptuous affair of peacock blue silk with gold and silver embroidery on the edges of hems and cuffs, and intricate lattice-smocking giving a delightful texture to her sleeves and stomacher.

"All of it," she replied softly. Beyond the supper room, the musicians tuned their instruments in preparation, and many of the people occupying the islands of tables rose and migrated towards the ball room. Out of another, narrower archway came the clack of billiard balls and the riotous laughter of the players. Raynes had remained mostly by her side this evening, and did not enter the billiards room this time.

Mr. Bellworth sat at a table by the window with a group of older ladies. The Halenwoods had opted to remain at home, as Lady Halenwood was too pregnant to move and had been enduring some pangs for the past days that the physician had assured her were *not* those of labor, but what he described to the Viscount as: "…merely the clarion announcing the arrival of the troupes, sir."

The Bellworths had gratefully offered to accompany Miss Nieve to the assembly and were all too happy to provide supervision of her as she partook in her subscribed activities.

When Nieve had filled her plate with all manner of mouthwatering bits of food, she wove her way through the remaining people to the table and settled down amid the Bellworth party where she was welcomed by the warm voices of the four ladies that had joined Mr. Bellworth to dine and gossip. Raynes sat beside her and they ate, half listening to the prattle of the ladies, and half-watching through the corridor and arches as the first dancers took their places in three lines of sets, all crushed together as closely as they could.

"We shall have to dance, Miss Nieve," Raynes said to her as he ate. "I haven't danced a step in all of the evening, and if I am to do so, it will *only* be with you."

Nieve nodded complacently, feeling obligated because they were accompanying her, and Raynes had so kindly dispatched with her other admirer. She ate the rest of her supper, and drank deeply of the punch that Raynes had fetched her, and then she conceded to his request and rose to her feet, accompanying him through the archways to the dance-room. The dance-master announced the name of the dance, and Nieve quickly riffled through her memory of the last dance classes to recall which movements the dance required as she settled into her place across from Raynes.

The musicians played the introductory notes, and Nieve curtsied to Raynes, feeling slightly warm towards him. He seemed so very intent upon pleasing her these days. He had ceased his tormenting, although he did occasionally tease. She imagined it was impossible to expect a complete reversal of his behavior when this was all that he knew. And it seemed that teasing was part of his very nature. She understood better why, after spending so much time in the company of the Bellworths these past weeks.

Mr. Bellworth was in private quite hard on his sons. But in public, or with the Viscount and his new wife, he was a gentle bear. At present, he was basking in the glow of attention from his retinue of ladies that had flocked to him on their arrival.

Raynes bowed deeply to Nieve, his eyes shining. She tilted her head and offered him a rare smile, which seemed to bolster him. He straightened his back and put his left hand behind him, capturing hers with his right in the first of the dance's movements.

She claimed his long fingers into hers, and they turned together to the lively tune. She skipped along to the music. They setted gracefully to one another and turned back to place. The other couple in their set mimicked their movements, and when they were done, she and Raynes cast away from their set and moved downwards into the place of the other couple as they moved up. A gipsy turn with the other gentleman, a single-turn for each lady, two balances, and they were progressed their new set.

Nieve loved dancing, and it flushed her cheeks and made her smile radiantly at her partner, who was as generous with his grins as she. He danced very well, and was as gentlemanly and graceful and poised on the floor as any lady could wish a partner to be.

She was enjoying herself, and it showed. She grasped her skirts and set again, giggling as Raynes spun her 'round by her right hand.

As they moved into their next set, Nieve's stomach lurched at the sight of none other than Tammin moving up the lines towards them. He was paired with an astonishingly lovely red-haired girl who seemed awash with affection for her partner in the way she smiled and blushed at him. Tammin was as impassive and brooding as always, looking slightly distracted and faraway. The girl was overt in her affection towards him, her eyes possessive, her regard one of happy attachment.

Tammin's expression changed entirely when his gaze passed over Nieve. First, they barely acknowledged her, as if he was just taking her in along with everyone else. But then recognition washed over his face, and his eyes widened and fastened onto her, astonished. His expression twisted into dismay when he saw who she was dancing with. He then peered at her in earnest, his brow crumpled and his lips tight.

"Look out, Miss Nieve," Raynes exclaimed laughingly, for she had forgotten a step. "You are distracted."

As they progressed into the next set with Tammin and his fiery-haired beauty, Raynes now realized why exactly Nieve had missed her movements. The gentlemen's' eyes immediately locked into adversarial glares, and their jaws rippled as they continued to dance. The only one unaffected by this at first was the redhead, but it did not take her long to realize something was amiss when her normally passive partner now stared angrily at the other tall, fair-haired gentleman in the set. When he made his turn with Nieve, his face softened and his eyes became glassy.

"Nieve," he whispered, barely audible above the music.

Nieve's response was strangled, as if by as sob. "Tammin, you're here."

And with that, Raynes reclaimed his partner and they moved down to the last set before they were out for the round.

Nieve was short of breath and close to tears. Her hands were trembling.

"Shall we retire from this dance?" Raynes suggested, his eyes flashing.

Nieve's attention was locked onto Tammin who was dancing his way up the sets. His curious redhead glared furiously down the line at Nieve, and then questioningly at Tammin, who remained stoic and forced, his gaze engaging nobody—even his flustered partner.

Nieve finally nodded to Raynes and he took her hand and led her away from the dance. She clutched his arm and stumbled along next to his long strides. She was awash with disappointment and scarce-contained misery.

Raynes took her to his father, bending down to whisper something to him. Mr. Bellworth nodded once and waved his hand at his son dismissively. Raynes led Nieve to the servant to reclaim their cloaks.

He gently placed Nieve's cloak and shawl on her shoulders, and escorted her toward the stairs. Nieve did not hear the voice calling after her at first, but Raynes did, for he ushered her urgently down the stairs to the foyer and bade the footman to summon a post coach in haste.

Raynes had counted on Tammin not being so discourteous as to leave a dance while they were in the middle of the set, for it would be rude to disrupt all the dancers by doing so. It was only acceptable to exit the dance if the couple was out at the top or bottom of the set. But it appeared that Tammin wasn't too concerned about being courteous to other dancers at the moment.

Raynes was about to guide Nieve through the door, when he was blocked abruptly by Tammin's arm which appeared like a barrier across the doorway, his hand gripping the doorframe, his body sliding between them and the outdoors. Nieve halted as well, still clutching Raynes's arm. Her eyes filled up with tears immediately upon the sight of Tammin's angry face.

"Where are you taking her?" Tammin growled.

"Home," Raynes replied curtly. He sneered at Tammin. "She is in a state of shock, as anyone would be to discover their favorite—after five years of being ignored and thrown aside by him—to be in the company of another lady, without the slightest warning or communication of the attachment."

Tammin opened his mouth to retort when the voice of said lady rose up and the clatter of feet sounded on the marble steps. "Halenwood, why have you run off like that? How could you abandon me without a word? I am mortified! The whole set was thrown into disarray!" Her desperate expression melted into panic at the sight of Tammin in near confrontation right near the girl that had evoked a feeling response from a young man who had never shown such emotion to anyone before.

"It wouldn't be the first time he's abandoned a lady," Raynes replied with a sardonic, disgusted smirk as the redhead approached in a great bustle. "Now, see to *your* lady. I will see to taking Miss Nieve home. She is unwell, thanks to you," He then threw Tammin's arm aside and led Nieve out the door to the coaches.

Tammin pushed past the red haired girl, who tried to keep him inside by taking his arm, but he yanked it free and vaulted down the steps to the post-coach where Raynes handed Nieve in. She was in shock, and hurt. He had found someone. Who was she to berate him for that? They never had an understanding between them. She had girded herself for this moment because she had to accept that his silence and his distance was a sign that he never truly regarded her as anything more than a child or friend. She had thought of all these things, and prepared herself for the possibility that Tammin never truly reciprocated her feelings—but it did not save Nieve from the heart-shattering pain of seeing him with someone else. She was struck dumb by it all.

"I arrived only this evening, Nieve," he told her softly through the door. "I was told you'd be here. I shall meet you at home."

Nieve sank back into the darkness of the coach, further confused by his kindness and the softness of his eyes, in spite of the red haired girl standing right behind him. She gazed at Raynes who had settled in across from her and yanked the little half-door closed.

"Park Street Circus," he shouted.

The coachman clucked his tongue and the coach lurched forward. Tammin stared after it, his eyes misty and angry all at once.

He turned and ran into Miss Glass. "Who were they? Was that *her*? The one you spoke of?" she asked in a jumble of desperate words. "She's chosen someone else, I see."

Tammin ignored her and circumvented her body, scaling the steps to fetch his greatcoat and hat.

"Halenwood! Where are you going?" Miss Glass shouted angrily. "You cannot simply leave us like this! You promised me two dances! That was your price!" She stamped her foot, making a spectacle of herself.

Tammin half-ran to the street and hailed a post-coach. In no time, he was in the rumbling conveyance heading towards his family's townhouse.

14. As Winter Ends

When Nieve arrived, there was a commotion about the house, and her early return went largely unnoticed. Landie was at last in the throes of childbirth, and the staff, midwife, and nurse were preoccupied with preparations. The circle of mothers that had befriended Landie, and who had promised to be present at the birth, arrived in a clutch of five to sit with her. They bustled in almost at the same moment Nieve entered the house with Raynes at her heel. She shucked her cloak and left Raynes alone, disappearing in the shuffle of silk and muslin skirts, absorbed by the small herd of mature women heading up to Landie's rooms.

Raynes tried to hang about a bit longer, but he was cast out by the butler who sent him home. Not long after, Tammin arrived, dismounting from the coach and stalking into the house without ringing the bell. He found himself alone in the foyer with nary a soul to be found. He heard noise below as the servants celebrated the moment in the basements. He heard more noise above-stairs. Then he heard a cough in the study, and he pushed the door open to find his father seated unseen by the fire, the back of the chair hiding his presence altogether. The door's creak brought his face 'round the edge of the wingback.

"Well, you're back sooner than I thought," he declared. "Where's the girl?"

Tammin stared at his father. For the second time, he was astonished by his changed nature. The simmering undercurrent of anger was utterly gone from his being. In its place was peaceful, albeit apprehensive, composure. He looked upon Tammin in a way he could never recall ever witnessing in his father before.

"I don't know," Tammin confessed. "The Bellworth idiot supposedly brought her home. But nobody is about. What's going on?"

"Landie is about to give birth to your younger sibling," the Viscount exclaimed with a satisfied smile. "I've been exiled from the room by the clutch of hens. I must wait down here."

"Ah," Tammin replied, sitting next to his father in the second chair by the fire. He peered at him in curiosity, as if meeting him for the first time.

"I'm hoping for a little girl," the Viscount said with a soft smile.

Tammin marveled at this. He knew his father had always wanted to be surrounded by daughters. But having children had always been a challenge for him. Tammin's appearance was a lucky one, but a disappointment to his father.

"I imagine Nieve must be with her aunt," he speculated.

The older man nodded at this conclusion and crossed his leg. "She's a good girl, our Nieve."

"How long has Raynes been hanging about the place?" Tammin asked his father.

The Viscount shrugged and shook his head. "Oh, I dunno. Since we arrived I think. The eldest boy seems fixed upon her, although our Nieve, she's not very receptive to it. She seems warmer towards the younger Bellworth, but that isn't saying much. She's been waiting for you to return."

"I'm here now," Tammin said matter-of-factly. "However, Nieve seems to have the wrong impression. As the Glasses used their seasonal subscription to the assemblies to grant me admission to this event as their guest, I was forced negotiate compensation for the favor. Two dances with Miss Glass," he grumbled. "Miss Glass has been… amorous and unrelenting in her pursuit of me since the early days of the draft. Her familiarity with me might have steered Miss Nieve wrong."

"I see." The Viscount gave his son a disapproving look. His tone was slightly accusing. "It probably doesn't help that you haven't written to her at all in five years. I would have castigated you for it in my own correspondences, but I thought it best to leave the matter for the two of you to work out."

Tammin's brows knit and he frowned. "Nonsense. I wrote almost weekly."

"If that is true, then I don't know where your letters went, my son. They never arrived. We received only the occasional one addressed to me, scarce as those were."

Tammin was perplexed, and stared into the fire with bewilderment.

"And the poor thing wrote nearly every week at the beginning. And then less and less as you failed to respond," The Viscount continued. "We could all see how much your silence pained her."

"I only received a few letters from Nieve in the early days," Tammin snapped. "They stopped completely after the first half-year."

The Viscount shook his head. "Oh, that's a falsehood, my boy. I paid for the paper. I paid for the post. I know what she sent. I was there to witness her growing disappointment and heartbreak. I had a mind to flatten you when you got home. But your little brother or sister, preferably sister, is about to enter this world and I won't ruin this joyous occasion with acrimony. You best fix it, young man. She might not be a sibling or a relative, but she is family nonetheless, and I've grown fond of her. And if she is unhappy, I am unhappy. Understood?"

Tammin nodded, tight-lipped. His gaze was cast towards the fire. He set his mind to ruminate on the subject of correspondence. He was befuddled by the notion that all of Nieve's and his own letters might have simply vanished just like that. His brow furrowed, and his jaw clenched as he tried to think. And then a strange memory returned to him. One that he had not bothered to think of at all until this moment.

Early on, the aspiring officers were asked to attend the first of many gatherings with Brigadier General Glass. He had taken a large house let by a local landowner which was about three quarters of an hour by horse to the site of the breach. It was a fine old place—an old keep that had been subject to many improvements over the years. Although still very much a fortification on the exterior, inside it was warm and welcoming, with wood-paneled walls, a plentitude of hearths to warm the place, and nicely appointed rooms with comfortable, modern furnishings. Although the round-houses were quite comfortable, albeit crowded and rustic, the young men, all highborn or rich, were delighted to bask in familiar luxury for this brief respite before going back out to battle the living sands.

Nine of the young officers-to-be and two young Fohomok from various battalions had been summoned to attend these gatherings, as well as a few of the lower-ranking members of the breacher force. The dining table stretched across the broad space, and the Brigadier General's wife had managed to round up a scattering of local girls to provide interest for the gentlemen present.

Miss Glass was the Brigadier General's niece. She lived with her uncle and his family permanently and traveled with them wherever they went. She was the loveliest of all the girls present, and the most accomplished and poised. She had grown accustomed to demanding all the attention and outshining any lady guests that might be invited to dine.

On this occasion, she set her lovely eyes upon Tammin the when she was introduced before dinner. She remained fast by his side the moment she had his name, and with a sharp wit and passive snide words, she drove away any other young lady that hoped to engage Tammin. She sat next to him at dinner, forcing another young lady change seats. She doted upon him throughout the meal and dominated the conversation with him, although Miss Glass did the great majority of the talking. Tammin was taciturn as always.

After supper, the group took to a large formal parlor where Miss Glass presented a song on the pianoforte she brought with her whenever her uncle and cousin were assigned to a breach. She sang a little tune about the fresh, bright feelings of a heart newly in love. She sang it with her eyes on Tammin for the duration. Even her uncle seemed uncomfortable for her unsubtle, rather tasteless display.

It was briefly after her song, when another girl was invited to play at her instrument, that she partook in a quiet conversation that Tammin was now reliving in his mind.

"You seem rather remote and reticent, Mr. Halenwood," she said, flicking open her fan and brushing her plump lips with the edge of it. She had taken a chaise beside him and leaned towards him, her broad neckline fully exhibiting her fine décolletage. "Do you not welcome my company this evening? All these gentlemen seem to very much appreciate the attentions of the ladies." She gestured to the others with her fan, and then closed it, resting it on the swell of her breast. "Am I not pretty enough to captivate your attention this evening?"

"I am not so unkind as to say that you are not pretty, Miss Glass. However, I am not seeking to gain the attentions of any young ladies," Tammin replied in a low voice. He leaned away from her, turning so that he could cross his legs, a barrier between his body and hers, which had inched even closer to him while she spoke.

"Why would you not wish to be lavished with interest from a young woman then? It must be that I am not pretty enough for your taste," she said ruefully.

Tammin did not like it when people fished for compliments or forced such sentiments with manipulative words. It reminded him of his stepmother.

"If my heart was free to accept the regard of a young woman, I would certainly not spurn you, Miss Glass. For you are indeed a lovely girl. However, there is someone I now realize that I already prefer above all others. Someone I left behind at the summon of the breach-draft. Although we have no formal understanding, as she is very young still, I will seek such a thing when I am released from this service. If she will still have me."

"A girl too young for an understanding, and yet you still prefer her over a girl your own age?" she asked him, her face painted with disenchantment.

"I do," Tammin replied levelly, taking his eyes from her face and looking instead at a group of young people that had assembled to dance while one young lady played on Miss Glass's beloved instrument.

Miss Glass exhaled through her nose as if almost bored with the idea. "It will be difficult for you to be apart from her. Breaches are difficult battles. Harder than actual war, in truth. The construction is inhibited by the advancing sands. They are as aggressive as any human enemy. But it still could be three, even four years of service for you and your fellow breachers. Breaches have been taking longer and longer to defeat, my father says. It is very likely your connection will not sustain itself with such distance and time between you." Miss Glass had a bit of smugness about her as she spoke.

"We will write one another," Tammin said matter-of-factly. "I do not doubt that Miss Nieve will be steadfast in her communication, as I will be with mine."

Miss Glass nearly rolled her eyes, but stopped herself. "We shall see about that," she said sourly into her fan.

She clearly was not a creature of subtlety, thought Tammin. He leaned back and switched one leg over the other, twisting his head this way then that to loosen his neck and shake off his exasperation. He pulled down the front of his waistcoat and then settled down, peering out at the dancers, his raised foot wagging in irritation.

"Letters always come with great frequency and alacrity at the beginning. Give it a few months," Miss Glass said with clear conceit. "This isn't my *first* breach. My uncle has raised me. I've seen many a heart broken by lovers who could not wait the duration—by those that grew bored or distant. Mark my words, the letters will stop." Her chin jutted out.

Tammin frowned at the girl and shook his head. He unlaced his legs and unfolded himself from the chair, walking away from the loathsome creature. As he did, he heard her sniff with laughter.

"I assure you, the letters *will* stop." The words rang particularly acid and bitter, with a lilt of amusement mixed in.

And, thought Tammin three years later, he realized that they did. But now he could only wonder if Miss Glass's prediction was not based as much on her experience as it was on her meddling. He would have to find out before he said anything.

As Tammin and the Viscount remained patiently waiting, Tammin mulled over the discussion with Miss Glass that first day. All correspondence for the breacher force came through the office of the Brigadier General. Tammin wondered if somehow...

He shook his head and frowned. *No, there is no way someone would do that*, he argued to himself. Would Miss Glass have had access to the letters at all? Would she have done that? He rose and walked to the table where a writing slope sat, full of paper and with bottles of various inks awaiting use.

He picked up a well-used quill and sat down, sliding a sheet of paper out of the slope and closing it again so he could write upon it. For a long spell, there was only the sound of the fire and the quill scratching pleasantly across the paper.

Iris Alia Halenwood was born not two hours later. A healthy, round-faced little cherub, smaller than the average baby, delicate and tiny, with hands that were immediately curious and grabby, and a eyes of a slate-blue that the midwife assured them would become sky blue in time.

The jubilant Viscount was dubious as he explained that Tammin's eyes started that same blue and turned emerald green. But he declared that they were indeed the prettiest eyes he had ever beheld (save for Landie's of course), and that her eyes could be yellow like a cat, and he would still think her the finest little baby to have ever been born. He tucked the tiny bundle into the crook of his arm and would scarce relinquish her until the nursemaid scolded him and insisted the little one be permitted to eat her first meal.

So the family gathered around Landie's bedside one with sweet, adoring expressions, watching her nurse the little. They admired the baby's little form, all gushing praise of the mother for her hard work, and at the baby for being so perfect. Iris was born with had a head full of dense, dark locks, and now they were already tufting out as they dried, forming small curls against her little face, which sent the Viscount into raptures. The family clustered around her as if Iris was a shiny hematite lodestone and they were all made of iron.

Nieve, who was sitting on the bed beside her aunt, peering down at the baby, was in awe of Iris, and she could not keep from reaching out to let the little fingers grip hers. "Oh, Landie she's as lovely as anything I've ever seen in all my days!" she told her aunt, her eyes misty and full of love.

Tammin's eyes could not leave Nieve's face as he watched her.

Tammin thought he was prepared for the shock of seeing Nieve at the assembly that evening after being apart so long. He knew she would be changed, but he never quite stopped picturing her as he had known her. Small and boyish, with a rounded face and large, childlike eyes. Her hair wild, and her hems stained from her various adventures each day.

The Nieve he encountered, although so very clearly the same girl in every way that he knew her at once, was also so altered that he could scarce keep his breath or countenance. Five years had turned her into a vision as far as he was concerned. Five years had hewn this wild creature into a young woman of the loveliest qualities. She was not much taller than she'd previously been; however, it was her lines that had changed most of all. The shape of her face, the delicate contour of her chin, the curve that shaped her back, the swell of her hips, the graceful column of her neck—all drawn together to create an image of elegance and beauty. Still possessing just a few lingering shreds of youthful softness around her face, it was clear that she was going to continue to grow even more beautiful and refined in the years to come.

He had been watching for her the moment he entered the assembly rooms and wanted to search every room until he found her. But Miss Glass insisted they dance, as he was obliged to. Irritated by the hindrance, he complied. His impatience almost made him overlook Nieve, for he was so furious he almost forgot to look for her.

Her movements, as always, were graceful and smooth. She danced as if she was made for it—like she had in the glade below his rock, gliding between the shade-witch trees. Her smile was unchanged, her lips perhaps a little fuller, her face slightly slimmer, her eyes luminous. And when they caught his, his heart skipped a beat.

And then his brain made the connection—that she was dancing with and smiling at Raynes—and his joy melted into ire almost immediately. Was she so cruel as to betray him? No, she might not have written to him while he was away, but she would not have abandoned him completely... *would she?*

The brief exchange of words, the expression of distress on Nieve's face, the tears forming in her eyes, these things passed too quickly. The thoughts churned as he continued down the line away from Nieve, with Miss Glass fawning over him as usual.

Miss Glass had become a fixture in his life whether he willed it or not. And when the letters stopped arriving, she had made a point of stressing this and attaching herself further to Tammin while espousing the notion that she was doing so out of concern and sympathy for a spurned, broken-hearted young man.

Tammin had planned to travel to the lakes alone, to return hastily to his family, but Brigadier General Glass, having heard of Tammin's destination, declared that the family would accompany him as they had fixed upon going to enjoy the winter season there as well.

The family persisted on including him in their party, Miss Glass insisting that he use her subscription to gain entry, and that she accompany him to the assembly where he would encounter his former love. He had not seen the motivations with any clarity until this moment. And he was angry at himself for not recognizing it sooner.

Tammin touched Nieve's elbow as she exited her aunt's rooms just before the family retired for the night. They were both still dressed for the assembly, and the clock was striking two in the morning. He had remained waiting by the door for some time for her to leave. She appeared startled to see him. Her face immediately looked drawn and afraid. She crossed her arms, and stepped out of his reach.

She was trying not to allow her anger with him for his silence and complete abandonment to further fuel her distrust of him. But she still felt so betrayed, and the sight of the redhead was another matter altogether. She did, however, harbor hope, that she could not shut him out completely. She bit her lip, and let her eyes fall to the ground, trying to find the words to articulate her hurt.

"I would have at least a word or two, Miss Nieve," he said quietly.

She dropped her chin and contemplated her feet for a moment. She then looked up at him and nodded once, her lips tight. He wondered what she was fearful of, to have such an expression.

He gestured her towards the parlor, and she followed, three small steps to one of his long strides. He opened the door and let her pass into the room before sliding it closed. He lit a four-armed candelabra and put it between them on a low tea table. Nieve had moved in front of the sofa, and now sat down, her arms still crossed, her expression one of hesitancy and trepidation.

He sat down across from her and gripped his hands together, putting his thoughts in order. "I did write," he finally said. "And now I know you wrote, too. I was led to believe that you had ceased corresponding with me."

Nieve's brows knit together and her lower lip pursed. In the light and shadow cast by the candles, her expressions seemed almost magnified. She wanted to him to speak. To explain. "I don't understand," she croaked.

Tammin sighed and rubbed the back of his neck. "My father was angry that I had not responded to your communications... but I had not received any from you for a very long time," he explained. "I wrote a quick note to the Brigadier General this evening to request a private meeting with him. For, you see, I have reason to believe that someone in his family might have interfered with our letters. I had not suspected a thing, honestly, until I found out you had written so faithfully, and that while I had sent you many letters over the years, I received nothing in return. I cannot express how exceedingly sorry I am for this, Nieve."

Nieve's took him in. Now her eyes were glassy, and she bit her lower lip, lowering her face as if to hide her distress. He could tell she wanted so very much to believe him.

"I don't know if I believe you," she said in a soft, cracked voice. "I feared you had forgotten me, and you are now feeling the guilt of it. I can forgive Raynes of cruelty because cruelty is expected with him. I don't know if I could forgive you of this, because I could never suspect you capable of it. I understand that you had no obligation, as you were merely being a kind friend to what was but a child at the time, but you promised you would write."

"That is rather harshly said, do you not think, Nieve? Have you not given me even the smallest benefit of the doubt? Me? Who has always been a friend?" he snapped.

Nieve was startled by his anger. But he was right. She let her selfish, wounded pride and anger make her mean and unforgiving of him, when he might not deserve it. He had not been given a chance to explain yet. She frowned, feeling the burn of tears. She dropped her chin again to hide it. But it was evident when she told him: "Please tell me you did not forget me for that girl." The words came out wavering and full of sorrow.

"Oh, Nieve, how could you think I had forgotten you?" He exhaled in despair. "The thought of returning home to you is all that drew me back here. I may have never come home, in truth, if there was not the prospect of you here, living under my family's roof. And no, I might add, I did not merely see you as a kindness. I have *always* thought dearly of you." He bowed his, his thick black hair tumbling over his forehead as he did.

"I think that because of your stepmother and her admonishment of me as a clinger-on. And of how young I was... and because in all, I was just a little child following you about like a shadow," she said. "What constancy would any right-minded young man have to such a creature? I can't half blame you, I suppose." She reached up and pushed aside one of her shining, chocolate-colored ringlets that had fallen in front of her face, using the heel of her hand to wipe away a tear that had welled up and flowed out onto her cheek.

"I shall do whatever I can to prove it to you, Nieve," Tammin could only reply. "And I am constant, and have always been constant, even when I believed you'd gotten bored of me and stopped writing. I thought I would at least return to see you, and ascertain for myself if your attachment to me had indeed changed. I was not going to take the silence as any true indication of your feelings."

"I waited, too," she replied.

"Can we please at least be friends again? Until I can show you that the silence was not of my doing, nor yours?" he asked quietly.

Nieve reflected for a moment, her arms sliding apart, her hands clasping delicately on her lap. She nodded once, and averted her gaze, her face flushing pink. That was all Tammin needed to hear. He stood and bowed to her deeply.

"I missed you, Miss Nieve," he said with a sort of formality before taking his leave.

Nieve's eyes brimmed with bright tears as she continued to look away. She remained fast in her seat for long after he had departed, sniffing and dabbing away the tears with her lace-edged kerchief. Although she had not replied, the words he said were few, but were not lacking in sincerity. The look of his eyes in the light of the candles was one of true affection.

"I will have to trust and believe him," she murmured to the darkness around her. "Because that is what one does when one loves another." She resolved to forgive him.

As she got up at last to go to her rooms, she paused. In the silence of the house, Nieve heard something. A whisper. And then another and another until she was surrounded by the din of it. Jubilant little voices hissing happy thoughts. It was like the day at the stone circle. The noises abruptly stopped, making the silence in the room equally as deafening. She was now surrounded by a bouquet of scent, also familiar. In the thick of winter, she picked up a loamy, earthy fragrance of humus and forest decay, another hint of the earth after a soaking rain. She smelled the perfume of a freshly blossomed flower. Her eye caught movement in the gloom. A mouse, perhaps. Something small. The rustle of something papery, the flash of something pale against the darkness. More tiny whispers. She seized the candelabra and advanced upon the source only to find emptiness when the shadow was illuminated.

Shaking her head as if to shiver away these strange illusions, she clutched base of the candelabra and used it to find her way to her rooms.

15. Letters

Breakfast was a quiet affair with only Tammin, Nieve, and the Viscount present. Landie was at rest and nursing the new baby. Nieve ate hurriedly so that she could join her aunt at first opportunity. She wanted to cuddle the little one—although the Viscount was stating the same intent as well.

"I want to behold that perfect little face and feel the weight of her in my arms," he said proudly. "She is indeed the sweetest little thing ever to be born."

Nieve was warmly in agreement, and smiled on her ridiculously proud and happy guardian.

"Would that you had shown so much adoration for me," Tammin said with a bit of a sardonic smirk.

The Viscount cast his son a strange look, and frowned. There was something in his regard. A look of pain crossed his face only briefly and his eyes dropped. He looked at the baby, and with a stubborn smirk he said: "You were not a handsome infant. Not beautiful like little Iris. And you did crow and crow a great deal. You were cross and disagreeable from the moment you arrived, and you did not like to be in anyone's arms except your mother's." He drained his coffee and silently jutted out his cup to the servant to fill it again.

"Have you heard even the tiniest cry from her? No. Only delicate little whimpers and mewls when she's hungry or her little nappy needs refreshing."

Nieve gave Tammin a quick, amused glance. Although the cry of a newborn was not as powerful as a more developed child, the little one could be heard squalling during the night and in the morning. The Viscount seemed oblivious.

"I suspect that little Miss Iris will be charmingly spoilt by the time she is Nieve's age," Tammin said, his face still expressing his bewilderment as his much-changed father.

"Oh, to be sure," the Viscount agreed wholeheartedly. "I will deny her nothing. I already spoil Miss Nieve, do I not, dear girl?"

"You do indulge me quite a bit. I shall feel it fairer if little Iris claimed the lion's share of that spoiling from now on," Nieve agreed.

"Shall I get her a pony?" the Viscount asked suddenly.

"Not until she has grown enough to sit on a sidesaddle," Nieve giggled.

Tammin exhaled, incredulous of the conversation and his father, and shook his head. The bell rang, and the servant brought a calling card to Tammin. He rose and took his leave, disappearing through the doorway.

Nieve and her guardian turned their attention to their breakfast. Above stairs, a tiny wail rose up against the quiet.

"Little flower must be hungry. She surely has an excellent appetite," the Viscount espoused.

Nieve bowed her head to hide her smirk and ate her boiled egg and toast and tomato in silence.

A short while later, as Nieve drank her chocolate; the footman came into the breakfast room and bent down to whisper to her. "Master Halenwood asks if you would join him with his guest."

Nieve set down her cup, nodding her assent. She excused herself from the Viscount and rose, bustling out of the room in her pale-yellow morning gown.

She followed the footman to the drawing room where she found Tammin seated with an older gentleman in a formal uniform. They both rose to their feet and bowed to her as she entered. Tammin gestured for her to join them. She circled a chair and stopped before them, her face a mask of curiosity.

"Miss Nieve, I would like to introduce you to Brigadier General Glass," Tammin said politely.

Nieve dropped into a curtsy, greeting him softly with, "Brigadier," before they all sank down into their seats.

The man appeared a little anguished at the sight of her. "I've come this morning early because of an act of selfish cruelty unkindness, Miss Nieve," he said in a gravelly voice. He suddenly looked quite ashamed, and his shaggy brow wrinkled. "Young Major Tammin wrote me last night with a question, which at first seemed almost insulting to my family. I have known this young fellow for three full years, and I have never known him to be anything but honorable and thoughtful. So it was out of character to imagine the letter was ill-intended or meant to inflict cruelty on anyone. So, I sought to confirm its veracity, and upon some insistence and a little sternness, I came to discover that there has been some wrongdoing on the part of my family against both you and this fine young fellow. I am here to apologize, and to make amends as best I can."

He reached toward a side table where there was a fancily-inlaid wooden box, picked it up with both hands, and offered it to Nieve, who took it with an inquisitive arch of the brow. She opened it under the shamed gaze of the Brigadier and found herself looking at a firmly packed stack of letters standing upright in the box. The wax seals had been scraped off to make them fit better and they were so tightly pressed together it took some effort to pull one out. When she did, it came with several others that shuffled all about the floor at her feet.

On their fronts were directions written in either Tammin's hand or hers. They had all been opened.

"I am so very sorry," the Brigadier General uttered. "My niece got it into her mind…" he faltered as he spoke, unable to finish.

Nieve was overcome with a rush of feelings and her eyes immediately began to burn with the rush of tears. She could not contain it, and her emotions burst out of her in a loud sob. She covered her mouth with her hand, as if to quiet the force of her relief and sorrow.

"The girl made a science of it, determining what she took and what she left at the beginning to make it appear that the communication simply ebbed. But all this time she has been hoarding all of your communications, unbeknownst to me. I understand this is a great trespass on our responsibility to the servicemen of the breacher force. How abused you must feel. I can only beg your forgiveness, Miss Nieve," the Brigadier said, his pale grey eyes expressing his mortification and regret. He reached into his pocket, withdrew a handkerchief, and offered it to Nieve who took it and used it to muffle her sobs.

"She confessed her actions, however—and is most repentant and desolated for having been exposed. That Major Halenwood would witness such low behavior of someone who only wished to admire him…" the Brigadier paused, realizing his words were not well chosen. "My apologies, I do not mean to make you feel sorry for my dear niece, for her actions are unforgivable and selfish. I mean only to explain that she likely never meant to carry it as far as she did. She was certain that your connection was fragile … as she's seen it so many times…" His voice tapered as he saw Tammin's livid gaze. He simply shook his head.

"I confess I have no words to express how I feel about this, or how shamed I am by the actions of a girl who is like a daughter to me. I never would have suspected her capable of such artifice—such manipulation and unkindness. I can only try to convince myself that these things were done without true ill-intent, for I love my niece so dearly and this has disappointed me so greatly. Such an abuse of her privilege, it is almost too much to bear." He paused and lowered his eyes, taking a deep, laborious breath. "Major, again, I cannot say I am sorry enough."

"I am appreciative that you brought this to me so quickly," Tammin replied levelly, standing as the Brigadier did. "For I returned to a state of affairs that was all confusion."

"I had no other choice but to embark first thing. I feel I must do what I can to rectify the harm this has caused. I came as soon as my niece produced the letters and made her confession." He turned to Nieve and bowed low.

Nieve was still weeping, clutching the handkerchief to her face with one hand, and the box on her knees with the other, letters scattered around her feet.

"I'll see myself out, Major. You tend to the lady." The Brigadier then moved out of the room and closed the door behind him.

There was a pall of silence for a while until the front door was opened and then closed, and the Brigadier was well out of earshot. Nieve then lowered her hand with the handkerchief and shot to her feet.

"What an odious little snot-nosed harpy! What kind of person does such a thing? She ought to be kicked in the head by a draught horse!" Nieve suddenly shouted wrathfully, glaring at Tammin.

He gaped at her for a moment, stunned by her words, and then he melted into his delightful, wonderful laughter that she knew so well. "Now *there* is the Nieve I adore!" he chortled, falling into a chair and throwing his head back in mirth. "I've missed her so." His eyes were awash with relief and happiness. He leaned his head to the side and peered at her. "If I squint my eyes, just so," he said while making his eyes into two narrow little slits, "you even *look* the same."

"You, on the other hand, haven't changed a jot," Nieve muttered, kneeling to collect the letters from the rug. She then slid down onto the floor and sat by the table. She began to sort the letters into separate piles. "How in the world did you connect yourself with such a person, Tammin?"

Tammin marveled at how much prettier she had grown. At how poised and delicate she could be, only moments after such an unladylike outburst. The thought made him smile, in spite of her question.

"I wouldn't call it so much connection as I would describe it like finding a leech on one's body after a swim." He sighed heavily. "It was five long years of rejecting someone who refuses to be rejected. What I am so astonished by is that if her plan *had* worked, there is a good chance I would have found out about these machinations. What kind of person would imagine that I would respect and care about someone who would be capable of such contrivance?

"I am relieved to be with my family again. I never thought for a moment I would ever utter those words together," he added. He rested his elbows on his knees, his eyes taking in the growing piles of letters.

She emptied the box and fanned the ones she had yet to sort out in her hand. "How long before you stopped writing?"

"A year, I think. Your letters stopped four- or five-months in. I suppose all the evidence of it is right there."

"Will I find angry words in these?" she asked, resuming the sort with an air of half-heartedness.

"Never," he said softly.

Nieve's gaze dropped, and she looked remorseful. "You will in mine."

"I will recognize whatever anger you needed to express towards me," he replied with an accepting, affectionate smile.

She returned the smile wanly, then put the last of the letters on its pile and stared down at them dejectedly. They sat in silence for a good, long while.

"Don't leave me again, Tammin. I don't care if the edge of the whole plateau breaches and we all slide into the desert," she said, her voice wavering. "You are my only *true* friend."

Tammin watched her eyes become soft and teary again, and her lower lip pouted out in such a way that made his stomach flutter. In a rash impulse, he leaned over the table and grasped the back of her neck, drawing her lips to his.

A wild wind blew up against the face of the townhouse and made the window glass shudder in the panes. This was followed by a frightful rumble of thunder that roared in the distance.

Nieve's eyes were first wide with shock as the warmth of Tammin's lips covered hers. Hers were momentarily frozen and tight, but then she felt the soft press of his kiss, and she let her lips melt into it. Her eyelids drooped and then lazily closed as every part of Nieve's consciousness spilled into that embrace. She leaned into the kiss, tilting her head and lifting her hand to rest it oh, so softly against his jaw—to feel him so close at last. Her heart was racing, and her skin was flushed and warm. The touch of the tip of his tongue on her mouth sent shivers through her whole body.

Outside, the clouds opened up and a storm of snowflakes billowed down on the untamed winds, blowing sideways and up and backwards with every gust and whorl. Thunder and spidery fingers of lightning cracked and flashed in thread-like fingers across the bottom of the clouds is if the gods were throwing great stones together.

Voices whispered again, giggling and cackling and tittering all around them, but neither could either hear it, or tear themselves away from the other. Not yet.

When their lips parted, Nieve's hot pink cheeks and heavy-lidded eyes were accompanied by a breathy stupor in which she remained for several lingering moments. Tammin was breathing heavily, too, his shoulders tight and his jaw rippling with restrained desire and excitement. He had to force himself to draw away from her, for he was sensing that it would be too easy to lose control.

He allowed himself fall back into his chair, his gaze resting languidly on Nieve's face with her somnolent regard and entranced expression. Her lips were still parted, and her lips remained jutting forward as if still engaged in the kiss. The hand that had been caressing his face was poised in the air as if he was still there. She gathered her wits about her and moved her fingers to her mouth, her gaze widening and locking onto Tammin's with the very look of affection Tammin had dreamt of when he thought of her.

Tammin felt both victorious and guilty for stealing the kiss. It was more than he had ever hoped it would be—but it was improper to do such a thing when there was not even an understanding between them, let alone wedding bands. He stood and tugged down his waistcoat. First, he gave her a stern look as if to frighten away that drowsy, flushed expression of bliss on her face. But then his regard softened, and he offered her a soft, affectionate smile before wordlessly stalking out of the room.

"Tammin, wait."

Her voice stopped him in his tracks in the center of the foyer. He turned, his frock coat flaring out elegantly as he did.

She proffered the stack letters she'd written him. "Here. Don't be angry at me if I wrote something untoward. I was still only thirteen, possibly fourteen at most."

He took them and nodded, reaching up to briefly rest his hand on her cheek. He tucked the letters into his pocket and vaulted up the stairs to his rooms.

16. The Burgeoning

The blare of the siren during lunch a day later startled everyone, and set little Iris to wailing. Nieve could not help but feel an immediate frisson at the memory of the last one which had taken Tammin away for so long. But Tammin had done his service. It was the turn of a new wave of young men to present themselves for the draft if it was indeed another breach.

The nature of the sound was different this time. It was not a long, uninterrupted tone. It was a rhythmic series of blasts over and over again. Half an hour later, the sirens quieted. As the family peered at one another in bewilderment, the sound of hoof-clatter arose in the street in front of the dining room, and they rose to see what that was about.

The sound was almost as deafening as the siren, and the source of it was line after line of cavalry riders passing through the circus, followed by more soldiers, both from the breacher force and the war militia. A field of bayonets paraded by the window, rising and falling in unison. The clatter of gaitered boots and the flounce of feathered helms and hats moved beneath them on the street.

"Where are they all coming from?" Landie asked, holding tiny Iris against her shoulder, patting her little back.

"The barracks at Evath. It's just at the lake's edge, between the town of Nayth and Adaskus," the Viscount replied. "However, there are breacher force soldiers in the ranks. This is most unusual." He reached up and delicately touched Iris's cheek absently. "I wonder where they're off to. I've never heard the sirens sounded in such a way before."

"Indeed," Tammin replied levelly. He glanced at Nieve, who was watching the soldiers intently from a few windows down. She then stepped back, and—without a word—slipped away. Tammin's brow slanted and he pursed his lips in curiosity, bowing to his father and Landie before exiting the room.

They did not notice, for they were still watching the parade of militia streaming by.

Landie and the Viscount watched as more horses had now joined the procession, this time, more breachers in their green coats and striped stockings, led by a little horde of Fohomok in their flowing robes.

Landie heard the front door close loudly, and she saw Nieve descending the steps to the walk while drawing a redingote onto her shoulders. She walked alongside the soldiers, her skirts flaring out behind her in the cold air.

"What is she up to now?" Landie sighed with irritation.

Then the door made another noise, and Tammin emerged. He tipped his hat onto his head, and buttoned the fawn-colored greatcoat that swathed his shoulders. He looked one way, and then the other before following Nieve's receding form along the sidewalk.

"Tammin will watch over her. Come, let us finish lunch. Here, give me the little glow-worm," the Viscount said, scooping the child out of Landie's arms. "Look at you, how lovely your rosy cheeks are today, my precious gift."

Iris responded to her father the best. Her little feet kicked happily under her voluminous skirts, and her little arms waved, grabbing at his mouth and chin. She seemed to love his booming voice, and became extremely alert. The Viscount's face was one of pure delight and contentment as he sat down to eat, one arm crooked to hold his precious offspring, the other holding a fork. Landie, who had only just this morning come out of her rooms, sat happily in her chair at his right elbow, watching them together and eating quietly. She was in a state of morning dress still, her hair loose around her shoulders in voluminous waves.

"You and Nieve, and now this precious treasure you have given me, what happiness you have brought," Viscount Halenwood murmured to his wife in a soft, contented tone. What a happy family we all make.

Nieve fiddled with the frogs on her redingote, desperate to close it against the icy air. She searched the seemingly unending procession of militia until her gaze fell upon a man with gold bars on his cuffs and epaulettes swinging with fringe upon his shoulders, leading a large complement of mauve-coated men. The fellow glanced at her as he marched in front of his company, and tipped his bicorne at her first.

"Miss," he said politely.

"Where are you going? What's the noise about? The sirens were not the usual peal…"

"We are dispatched to the edgelands. The higher-ranked Fohomok Earth-masters are calling it a Burgeoning, and we are tasked to protect it. I've never heard of what that is, but the orders have been issued from the royal congress," he called out over the din. He then tipped his hat again and marched on.

Nieve stopped, and Tammin was finally able to catch her. She stood by the edge of the walk, watching the flow of military and breachers, horses, and—to Nieve's disgust—three squads of biped Ynbrent'nede dragons.

Nieve shrank back, immediately horrified by the sight of the tall, bird-like dragons stomping behind the soldiers. She turned, running straight into Tammin, and huddled against his torso, hiding her face from the dragons. He put his arms around her protectively, resting his chin on the top of her bare head.

"They're just the minor dragons, Nieve. Nothing to fear," he said softly.

"I hate Ynbrents," she whined. "I was attacked by a clutch of hatchlings when I was very little. If my father had not intervened, I would have ended up being torn into little strips and gobbled up by the disgusting things."

These were desert dragons rarely found on the plateau. Sometimes if breachers found them, they would collect eggs from the warm sands and send them to the mounted division of the army where the hatchlings would be raised to serve as mounts.

These were magnificent specimens. Raised on healthy diets of mutton and rabbit, their polished and groomed scales flawless—no etched wear from the sandy desert winds, none missing from scraps with other dragons and desert creatures over food. Their scales looked like mail made of scarab wings with a deep, dark base of near-black, a vibrant metallic emerald and sapphire iridescence, with hints of gold here and there. The very edges of each scale were serrated and almost feather-like in appearance.

The largest of the dragons in this group was at least eight feet tall at the shoulders—not to mention the long, upright neck and delicately formed head. Their narrow, sea-horse-like muzzles with broad foreheads and huge golden eyes made them look rather disarming and adorable, especially with the intricate silver-decorated bridles over their faces and brows, and the two fans of shining scale blades that swept off the sides of their heads like magnificent headpieces.

They displayed tidy, perfect rows of razor-sharp teeth as they snapped their jaws against their nosebands and chewed on the strange, shining bits that were in their mouths, throwing their heads against the curbs and martingales. The riders of these sinuous, graceful creatures held their reins tightly, and sat deep in their wedge-shaped saddles. They were elegant in their long boots and draping coats of vermillion dripping in bullion braiding. The sheer volume of this exodus was enough to set all the mounts on edge, and horse and dragon alike were skittish and spooked. They danced by on their two feet, swinging their long, serpentine tails.

"They must certainly be heading to the sands with these riders in tow," Tammin surmised. "The dragons are usually brought out only when there is to be action on the sand itself."

"Are they gone yet?" Nieve asked, her voice muffled by his wool coat.

"They've passed by," he assured her.

Nieve peeked out and took a quick glance down the road. The bulk of the force had gone by, and it was now mostly slower-moving ox-carts carrying the round-houses and other supplies.

"I have a great curiosity about this whole thing," she said after a while. "I want to go and talk to someone who might know a bit more of what this Burgeoning is. She knows a great deal about the sands and the breaches and the greenlands," she told Tammin. "She also thinks something special happened to us at Winden that day. I'm not sure I understand what she is describing but perhaps you might."

"I met someone who also spoke of Winden," Tammin interjected. "I take it you haven't read all your letters yet?"

"No. I've been taking my time to digest them. I think they deserve careful review after being held hostage for years by that nasty harpy," Nieve snapped.

Tammin smirked and crossed his arms. "So who is this mysterious person? Shall we go visit her?"

"Yes. She is Lady Parendil. She has been my friend since our very first winter at Adaskus, and comes to visit me at Halenwood as well during the warmer months. She is an odd duck, I warn you. But she might have insight. Come, she lives in the circus, too. This way." Nieve broke into a half-run, her coat flaring out behind her in an elegant billowing fan.

"Why did you not wear a hat, Nieve? For the sake of the gods, you're going to get sick," Tammin cried after her, breaking into a jog to catch up yet again.

The young couple arrived at Lady Parendil's threshold as the soldiers filed out of the city to the east road. The old woman was all too keen for a visit from her favorite person.

"I haven't seen you in two weeks at least, little Saed," she scolded Nieve as they were invited inside.

"Much has transpired since we last met. Major Halenwood is now returned, and my aunt has given birth to a lovely daughter," she told the Lady.

"Oh, a Saed! At last, how delightful. With hopes that this new one is fruitful, too," the woman murmured nonsensically.

Tammin thought her to be a stately, handsome old lady, in spite of her ramblings. He had remained standing for a bit when they first entered the parlor—positioned behind Nieve, with a possessive air about him. But he finally sat down beside her and accepted tea from the Lady when the servant brought it.

"He's a fine young man, this Wyldwaerd Mennin rake," Lady Parendil informed Nieve. "This is the bond-mate that was with you in the circle… when you were blessed?"

Nieve gave Tammin a worried side glance. For his part, he was bemused by the strange ramblings of the old woman.

"The Saed have a power that brings the best out of greenborn men. They make them better people, against the man's ingrained nature," Lady Parendil told Nieve. "The worse they are, the nicer they become when they are in the company of such rare and valuable creatures." She then turned to Tammin and gave him a critical sweep of the eye. "Was this boy, too, a heathen and a boor like his father when you met?"

The girl did not reply immediately, she merely reached out and accepted the rattling cup and saucer from the old woman, who proffered it to her with a shaking hand. "I don't think so," Nieve finally replied, lifting the cup to her lips. "He liked to fight and bully people. But I'm fairly certain that deep down, he was always kind. He was certainly kind to me."

Lady Parendil looked upon him with an expression of misgiving, and then said, "Hmm," and drank her tea. She studied Tammin quietly, and for a spell, there was only the sound of tea being slurped from the fine china, and the cups clinking onto their saucers.

"The burgeoning siren has sounded," the old woman suddenly said with a dreamy smile. "I am ever so grateful to be witness to the wonders of our natural world and its rebirth. And its very essence is taking tea right here. Was it a kiss? It could not have been much more than that—for this is only a burgeoning. The wildening, well, that…" she made a laughing sound that almost had a suggestive air to it.

"What is a burgeoning?" Nieve asked.

The old woman put the tea cup down on the table and leaned her head back, staring off into nowhere for a moment. "The greenlands experienced a burst of growth. They have thrown out their fertility onto the living and the dead sands alike, and taken root.

The vines have wormed their way through the arid spaces, down the cliff-sides and mountain ranges of the plateau. Over the breach walls, through the gates, they will burst-forth. The sand-ships will come, and there might be a brief war, for there will be a ring of fertile lands to farm, and the duchies of the sand will battle over who might possess them. The royal congress will have to choose and choose and choose custodians who will cherish this new land, and they will have to manage the oversight of the new sources of water wicked up from below the deserts by the power of the unfurling green.

"La! There has been no such thing for many, many years," the old woman explained, pouring more tea for everyone. "We have raped our natural world to its very limit. We have made a desert of a world that was once as green and lush and leafy as this cherished plateau. We allowed our greed to give power to the living sands, and to help it consume the very life that sustains us. We tipped the balance, shame on all of us.

"But that is all soon to be past. Soon, we will have a verdant world for all again, you delightful children. More kisses! You must have more of those, at least," she exclaimed. "A few more charming kisses. But you must not part or the unfurled tendrils will dry up like so much dust and become more living sands that will, in part, encroach further, and cause a cascade of breaches. So take care, little ones. Take care."

17. An Understanding

"What a mad old bat," Tammin observed rather crossly, throwing his hands behind his back and gripping his wrist there. He walked with a slow swagger, his coat swinging around the legs of his stirruped trousers.

Nieve peered up at him and made a face at him. "That is unkind."

"*Unkind?* No. Honest. What in all the world was she blathering on about? Kisses and water wicking—clearly she's never been to a breach. There is no way the growth can reclaim land the way she describes. Not without our intervention. We must add all that is dead to the soil to give it life again. We must dig trenches and build viaducts to carry the water out. That is simply to reclaim just what the breach took. To claim new land below the plateau, the idea of it is impossible. There's no way. She is mistaken, or barking mad," he said.

Nieve turned her gaze to the broad slate pavers that made up the sidewalk, and the thin layer of snow and ice that coated it like powered sugar. Lady Parendil had been a strange friend these past years, since they met in such an extraordinary way on the night of the promenade. Nieve took tea with her at least twice a month while she was at Adaskus—for the old lady, once having known Nieve, had pestered her relentlessly to visit. The Lady sometimes wrote when she was unable to visit them at Halenwood for the warmer months as well. Mostly letters that were not easy to decipher.

Lady Parendil, although sometimes appearing to make no sense, somehow seemed to know things that nobody else could know. The stones at Winden. The voices. And she had also described the same little rustles and squirmings that Nieve sometimes thought she witnessed from the shadows in her room. Nieve was not sure if perhaps they simply shared a similar delusion, or if the old woman was some sort of oracle or sorceress who knew a great deal more than anyone else, and whom everyone thought to be mad instead. It irked her that Tammin had dismissed her so easily.

"She knew about Winden and the stones. She knew about the lost day simply by looking at me. I don't think she's completely mad. I think perhaps she is speaking to us in a language with words that are familiar to us, but have different meanings. A language that only she understands," Nieve told him with a hint of defiance in her voice.

"When I left you for my school, a classmate of mine who is fascinated with all things Mennin, heard of what we experienced together on the hilltop at Winden. Effrid Finn is a worthy soul, and I have never mocked his belief in the ways of the Mennin. He took me to what he called an Auspex. It was a rather dashing looking fellow of about forty, married with a veritable army of children running about the place and climbing on things.

"He sat us down in a small office in his home, and while his children toyed with the tails of our coats and climbed onto our laps and tried to pry small soldier figures into our ears, he listened to my tale. And he spoke in that same language. Perhaps plainer. He and Finn called it a Consecration of Binding. They said that we were married, of sorts, that day. That the old fae-folk had chosen us to bond. And that it happened in the center circle was significant. It took this as a way of saying that you and I, we are meant to be. Fated, perhaps. To be a pair, in whatever form that may be. We are to be the beginning of something. Of a great change. That is why I never worried when your letters stopped arriving after the draft. Because I had this notion that we had been bonded by the power of the land itself, and that it would take a great deal more than lapsed correspondence to rend us apart," he told her.

"Did you truly feel this way about me, even then, when I was so young?" she asked, her brows high in curiosity, and her eyes wide and searching.

He stopped on the sidewalk and peered down at her guileless face. "I think I loved you the first moment I saw you. Sopping wet, half-drowned little squirrel, and as obstinate as anything in spite of it. Deigning to dress me down for brawling." He laughed softly at the memory, breaking a crooked smile. "There was never a time in my life before you that I ever questioned my actions or felt remorse for being a bully and a tormentor. I was who I was shaped to be before you. I was like my father. In fact, I cannot even think of time when I ever volunteered to help anyone in need. It never was my nature to throw myself into the water to help someone who was drowning. Why I did it that day still puzzles me.

"But I recall that look on your face with a clarity I wish would fade. How it melted so painfully from open trust and happy engagement to disappointment when you asked me about the fighting. How that single expression sliced into me." He lifted his hand and made a fist, hitting his chest. "After that moment, I just wanted to be a better person so that you would never look upon me like that again. You might have been only thirteen, and I only sixteen, but I don't think the age we were and are..." He shrugged with one shoulder to express that it was unimportant, or even irrelevant.

Nieve's cheeks had flushed a lovely rose-pink, and her eyes were misty. She blinked, and the moisture welled along the lower lids.

He reached out and clasped her hands in his. "We are still young. You haven't even come out yet..." he murmured, dropping his chin, looking at the ground between them. "But I would like to make myself clear, Nieve. Wherever we end up in life, my intention will always be for us to be together—whatever life throws at us."

She gazed up at his bright emerald eyes, and the dark curls of hair falling onto his handsome brow. The deep folds of his eyelids shadowed so beautifully below the brim his hat. She loved this face so.

"*Your* intention?" she repeated, an amused smirk on her face. "Is this one of those infamous moments from the novels, where the couple settles on an understanding?"

"If you wish to think of it that way, then yes. I don't want to worry that in the span between this moment and when we marry that you will think yourself available to other offers," he said this haltingly, as if trying to find the right words.

Nieve tilted her head and crossed her arms with an expression that looked like a combination of being unconvinced, nonplused, and exasperated all at once. Her brow was arched at him with an expectant air. "So you are saying you want to mark me as taken so I don't get swept away by some other fellow?" she asked.

Tammin's brow darkened and he crossed his arms. "I don't want Raynes or that detestable, slimy dandy of a brother of his following you about like a pair of hungry wolves. It was *not* pleasant to witness him behaving with such familiarity and possessiveness towards you of you that night."

"And you simply assume that this is what *I* wish as well? Maybe I *want* to have Raynes and Alderny hanging about," she said provokingly. Her face was now a mask of defiance and humor. She delighted in this teasing of Tammin because she found this benign, almost child-like possessive jealousy so very charming. Another part of her wanted to jab at him a little for not trusting her to be true to him.

"How in the world did Raynes worm his way into your life?" Tammin suddenly barked, shaking his head. "I imagined he would have tormented you to no end and made your life as hard as possible because he hates me, but instead, he's looking at you with soft eyes, and placing your shawl onto your shoulders with delicate care." He used his hands to mimic this in a sarcastic, contemptuous way. "How is this possible?"

Nieve exhaled loudly and shook her own head, looking at her dearest Tammin who was acting like a petulant child. *He is a Major and look at him.* "Raynes is not a terrible person…" She paused, and then thought it through with a furrowed brow. "No. I am correcting myself. Raynes is not a *kind* person. But he is trying. He simply doesn't know how to be such a thing. I think he hopes I will be the one to show him the way. The way he goes about doing these things, that is where he fails—for he tries very hard to do right—only to do so by doing wrong. He did indeed torment me. For almost all the years you were absent. But he claims he did it exclusively to me so that nobody else would. He hoped to capture my attentions by any means possible. Even if that meant being a downright prat to me all the time. But that changed this fall when we arrived at Adaskus."

"Because he saw how remarkably beautiful you've become," Tammin concluded. "And he is also bent on doing things to harm me."

"I am quite certain his interest was fabricated merely to provoke you. At least it *was*. I think now Raynes genuinely likes me," she told Tammin.

"Who cares?" Tammin retorted bitterly. His arms crossed obstinately again, and he frowned childishly at her. Then his mouth dropped open. "Wait… do you *like* Raynes?"

"Oh, stop!" Nieve snapped. "All I am saying is that you shouldn't vilify him for being protective of me. He knows the hurt your silence of nearly *five* years caused me. He might have made fun of me for moping, and teased me that you were unreliable and selfish. He reveled in your failure on that end. But he knew how sad I was. And it bothered him. It fed his dislike of you, I think."

The pair stood quietly for a moment, drinking in these words. Then Tammin frowned. "Would you please stay away from him? For my sake?"

"Do you not trust my affection for you?" she asked, a little angry and a little hurt.

"I don't trust *him*," Tammin retorted. "He's a snake in the grass, slithering to you as soon as I was absent."

Nieve's ears grew red and she frowned darkly. Tammin was disappointing her, and she did not like the feeling of it. She did not want to bicker with him in the street, and her disillusionment was almost strong enough to make her want to cry. She turned on her heel and began to walk again, circling around a slowly promenading couple, and scurrying along the gentle curve of the circus walk, passing face after face of the townhouse buildings. Tammin followed a few steps behind, his hands again behind his back, one in a hard fist, the other clamped tightly around the wrist of the other.

When they reached their home, Nieve raced up the steps and pushed the door open. Tammin followed only to be called as he walked through the door.

"Major Halenwood?" a voice asked. "Is this the residence of Major Halenwood?"

He turned to see a young man in army slops standing at the threshold behind him.

"Aye," Tammin replied, his brows shifting from expressing his anger to curiosity.

"Message for him, sir," the fellow said, handing Tammin the envelope he clutched in his fingers.

Tammin took it, and the young man bowed and left. Tammin closed the door and allowed the footman to help him with his coat and hat. He then took the letter and opened it as he walked towards the drawing room. By the time he had entered the room and sat down, he had read it. The look on his face was one of despair and anger. He sat for a long time in silence, his elbows resting on his knees. The Viscount and Landie were present, both engaged with Iris on the sofa. Nieve was not. She had stomped up to her room.

The Viscount finally peered at his son, and raised a brow. "Good gracious, Tammin, why the long face?"

Tammin lifted his eyes to his much-changed father, taking in the ruddy, happy face. His gaze then shifted to the lovely Landie and the baby clutched in her arms. He heaved a great sigh and dropped his head.

"I've been drafted again."

* * *

Nieve allowed Tammin take her hand and draw her into the dance room. She followed almost listlessly. Scarcely able to look Tammin in the eye since their little spat and the subsequent news of the morning before, she had barely spoken two words. The desire to attend the last of the winter assemblies was next to nil, but Tammin insisted as he would be leaving soon again.

Nieve could not bear the tightness in her chest and in her throat. It felt like she was going to fall down and die at any moment. She had dressed as prettily as she could muster, for Tammin had never taken her to a ball before, nor had he ever had the chance to dance with her. Her glassy, puffy eyes were all that she could see in the mirror as their chambermaid helped her dress. She did not see her vibrant ruby gown of papery taffeta with its pearl and gold beaded trim. She did not see the matching parure of ruby stones dripping from her ears and draping across her graceful neckline. She did not see the golden slippers that she had only just purchased, nor the beauty of the delicate coif that the girl had arranged on her head; such a lovely weave of plaits and wefts of mahogany hair, peppered with pearl pins surrounded by little diamonds that sparkled in the candlelight like stars.

She did not see Raynes gaping at her with his longing in his eyes as she entered the space, her goldenrod gloved armed wrapped around Tammin's possessively—even greedily. She was still seeing her puffy eyes and her wan features from the mirror. And now they stood one across from the other, preparing to dance the Rowan Tree Waltz. She stared at Tammin now—watching him bow to her during the introductory notes while she offered a half-hearted curtsey.

He stepped forward and took her hands, turning with her twice 'round. It was then that she could see him. Her eyes on his, his gaze grieved and exhausted. She was parted from him briefly, paired with the second gentleman, but her right hand found his again soon after, and she turned to cast away and recaptured into the intimate promenade hold where they danced side-by-side, shoulder to shoulder, with holding hands in a crossed fashion between them. The couples sailed forward and then fell backward into a turn.

As they spun shoulder to shoulder, the room fell away from around them like a theatrical scrim dropping from above to reveal a darkness and silence that seemed to exist inside the reality only they knew. They stopped dancing and looked about in shock.

The darkness was more than just darkness. It was the lush growth of a forest, someplace entirely wild, with trees and thick, fragrant humus and a night sky that hung over it all like a great sparkling mantel. There was the sound of nocturnal insects trilling, and frogs croaking and singing. There were rustles and scratches, and the sound of leaves and limbs stirring in the soft breeze that now brushed the couple's warm cheeks.

"What?" Nieve murmured, turning around once more.

Tammin had stiffened and was warily circling the small clearing in the darkness. As he did, a tiny light blinked softly into existence in a luminous greenish yellow. Another appeared, and another, blinking for long spells before fading gently into darkness. Soon the clearing was filled with such firefly lights, and the sound of tiny wings could be heard fluttering by their ears.

As Tammin spun to take in this view, he stopped short. His gaze fell upon Nieve who stood with her back to him, peering out at all the lights gathering around them. She was beginning to generate her own light. He shook his head as if to rattle his brain back to its senses, but it changed nothing. What he was seeing was real, and Nieve was seeing it too, her face aghast and full of wonder as she swung about to take in this magical world.

Tiny luminous speckles formed at the center of the small diamond-shaped back of her gown, like illuminated motes of dust. They moved with purpose and pattern, blowing down and raining from the wings of the firefly lights that clouded around them. Tammin's brow wrinkled in wonder and confusion, and he watched as the glowing dust from the fireflies fell upon an invisible structure, and gave it shape to look like wings. The more the dust fell, the more it settled upon Nieve's invisible wings and the more they took shape until he could see all four of them. Almost as wide each as she was tall, they looked like dragonfly wings, which—as Nieve moved slightly to peer around her in awe—twitched and flicked as if they were part of her being.

She turned to him, her skin aglow in the same pale greenish yellow of the fireflies, and her smile of amazement melted away into shock. Her hand rose up and she gasped. "Tammin... You've got horns!" She then started to laugh.

Tammin reached up and his fingers fell upon the base of a hard, bony structure flaring off the side of his temple. They coiled against the side of his head like ram's horns. His brows shot up and he barked out in laughter.

"You have wings," he told her. He reached out to pass his hand through what seemed like an illusion only to have it fall upon a papery surface. Glowing powder poofed into a cloud.

Nieve squealed and jumped. "I felt that!" She turned and turned again to peer over her shoulders. Her wings brushed his face as she did. They both laughed hysterically.

"What is this madness?" Tammin chortled. He wrapped his hands around the curl of the horns on each of his temples and then shook his head, sending glowing powder up again in a tiny storm of whorls and eddies.

"Look!" Nieve exclaimed in glee. She stood in a glowing cloud, the fireflies and their dust surrounding her in a languid dance. With a little hunch of the shoulder her wings fluttered, making a loud percussive sound and sending the golden dust into swirls of dancing motes.

As she did this the forest around them began to titter and rustle. Suddenly, the noise grew louder and louder until the leafy surroundings exploded with tiny creatures flying and running along the forest floor.

"Tammin!" Nieve squealed in delight, lifting up her hand.

Perched on her dainty index finger was what looked at first like a butterfly. But upon closer inspection it was a marvelous little oddity. A minuscule thing, the shape of a person, with shimmering skin and two large, beautifully slanted black eyes that consumed the better part of the tiny head. The wings sprouted from its back. It peered at Nieve and then Tammin, walking along her finger, clutching her other finger to steady itself with minute, sticky fingers as she walked onto the palm of Nieve's hand. The little fairy creature then leapt off Nieve's hand and fluttered away into the cloud of similar creatures flying around them.

"What is happening?" Nieve asked.

"I would say we must be going mad, but this is not the first time we've been here. This is the same world that we touched at Winden," Tammin murmured in puzzlement, reaching out to try to touch one of the passing creatures. They flew by on butterfly and dragonfly and bees' wings. "We must somehow be summoning the world of the Mennin."

Nieve looked down and saw a small wood sprite climbing up the skirts of her ballgown. She reached down and picked the little thing up. It almost looked like nothing more than a splinter of wood, but it possessed little arms and legs, and eyes that looked like glass beads of shining black, and its fingers and toes and the top of its head sprouted with thread-thin vines and buds of leaves. It squirmed in her grasp, and then escaped her fingers, running up her arm and onto her shoulder. It then joined another that had made it to the top of her head. She giggled and reached up to grasp at them.

"Why are we experiencing these things?" Nieve asked in wonderment, plucking the little creatures that had tangled into her hair. "I shall have to ask Lady Parendil."

"Do you think that old bat would have anything of sense to offer if we told her of this?" Tammin inquired.

And just like that the world disappeared and they were standing at the top of the set while the other dancers continued unperturbed. Tammin's curled horns were gone, and Nieve's wings were no more. They were back in the world where Tammin would be going away and Nieve would be left without him again. She lowered her head and then rolled her eyes up to look at him sheepishly.

"Is it terrible that I wish we could be in that other place instead?" she asked.

Tammin stiffened and bowed his own head, clutching his hands behind his back. He said nothing in reply, but instead looked uncomfortable and angry all at once. He could not express that he too wished escape to that world. To be with Nieve. To never set foot at the edgelands again. But he was burdened with this obligation to return, and to leave her again, and it made him miserable to think of it.

The dance ended at length, and the couple walked back to the supper room where the family party awaited them. The Viscount had come out with them and was in the company of Mr. Bellworth and his sons. Raynes stood stoically by his father's side, his pale eyes on Nieve the moment she appeared on Tammin's arm.

He bowed deeply to Nieve, and so did Alderny. "I hear you are to be dispatched again," Raynes said in a mocking tone.

"I imagine you would be obliged to go, too, but you somehow manage to escape responsibility each time," Tammin replied snidely, taking a glass of port from the tray of a passing footman and sipping from it at once.

Nieve settled down next to the Viscount who thoughtfully poured her a glass of water and handed it to her. She drank, watching awkwardly as Tammin and Raynes spoke to one another.

"I have a legitimate excuse from it, but that is none of your business. I, thankfully, will be here to watch over Miss Nieve's welfare."

"I have my family," Nieve said quietly. The Viscount patted her arm affectionately.

"You will need someone at your side when you are out and about in society, Miss Nieve, and I am happy to accompany you," Alderny piped in.

Nieve merely bowed her head shyly and sipped her water.

"What is it that exactly that excuses you two from the draft?" Tammin blurted crossly.

"The Bellworth name is listed in the Mennin Book of Commons," Mr. Bellworth replied curtly. "My family line has been marked, and so we are bound to the living sands. They will seek us out as soon as we are near it, and consume us."

"The sands seek you out? Mennin book? What nonsense is this?" Tammin laughed mockingly.

"It isn't nonsense. There are family lines that have been cursed. There is nothing that can be done. If we approach the sands, we are made part of it. It is not uncommon if you are not a landbound family in the greenlands." The gentleman lifted his drink and drained it, looking Tammin up and down. "We cannot all have direct lineage to the Menninfolk, with titles and land and all that."

"Not all land-bound families have direct lines to the Mennin. But most do," the Viscount observed. "In the case of the Halenwoods, we do indeed have a Mennin bloodline, and our land has been bonded to us for as far back as we can find in our family tree."

"Indeed. And the Mennin Druids did not care much for the common folk," Bellworth said. "They castigated them for tarnishing the lands, and for abusing of the resources that they offer. And so they made their list of those living in the greenlands. They wrote the names in the cursed book, and any one of those born from those family lines are sought out by the living sands. Some say the sands are made up of all the cursed people through the generations. We will stay safely in the greenlands, thank you very much. And my boys, like many of the cursed lines, do not serve at the breach. They might serve in other capacities, but my fellows have yet to be called."

"How convenient for you," Tammin snorted bitterly, grasping a goblet from the table and drinking from it—his gaze falling upon Nieve who peered at Mr. Bellworth as if awaiting more information about this curse.

Raynes looked out into the room where the guests were milling about and circulating between dances, and having set his eyes upon two ladies approaching their party, he lowered his glass from his lips and cleared his throat. The discussion was dropped as the ladies approached them.

Raynes instead said, "I nearly forgot, Miss Nieve, as the Major is off tomorrow and you will be bereft of things to do, I thought perhaps you would like to join us. Miss Gillian here is, I believe, a friend of yours, and she has been talking of hiring a great sleigh at the end of the next week, to take a turn through the lakelands and to picnic at the falls under blankets. Will you come?" Raynes gave Tammin a derisive little smirk.

Nieve turned her gaze to Raynes and then Tammin, before declining quietly. "I would rather not."

Miss Gillian then joined them with none other than Miss Glass. Nieve wondered if Miss Gillian was unlucky in her friendships to find always the most awful of creatures to accompany her. First Miss Morrie, now the hateful Miss Glass.

"*Here* she is," Miss Gillian exclaimed when they merged into the little circle of young people. "Dearest Nieve, you've been hard to find about town these days. Where have you been hiding? I heard you have a little sister-cousin now. How wonderful! I'm so glad to have found you. I dispatched Raynes to ask you to join us on our sleigh ride and picnic in the snow. I hope you will come!"

"He has only just now asked me," Nieve said. "This is my first assembly in so many days. I have declined. I simply don't think I will be good company over the weeks to come."

"Nonsense, you should get out more if you are feeling aggrieved about the draft, dear girl," Miss Gillian argued.

Miss Glass looked on, her fan resting on her breast, her hand listlessly drooping while holding it, the other arm wrapped around her lower bust, with a hint of acrimony in her regard when she looked at Nieve and at Tammin. But she said not a word.

"You ought to go," Tammin said gently, his hand falling upon Nieve's shoulder. "You will feel better if you are engaged with friends and enjoying yourself."

She glanced up at him, and nodded once. Miss Gillian threw up her hands and celebrated with a little squeal.

"Oh, we shall be such a merry party, shall we not?" she gushed.

"I will be accompanying Miss Nieve," Raynes added before Alderny had the chance to say anything. He gave Tammin a rotten little smirk, and crossed his arms triumphantly.

The hostess smiled broadly and patted Raynes's arm. "You are so attentive to Miss Nieve, are you not, Raynes? Excellent. You are lucky to have a gentleman to cling to, for so many of us ladies must see our beaus off to this strange event at the plateau's edge," she lamented. "Well, we will be off first thing on midweek day. We will be leaving from Tarleaf Park by the boathouse."

Then she and Miss Glass curtsied and sailed away. Tammin watched as Miss Glass turned back and shot him and Nieve a strange look.

He turned to Raynes. "If you can manage to do anything right, please try to keep that Miss Glass far away from her." He then bowed to the party, reached out to take Nieve's hand, and led her away to dance again.

The following day, Nieve remained in her room most of the morning. She was summoned down by her aunt who castigated her for being so remote when Tammin would be gone for so long. But the family managed to spend an hour together in sedate, quiet conversation with Tammin as he, in his full uniform, girded himself for his second removal from the family. Nieve sat quietly on the long chair, her hands clasped on her lap, her eyes downcast.

A few moments before the clock knelled the eleventh hour, Tammin asked if he might talk to her alone, and the family departed. Nieve did not see the expectant, badly hidden smiles on the faces of her aunt or uncle as they took the little one and exited the room. She was busy staring at her hands and trying not to cry.

Tammin approached and knelt before her, taking her hands. "I will return. I don't know when, but I will return to you," he told her.

Nieve's throat tightened to the point that it hurt, and she felt the burn of tears in her eyes. She blinked and a tear dropped onto the back of Tammin's hand.

"Nieve, because of the uncertainty of when I return, I think we should perhaps have a word," Tammin said.

Nieve peered at him with her bleary eyes and she sniffled, but otherwise said nothing, only waited for him to speak.

"We should perhaps clarify things so that there is no doubt or confusion. You see, I fully intend to be your husband, Nieve, and I think we should both perhaps come to an understanding so that we can both suffer this parting with at least the knowledge of our mutual intentions and affection. If I am being unclear, I am asking to you— upon my return—to marry me."

Nieve stifled a sob, and bent over even more, covering her mouth with her hand. Her heart felt as if it was going to explode. They had already settled into the idea that they were meant to be together. But to have him ask, so formally and lovingly. And to know she would not see him for some time, all of these things culminated into a rush of feelings, both good and bad, sending burning tears into her eyes. Her hand shook, and her throat was strangled by emotion.

"Will you consent to be my wife, Nieve?" he asked her.

Nieve nodded and she bit back her feelings of both elation and misery. Tammin, with an expression of joy and regret all at once, took her hands and stood, pulling her to her feet.

"Then we shall seal this vow with a kiss," he told her, and he bent down and planted his lips upon hers.

It was so quick, she scarce had a moment to prepare, and she gasped a little, her body shuddering from the shock of it. At first it was but a benign press of the lips, her lips unmoving and tight in confusion, his warm and soft, melting against hers. But then she softened and leaned into it. They scarce noticed the blowing wind and violent gusts outside, or the sudden squall of snow that hissed against the panes and streaked across the sky. Their ardor made the rumble of thunder and clap of lightning nearly unseen.

When he withdrew, her cheeks were flushed pink, and her eyelids were droopy.

"One more," he said roughly, and he bent down and took another sip at her.

This time, there was an immediate flush and heat, and the kiss was filled with motion and reciprocation, along with just the brush of a tongue. Nieve's hands slid up the line of his jaw and she gripped his face, pulling him towards her. She felt the wetness of his tears against her intermingled with a few of her own.

Outside, the weather lashed out at the earth as if in a fervor. But the pair did not notice it. They were lost in their kiss, seasoned in the salt of Nieve's tears, heated by the flush of two young lovers.

When they parted, Nieve submitted to her sorrow and collapsed back into the chair, wiping her eyes with the back of her hand. Tammin reached into his pocket and withdrew a kerchief which he used to blot her tears as he knelt before her.

"I will return, my love," he told her. "As soon as I can manage. And I will write, and you will too, I hope. I will do what I must to insure that no person intervenes with our communications again."

"Tammin," Nieve finally spoke, her voice broken and hoarse, "you should know how deeply and passionately I love you; and how much I will miss you."

He leaned forward and wrapped his arms around her. "I can only express that I feel the same, and that my thoughts will be with you every day. We are engaged to be married, so be sure to tell everyone this. I don't want to imagine Raynes looming over you like some great, ugly, fair-haired spider in a web."

Nieve snorted a laugh through her tears and took his kerchief to blot away her sorrow.

"I will send you my directions the moment I arrive," he told her. The clock knelled and Tammin's shoulders fell. "It is time," he said regretfully. He rose again, and took her hands, pulling her up into a deep, warm, melting embrace.

They lingered there for as long as they could before he withdrew, a wash of cool air wafting between them. He gave her one last, lingering kiss and walked out into the stormy weather with stiff shoulders.

18. *Away*

The heavy sleigh waited underneath a tree that was flocked in ice and frost. It had been enrobed in a thick mantel of fog that had settled after the storm had passed, and it had covered everything in a coat of crystals. Puffs of steam rose up from the passengers and the team of four heavy horses that were harnessed to the long vehicle.

Miss Glass slid over on the bench a bit to allow for Nieve to sit down. There were eight people—Miss Glass and Raynes among them—in the large sleigh in addition to the driver, who sat beside Miss Gillian. Raynes made a point of sitting between the ladies, and he was attentive to Nieve, placing a second blanket over her knees and serving her a mug of hot grog from a thick clay bottle he produced from a hamper that was squeezed in front of their feet.

Nieve was not feeling quite up to the activity, but she felt obligated because she had accepted the invitation. She sat curled slightly in on herself, wrapped in the blanket that Raynes had gently laid over her shoulders before she sat down. She closed the ends over the front of her body, and huddled down, her face sinking into the ring of fur that edged the hood of her woolen cloak.

When everyone was settled in and rightly bundled up, the sleigh was set to move, and the horses drew it along, their hoofs crunching on the thin layer of snow left behind by the heavy plough that had taken away the bulk of the night's snowfall from the streets of Adaskus. The wind was rather brisk, and the cold was biting. She held her cup of grog gingerly with one gloved hand, and sipped from it as if it was the thing that required all her concentration.

She could scarce keep up with the idle conversation that filled the air around her as the sleigh cut through the snow towards the falls. Her mind was on the last moments with Tammin, and how it felt as if he'd torn out a large piece of her heart and taken it with him. She felt hollow. He'd been gone a full week already, and it felt already like an eternity.

As the sleigh carried them along, the weather grew worse. It began to snow and the wind picked up the delicate flakes and hurled them with such strength that they became tiny missiles and stung the exposed skin of their faces. As she sank into her hood even further, Raynes put his arm around her shoulders and pulled her in close, lifting a cape of his greatcoat to shield her from the snow.

She would have normally squirmed out of this attempt at an embrace, for this was not his first time, but he was shielding her from the icy pellets, and there was nowhere to squirm to anyway, as they were all squeezed so tightly together on each seat. She ducked down under the protection of his coat and shivered.

"Perhaps we might consider that this outing is ill-advised for today," Raynes suggested. "It seems the weather has taken an unfortunate turn."

"Nonsense," Miss Glass shouted from the depths of her own hood. "We can stick it out."

Miss Gillian thought otherwise, and conceded that it was indeed not a good plan to move forward with a picnic when the wind was creating something akin to a blizzard. But instead of suggesting they turn around, she offered another option.

"Perhaps we ought to go to Wolf Hall," she suggested. "It would be an ideal place to retrench as a party and still enjoy an outing. And if the weather worsens, we would have a safe place to rest."

Nieve had heard of the old place two or three winters before. She had yet to visit it. From what she understood it was a protected, historic site, preserved with funds provided by the throne. It was an ancient edifice; an old earth-lodge, which now served as a guest-house for those who wished to visit it.

"Barring it is not already full-up with guests," a Mr. Almoth murmured. To Nieve, he seemed a negative sort of person who always had a worse scenario to offer no matter what the subject. This was the first time she'd ever met him, and from the moment they set off, he had some contrarian remark or other for anything anyone had to share. She found him tiresome.

"Well, it's close enough that we can stop and check, and perhaps take a pot of tea or chocolate. If we do that, and the rooms are all taken, then we still have time to return to Adaskus. But if there is room, we can simply stay and send notes home if possible, to let our families know the change of plans. Then we still have a lovely outing for our party, and we are not forced back into our homes for another spell of awful weather," Miss Gillian offered. The group seemed to agree to this, and the driver was directed take Lodge Road to the hall.

Nieve was huddled against Raynes, stiff and uncomfortable at first, but then she unconsciously gave into the warmth, and melted against his long, lean body, simply grateful for his consideration. It was more than three years since she'd experienced her first winter at Adaskus and she was still not accustomed to the harshness of it. She rarely longed for the hot nights of Rethros, but at times like these, she did.

Wolf Hall was a great house that once belonged to an old Burl-Mennin Duke. The Burl were among the oldest cultures of the Mennan highlands after the devastation of the sands. They were an ancient culture of warriors and poets. Greater Adaskus had once been part of a large Duchy before it was resorbed into the empire. It was an ancient Burl-built lodge, large and rustic, made by the Mennin aristocracy, one of the few surviving relics of an ancient past. Its very bones were cut from the massive logs of old-growth stone-oak which had mostly been harvested, leaving only thin, anemic-looking relatives in comparison. The behemoth logs were rarely found anymore, for such size took at least a thousand years to grow. Those that did remain alive were no longer allowed to be harvested. They were a cherished and protected tree now.

The lodge was partly beneath the soil, its great face rising up like a cliff side, with its mantel of life and greenery and snow resting on its shoulders. The tall edifice was an elegant conglomeration of silver-grey stone-oak beams interspersed with patterned masonry made with alternating bricks of gneiss and basalt, giving it a grey and black checkered appearance. The two towering windows flanking the sizeable carved wood door had been added later, as most earth-lodges lacked them. These had been added by the Berralths, the culture that followed the Burl by a century or two, who preferred elaborate tracery and dramatic lines in their architecture. The windows ran nearly the entire length of the building's face, two long, narrow, pillar-like openings with arrowhead arches at the top, and thick glass embedded in stone mullions stylized into the shape of tree limbs. The great door itself was also carved with an elaborate stone-oak, with a smaller man-sized inset door that was infinitely more practical to go in and out of.

Directly behind the face was a long, open space which—with all its trusses and beams—looked like they were inside the skeleton of a great beast. At its end was a cave of a hearth made of stone with a colossal fire crackling within it. The open space was interspersed with modern furniture, but made to suit this ancient place, with careful, elegant lines, but with the weight and feel of the heavier Burl aesthetic. The flagstone floor had been scattered with a patchwork of stylish rugs that divided the open space up into smaller ones, the furniture arranged in little groupings around low oak tables with fat bristles of candelabrum made of antlers dangling over each one.

There were arched passages also lined in wood and stone leading off to the variety of rooms that were connected to the great hall, all hidden underneath the structure's slate and earth roof, which was so established and ancient that root systems of trees that had grown atop the lodge had taken shape around them, making them nearly indestructible and impermeable. It also made for an oddly cozy space, in spite of its size and scale. It was warm, and smelled of wood fire.

"Oh my word," Nieve muttered upon entering the building, her eyes rising up the long ribs of the building to the trusses and the hanging antler candelabras.

Mr. Almoth's prediction had been inaccurate, for the lodge was mostly empty. The keeper—a jolly, round, sweet woman by the name of Julla—explained that a large party had taken reservations for most of the rooms but had sent word that they were waylaid by weather at Mormack, and that they would not be staying. Miss Gillian's party had come at a fortuitous time. She was pleased to have them, and helped them to rooms, offered to launder any clothing they would require, and directed them to the desk where they would find paper and ink to send word to their homes.

"The roads are still passable, so be quick about it, young ones," she called to them.

She directed the coachman to bring their hampers to the kitchens where she would direct her staff to serve their picnic by the fire, and she told them what time dinner would be served that evening.

Nieve remained locked against Raynes, whose arm remained fast upon her shoulders, but when Mrs. Julla assigned them their rooms, she was freed from his grasp and allowed to venture off on her own. She entered her room and closed the door behind her, exhaling a shaky sigh. She stripped off her cloak, which was now sweltering in this warmed under-earth space.

A young child lit a fire in her hearth as she removed her outerwear and stripped down to the simple wool walking gown she wore beneath all of her layers. When the child left her alone, she sat down in the small, rather shadowy room, with its bed nook built into the stone walls, and heavy furniture edging the perimeter, and stared blankly at the space for a long while.

Then a feeling crept up on her. Her body suddenly felt heavy and her heart began to hurt, her throat tightened until she could only squawk out a sob. She slumped onto the mattress in a heap and succumbed to her misery, sobbing out all the sorrow she'd barely kept inside all this time into the soft pillow, until she was spent and could not cry another tear.

When she turned onto her side and exposed her red, ruddy face, and opened her eyes, she made a little hoarse squeal and drew further back into the bed-nook.

The wide columns of stone-oak, smoothened by centuries of use, had flushed green in the candlelight, and there were small buds swelling up on the dense grain of the wood, some bursting open and unfurling little clusters of pale green oak leaves. From the corner of her eye, she spotted a little wood sprite making its way up onto the mattress towards her.

She sniffed and wiped her eyes with the heel of her hand which was covered in the long cuff of her woolen gown. She stared at the little thing as it ambled towards her. When it came within reach, she splayed her hand before the creature. It scrabbled up onto her palm and tickled her skin as it settled down to sit with its strange little wood-chip legs and curling tendrils of green vine sprouting from its toes and hands, so small they looked like fine silk thread.

She drew it close and gazed at it in wonder. It gazed back, bracing itself with its little arms, its beady eyes—tiny, black, shining orbs—resting upon her face. It was without the doubt the cutest thing she'd ever beheld.

"Well hello there, little sprout," she greeted it.

It opened a little mouth hidden in the grain of its wooden body, nothing more than a small knick in the bark that covered it. It said nothing, but made only a little squeaking sound. She giggled.

"Will you disappear like last time?" she asked.

It did not reply. Instead, it climbed back onto its little feet and skittered down her wrist and arm, which she straightened for the sprite to make his passage easier, and it climbed up onto her shoulder and tangled itself into her hair.

"What is it with you little things and hair?" she giggled, reaching to untangle him from her carefully coiffed tresses.

She felt something strange when the little creature stopped struggling about in her locks. A liquid movement that was unlike the little sprite's scrabbling. When her fingers found purchase to pull the wood sprite out, she was holding a long, tapered wooden shape of a lovely hairpin carved into an oak leaf at the tip. It slid smoothly from her hair. She turned the thing in her hands, studying it in wonder. It was shaped like a two-tined fork, with only the faintest indications of a sprite etched into the pin. There were faint carved lines indicating the little arms pressed tightly to its side, and the legs were the fork, where tiny tendriled lines curled stylistically against the grain to represent the vines that sprouted from the toes and fingers. The eyes were simply tiny rounded points, and the oakleaf sprouted off the top of its head.

"There you are," she whispered. "Look at you."

The little eye dots blinked at her.

When someone knocked at her door, she slid the wooden hairpin back into the mound of hair piled on her head, and slid off the bed.

"Who is it?" she asked. But she already knew who it was.

"Raynes," he replied predictably. "May I come in?"

"I'll come out. Give me a moment," she replied, anxious to not allow him inside her room. She felt he might abuse the privilege.

"You *must* come out. You won't believe what is transpiring out here. The lodge has come alive!" he called through the door.

Nieve froze and peered at the wood that had become living wood again, thinking it was the same transient illusion only she and Tammin shared. How would the others see it? She peered quickly in the mirror to see a slightly puffy-eyed girl peering back at her with a little oak leaf sticking up from the top of the bun on her head. It was sufficient, she thought. Her ruddiness could be excused by the exposure to the cold.

She opened the door to find Raynes grinning at her. He held a little sprig of fresh oak leaves in his hand. "These sprouted from the mantelpiece," he informed her impishly. "Come look!" He grasped her hand and led her to the main hall, not giving her the chance to close her door.

Indeed, the wood had come to life. The ceiling was festooned with boughs of spring leaves, acorns swelling into existence one after the next from the newly formed twigs that had sprouted from the time-hardened oak beams and trusses. The barkless wood was flush green, like the ones in her room.

"Good gracious!" she exclaimed, peering up in awe, spinning slowly to see it all. The whole party was gaping up at the ceiling and the walls.

"What could this mean?" someone asked.

Nieve lost track of the exclamations of shock and wonder. She saw only the growth, bursting and budding forth from the long-dead wood. She felt little splinter-legs kicking against the back of her head, and her headpin shifted in her hair, settling back down again. It seemed her little friend wanted a better view of this incredible moment, too.

"It could mean that the Mennin have not all gone from this place," Miss Glass suggested.

"They were never gone," Miss Neery exclaimed. She was not a talkative creature, and had remained a bit of a non-presence amongst the party's revelers. She was understood to be the girl most suited to the morose Mr. Almoth, and so far, they'd scarce exchanged two words. "My uncle is Mennin," she told everyone rather loftily.

"Nonsense. Anyone who claims such is but a pretender," Raynes exclaimed.

Miss Neery glowered at him and shook her head in disgust. "You know nothing. The Mennin never went away. They just took their ways and made them secretive after the Ouros Dynasty. It's common knowledge amongst the Mennan-born families."

"Well, that explains it all, for I am common blood," Raynes declared affectedly, acting as if he was suddenly enlightened. Then he dropped his shoulders and laughed. "Understanding that a better part of the people in the greenlands are common-blood, it's no wonder nobody knows what you're talking about."

"Better part? That is nonsense if anything is. How do you think the breaches are managed but by Mennin-born soldiers. Why are you and Mr. Almoth and Lamb over there able to join us today, and are not marching into the tentacles of the living sands like Miss Nieve's beau is at this very moment?" Miss Neery flared.

Nieve's gaze dropped from the ceiling and she took in the scene developing around her. Miss Neery was standing by the fireplace with her arms ramrod-straight against her sides, and a very cross look on her pretty, fair face.

"It is the greater majority of Mennin-born who have struggled to keep the sands at bay all these centuries as the sands encroach and shrink our greenlands!" she shouted.

Mr. Almoth, who had been quietly observing this interchange, moved quietly to Miss Neery's side, all while nodding thoughtfully. "It is true. Only the Mennin-born can safely approach the sands without being consumed by them immediately. And there are often few of us remaining when there are breach-drafts. They are the ones whose efforts have prevented the remaining greenlands from being overtaken completely."

"And a grand job they've done," Raynes sneered dismissively. "There's naught but this small patch of green left in the known world. But let us not confuse the Mennin-born from the Mennin. A bloodline legacy to this green land does not necessarily make them Mennin. What evidence is there that the Mennin exist at all anymore?" Raynes crossed his arms and gazed about at the growth.

"The Mennin-born are Mennin. They are named for their land—the land is named for them. It is the family lines that determine if they are directly descended from the Mennin. And do we need more evidence than this? This lodge has been standing on these wooden logs for centuries. They are nearly petrified. But look, there is life pulsing through them now. Only the Mennin could do this," Miss Glass exclaimed.

Gillian entered the little circle of young people from the corridor, carrying a thick mug of ale. She said nothing, but peered at everyone in curiosity.

Nieve remained quietly removed from the debate. She stood a bit apart from the group, her hand resting on one of the great wooden columns that supported the weighty ceiling trusses. She could feel movement beneath her fingers. A soft throbbing in the grain, as if somewhere deep in the core of the oak, a heart was pumping. Small filaments of a spriggy moss began to grow around her fingers, unfurling gracefully before her eyes. She stared wondrously upon it.

Outside the tall windows, the snowfall had gone from thick, blowing flakes, to smaller, violently pelting ice crystals, which *tick-tick-ticked* on the window. Inside the warmth of the lodge, the cozy burning wood scent was now being overpowered by the scent of loam and humus, of fresh green things and the lushness of a forest, which was slowly thickening all around them. She turned to look at the party of ostensible friends, and studied each person in turn. The defiant Miss Neery, glaring at Raynes. Her companion, Almoth, gazing down upon her with what looked like sudden interest. Miss Glass stood by the fire, her arms crossed. Mr. Lamb, Miss Gillian, and Mr. Braice looked on in silence.

Nieve frowned. "I feel like we should be honoring this moment, not debating it." Her voice cutting through the momentary pall.

The others all turned toward her and their faces transformed into expressions of wonder and awe when they fixed their eyes upon her. She then caught her reflection in the darkened, besieged window, and a soft, strange little smile crossed her lips. For all around her being the great oak had grown thick with mosses and tiny plants, all of which had blossomed into a riot of flowers.

19. Besieged

Tammin and his new friend Rett drew back. The violence of the motion was so that they nearly fell. An arm of sand arced over them and then slammed down in an explosion of grains that stung their eyes and filled their mouths. His sand shield was almost immediately scooped up by grappling arms and gobbled up by the earth.

"Upon my oath!" Rett shouted, scrambling to grasp his shield before it, too, was taken. Tammin managed to grab hold the hilt of his sand cutter and got back onto his feet, staggering as the sands shifted beneath him.

A sand arm reached out to envelop his companion, and Tammin reacted. He lunged forward in front of his friend, grasped his sand-shield, and deflected the blow, both huddling under the impact of the strike and then the raining grains that ensued.

Further out, a dark froth formed on the advancing desert and they could see that it was a school of sand-hags, hoping to ride the next arc of living sands in.

"CUT IT!" Rett called out.

Tammin spun in time to see another arm of sand rising up from the ground. He ran forward and swept his sword through the wide base of it, cutting it dead before it could reach out and fall upon the greenery. Sand-hags tumbled all over the hardened, mossy soil, hissing and wriggling in defiance. Tammin chopped their heads off one by one until they were but oily streaks of black against the sand-dusted greenery.

Calls and cries could be heard all along the crescents of Burgeoning land, as the living sands aggressively reclaimed them. The Fohomok seemed almost powerless against the onslaught, and their Mystics were flummoxed. "How can this be? To have the green reach out so boldly, and then now be so vulnerable to the sands?" one shouted in confusion.

The Fohomok had been operating in a state of disorder since the troupes had arrived. The sands and the burgeoning greenery were acting in such a way nobody had ever experienced before. The scene was one of chaos. The breach soldiers were besieged by the sands, and the greenery was lashing back, which was unheard of. But the greenery did not appear at the advantage, and the living sands were taking it back almost as quickly as it could create a swath of lush land. The living sands were looking as if to use this moment to breach the old embankment and invade the highlands. The onslaught appeared unstoppable, and the fervor with which the living sands retaliated against the greenery was of the like never seen before.

The call for the more powerful magics had already been made, and the soldiers and Fohomok now battled to at least prevent further incursion until the backup arrived. They hoped soon, for the sands had taken on a fresh new assault and the greenery did not appear to be as lively as it had been only a few hours before.

The Fohomok along the line were battling the arms of living sands, and the terrible creatures that came inside them, all the while simultaneously attempting to conference with one another in a succession of shouts and barks along the front line of this strange, otherworldly battle, as to what they could possibly do, what magic they could possibly use, to slow this incursion. The greenery struggled as the living sands did, with the same sentient, sinuous action, tentacles of growth sprouting up into the edges of the desert, pushing up violently in tapering arms to be cut off by arcing falls of living sand.

Another smaller arm rose up, and Tammin swung toward it only to be blown back by the force of a Fohomok's magical blast, which had reached it first. Tammin stumbled back and then collapsed onto his backside into a thick tuft of tiny leafy growth, which was seething with living grains of sand. He felt the crystals beneath his hands, burrowing and digging into the growth, cutting through the tender new leaves and regrouping into little tendrils that flowed into bigger ones, moving back towards the incursions of undulating, heaving waves of sand that surged against the shores of greenery that fought so hard to keep its foothold.

He staggered to his feet, but he was now simply enraged by the whole seemingly futile battle. With a scream he lifted his sword and thrust it into the earth. To his shock, the sands splashed away from the force of it, like a large rock thrown into a still lake.

"Give me back my shield!" she screamed at it. He yanked his sword from the soil and drew it back, thrusting it again point-first into the soil closer to the edge of the greenery. A little spray of green arced out from the impact of it and rolled into the living sands, finding purchase and digging roots in. He gaped at it, and then pulled his sword out again.

A shout was heard. "Fohenwicke approaching!"

Tammin twisted and then threw himself behind the line just as the thundering hoofs of a great draught horse pummeled down where he had been and skidded to a halt at the edge of the greenery. The massive animal was armored almost entirely in protective leather plates, save for its snout, eyes, and ears, which were covered instead in a silky, gauzy mesh. It made for a strange image, for the horse appeared mechanical.

On its back was one of the most powerful of the Fohomok. An elder and the highest of the order. There were few of these old creatures. They, like their lesser brethren, shared many of the same traits. Tall, gaunt, with hollow blue-black eyes that seemed to look through a person. From their wizened lips fell skeins of silky whiskers that brushed their knees, sometimes plaited in a variety of ways, other times loose and gauzy like a wispy cloud. Their pale white hair was tied back with a silver cone into a flawless, perfectly coiffed queue that, when riding, would fan out behind them like their mount's creamy tail.

They carried with them long staffs that they kept hooked to their saddles lengthwise on the offside and wielded them with flourish when called upon to do so, when the sands were particularly war-like and the ordinary Fohomok could not manage it on their own.

The old man, with the movements of one fifty years younger, snatched up his great wooden staff, spun it twice before arching it high above him. He shouted out some words that Tammin did not understand, before planting its end into the earth from his horse. The force of it made the living sands and the burgeoning growth shudder as if the earth was quaking.

The soil and sand seemed to simmer and then boil around the large hoofs of his mount. The horse was implacable and calm through the chaos, and waited intently as the earth settled beneath it. But then, the sand wizard barked out another spell, or command, or whatever it was, and the sands appeared to draw back at the force of his declaration. To Tammin's shock, the horse suddenly rose up on its back feet and kicked out its forelegs before bounding in long, heavy strides forward towards the sands. The rider gripped his staff and hunched down over its neck, holding the staff horizontally like a lance. The horse dove into the sands as if it was diving into water, and it cut through them like a sand-ship. Two curtains of sand exploded from its sides, and Tammin observed in amazement as the grains turned to soil as they arced through the air. A wake of green and loamy brown followed in the animal's wake as it swam through the tawny sands as if it were nothing more than water. The wizard, now knee-deep in the waves of living sands, thrust his arm, staff and all, into the roiling particles around him and the earth shuddered again.

From where his staff slid through the sand, great vines began to burst out of the roil behind him, and from their bases, ripples of green spread out. Mats of thick, clover-like growth breached the surface and grew upwards towards the sky. The rider made a broad arc, following the edge of the Burgeoning, and created a sea-wall of sorts, a barrier of thick, high growth to keep the surging living sands at bay. It grew high enough so that the arms of living sand would not be able to batter the fragile edge of the green lands.

The other Fohomok were able to step in now and to take up where the old man left off. They filled the gaps with new growth to fortify the new living barricade. Tammin gaped in amazement as the elder and his steed scrabbled back onto solid land and turned to look at the product of their work, and with a shout, rode off to do it again at the next crescent of Burgeoning.

"They will stand for now, at least, against the entire ocean of sand. I cannot say for how long," a gravelly voice said in careful, accented words.

Officers, including Tammin, had been summoned so a new strategy could be formulated. The Fohomok and their elders met with them to assess the damage and to discuss some way to sustain the new growth, which had fought so hard to come into existence. After so many years of a virtual stalemate, they were daring to be hopeful.

Tammin had arrived with other officers during this discussion. Hearing that the barrier was only temporary was disheartening. He settled along the side of the table where the younger officers stood, looking on where the elder officers, Fohomok leaders, and three of the Fohenwicke sat.

"The problem is, whatever fueled the Burgeoning is no longer emitting power," the Fohenwicke that Tammin had seen exclaimed. His eyelashes, the corners of his eyes and mouth, and the edges of his nose were dotted in grains of sand. His hands and his long robes were pale from the dust he had forged through. "In order to sustain this growth, whatever prompted it must continue. We must discover what that is." His black gaze roved across the space. They fell, oddly, upon Tammin, and his silver brow arched, taking him in. "You. Come here."

Tammin up and tapped his own chest, a look of confusion on his brow.

"Yes. Come here. I saw you out there. You were the boy with the sword," the Fohenwicke observed.

"I suppose..." Tammin was at a loss.

"Come with us." To the remaining officers and wizards, he said, "Continue to strategize." And he, along with the other two Fohenwicke, rose.

They waited for Tammin to follow. He did, but he did not understand why. The old men in their split riding robes, all covered in the sand they had battled so aptly, led him to another of the structures that had been hastily assembled. They waited until everyone was inside before even acknowledging Tammin.

"You know," the first Fohenwicke said the moment the little door was shut behind them.

"I know what?" Tammin asked, wide-eyed and bewildered.

The three old men peered at him, each one the same yet so different in turn. One had his beard and mustache braided into hundreds of tiny plaits. The other was a shaggy, thin-faced, sand-covered mess. And the third, the one that had come to Tammin's place at the front, peered at him as if he was not to be fooled by the likes of this boy. They all three crossed their arms and glared at him impatiently.

"You know the source of the growth boy. You touched it. You had something to do with it, because I saw you today. You were driving that sand back by will alone, and only a Fohomok can do that. Or a Mennin Wyldwaerd. But there are no more such creatures, are there?"

"I have no idea," Tammin blurted, all-mystification.

"Then there is another reason why you are able to do what you did today. You and the source of this Burgeoning are connected. And if it were with you, you would likely be a great deal stronger," the wizard that looked the biggest mess barked at him.

"I saw you spread life-bursts out there, weak as they were. You are not Fohomok, so there is only one other possibility," the Fohenwicke that knew him repeated. "Whatever it is that has freed your magic—brought out whatever it is the Mennin stored in the line of the Mennin-born boys, it must be empowered again. And we three think that it can only do that if you not separated from it. With it, you are Wyldwaerd. Without it, your magical blood is weak."

"And whatever it is, or who it is, you must return to it," the braided one added.

"I don't understand. The greenlands have remained steadfast for I cannot say how long. Why now does it stand to be weak enough to be won by the living sands? Why now? When the greenlands have clearly grown forth back into the sands? I can only say, with all due respect, that none of you make any sense."

Six arms dropped impatiently to the sides of their dusty robes and they dispersed about the small space, one grasping a goblet and pouring himself some water from a jug, the other sinking down onto the edge of a cot, and the third took a step towards the stove and warmed his hands. He took a deep, intolerant sigh, and shook his head. Tammin had disappointed the three and lost their interest it seemed.

"You know *something*. Or you *suspect* something, of that I am certain. No *Wyldwaerd* could make his magic without some inkling of it. It's coming from inside you, and you are connected to it. Perhaps you have yet to look at that truth in the mirror and admit to yourself that it is there. But you know." The old man reached up and wiped away the sand from his face. Tammin could hear it falling onto the wooden slat floor with each brush of his raspy fingers.

Tammin's brow darkened and he put his hands on his hips, his gaze dropping to the floor. There was no mistaking that he had indeed pushed back the sands by the sheer power of his anger at it. And that his sword had caused bursts of growth every time he had thrust it into the soil. And his mind kept slipping back to the conversation with Nieve, and that odd old lady whose name had slipped his mind. She had used that word, too. *Wyldwaerd*. But another word popped up instead.

"Mennin-saed," he murmured.

The old men all turned to look at him at once, and their sandy skin grew waxen in the pale flickering light of the lanterns. He had their attention again.

The Seed of Winden

20. Saed

Raynes looked stricken. He stood a way back, watching her as Nieve peered at herself in the window, her aura of flowers still rustling and blossoming. She moved, and the blossoming followed her along the trusses and the walls, around the columns as she passed the great wooden oak beams. At her feet, the cracks between the slate pavers exploded into little veins of green that snaked in the joints between each stone slab. She moved languidly, her hand brushing the wall as she made the perimeter of the space.

"Do you think I could go out there and put the winter to a halt?" she laughed uncomfortably.

The company peered at her in wonder. She reached out and touched the doorframe of the main entryway and sent a little burst of growth forth, with buds popping open and unfurling into blooms. She smiled stiffly, discomfited with the whole thing, trying to be humorous about it while the others stared on, astonished.

"What do you think this is all about?" she asked them. She waved her arms and spun, and the flowers blossomed wildly.

Abruptly—it all went away. The greenery began to shrivel and turn brown, the flowers lost their petals, and they were naught but little motes of nothing before they reached the floor. The leaves fell in autumn colors and crumbled to dust. Within but a moment or two, in the time it took to gape up at the ceiling and gasp, it was over. A rain of dust fell upon the guests of the lodge. The magic had gone.

Lamentingly, Nieve reached up and touched her hairpin. To her delight, she felt a little twitch and scrabble from her tiny wood-sprite. It wasn't completely over. She retreated to her room, mostly cowed by the looks on the faces of her companions. Raynes, who had always been so relentless, took a distance from her.

They ate dinner in a restrained silence. After dinner, nobody seemed inclined to leave their rooms, but Nieve wanted to. So she slipped out and walked gingerly to the common-room where the fire, which had been briskly crackling and dancing a few hours before, now snapped and popped mutely, quietly consuming the core of the oak log that had been put in earlier that evening. Now it was less flame and merely a riot of dancing orange embers tracing their way across the scorched wood grain. It was beautiful. A blue flame would emerge now and again, or a little hopeful yellow one that would inevitably flicker out.

What happened to the magic? Nieve asked herself. She sat in her bodiced petticoat, wrapped in a shawl. The lodge was warm and dark. There was brown leaf-dust on the bottom of her silken winter stockings. *And why did this growth originate around me?*

Her wood-sprite friend was still and quiet in her hair, holding it all up against her scalp. If the others had not seen it themselves, she could have marked it a dream. Just like the night of the ball when Tammin was departing, and she had grown wings and he had grown horns. She drew her feet up underneath her on the sofa, and stared at the embers. They flickered and danced, crossing the wood and extinguishing with the occasional flame before being reborn elsewhere.

As she watched this impassively, half-lost in her thoughts, she noticed a pattern taking shape in the dance of the embers. There was a face amongst the flickers and flashes along the blackened wood. A pair of eyes, a long nose, and a soft mouth that smiled at her with a flicker of orange.

Nieve furrowed her brow and leaned forward, peering at it as the fire-sprite peered back at her.

"Are you real or my imagination?" she asked it.

The sprite's eyes turned into little crescents and its mouth into a smile. It seemed to be laughing at her. Its eyes turned upward, and it made an explosion of flames that appeared like its hair. It smiled at her again for approval when it was finished with the display.

"Can you not speak at all?" she asked it.

The embers flickered and moved, and it shook its head. But it pursed its fiery mouth and arched a burning brow, as if to think. And then its brows arched in elation and it shut its eyes, and the flames erupted again over its head.

"Return." In the gaps and flickers of the flames, the word appeared.

"Home?" Nieve asked.

"Stones," the flames spelled momentarily, before extinguishing and causing a renewed fervor of embers to scatter across the log.

"To Winden?"

The face nodded emphatically, its eyes in happy crescents again. "Give sprite," it said. "Hungry," it flickered.

She reached up protectively to the little pin in her hair and she shook her head. "I'll give you firewood, but not my sprite," she told the ember-face, which pouted at her. She felt her hairpin wriggle.

"Now, now," she shook her finger at the face. "Here, this will suit you just fine." Nieve reached for the basket and found a thick piece of fruitwood. She put it on top of the blackened log, and watched the little fire-sprite smile at it. The eyes squeezed into two little lines and flames popped into life below the fresh wood, its tongues lapping around it happily.

Day rose with a clear sky and a bright, low sun that shone across a frozen, white-blanketed land. As the group emerged from Wolf Hall to climb back into the sledge and return home, they experienced an astonishing sight.

The Eighth Colossus, which they could see it from the hilltop as they descended towards the city, had stood the test of time and endured centuries, keeping the desert at bay for as long as anyone could recall. As they stared at it, just a tiny little figure far in the distance, an arm of sand the likes of which no one had ever seen swept out against the statue's leg. It wobbled, then buckled under its own weight and dropped before a great ocher sand-cloud rolled over its ruin.

The driver drew the horses to a stop.

"Oh gods," Miss Glass muttered. "The sand has breached."

All around the countryside, the sound of the sirens rose up chillingly against the frosty morning.

"Tammin," Nieve whispered, her gaze falling upon Raynes with desperation. "I must go to Tammin."

"You cannot," he replied, his eyes imbued with a confusion of emotions.

"Then I must go home to Halenwood," she exclaimed.

Part Three

The Seed of Winden

21. Summoned

Lady Parendil was impatiently awaiting Nieve when she arrived home. The girl bustled in; her cheeks still red from the icy cold. She did not know about the guest, as the party had only lately dropped her off in front of the house, the sled moving briskly away as soon as she had set foot on the snowy ground. Raynes went along with it, dismay upon his face.

All Nieve wanted to do was to go and wash up with some hot water, and to change into fresh clothes; the scent of the lodge and its smoky air still lingered on her garments. She aimed for the stairway, but she was redirected the moment she set foot into the house by the housekeeper.

"You've a visitor, young Miss. She has been here all morning," Mrs. Fennig told her.

Nieve emitted a sigh and moved towards the parlor where Mrs. Fennig directed her. She found Lady Parendil and the Viscount sitting quietly together. Her guardian was sipping coffee from a tall, thin mug, and the Lady was ignoring a setting of tea and refreshments laid out before her. She rose to her feet with some difficulty the moment Nieve entered the room.

"My dear, dear girl, this is disastrous. Utterly disastrous! You must go to the stones. You must go and your bond-mate must go, too! What shall we do? What can be done?" She immediately began to fuss and fidget.

"I informed the Lady that there will be no travel today for any of the Halenwoods. The baby is not ready for such a thing yet. We will be staying here," the Viscount grumbled.

"Then I shall take her," Lady Parendil said. "You do not oppose me, too?"

Nieve's eyes fixed upon the old woman's face, and she blinked and shook her head. Nieve was at once relieved. She had worried on her way home about how to present her need to return to Winden to her aunt and uncle. They would not let her go alone, without them. With the new developments at the edgelands, she thought she might be able to persuade them to go back to Halenwood. But Lady Parendil had spared her the work of persuading them. She could return to Winden at immediately, and her family could follow whenever it suited them. She turned to her uncle.

"No, I do not oppose this plan, ma'am. I am desperate to go home. Would it be acceptable for me to return to Halenwood early, my Lord?"

The Viscount lowered the book he was reading and arched a brow. He did not know that he was powerless against Nieve or her aunt. But he was. With a bit of a grumpy frown, he nodded his assent. "I'll send word to the house to prepare for your arrival, and that of your guest."

"Excellent. I will go and summon up the coach at once. And you must pack up your things, dear. I will be ready to collect you in oh, let's say two hours?" the elderly woman exclaimed.

Nieve nodded and ushered her out. She watched the old woman shuffle down the snowy sidewalk with her train of wool behind her.

"I won't ask what sort of nonsense that was. I agreed because it was *you* asking," the Viscount said from behind Nieve.

"It is a matter of some complexity. It is difficult to explain," she said, turning to face him. "I will go and pack. I will see you and my aunt before I leave, and then I will see you again when the little one is strong enough to travel."

Her guardian assented again with a softer expression, and watched his step-niece scamper from the room, her voice calling for a chamber-maid.

As promised, two hours later Lady Parendil's rather large, shining black and robin's egg blue coach appeared before the door of the Halenwood Townhouse complete with elegantly clad livery, all in caped garricks and broad, gilt-edged tricorn hats. They wore powdered side-curls and queues and sported bullion cording on their frock coats.

Nieve had made her farewells to her family, and the fashionable footmen hastily placed her trunks on boot of the four-in-hand. The four bays, their winter coats like a thick-piled velvet, all matched perfectly, with shining black points and their manes done up into pretty rolled plaits. Nieve waved to her family in the window and was handed into the coach. And soon enough, the horses, their spiked shoes sparking on exposed cobbles, drew the coach inland towards Halenwood.

About half an hour out on the Lyan Road, they were overtaken by the sound of clattering hoofs. Nieve peered out to see what the hullabaloo was about, only to find Raynes drawing his horse up next to the coach, the poor thing slick with sweat, its body steaming from the exertion. The young man offered no explanation. He merely let his horse fall slightly behind the coach. Nieve stole occasional glances out the back window at him as he rode along, but he did not engage her until they had disembarked for the night at the inn at Rochdorp.

Lady Parendil was tired and so was Nieve. She helped the elderly woman descend from the coach, and clutched her elbow as the she stiffly made her way through the doorway of the posh inn they'd chosen for the night's rest. Raynes followed them in with a swish and swagger of his greatcoat, and waited to speak to her until Nieve had secured the rooms and helped Lady Parendil to hers to refresh herself and rest before dinner.

Nieve closed the door to the Lady's room to find him leaning with his back against the wall in the corridor. He looked down at his gloves and hat when she peered at him questioningly.

"Why did you follow us, Mr. Raynes?" she asked him pointedly, picking up the hems of her skirts and moving past him towards her own room.

"I have come to realize this winter that I cannot be anywhere where I am not by your side, Miss Nieve," Raynes muttered.

The young woman, in all her fatigued loveliness, paused in her step and then twisted towards him. Her hands fell, along with the train of her skirts. "Mr. Raynes, I am not..."

"Do not say it," he interrupted her, his hand rising up flat between them. "For we do not know. We do not know yet what may come." The fair locks of hair on his forehead fell forward onto his brow, and he picked at his hat, which was clutched in his gloved hands.

"I do know," she replied softly.

"I will be with you until the very end, Miss Nieve. Any chance I can remain by your side, I will take it." He expressed this only after lifting his eyes to meet hers, and after chewing on his teeth for a moment, his jaw rippling.

"I cannot stop you from following us, Mr. Raynes. I appreciate your..." she paused, her eyes searching, "...your devotion. However, I believe whatever is happening, I am connected to it, as the Lady Parendil has so zealously warned me. After the lodge... After all that, I am convinced of the truth of it. And I believe Tammin is connected to this, too. We will be... No," she hesitated. "We *are* together. In this. And in us. We have an understanding, Master Raynes. To follow me and to continue this pursuit, it is fruitless, and it will lead you only to disappointment. I have shown you clearly that a romantic connection between you and me is impossible. I love Tammin. I belong with Tammin. You are best served to go back to Adaskus to your family and your party of delightful, dutiful friends."

Nieve turned and entered her room before he could reply. He remained in the corridor, fidgeting with his hat, staring down someplace beyond it, ruminating on her words. After a bit, he threw his hat on his head and stalked out to the public house across the street, where he remained well past dinnertime.

After the ladies took supper in the common room at the table with the Inn owner and four other guests, they took to a large parlor to soak in the heat of the fire. Here it was not as cold as Adaskus, and the snow had melted already. Away from the lake, in the lower elevations, closer to the center of the greenlands, spring was coming. And along with it the green and lushness that Nieve had so grown to love, and that made her feel she was where she belonged at last.

She wished only to be home at Halenwood Hall which, over the past few years, had sunk into her skin and taken root into her soul. She felt tired. Exhausted, really. Her spirit was heavy, and all she could do was recall that moment when the colossus fell, and the sound of the sirens wailing. Inside her heart there was a sense of urgency to get back to Halenwood. To Winden. To Tammin. She only hoped he too knew it. And he too was on his way home—for she had no idea where he was at the moment.

In the greenlands, it seemed like life was simply going on while the living sands encroached upon the center of this last vestige of healthy flora. What else could people do but send their ablest to fight the onslaught, while those who stood to be absorbed and consumed by the sand fled inland in fear. She expected more alarm on the roads. More noise and panic. But there was no such thing. Instead, it was almost deathly quiet at this inn—and on the roads. It was peaceful and restful here. The fire snapped and the conversation lagged and then failed completely. Lady Parendil's usual loquacious nature had become subdued and thoughtful, and Raynes was at the public house, likely getting drunk.

She leaned back in her chair, her hands without occupation or project to work on. She stared instead at the fire, recalling the fire sprite's face as it told her to go home. Her little hairpin had scarce moved for days, coming to life only once after the incursion of the sands when the sirens stopped. She kept it in her hair at all times. At present she reached up and plucked the wooden thing from her hair, and ran her thumbs along the delicate grooves carved into the surface of the hairpin. She brushed the little barky cheeks and caressed its little head. It remained rigidly in its shape, and did not stir.

"What is it?" Lady Parendil said in a low voice, her watery eyes falling onto the pin, her papery-skinned hand reaching out to take it. Her skin felt soft and rough at the same time as her fingers slid over the pin and she took it to peer at it through her quizzing glass which was hanging from a delicate silver chain on her neck.

"Isn't this a delight?" she smiled, peering at it in the light of the candelabra. "It looks like a little wood man. Where did you find such a whimsical little hairpin?"

"It's not a hairpin," Nieve confessed in a half-whisper. "It's a wood sprite. He's been holding this state for so long now, I'm worried he won't come out of it."

The old woman took this information in stride, and studied the thing closer, tilting her head, twisting it in her hand. "Oh, magical things of the Mennanfae do what they do, my dear girl. They do not abide by the same rules we do. There is nothing to worry yourself about. Where did you collect the little fellow?"

"At the great lodge. During the blossoming I described," she replied.

"I see. Then this little chip of wood may be a custodian for you," the old woman speculated. "I read about them, long ago. Tasked to watch over you. To keep you connected to the veils of the Mennanfae world as you traverse this one. They use him to watch you."

"They?" Nieve asked.

"Why the Mennanfae themselves, dear girl. The originals. They are watching you. For certain, Tammin might have his own little companion, too, guiding him as others might be. As you said the fire did for you."

"My Lady, I do not understand. The Mennin, do they exist still here? In our world? Or only in the veiled world?"

"In both, my child. In both blood and in spirit. They have hidden themselves in the veiled lands for so long now, but there they are powerless, as powerless as the veil itself. It's like a living image. A tableau vivant. Pictures of spirits and time long past. The veil. If they come through here, they can influence this world. So there are some here, living as we do. Using the family lines… Living as Halenwoods, and as Parendils. Some have forgotten their purpose and their grudges. Others have not. The Greenborn are the life of the world in many ways, but without you, without the Saed, their power shriveled. They become ghosts of what they used to be. Dark, bitter, angry fragments of what was once a whole, joyful, vibrant living race turned sour by betrayal and destruction. Just as the world mirrors their fates.

One half, another to make them whole. To make the world whole again."

Nieve wanted to scream and tear out her hair. The Lady spoke in nonsense. She could not wrap her brain around what she was being told. She took back her hairpin and slid it into her coif.

"My Lady," she began, "are there any Mennin that you know of. Ones with whom I can speak?"

The mad old lady mulled upon this thought for a long while and nodded slowly. "I fair think there are one or two that are still about, and that I know of. Should we visit one? If he's still alive, that is. He was old when I was not even fifty years myself. They are long-lived by nature though," she assured Nieve. "He is at Revechelle. It is only another half-day from here I estimate. We shall go upon the morrow, eh?"

Nieve nodded.

Lady Parendil lifted her shoulders and then sagged them, timing it with a sigh that sounded more like a yawn. "It is time for me to retire. Are you going to wait up for your friend?"

Nieve shook her head. "Do you wish me to assist you to your room, ma'am?"

"No, no, no, child." the Lady waved her away as she struggled to her feet. She shuffled away as she bade Nieve a good night.

22. The Truth

Nieve had resolved to go to bed soon after Lady Parendil, but instead, she remained in the common room long after the rest of the guests and the owner had retired to their beds. She sat by the fire, absentmindedly watching the flames lap up the sides of a dense beech log that the innkeeper had placed on top of the coals before going upstairs. The resilient mosses that were growing on the bark had been infused by the fire and blackened, but held their shape still, while the fire's embers danced through the lacy structure and made a beautiful display of it all. It was mesmerizing.

Nieve's rubbed the surface of her wooden hairpin. Her dormant wood-sprite. She felt so very tired but she could not bring herself to move. She could not keep warm in spite of having her feet, in her favorite emerald-green parlor slippers, propped on the brass fender before the fire.

She was startled by the tolling of the clock when it informed her that it was midnight, and jumped again when the bell jangled at the door, and a cross footman stumbled to open it. From the parlor she could see Raynes stagger into the vestibule, and stop short at the round table with the flower vase on it, nearly upsetting them both as he used it to prevent himself from falling. He stood as the footman left him to his devices, and swayed on his feet, staring at the tabletop where he was bracing himself from tipping over.

With a sigh of resignation, Nieve got up and padded softly to Raynes whose pale face and watery, bloodshot eyes pivoted towards her in a drawn, sluggish speed. "You. You, little thing, should be resting, should you not?" he slurred, cracking that smile that, in spite of it all, quickened Nieve's heart. It was charismatic and bright, raffish and earnest all at once.

He was terribly handsome, she thought. Even when he was three sheets to the wind.

She put the hairpin on the table and braced his arm.

"I think we ought to consider that you are in the most need of rest and bed between the two of us," she replied, smiling softly at him in the golden light of the two candelabras still burning against their dish-reflectors on the wall sconces.

"Why must you be so adorable?" he asked her, trying to straighten himself, but instead swinging his weight backwards and nearly stumbling onto his bum. Nieve reached out and grasped his arm, steadying him. He threw his arm around her shoulders immediately and hugged her to his side tightly. "You're so tiny," he added, leaning heavily into her.

She grunted and bore it, hoisting herself up against his underarm, wrapping her arm around his middle.

Raynes paused and stared at the table for a moment. "Your hands are full," he slurred. He reached for the hairpin and pocketed it. Nieve ushered him towards the stairway.

"You are *not* tiny," she replied. "You are heavy."

"You are beautiful. And sweet. And delightfully rude. And amusing as anything. And I love you," he bellowed, laughing afterwards.

She guided him along, suddenly silenced by his exclamation. He staggered, nearly dragging Nieve along with him, but she stood her ground and led him to the foot of the stairway, giving it a good, long, challenging stare before girding herself and pushing forward with the wobbly Raynes leaning so heavily upon her.

One step, and the next, and he kept rambling loudly. "You cannot love someone like Tammin. It cannot be. You know what he did? He destroyed my family, is what he did," Raynes spat bitterly.

"I am quite confident you are mistaken on that end, Raynes," she replied, giving him the side eye.

Raynes stumbled over a stair and reached out his free hand to catch himself. Nieve stopped until he regained some semblance of equilibrium. He wavered on his feet, turning his face down to look at her. His eyes, red from the drink, were now brimming with moisture.

"My mother fled her disappointment in me. And in herself," he said. "Because of what Tammin did. Because of Miss Flowers."

Nieve listened, her curiosity leading her to remain on the stair with him, with his arm wrapped tightly around her shoulder. "Miss Flowers?"

"The first girl we fought over before you," he explained. He sighed heavily and cast his gaze out into some not-too-distant past. "Compared to you, she was nothing, now that I consider it. But at the time, she was oh, so charming. I delighted in her company. She was not as clever or wise as you, but she was right pretty, and she laughed a great deal. We all of us friends admired her in one way or another. But she was my girl."

"I heard her name once, uttered by the Viscount, now you mention it," Nieve said with puzzlement.

"Yes. She was a regular of the party then. She traveled in our circle, and sat in all of our parlors."

"Did Tammin like her, too?" Nieve asked.

Raynes lost his balance and righted himself, putting both of his arms around Nieve and hugging her close. He groaned shakily and propped his chin on the top of her head. "No, not like I did. He, like most everyone else, disapproved of her as a prospect for anything other than a season's lark. Miss Flowers was but the companion to one of the young ladies of note, and entered our circle because of her superior's status. Miss Flowers's father was merely a saddler. Mind you, he makes the *best*, most *expensive* saddles and tack to be found in the region, but she was merely a daughter of a saddler. As well-liked as she was by our circle, she was still regarded as what she was: a commoner. Not by me. I had come to adore her."

"How did this pull your family apart?" Nieve asked.

Raynes stepped back, gripping the railing. He climbed a few more steps before continuing. "I never looked down upon Miss Flowers, because my own father came from common stock. My mother from a lower place. It was not generally known, but my mother came from a family whose patriarch was but a silk seller. I never saw the match with Miss Flowers as impossible as the rest of my peers did because of this. I assumed that my mother, out of all, would have a unique understanding of this. I thought neither of my parents would discourage me. Because they too had experienced this kind of match.

"But to my shock, my mother of all people objected the most. And her frantic, public objections ultimately exposed her own past of common blood. My father's sister—who has always despised and resented my low-blooded mother—upon hearing mother decry the match during a night of carding, stated quite frankly in company that my mother ought not be so discriminating and show such snobbery when she herself elbowed her way into a marriage above *her* station as a silk-seller's daughter."

Raynes stopped again, let go of Nieve and turned, sinking down to sit on the top step. Nieve sat down next to him, her brow knit in confusion. But she listened regardless.

"Nobody in our circle knew of my mother's previous station in life. And the discussion then turned to how such a remarkably well-mannered lady could have such airs and poise when she was but a merchant's girl. She made the mistake of defending herself by naming the lowly finishing school where she had learned the necessary skills. The guests were all greatly amused by this, and their ridicule shamed my mother so greatly, she never recovered from it. Her circle of friends diminished almost at once. A few months after this day, after being left to preside over her salon alone without the usual condescension and society of her peers, she faded. One day, she declared she was going to the lakes. She packed up all her precious things and took a post to somewhere, and she disappeared. She has never returned."

"I still fail to understand how Tammin was party to all this," Nieve interjected.

"He exposed Miss Flowers to my family as my intended. *He* told them. Had he left that to me, to do on my own, to work it in a way where nobody was hurt or ridiculed, so that none of their secrets were publicly aired as they were, my mother would still be here. I love my mother, Miss Nieve. I loved her, but she chose to abandon me over her own pride." He swallowed his last words, his voice gone gravelly. He bent forward so that his head nearly touched his knees. His shoulders shuddered. "He was the only one who knew of my intentions with Miss Flowers. Everyone else thought I was but engaging her as I often did with pretty girls—harmless flirtations and the like. It all came to nothing anyway, for when Miss Flowers got wind of my mother's ardent disapproval, she went to Sands-Upon-Muldoon to stay with some relatives. She chose to go to the sands rather than to stay here in this sacred place to be with me."

Nieve's brow furrowed and she shook her head. "But Master Raynes, that isn't true."

"With all due respect, my beloved Miss Nieve, you were not there to know," he snapped defensively.

Nieve reached out and put her hand on his shoulder and shook her head. "But that's the thing. As I said before, I heard Miss Flowers's name once when my uncle, the Viscount, was talking to my aunt. He was speaking about the dissolution of your father's marriage, and how unusual it was for a divorce to be granted—to a woman, no less. And then to top that, the House of Lords approved an order of an annual stipend to be paid by your father until the decease of one or the other." She carefully measured her next words. "My uncle speculated that perhaps this Minister that spearheaded this unheard-of divorce was the man your mother ran to. For my uncle stated that the marriage had been unhappy for a very long time on your mother's end. That your father's undying love for your mother was not reciprocated, and there was suspicion that she was cuckolding him for someone else. The shame of her low birth might have been difficult, but according to my uncle, it is not *why* she left your family." She stopped, peeking at Raynes to gauge his reaction. He merely sat with his elbows propped on his knees, staring down at his feet.

Nieve cleared her throat. "My uncle praised the gods that you did not fall into the same trap," she said carefully. "He told my aunt that you had run with a girl named Miss Flowers, a common little thing, the daughter of some tradesman or whatnot, and that if the connection had been allowed to continue, the precedent created by your mother might have inspired Miss Flowers to do the same to you. But he then said this:" Nieve lowered her voice into a gruff imitation of the Viscount and continued. "'Damned fortunate that the wife saw the boy in intimacy with this little commoner girl, kissing her in the gardens, thinking themselves unseen. Once she saw that, then all the ballyhoo and hurly-burly arose over it, and the fervor drove the little lady away. Sadly, the Mrs.' reaction to her son's connection with this girl enraged Bellworth. He held her accountable for the hypocrisy of her objections. For he, too, perhaps not quite so low, rose on his own grit from a common birth.

"It was his goodwill and devotion that was holding that marriage together. The loss of it simply widened the rift between them and it was all the impetus the lady required to dissolve her connection to Mr. Bellworth. A few weeks later, Mrs. Bellworth was gone.'

"You see, Raynes. It was not Tammin that exposed you. *You* exposed you. And it was not your connection to Miss Flowers that did the family in, Raynes. The cracks in the foundation were already there. It was merely the circumstances that allowed the great house to crumble entirely."

Nieve was forthright as she always was with Raynes. She knew it was the only way to make him hear her sometimes. She had to acknowledge that there was something to respect in his bearing of her brashness. She had always been rather brutal with Raynes when it came to stating her truth, and he absorbed it unwaveringly—he might have been even slightly buoyed or amused by her frankness, had the subject not been so grave. Even in this drunken state, he listened. He measured. He processed it. His head hung low.

She heard a tremendous sob boil up from deep inside him and he buried his face in his hands. "Damn you, Miss Nieve," he blubbered between his fingers. "That I must bear all this. To know now that my greatest friendship was destroyed over such a stupid misunderstanding. To know that my mother was not innocent. And to accept that you... That you will never love me..."

Nieve's heart sank inside her chest, and she bent her head too, the hand on his back sliding off and falling to her side. "I am sorry, Raynes. I cannot change my heart. I have loved Tammin since

I was but a little girl. He's in my blood. I cannot change my heart, but I do cherish you now, Raynes. Even if I did despise you once, I have come to know you better. To trust you. To value you. It is not the essentials that I cannot love. It is not *you* I cannot love. It is that I cannot stop loving Tammin."

"I'm going to bed..." he croaked. He rose with some difficulty, and glanced down at Nieve as he turned back towards the corridor. "Goodnight Nieve."

He stumbled off and vanished with the click of a door latch. Nieve remained on the steps for another few moments, trying to organize her mind after all this. With a sigh, and the hopeless shake of her head, she got to her feet.

She was so, so tired. And she was cold, too. She shuffled to her own room, and fell into her bed. Exhausted by everything.

23. Mennanfae

Mardlan House was very old. One of the oldest houses Nieve had ever seen. Even older than some of the great houses of Rethros which had been built when the lands they sat upon were still green. They had survived the sweep of the sands and now stood amongst the dunes like lone sentinels.

Mardlan was so aged it had no particular style to it. It was a great stone drum, the flat, crenelated top dripping with vines growing from the stone roof which had accumulated so much debris and matter over the years, that it sprouted its own wild garden. The odd chimney rose up here and there, added many years after the house had been built. The windows—once been small, glassless slots but now modern panes—were many, circling the cylindrical building in three tiers, looking out on a murky moat which looked more like a lawn from a distance, the duckweed was so dense and thick, floating on the water.

Someone had built out a portico with a smooth eyebrow roof over it to shelter the massive wooden doors, and to shade the stone stairs leading up to them. The park around it was wild with growth, many of the bare branches already budding, many evergreens shining leafed and leathery, bright against the dark, rainy, mossy backdrop. The whole estate sat in the very bottom of a narrow valley, nearly a canyon in its own right. A rushing river dominated the floor of these narrow flats, and roared at the front of the house, where a slick stone bridge crossed over it leading to a circular driveway made of cobble. A folly had been built by the riverbank in the past decade or so, to give the place interest. The white sandstone was now green with algae and moss was covering the lower portion of the foundation stones. The little circular shelter looked like it had not been sat in or attended to in years.

"This place is so wet," Nieve muttered. "It reminds me of Andenswegg."

Raynes nodded, and peered at her wan face, which caught the harsh light in this dark place in a lovely way. She looked particularly drawn and pallid this morning. He had pointed out that he was worried about her health and that she might be coming down ill.

"You look a bit peaked, Miss Nieve," he observed.

She dismissed him with a shake of the head, acting slightly cool and shamed since their conversation the night before.

They disembarked, and helped Lady Parendil down. She hobbled up the steps to the door and rapped loudly upon it with her cane. She then let the cane slide down in her hand, and she caught the handle, leaning immediately upon it to wait for the door to open.

It did rather quickly, and they were met by a particularly handsome woman with smooth black hair tied tightly back into a low bun, two little curls dangling on her temples on each side of her pale face. She had eyes the color of richly stained and lacquered cherry wood. She wore a demure black gown with a thick cotton chemisette and a ruffed collar, and on her bustline at the gown's waist hung a bright shining chatelaine. It was shaped to look like a delicate spider with its legs curled down, little rings at the tip of each spider-leg, and a chain dangling. Each chain had something clipped to it: keys, a tiny pair of scissors designed to match the spider and engraved to look like a fly, a quizzing glass, a snuff spoon, a melting spoon, a wax seal stamp, and other such things. All were embossed to appear as insects caught in the spider's web and rang together pleasantly as she moved. She had long sleeves of the sort that hung to the knuckles, with a pop of a white cuff beneath. Her mouth, although set in a neutral expression, curled just a mote when she set her eyes upon the Lady Parendil.

She curtsied kindly to Lady Parendil, and stepped back, widening the door to allow them in. "It's been half an age, Ma'am," she said with good humor.

The old woman snuffed through her nose. "To us elders, half an age is nothing."

"The Master's in the conservatory this afternoon," the woman—who was clearly the housekeeper—informed Lady Parendil, gesturing them to follow her.

They cut through the massive cylindrical building into a darkened corridor, and then hooked right into another hall where light shone brightly at the end of it. It brought them to another vestibule like the small one at the entrance, but this one was capped by double doors that were made entirely of glass panes. The housekeeper opened them, and they entered a small space where another set of identical doors faced them. She closed the first, and then opened the second in a gust of warm air. The visitors filed out of the great building into a greenhouse that was built up against the back of the building. It, too, was circular, with a faceted glass gem of a roof which was slightly green with algae. It was hot inside, and there were exotic trees rising up into a misty fog that lingered up near the roof of the conservatory.

There were countless islands of stone beds lining a labyrinth of pathways through the space, all overhung with greenery, with a small central sitting area. Inside, there was the exotic song of birds long extinct outside this glass house, and flashes of brightly colored feathers zipping between the trees.

"Make yourselves comfortable in the sitting area. I'll find the Master. He's in here somewhere," the housekeeper declared. She gathered up her hems, and clattered off down one of the many paths.

The group of three walked to the little central plaza where a small round table and chairs were placed, as well as several shabby armchairs and a sofa. The sitting area had a round awning over it, protecting the furniture from the constant drip of condensation and droppings from the birds that occupied this unbelievably lovely hothouse.

Nieve found the high wingback to her taste and sank down into it, closing her eyes and exhaling heavily, almost too tired to move. She was wearing a linen gown this morning, with several petticoats, and was wrapped up in a shawl to keep warm. Even in this hothouse, she was bundled up, her little brown boots peeking out from her skirts.

A small bird fluttered down onto the armrest and then hopped onto her hand. Her eyes opened and she peered at it impassively. It was a variety of bird she'd never seen before. A body of bright, vibrant blue with patches of green and yellow and purple, with a ruby cowl. It had a wide, short vivid orange beak and bright watchful eyes. It hopped up onto her wrist, turning its head one way and then the other to take her in with each beady little eye.

Another one landed. This one was of plain, pale grey colors with just hints of blue under the throat and on the crest of its head. A third, fourth, and fifth bird landed. The next two were of a different variety, with teal and robin's egg blue straps around their heads, and bright violet wings. Raynes and Lady Parendil watched the little flock gather on Nieve's hands and hop along her arm.

"The strapped warbler and the jeweled finch—these are no longer found anywhere in this world but here. These are bred from a few lines kept by the most dedicated preservationists in the greenlands. There are few of us now. And even fewer of these delightful creatures." A hoarse voice broke the silence.

The sound of it sent Nieve's little avian retinue to burst into flight and to disappear into the branches of the foreign trees that filled the space. The party turned to take in the source of this information.

The fellow was very, very old, with a mop of silver hair that had been styled carefully into double side-curls and a queue. His face was a map of a lifetime of laughter and expression, a beautiful record in wrinkles and folds, with a pair of bright, clear, sparkly sky-blue eyes nestled in the heavy folds of papery eyelids. His back was hunched, and he leaned precariously onto a cane which he clutched tightly in a knobby, blue-veined hand. He shuffled slowly.

His gloved fingers were brown with dirt. In his free hand he clutched a pair of clippers and a bright yellow blossom that looked something like a cross between a lily and a rose. He shuffled to Nieve and offered the flower to her. She sat up and bowed her head in greeting, quietly taking the bloom from him and putting it up to her nose. It smelled like citrus.

"The Andrave flower. There are only four shrubs that I know of that remain. All of them are hundreds of years old. The older they get, the better the fruit. These are just blooming. I'm excited for this year's crop, for it could be my very last," he lamented. "Mrs. Gees, if you would be so kind as to furnish us all with some tea while I introduce myself to these lovely young people? Oh, wait, it's time for a nuncheon, isn't it? How about we have a nice meal out here? Eh? Can we do that Mrs. Gees?"

"Of course, Master Abris," the housekeeper assured him. She curtsied and left him with his visitors.

He moved to the seat across from Nieve, studying her first, and then moving to Lady Parendil, who watched expectantly.

"I never imagined you'd come to see me in the company of such a gift, dearest Lady Parendil," he exclaimed, a smile crossing his nearly toothless mouth. "I never thought I would ever see one in my lifetime." He stuck out his hand. "I am Bern Abris, and your name is?"

"You may call me Nieve," she said. "And this young man here is Raynes Bellworth."

Master Abris turned to Lady Parendil after shaking Raynes's hand and gave her a gap-toothed grin. "This is almost better than what I imagine it would be like, witnessing everything that has lived in this hothouse for so long, surviving freely in a wilderness made for it."

"One would beget the other, would it not?" Lady Parendil told him.

He nodded, his eyes resting warmly on Nieve. "You are a beautiful thing to behold, dear girl. Something so many of us preservationists hope to see in our lifetime. What a gift indeed."

"If I may sir," Raynes interjected, "I find what the Lady describes Miss Nieve to be difficult to understand. Can you perhaps explain it?"

The old man tilted his head and stared at Raynes for a good long moment. He then leaned back and clutched the cane's pommel to his belly. He exhaled, chewing on his gums for a moment. "The low-folk cannot often understand the ways of the Mennin, dear boy. And those with the connection of blood to the Mennin cannot easily explain it. How does a frog explain a river to a sand-serpent? It is a conundrum. But one I've spent many years ruminating upon.

"You see all this?" He gestured to the conservatory and all its exotic contents. "This place holds the last vestiges of a world that no longer exists. There are a few of us, all those of the sacred bloodlines, who have dedicated our long lives to preserving what we could of the far-lands as the sands closed in upon the protected lands of the colossus."

"Preserve it for what reason? If the sands are to simply devour the land?" Raynes asked bitterly.

"Some claim for the regrowth. To have these treasures seed the new life once the curse has passed. But I am confident that the world of the veils has preserved the things the sands took away, and once set off, the regrowth will bring it all back.

"For my sake, all this is to preserve the memory of it. To keep the dream of restoration alive. To remind us what it was all for—this curse and the sands. To help us all work towards the ultimate goal; to return this world to what it once was, my boy. That was the plan from the beginning. For the land to return to its state of fecundity and lushness. For the clouds and rains to bless the dry lands, and for life to remerge again in full force. Only this time without the scourge that destroys it." The old man's last words were imbued with both anger and with disappointment.

"The sand…" Nieve muttered.

"No. Not the sand," he replied with an ironic chuckle. He lifted his cane and pointed it at Raynes. "That is your scourge, right there."

"Eh?" Raynes asked, his brows rising up in astonishment.

"You common-blooded people. The unpowered. The unconnected. The *lowest* kind of human. The one that destroys its own home. The one that puts its own personal desires above the welfare of the whole world. *That* scourge." The old man lowered his cane and gripped it again against his stomach as he gazed out at the greenery. "The Mennin always resented their common-blooded cousins. Because they possess no spiritual connection to their mother world. No sense of gratitude or deference for the gifts she bestows.

The common-blooded creatures, they stumble about, pillaging this paradise, leveling the forests, poisoning the waters, never giving back, or giving due for what they take. In the days before the sands, these were dark times. There are few records that document how bad it actually was. The civilizations then were advanced beyond our modern understanding—with wonders that we can scarce dream of today. But it was untenable, and unsustainable. The common-bloods were the largest portion of the people. And they were a scourge. Waging wars that destroyed everything. Raping the land for everything they could squeeze from it. Destroying entire species of animals for sport. Poisoning the air and the water and the earth. Yes, we are all related, all peoples. But we were, and still are, nothing alike.

"The living sands, those are a result of that resentment. *They* are the curse. The means to end their reign of destruction. Every man, every woman, every child of this people that have been consumed by the sands to become part of it—they have been destroyed for a reason."

Miss Nieve gasped in shock and her eyes grew wide. The color drained from Raynes's face. Tears brimmed Nieve's eyes and she lifted her hand to her mouth in horror.

"The living sands grow with strength and power with every low-human it absorbs. It will only stop when it has overpowered and incorporated the life-essence of the last low-human in the world. Only then will the world be left to restore itself. It will be restored for those that live in harmony with it. The mennanfae, which are the Wyldwaerd and the saed, and the lower magical people." The old man turned and set his eyes upon Nieve. "She is the first Saed I have ever seen with my own eyes. But I have never left the greenlands. Your kind fled to the sands when their counterparts, in a rage of anger,, created the curse of the living sands."

"I don't understand what you are saying," Raynes interrupted, his brow furrowed in confusion and distress

"The highest kind of Magical being are the Mennanfae. The men are called Wyldwaerd and the women are the Saed. The Saed are known to temper their counterparts, for the Wyldwaerd are rather violent and horrid by nature. The magic of the females is made to balance them.

"Just before the time of the division, there was a terrible plague that somehow only harmed the womenfolk; and it decimated the Saed. It took such a number of them that the Wyldwaerd that were left behind fell into imbalance, and a faction rose up from them that believed that the Saed did not balance them but made them weak. This faction, bent on their natural acrimony and anger, began to act in reckless ways.

"The better part of them left the veil. It was during this time that the common-bloods were at their worst. Without the balance provided by the Saed, the choice to act was taken in the most drastic fashion. They formulated a plan to eliminate the existence of the low-humans altogether. You must understand, the Mennanfae, they are stewards of life itself. To suggest such a thing is simply beyond the pale. No matter how awful the low-humans were, no creature deserved to be wiped out.

The Wyldwaerd reveled when their remaining counterparts rebelled against them for this terrible plan, and abandoned them. The Saed would not partake in this wholesale destruction of an entire people. The Saed took to the veils, or fled the center-lands, venturing into the newly forming deserts as the Wyldwaerd enacted their destruction upon the world.

"Once all the Saed had abandoned the center-lands and the circle of colossi, the congress of selection was created to keep them out and keep the Saed from making the Wyldwaerd weak. With all their balance-makers absent, the Wyldwaerd became even more indifferent to others. Without their counterparts, the world-bound Mennanfae used the low-humans and low-magic humans to procreate their lines. It diluted them a little.

"My family, Lady Parendil, even you, Miss Nieve, are a product of those watered-down family lines. The infamous Wyldwaerd rage has been distilled into them simply being unpleasant people." He laughed. "I have been an unpleasant person most of my life. There are still the Wyldwaerd who support the original objective of the faction, their hatred for the common-human as potent as ever. They will find ways to undermine you, Miss Nieve."

"How?" she asked. "And more importantly, what are they preventing? I do not understand what my role is in all this. What am I to do?"

242

The old man shrugged and emitted a burdensome sigh. "I do not know a great deal about those things. I just know what I now. But be warned. A Saed in the center-lands is a dangerous thing for these descendants of the bitter faction. They would be incensed to know that you have bypassed their congress. Be prepared for some kind of resistance."

Nieve could not take her eyes from the old man.

"This is how the world is now. The world-bound Mennin blood is diluted with lesser blood. But the magic remains. The Saed, and other magical peoples, like the Morsded and some others, they live in the deserts. No pure low-human can without risking becoming part of the sand. So the ones that remain are all here in the greenlands. And the living sands will not stop seeking them until they are all gone. The veil preserves much of what has been taken by the sand. It holds it in expectation. But it cannot be freed until the curse of the Wyldwaerd has come to fruition and all low-humans are gone. Or…" He paused and leaned forward, leaning his elbows on his knobby knees.

"Or there is a great burgeoning," Lady Parendil interjected.

The old gentleman nodded. "One that is great enough to send the greenlands out to the desert countries, which will summon more Saed to return to the protected circle of the colossuses. These center-lands, where their counterparts are. They will make the race of the mennanfae complete again. That alone could overpower the curse and send the green back without the complete annihilation of the low-humans."

"The old Mennin, those who created this curse, did not know this could happen when they first began their siege against their own counterparts and the low-humans. But the ancestors in the veils knew. And they've hoped for it to happen. The Wyldwaerd, once they realized that there was a flaw so great in their plan, realized the only way to keep their curse from being undermined was to stop the Saed from entering the greenlands. So the selection congress came to be." Lady Parendil said.

"How did I get through the selection congress if I am this Saed you speak of then?" Nieve asked. "Or my aunt, for that matter, for she would be Saed, too, would she not?"

Master Abris paused and reflected on this. "I imagine the ancestors of the veil had a hand in it. The other lower magical people can come and go freely. The Morsded. The Brill. The Torised. The Sylphians. There are many. They live wherever they please. They are the blessed people. The ones deemed worthy to live in harmony with our sacred world."

Nieve had been so filled with doubt when he began his narrative. It sounded all nonsense to her. But a little scratching, scraping wiggle of suspicion began to consume her, one where she believed the words uttered by this old man were true.

"Why do you pin so much hope on one Saed?" Raynes asked. "She is but a girl. What is it that she can do that makes her so important?"

"The magic that sustains the world, the life, the breath of the land, it is all the work of the Mennanfae. The veil now serves the Saed alone in its way. The Wyldwaerd hoped to use it to restore the world after the sand had cleansed it, but it is only magic that can work when the Mennanfae are complete. When the feminine complements the masculine, when they are joined. Separated, they are nothing. The world is starved of their magic.

"The Mennin understood that it is the very nature of the Saed to protect *all* life. And that they would not tolerate such a plan to destroy the low-humans.

"When the Saed had all fled in rage, their counterparts erected the ranges and lifted the plateau from the sands. The colossi kept the Saed from the source lands. Until the Wyldwaerd *wanted* to let them in. They allowed the sands to consume everything else first, and to spare these lands until the very last where the Mennin would take shelter and foster the bits of life they could spare that was not relegated to the veils.

"But the ancestors of the veils, they are the ones who desired a different outcome. And they must have found a way to deceive the congress of selection. To finally let the Saed return before the curse played out entirely. Perhaps it is because it was always this young lady's fate. I do not know on that end. The opportunity may have presented itself to the ancestors. Who can truly know?"

Abris paused when the housekeeper entered with a chamber maid to bring them a lovely meal of cold meats, cheese, a delightful vegetable potage, and a savory, tart salad of pickled summer yields, and chopped cellar vegetables that accompanied the smoked and cold-baked meats delightfully. There were also rolls of freshly baked bread still warm from the oven.

The four of them arranged themselves around the small round tea-table and served themselves from the little wheeled cart the housekeeper had rolled into the conservatory. The conversation had stopped for the time being, and there was just the sound of silverware on good china, and the occasional mumble of appreciation for the meal. Nieve helped Master Abris to serve himself of the soup, and passed the bowl to him. He slurped noisily and grunted in approval. He then put the spoon down after a few more slurps, and looked at Nieve. Then at Raynes, who was watching Nieve with a gentle, affectionate gaze.

"One can only speculate how this Saed entered the sacred lands. But what I do know is that you are not the right kind of man to be with this girl."

Raynes's eyes pivoted with no shortage of annoyance upon the old man that scolded him.

Lady Parendil nodded emphatically. "Indeed. She needs a nice, healthy, hardy Mennin-born man. And they need to be together. And their affection will turn into magic. And their love will empower the growing things to reach out and defeat the sands, and in turn, to break through the great walls and summon back the Saed who left willingly, but who were ultimately, banished. She is pivotal. So, so important." She reached out and patted Nieve's hand.

"If you wish to save what's left of your kind, boy, you best help her get where she needs to go." Abris exclaimed. He then snatched up his spoon and drank from it.

The old man had to be somewhere close to a hundred years old, but there were no bleary, watery, cataracts to dull the sharpness of his gaze, and there was no senility to dull the cut of his words. Lady Parendil, on the converse, although bright-eyed and bushy-tailed, had an almost child-like air to her. She wasn't as sharp, or clear-minded as the old man. She ate a roll, her eyes fast on Nieve..

"Wait a moment," Nieve interjected. "How can the Lady Parendil have the power of Mennin sight if she is a woman?"

"She is Torised," the old man replied matter-of-factly. "But her father was Mennin-born. The Torised are few now. They were the keepers of the freshwater seas. They dwindle as those seas are now under the sands, but they are gifted to see what many cannot."

"And what I see is that you must find your counterpart that the circle bonded to you," Lady Parendil insisted. "The colossi are falling, and there is no going back now. The Saed are free to enter the source lands as easily as the sands now. The sands will either achieve their purpose or they will be stopped. The only thing that can do that is the union of the Saed with the mate the veils chose for her."

"Then we ought to finish eating and be on our way," Nieve concluded in a near-whisper. She put her fork down. She'd hardly eaten two bites. Not half a moment after she uttered the words, she fell from her chair onto the ground, and collapsed into unconsciousness.

24. Devotion

Raynes buried his face into his hands and groaned loudly. Outside, it had begun to rain, and the sound of it battering the windows was almost deafening.

The room was curved gently, like a bow, with four tall windows looking out on the gloomy park of the Mardlan House estate. The green folly was in full view behind the pale, gauzy curtains that let in the spare light of this strange, humid cleft in the earth.

Nieve was in the bed, her face covered in a sheen of perspiration, her breath labored and wet sounding with a little wheeze. The doctor from the village had come by and dispensed an electuary of herbs that he directed them to dissolve into hot water and to give her four times a day. She'd just had her first dose of the honeyed liquid, supplied by the spoonful by Raynes who had not left her side for even a moment since she had fainted.

She had regained consciousness when Raynes lifted her shoulders onto his knees, but was weak and woozy. To add to the moment, every bird in the conservatory had fluttered down from the branches of the hothouse trees and settled on her person. Over her legs and on her lap, on her fingers and arms. Their song was silenced. Raynes's hand fell upon her damp brow and he frowned.

"I think we need to summon a doctor," he told the old man.

"I'll find the housekeeper," Lady Parendil offered. She got up and scuttled off as quickly as her old legs could carry her.

Master Abris immediately called for a bed to be prepared and for a fire to be lit when Mrs. Gees arrived with the Lady, for Nieve was shivering now, her teeth clattering.

She was brought to a room upstairs by the servants and undressed. She was tucked into the bed in her shift and heaped with blankets to keep her warm. Raynes washed her brow down with cool water to soothe her, and whispered to her quietly of things she had talked about before. Of her horse at Halenwood. Of the places she loved there. Of the Narroway Grange that she hoped to live in one day. Of everything but Tammin.

Her lucidity came and went. Sometimes, she would utter a word or two. But it was Tammin's name he heard the most, and with each utterance of it, his heart broke a little bit more. He did not let it discourage him from caring for her. He remained fast by her bedside as both the Lady and the old man came in to check in on her.

Raynes stayed with her through supper and had soup in a mug while reading to her from a book about the once-great river and waterfalls that had existed on the eastern valley which was now a but a basin of sand with only small oases strung along the old riverbed.

The old man shooed him out after supper. "Go and have a glass of sherry. Sit with Lady Parendil and clear your mind, boy. I shall watch the beloved Saed."

Raynes left reluctantly, threading his way down the spiral stairwell. He navigated the dark corridors with a candelabra in his hand. He found Lady Parendil dozing off by the fire. She shook herself awake when she heard him come in, and sat up. When he served himself of the dark ruby liquid from the decanter, she begged him for one of her own, which he supplied readily, coming to sit beside her.

"Is she better?" the old woman asked, accepting the offered cut-glass goblet and drawing from it. She closed her eyes to savor it.

"Slightly. The honeyed medicine seems to be helping. Her breathing has softened. The wheezing has stopped. She is still feverish," Raynes replied, sipping his drink, thinking for a moment how much he had changed since he had met the girl.

He lingered upon these thoughts, while Lady Parendil sipped her drink.

"You are kind and devoted young man. But you must hope no more, for it is not your lot," she warned him.

Raynes let the words sink in a bit. He drained his glass and put it on the narrow table between their two chairs.

"I love her. I *truly* love her. If what you say is true—that greenborns or Mennin born or whatever they are—if they are made gentle and made kind and swayed by the power she wields, to love her—then my love is the only *genuine* one. Not his. His is a love assisted by magic. Mine… it is true. Halenwood—he is not what is best for Nieve," Raynes uttered.

"He what is best for the world, my dear boy. And you must never decide what's best for someone you love. You must know that! The most tragic and unnecessary of divisions that can intervene in true love is the idea that one of the lovers might decide independently what is best for the other," Lady Parendil said defiantly. "It speaks of a distrust of the other's choices. And trust is paramount. Trust and acceptance." She sighed deeply and shook her head in resignation.

"Her fate is sealed, young man. Sealed by the very fate of this world, which itself is calling her to save it. You *must* accept this. And you must accept your role in it all. For you do have a role in it, boy. Will you unselfishly stand against the sands and fight for the fate of *your* people, or you would allow your self-interested desires to allow the sands to consume what is left of the world, along with what is left of your people?"

"My people…"

"The ones the living sands hunger for. The ones they seek to consume and absorb until there are none of you left. The ones the Wyldwaerd have cursed." Lady Parendil reached out and picked up her glass.

"I should return to Miss Nieve's side," Raynes murmured, his eyes fixed sadly upon the old lady's wrinkled hands.

"You should enjoy that coveted position for now, for your place at her side will soon be occupied by another. And it is something you must allow for the sake of all of us. This is your fate. This is your role. To ensure that they are united, and that they can be who they are meant to be, and do what they are meant to do."

Raynes stood and gazed at the old woman, looking past her for a fleeting moment. He then dropped his gaze to the floor and shook his head. "I changed the very essence of who I am to be acceptable to her. Of my own volition. Not under the influence of the Mennin blood. And she still does not see me." His voice took on an edge of vulnerability that was unlike Raynes in every way.

"This is not a lament sung by you alone. There are lovers all over this world who love someone who cannot love them back. She loves who she loves. Magic or no magic. If you do indeed love her as you say, you must let her be happy. For her happiness should mean everything to you."

"It does," he croaked, his voice breaking. "But it hurts here…" His hand curled into a fist which thumped repeatedly, hard upon his chest. He fought back emotions as he spoke, his eyes going glassy in the firelight. "From the beginning, those bright eyes, and that cutting, truthful way about her sliced my very core out of the beast that had grown around me like a prickly shell. I loved her, and I never knew how to show her, how to make her to turn her eyes to me. I only knew then cruelty and shock would capture her attention for fleeting moments. Even those moments were cherished to me. I wonder, if I had known better, known to approach her in the way Tammin did. With openness and kindness… I wonder if I could have captured her heart then…?" His voice was hoarse and bare. His emotions rode just on the edge of his expression.

"You will never truly know. But in my experience, Mr. Raynes, true love like theirs is there at the start. I think you never *had* that chance. And if we look now at what they are, you two were *never* meant to be." Lady Parendil drained the last of the libation and daubed her lips with a sheer white napkin. "You have your own fate to follow, young man. You will walk away from this a better man, thanks to her. Perhaps better prepared to be what the world needs you to be, eh?" She arched a pale brow at him, her wizened face offering him a conciliatory smile.

Raynes bit back the painful pressing of his hurt and pivoted on his heel. He vaulted back up to the chambers where Nieve lay quietly slumbering on her side. The old man got up and they exchanged quiet greetings. "She's just had her medicines. She's resting again, don't wake her."

As he left, Raynes sat down in the chair, still warm from Master Abris's narrow backside. Nieve's fever seemed almost abated now, and her sleep was restful and deep. He crouched by the bed and peered at her face closely. Her nose was red, and her cheeks ruddy from the remnants of this illness. Her lips, slightly parted, were pink and full. Her eyelashes rested just above on the swell of her cheekbones—dark crescents that seemed in that quiet, intimate moment, to encapsulate everything that Raynes found charming about her.

"You are so very precious to me, lovely Miss Nieve," he whispered to her. "How will I ever reclaim my heart from you?"

Nieve took a deep breath and closed her mouth, exhaling through her nose. She stirred, twisting slightly, and curling deeper into herself, burying her face even more deeply into the pillow. Her hands slid up under her chin still clutching the blanket.

Raynes let his knees fall to the floor, and he stayed there, staring at her, unable to stifle his sense of loss anymore. Unknown to Nieve, he allowed some tears to fall, grieving the love he would never know.

The morning came with another rainstorm, but it also brought Nieve back to life. She was rested and feeling slightly better, eager to get going. She insisted she was well enough to continue the journey toward Halenwood. She did not want to delay her voyage another minute.

She was dressed warmly, and a clay bottle was filled with hot water and some of her medicine and placed next to her on the coach seat. The three of them sat inside the coach with Raynes' horse tethered to the back of it. Their trunks were loaded, and they were sent on their way with a kind farewell, their stomachs warm with porridge and tea.

Nieve remained slightly under the weather and quiet for the next two days. Her constitution slowly improved, but she was still weakened and frail from the day she fainted. She kept herself wrapped up in a quilt borrowed from Mardlan House. Lady Parendil insisted that they ride no more than eight hours in a day, so they retired early at whichever most comfortable inn they could find each night.

The news from the edgelands was grim. The sands seemed to be winning the fight wherever there were breaches. The edges of the plateau were sliding into the sands, and the ridge-walls were crumbling. From the talk at the inns from other travelers, the number of breaches varied. One person said there were nine, another claimed there were twelve. The drafted soldiers were overwhelmed and the breach force was spread thin. There was also word that two more of the colossi had fallen.

The news had a draining effect on Nieve, and it was almost like it served to undo the progress she'd made in overcoming this wasting illness. Raynes watched over her and fussed at her until she ate something and was forever tucking her blankets and shawls around her. When she complained her feet were cold, he lifted her ankle boldly, slipped off her boots, and warmed her feet with his hands while the old lady dozed beside her.

Nieve was too weak to protest, and too grateful for the care. She hated that it gave leave to Raynes to position himself so close to her, and to be so informal and comfortable with her, but in all honesty, she was too glad to have this attention when she so needed it. In fact, the warmth she felt towards him was a little alarming. She stared at him a few times as he sat across from her, rubbing her feet absentmindedly while peering out at the greenery going past the windows, and she reassessed her impression of him.

He had indeed changed in all the essentials. This clumsy bully who had made her life so difficult these past years was calm and thoughtful. Attentive and kind. Considerate and gentle. He was so good-looking. She had always thought so. Tall and graceful even. His narrow waist and wide shoulders, his lithe way of moving about. Fashionable in his clothing, brightly colored waistcoats and gold edging. The finest of nankeen breeches and shining top-boots. He fussed with every deliberately wayward lock of his blond hair, and preened like a young woman with his cravat, but never for a second was he anything less than manly. She had noticed the longer she was in his company at inns and public houses that his eyes were ever on her. For there was invariably a handsome, pretty girl to be found, but he never noticed them, even if they noticed him.

She wondered what prompted this change in him. Surely it was maturity that had brought him 'round and showed him a better way of getting someone's attention. She lamented that it was hers he sought. The truth was, Nieve had come to like Raynes quite a bit. She had resisted it, but he had spent so much time doting upon her when Tammin had gone. Whether it was doting with laughing bullishness, or doting like this, it was earnest and well-intended. He loved her. She knew that. She wasn't sure where her feelings fell for him on the spectrum of affection, but they were warm. With Tammin's absence it was easier to recognize the qualities that made Raynes appealing, mostly because she missed these very things about Tammin.

She glanced down at her hands which were lying slightly curled on her lap, barely clutching a small book she'd been trying to read. Her feet were still in his hands, but his eyes were closed, and his head was tilted back. His hands were slowly falling quieter and quieter until they stopped moving at all. With a little pig-snort, he slumped over a bit and was in a deep slumber thereafter.

She suddenly wondered, in passing, what happened to her little hairpin. She last remembered having it at the inn before Mardlen Hall. She wondered with regret if she'd left it there or dropped it. She worried for her little sprite.

The coach reached Halenwood at the eleventh hour of the night. Lady Parendil did not want to stay another night out on the roads, and opted for the coach to continue until it reached Nieve's home. The staff was awake to receive them, and had prepared rooms well ahead of time, having gotten notice from Adaskus from the Viscount.

The housekeeper helped Nieve down from the coach, but it was Raynes who caught her when she wobbled.

"Watch yourself. You need to get inside and rest," he told her.

"You should go sleep in your own bed tonight. That ought to be a comfort," Nieve replied. "Take one of our horses if yours is too tired."

"I shouldn't leave you," he said.

"I am fine," she assured him. "I have the staff. They are all familiar and comforting to me."

With a reluctant sigh, in the light of the coach-lamps and the house-staff's candlesticks, he put his arms around her again and hugged her to his chest. "I'm worried about you."

"You are not drunk this time, Mr. Raynes. You don't have a good excuse to be so familiar with me," she warned him, half smiling.

"I will take every advantage I can," he replied laughingly. He then stepped back and bowed. "I shall see you in the morning, first thing."

"No you shall not," she warned him. She then put herself into the care of the housekeeper.

Nieve was ushered to her rooms and the local physician was called at once by Mrs. Yaymes, Halenwood's housekeeper. She had been hired shortly after the Viscount married Landie. She was a wonderful, warm, kind woman who adored Nieve, and she was not pleased to see how wan and ill the girl appeared upon arrival.

Nieve was tucked into bed at once. There was a relay-letter awaiting which the housekeeper handed to her as she tucked her in. She opened it listlessly, just happy to be someplace familiar and warm. The letter informed her that the Viscount and her aunt were going to opt for travel regardless, because there were sand-clouds to be seen on the other lakeshore. They had set out only two days after Nieve had left, which meant they would not be far behind. She felt greatly comforted by this. She would not be alone here for much longer. She only wondered where Tammin was, and if he was safe.

Tammin, who had arrived only the day before, was unsure of what to think of the display he witnessed as he stood in the darkened room, looking out at the driveway below. The angry, dark, jealous feelings bubbled up with the same fire and fervor he had experienced in the days before he knew Nieve. It was that same blackness that had fueled his thuggery. He bit it back as best he could as he watched Raynes finally step away from his embrace with Nieve.

When the servant arrived to inform him of their arrival, which Tammin had just witnessed due to his sleepless worry, he learned that Nieve seemed ill.

"The Miss has come home, Master Tammin," his man muttered. "I was not going to wake you, but Mrs. Yaymes said the girl looks a might more than peaked. She said she's lost some weight and she's pale as death. She suspects the girl is very ill. She sent for the doc. I hope that's all right," he rambled.

Tammin could only set aside his covetous heart at this news, and put on a banyan and slippers. He would see to Nieve himself, and hopefully, clear his worried mind of all doubts.

25. Infirmity

Nieve had only just folded up the letter, and was pulling her covers up over her shoulders when there was an insistent tap on her door.

"Who is it?" she asked in a faint voice.

"It's me, Tammin," a familiar voice replied.

She sat up, and then carefully covered herself with the blankets. "Come in!" Her heart, which had felt nothing but heaviness and sorrow for days, suddenly lifted and pit-patted in her chest. Even in her weakened state, she felt heat rush to her cheeks. He was home! Her heart swelled even more at the sight of him sliding through the doorway. Her stomach fluttered and her eyes grew glassy. "You're here!"

At first glance, Tammin looked angry, but the sight of her seemed to dissipate it. He advanced and sat boldly on the edge of the bed, reaching to embrace her closely. "You're thinner," he remarked when he drew away. "You look ill, Nieve."

"I haven't been feeling well at all," she confessed, grasping his hands. "But seeing you has made me feel much better. When did you arrive? How did you manage to escape the edgelands when they are so under siege?"

"The Fohomok sent me," he said. "They said I had to be here. I knew they were right."

"I'm *so* glad to see you, Tammin," she said with gushing happiness and familiarity. "I wish Mrs. Yaymes had mentioned it. I'd have come to say hello the moment I arrived."

"I saw you arrive with Raynes," he ventured.

Nieve had no reaction of guilt or anything untoward when he made this observation. "Yes, he insisted on accompanying us when we left Adaskus, the Lady Parendil and I. But I am now so grateful for his company. He was so attentive and kind, and made withstanding this illness in travel bearable," she confessed, still easy and happy—pleased to see Tammin. "I was determined to come back to Halenwood. There was a time where everyone was persuading me to rest at Mardlan House in Revechelle. I did *not* want to stay. No matter how awful I felt. I hoped you would be here, or you would come home soon, and I didn't want to wait another day."

"I don't know if there was great wisdom in that decision. You might have made yourself worse for it," he scolded her, reaching out to caress her cheek. "But you are home now. And according to the Fohomok, you and I, we have an obligation to fulfill. We must return to Winden. But we can do no such thing until you are well."

"But the sands, Tammin," she exclaimed weakly.

"The sands will do what the sands do. We cannot endanger *you*," he muttered decisively.

"I suppose another day, but no more," she murmured.

She slid down, tired, but her gaze was fixed on Tammin as she rested her head on the pillow. Tammin kicked off his tapestry slippers and brazenly moved to lie beside her, turning onto his side to gaze at her.

"I missed you," he told Nieve.

She reached out with her warm hand, and laid it upon the side of his face, her thumb tracing the line of his nose and then resting gently on his lips. "I missed you too," she replied in a whisper. "Every day."

"Now, what is the meaning of Raynes putting his big, dirty mitts all over you like that? I was not happy when I saw that," he grumbled, crossing his arms.

She gazed into his green eyes which caught every shred of light cast from the candle on the table, and the flames of the fireplace, and his gleaming black hair, which was a bit too long, and needed a cutting. His face was also unshaven, and he had dark stubble on his jaw line, something she'd never seen before.

"You almost have a fine moustache, Tammin," she giggled, making it rasp with her thumb. She then yawned and shook her head against her pillow. "Raynes is clumsy. He has confessed that he loves me. And he has begged me to forget you. But he understands those are impossible things. He has been forward and affectionate. I confess I have allowed it. Because I've grown to respect and like him very much, and I feel sorry for the heartbreak I am causing him."

"Correction: the heartbreak he is causing *himself*. Has it progressed to anything more than such embraces?" Tammin asked cautiously.

"Like what? A kiss?" Nieve asked, a wry smile forming on her lips. She was mocking Tammin a bit.

He did not reply.

"Rest your worries. The most intimate thing he did was to warm my feet with his hands in the coach, and he fell asleep doing it."

Tammin laughed softly.

"He learned something about you, about the matter that drove a wedge between you as friends. And he knows it was a great misunderstanding," Nieve told him.

Tammin's brows rose in curiosity. "You know *why* he grew to hate me? I never entirely knew. I suspected it was because he thought I interfered with his relationship with a girl he was interested in. She was below him, yes, but I never did anything to stop him. I always thought it was why he hated me."

Nieve frowned, saddened that *both* of had severed their friendship over such silly misunderstandings. She quietly explained it to him until she grew too tired to continue. Tammin shucked his banyan and slithered under the blankets, wrapping her in his arms. She melted into him without the slightest hesitation. She fit as if she belonged. With a tremulous sigh, she succumbed to sleep in her Tammin's arms, neither even remotely concerned about the propriety of it. They'd loved one another too long to care. Just before slumber took her, she slid her hand up under his arm and across his back, notching herself in under his chin, slipping a leg over his.

"I do love you so, Tammin," she whispered. And with that, her arm fell heavy, and she began to snore softly.

Come morning, the chambermaid entered, and upon seeing the two cuddled so intimately, she blushed and scurried out of the room. Mrs. Yaymes entered a while later carrying a tray with a teapot and two cups. Tammin was awake but dared not move with Nieve sleeping in the crook of his arm, her hand lying on his chest, and her warm breath blowing on his neck.

"Has the doctor not yet come?" he asked Mrs. Yaymes in a soft voice. "She's like a hot coal."

"I received a note last night. The physician has been attending a difficult birth with Madame Vorenne. He assured me that he would come as soon as he can, Master Halenwood," she said. "In the meantime, I've made her tea with the concoction sent by the last doctor to see to her a few days ago."

The woman took the situation in stride. She was aware that Nieve felt great affection towards the young son of the Viscount. Before she brought them breakfast, she gathered the staff to put a quick stop to the talk and chatter that was already going about below-floors. She nipped it all in the bud and firmly with the support of Mr. Neyalm, the elderly Butler, and commanded the house staff to respect the privacy of the family.

It was clear to Mrs. Yaymes as she delivered the tea that this was merely innocent cuddling and nothing more. Even if it had not been so, it was nobody's business except perhaps the Viscount's. And according to the staff that had been here longer than she, he had grown to be rather permissive and soft over the past few years, and would likely show little concern about the two young people.

She set down the tea tray and served a cup for Tammin. He took it with his free hand and tried to sit up a little. His stirring woke Nieve, who groaned and rolled onto her other side, freeing his other arm. She saw the housekeeper and slid deeper into the covers.

"Can we not call the physician from Istril instead? She's extremely unwell," he asked.

The Housekeeper sank into a curtsey and withdrew to do just that. Only a few moments later, the sound of hooves could be heard retreating from the livery.

"You stayed all night?" Nieve asked, her voice weak and raspy.

"I could scarce abandon you when you are so ill," he grumbled, his hand falling upon her forehead and her cheeks. "You have a fever."

"Again?" she whined. "Why will this fever not go away?"

"There is a doctor coming. We will see. I will go and dress, and then I will bring you some breakfast. You must eat."

He withdrew from the bed, leaving a cool void beside her. She shivered and rolled herself up further underneath the heap of blankets, and dozed while Tammin left to prepare himself for the day.

The sound of hooves brought hope for a physician, but instead brought Raynes, who entered the home without knocking and quite boldly vaulted up the stairs, his greatcoat flapping at his heels, a tall topper on his head. He was surprised to find himself face-to-face with Tammin when he reached the top.

"Good gracious, when did you drag yourself back from the sands? You look a fright," Raynes blurted, laughing uncomfortably, removing his hat.

"Why are you here?" Tammin snapped.

"To see Miss Nieve of course. She was not well yesterday, and I am bringing her back her charming little hairpin that I forgot was in the pocket of my green coat." He pulled his hand from his pocket to reveal the wood-sprite hairpin that Nieve thought she had lost. "She seemed to like the thing a great deal. She will be happy to have it back. I'm unsure how it got there. My man found it this morning when he was preparing to clean my travel clothes."

Tammin reached out and snatched the thing from his hand. "Thank you. She's in bed sleeping. You best go home now."

He gave Raynes a sidelong glance as he guided him down the stairs again. Raynes could almost feel it burning his skin. When they reached the bottom of the stairs, Tammin stopped and faced his old friend.

"Nieve explained some things to me last night when the two of us were in bed, preparing to sleep," he said wryly. Raynes bristled, which made Tammin smile a bit. "Seems we must reassess the events that created our enmity. If there is a need for it, of course. There might be something to benefit from the two of us needlessly hating one another."

"You have Nieve. That's reason enough for me to continue hating you," Raynes murmured bitterly. The two stared at one another for a brief moment.

"You have her, too, in a sense," Tammin said in a surprisingly softened tone. "She seems to cherish you in her own way."

"It's not enough," Raynes replied hoarsely. "It pains me to even think of the two of you together."

"Then go home," Tammin replied. "Forget our friendship, forget her. Go."

Again there was a pall. "She needs me," Raynes finally exclaimed. "Whether she knows it or not. With or without you. She needs me."

"Then figure it out for yourself, Bellworth. Figure out where you will stand with her and with me. And make your choice. We're both here, whatever you decide." Another long span of silence fell between them.

"Is she better?" Raynes asked, moments later.

"She's worse than she was last night. She became feverish during the night," Tammin replied.

"Then we must do what we can to fix it. I shall ride to Menrach. See if the Aldech Shaman will come. If the physician could not cure her, perhaps a mage-healer can," Raynes suggested. "She is a magical creature, after all."

Tammin tilted his head. "No use in not trying. That's an idea with merit."

Raynes bowed to his old friend, offering him a wan smile. "Then I'm off." And he threw his topper onto his head and stalked out in a flare of a greatcoat.

26. Hexis

The Shaman was a flamboyant fellow of about thirty-five with a pair of impressive sideburns that consumed most of his jaw and were brushed out like a fox's mane. He had a set of eyebrows that were nearly as remarkable, which had been combed upwards into a stylish swish above each eye. He wore a shining silk taffeta waistcoat the color of the sky with narrow, matte stripes cutting through the shining weave and lovely silver buttons on the double-breasted front. Over that he wore a fashionable blue frock coat with the most extraordinarily tall collar that brushed the tops of his ears and sloped down over his shoulders almost to the seam of the armscye.

His stockings were robin's breast red with ornate clocking that rose up from the shining patent leather of his expensive slippers. His breeches were black with little rows of those astonishing silver buttons at each calf-hem along with ribbon ties. He arrived on a stylish curricle with a handsome pair of matching dapples driving it. He swished into the house in a forest-green greatcoat with no fewer than six capelets stacked on his shoulders and threw off his elegant beau topper with its swept brim into the hands of the footman with the flourish of a stage performer.

To Tammin's shock, he also wore two small silver hoop earrings. Like a pirate. And had an indication of some kind of tattooage that peeped out occasionally under his ear, just above the edge of his stiff shirt-collar and densely pleated and tied cravat. He had the airs of a dandy, but the feel of a brigand in a gentleman's clothing.

"I am here to see a lady, I understand?" he intoned in patrician, stiff-upper-lipped tones.

Tammin, who'd barely made it to the bottom of the stairs to receive him, merely arched a brow in astonishment at this character who'd invaded his home. Raynes, who'd just followed him in, gave Tammin a look of cynicism that nearly invoked laughter. They both stifled smirks as the Shaman, having heaped his heavy greatcoat onto a staggering footman, demanded in the haughtiest voice to be taken to the lady at once.

Tammin nodded and swept his hand toward the stairs. The peacock of a man climbed the steps like a dancer, prancing to the top to impatiently await the other two gentlemen, fussing with the buttons on his cuffs with a look of irritation.

He swept into Nieve's chambers as if returning to the stage for an encore, and moved to the bed with his brow arched in curiosity. "Oh my, oh my..." he murmured, reaching for the fob that hung from the watch pocket of his fall-fronts. He withdrew not a watch, but a quizzing glass, which he wedged into his eye socket as he bent over Nieve's sleeping form.

"It is wise of you to have summoned me. There is nothing a mere physician can do for this lady's ailment," he told the young men who stood with their arms cross, gazing dubiously upon the man. He put one knee on the bed to get closer and put his face right up near Nieve's, sniffing deeply the air around her. "Hmm... Mmm yes. Yes. I will need my bag. Send a man to my conveyance please," he ordered them with a wave of the hand.

Tammin, incredulous, still complied. He rang the cord and gave the orders when the chambermaid arrived, all while watching this man closely as he now crawled on the bed and hovered over Nieve, peering at her with his quizzing glass. Tammin could see Raynes barely containing his irritation at the scene.

"I've seen this before in other forms. None quite so severe. *This* form… it is new to me in so much as I've never witnessed it firsthand. This is a thing of the past. Something the cunning-folk of the olden days would see, before the time of the sands. I have, however, read about it in the Codex of my predecessors.

"It is *Hexis*. She is in possession of something that does not belong," he explained, dropping his airs for all-seriousness. He slid back to the floor, and popped out his eyeglass, tucking it back into his watch pocket. He unfastened the multi-colored, massive death's-head buttons on his frock coat and stripped it off. "Someone means to waste her away. Someone wishes her harm." He loosened the cuffs of his shirt and rolled up the sleeves. In doing so, he revealed a festooning of tattoos covering his arms. "And it is not someone of middling power. This is someone of the ancient sources. Someone of consequence and authority. Someone the like we have not seen in, oh, a century at least."

As he finished rolling up his second sleeve, the door opened and a footman entered carrying what looked like a traditional physician's bag. It proved to be anything but traditional when the Shaman opened it. He began to remove a panoply of magical items. In particular, he removed a large tome from the bottom, spilling out bones and crystals, talismans and a stack of folded papers that shuffled to the floor. He put the book on the bed and threw it open, turning pages, turning them back, licking his finger for traction, leafing away through until he came to find what he was seeking.

With his back to Tammin and Raynes, the Shaman clutched his elbows and rocked on his hip as he read, murmuring under his breath as he did. The back of his breeches was particularly puffy at the gather, making it look rather like a wrinkled pumpkin as he balanced back and forth in concentration. Tammin and Raynes were barely unable to contain their amusement.

Nieve, who had managed to sleep through most of it, stirred and rolled over, cracking open her eyelids long enough to take in the stranger at her bed. This woke her, and she tried to sit up. She gaped at him, her pale face making her eyes appear even larger than they already were.

"Who are you?" she croaked in a raspy voice, rubbing her eyes with the heel of her hand.

"I am here to help you, my dear," the Shaman replied absentmindedly, turning the page on his book. "Someone doesn't care for you to have a happy, long life, it seems." He glanced up and gave her a strange little smile and then returned to his reading, his finger tapping the book as he did.

After a bit, he exhaled in resignation. "Well, we shall have to give it a good old try, shan't we dear lady? Can't have that Hexis thing burdening you with something that will continue to do you harm, can we? I will need you to unclothe yourself entirely."

"I beg your pardon!?" Tammin barked. His fists balling up, he threw himself toward the man.

Raynes was quick to grab onto Tammin's arm and to keep him from throttling the strange fellow.

"For this to work, she will have to present herself to the world as she would have done on the day she came into it." The Shaman turned to Tammin and gave him a look of resignation as if this request were a great burden to him. Only then did he seem to notice the expressions of ire on the faces of both of the young men.

"You needn't fear young man. I am well versed in the anatomy of the body, and I have seen my fair share of them in this trade, just as many as a lowly physician might. It is of no shock to me." He waved his hand dismissively. "And in the state of torpor I will be in, induced by the magical work that I must do, I would scarce notice it anyway. It is necessary. The instructions are quite clear here." He tapped on the page of his book. "She cannot have anything foreign upon her body. No jewelry, no clothing. She must be in her fully natural form."

"Then we shall have chambermaids to shield her with a sheet," Raynes barked.

"I am not comfortable that you are applying magical treatments by written instruction alone. Have you no experience at all with this?" Tammin asked.

"This is old magic—*that* I can confidently affirm. But it isn't impossible for me to perform what is described here. It is something of Mennin origin. The illness that besieges her, that is. The cure for it is listed here quite explicitly," the Shaman assured them. "It was written by one of my predecessors whose magic was very likely no different than mine. It can be done. As I've said, I've performed *similar* arts before."

"You will respect her privacy, and you will allow her to stand behind a sheet," Raynes repeated.

Tammin didn't seem like he was finished expressing his trepidations.

The Shaman ruminated for a moment or two and then assented with an irritated wave of the hand and instead set to eviscerating the contents of his bag and arranging things here and there along the edge of the bed where Nieve, already fatigued from this minimal effort, was huddled underneath her mountain of blankets, clutching the edges underneath her chin.

She watched him with drowsy eyes, a slight look of alarm on her face, her gaze shifting between the flamboyant, tattooed interloper and the two young men who were scarcely keeping from assailing him. When he was finished riffling about, and fussing with his things—between pauses to reference his codex—he straightened and reached up, flatting down the wild tousle of his auburn hair.

"It's time for your maids to come," he commanded, shifting his hands to his hips.

Raynes summoned the chambermaids and the three men exchanged loaded glares between them.

The chambermaids arrived in due time. When they did, a large bed sheet was spanned between them, and Nieve was told to go behind it.

"Take it all off. Leave not a stitch on her skin. That little pendant, too. All of it." The Shaman commanded.

Tammin's rage bubbled up, and Raynes gritted his teeth. But they both crossed their arms, and looked on, trusting that the man had some idea of what he was doing..

Nieve shivered, her smooth skin rising up into myriad goosebumps. Even with the fire blazing warm in the hearth, there was no relief from the fever-induced chills that already possessed her body. Adding to it, she was now standing near the fire without a hair of clothing upon her, holding her forearm against her breasts and her other hand covering her most intimate parts. She trembled in solitude behind the sheet the chambermaids—who looked as bewildered as she—were holding up, trying to quiet her clacking teeth.

"It would be ideal if we were in a period of syzygy—when the bodies of the sky are in proper conjunction, but alas we are not. We will make do," mumbled the Shaman as he fumbled about with his supplies.

"How long must I stand here? It is cold and I'm tired," Nieve whined.

"Another moment, girl. Patience. One does not exorcise a Hexis easily. There are preparations to be made," the Shaman replied intolerantly from the other side of the sheet. There was more noise of things being moved about. "Ah… may I use your drinking water? It will save the maids another trip downstairs."

Nieve did not reply as she heard the water being poured into some vessel from the decanter that had been on the side of her bed. "Do you truly comprehend the magic of the Mennin?" she asked instead.

Silence fell.

"Magic is magic," he barked after a lengthy pause.

His replay did not exude the certainty or assurance that Nieve had hoped it would. She shivered, chewing her lower lip. "That does not inspire my confidence."

Nieve's patience for all this was at its end. She was miserably cold, she felt herself weakening by the moment, and the sense of urgency to get to Winden was growing with fervor. Especially now that she knew her ailment was inflicted by magic and was aimed to stop her from achieving whatever it was she was supposed to do at the stones. To wait any longer was madness. To remain, and risk having this quack of a sorcerer perform magic upon her that he did not fully understand was even more worrisome. She frowned darkly and was overcome with an irrational desire to flee immediately.

After a moment of listening to the man fuss about with his supplies while whispering the instructions as he repeatedly returned to his codex to read them, Nieve straightened from her shivering huddle. She caught the eye of one chambermaid, and then the other. Her finger rose up silently to her lips and she furrowed her brow. Each girl gave her a subtle, acknowledging nod.

With that, Nieve quietly moved towards the door of the dressing room which was hidden by the stretch of cloth between her and the Shaman and slid through it. Her maids remained in place, one smirking to the other as their ward crept away. And there they remained while Nieve closed the door silently behind her.

The naked girl proceeded to rummage through the drawers of her armoire in search of clothing. She furnished herself with silk stockings and then drew a set of wool ones over those and put on a thick linen chemise. Nieve's head was swimming from fatigue and weakness, but determined, she continued to dress.

She put on some old, yellowed stays, and over that a wool petticoat. She did this quickly and by herself, opting for a drop-front gown so she could dress without the assistance of a chambermaid, who was at present occupied holding a sheet to hide the fact that Nieve was no longer there.

She furnished herself with her walking boots, and a heavy cloak, and her last item, the little wooden hairpin that Raynes had only just returned to her via Tammin. She clutched it in her hand and exited through the servant's entrance which was blended into the pale green paneling.

By the time anyone realized she'd slipped away, Nieve was trudging up the steep path towards Winden, hoping Tammin would know where to find her when they discovered her absence.

27. The Whispers of Winden

Nieve could scarce breathe without a sharp, rasping pain in her lungs. The effort of running away had taken its toll early on in her escape, and she found her progress to be frustratingly slow. She fell short of air quickly, and dizziness consumed her senses. She staggered past the path to the quarry and around the glade overlooked by Tammin's rock. She had to stop and lean on the smooth bark of the white-barked shade-witch trees to catch her breath. It felt like the closer she got to Winden, the more her weakness grew.

Damnable Shaman, she thought to herself. *Useless idiot.* He served only to enlighten her of one important thing… she was cursed. She was certain beyond all doubt that it was Mennin magic— the purest of its kind—that was crushing her. She sensed the urgency of the moment. She understood what the curse was meant to achieve, and what she risked if she did not reach Winden in time. She counted on Tammin to follow. She could not get him, since he was present in the room when she escaped the Shaman. But he would know where she had gone, of that she was certain.

She gathered her willpower and forged forward, stopping only briefly to catch her breath. She would not be responsible for the demise of all common humans. Not if it was within her power to stop it. She set her teeth and forged on.

"What do you mean?" Tammin roared, his face flushing hot red in his rage.

He stormed across Nieve's room and burst through the door of the dressing room, witnessing where Nieve had left the door ajar in her stealthy escape. It only took Tammin a moment to register what had happened and he was scaling down the stairs in haste only a few seconds after. He did not bother with adorning himself with a coat, and he strode right out into the misty day after Nieve.

He did not expect what befell him the moment he set foot out into the garden. Whatever it was, it was powerful. He dropped like a sack of coals, and crumpled to the ground.

Raynes, who'd followed Tammin out into the cool, wet morning, gaped at him in confusion. "You need help, Halenwood?"

"Good gracious, this household is besieged by the cursed," the Shaman observed casually from behind Raynes, giving Tammin a rather dismissive look as he languished on the ground in a sudden bout of weakness.

The younger man turned to glare at the magus.

He pointed listlessly at Tammin. "I take it you do not have the eyes of a magic bearer if you do not see the drain curse that is enveloping your friend," he informed Raynes impassively as he donned his overcoat. "The more of his strength he expends trying to move toward his goal, the more his body will become powerless."

A footman handed the Shaman his hat, which he placed on his head. A chambermaid also came in tow, carrying the man's heavy bag of paraphernalia.

He had thrown a bit of an ill-tempered fit when he discovered Nieve had made her escape, throwing up his hands and declaring he was finished with this madness. "I leave you to your own devices then, if you cannot respect my diligent efforts," he had bellowed, throwing his magical items back into his bag.

"What can be done?" Raynes asked the man as he clattered down the granite steps to the gravel towards his waiting coach.

He paused and peered at Raynes with a look of incredulity on his face. "You're a powerless common human, I take it? Do the only thing you can do in this sort of situation. Walk through all the magic that can hinder *us*. That is *your* power." He sneered as if he was disgusted by his words, or even just by the existence of Raynes himself and swept away like a lady in a huff.

Raynes frowned and walked up to Tammin as he lay there, trying to get up, standing over him with crossed arms and a rather amused look on his face. "Problem?"

Tammin, irritated by Raynes's flippancy, roared out in anger, and tried to get up again.

"Seems like I'll have to step in and fetch your girl myself." Raynes grinned cruelly.

"You touch her and I'll…." Tammin growled, glaring up at him from the ground.

"Oh, stop. I won't touch her." Raynes shook his head and sighed as if he was bored with Tammin's outrage.

"I must to be with her. That is why we are here. I *must* go to Winden," Tammin roared.

"Then let us go to Winden Hill," Raynes said lightheartedly. "I'll get you there." He loped off to fetch a horse or two.

* * *

Nieve heard the whispers of Winden long before she came to the hilltop. The forest seemed to close around her on the narrow, steep path as she struggled to take each step towards the stones. The soil felt as if it was turning itself to muck beneath her feet, making it even harder for her to walk. She heard the voice of a raven as it hopped through the boughs of the trees above her, and the flutterings of other creatures around her, as if their existence had somehow surged forward into her awareness and filled her senses with their noise and movement. She could feel the life and strength of the trees, both enveloping her with their canopy of boughs and their sprawling tangle of roots beneath the soil, almost bursting with energy and power and life. As she felt the world's life surge, she felt her own strength drain from her body. As she walked, she felt as if the roots of the trees themselves were trying to keep her stable even while the soil eroded beneath her feet.

In her hand, which had been clenched white-knuckled around her hairpin, there was movement. She staggered to a stop, wheezing and gasping, leaning against the ancient retaining wall, her breath ragged and heavy. Her fingers were numb from the strength of her grip, and she had trouble opening them. But as they peeled away from the wooden chip, she saw that her little friend had melted into its living form and was elated to be released from her iron grasp.

It clambered to its vine-riddled feet and quickly escaped the palm of her hand before she could trap him again, climbing up her arm to her shoulder where it reached out its little hand. Its little vine fingers sprouted more tendrils, and they stretched out to grasp the ferns that were growing from the cracks on the stone wall. Nieve collapsed onto her calves, slouching against the wall, too weak to continue. Tears formed along the brims of her eyelids. It was as if she was going to fail the whole world. She ought to have asked Tammin to help her. She ought to have known she would be impeded by this curse.

The sprite leapt off her shoulder and swung to the wall using his vines, and then climbed up towards the roots of a towering walnut. To Nieve's astonishment, as soon as he gripped the surface root, the little sprite hugged it and disappeared into the pattern of its rough bark as if he melted right into it.

Within a moment, the great tree shivered and trembled. Its leafless limbs quivered and twitched. Suddenly a great bough swept down, and the branches flattened into a scoop, sweeping Nieve up like a mother snatching up her baby. She found herself being lifted into a basket of twigs and branches. She rolled onto her belly as she was brought aloft, and watched below as the roots of the tree yanked themselves from the grip of the soil in order to move closer to the next tree.

Accompanying the tree was a flurry of small creatures. Birds and squirrels, badgers and mice, forging a path ahead as other trees, somehow, reached out their branches. As one tree touched another, the animating life-force of the sprite was carried along, giving their movement strength and purpose. From tree to tree, each one carefully passed the listless, weakened Nieve along like a delicate doll, from one heavy bough of carefully spread branches to the next. From bare-limbed deciduous tree to prickly spruces, she floated up the hillside in the arms of the forest, accompanied by a small army of fauna.

Meanwhile below, rocks dislodged and rolled down the hillside, battering at the foot of the trees, and a small piece of the retaining wall gave way, making one of her bearers slide down just after passing her onto the next. The land was rebelling against the living things—working to prevent what was happening from succeeding.

The whispers grew increasingly frantic. The desperation of life itself, of the trees and the animals. The few that remained as the sands advanced expressed themselves in a din of voices around Nieve. They needed her. As the trees passed her along, one after the next, she rose to where the timberline ended and the trees could no longer carry her.

She was deposited carefully onto the ground by a creaking, crooked pine, and she tumbled into a tangle of limbs and skirts onto the gravelly path, gasping out. Her body felt as if she was made of lead. The land shivered beneath her, threatening her. The circle of stones was so close.

The wind lashed at her here, blowing her skirts around her legs and body, chilling her to the bone. She could scarcely breathe, and she was gasping through what felt like a strangled throat to swallow even the smallest bit of air. She lay on the ground on her side, wheezing. The animals fussed around her. Some pushed her towards the hilltop and the stones with their heads, but none were large enough to budge her.

It was then she heard the sound of hooves, cloven, delicate, and tentative. A small herd of deer appeared along the path, with two wolves, several wild boars and a great rock cat which slinked along, its muscles sliding beneath its smooth, deep brown hide.

We are the life, the breath of the land, the voices called to her. *Beware the water and the soil, the stone and the winds.*

Stones rolled as the animals approached, taking two deer with them down the steep hillside. Another small landslide took a bite out of the hilltop and part of the path. But the magic of the standing stones held true, and the ones that escaped the assault by the elements of the land and the air arrived to help Nieve.

The big cat circled her, its golden eyes watchful of her as it studied her body. As gently as a mother cat, the predator wrapped its mouth around her upper arm and gingerly locked its teeth around it. It began to tug her towards the circle. The wind became more violent and insistent as the wild cat pulled her along. The wild pigs nosed her, shoving her rather brusquely. The deer were gentler.

They drew her over the lip of stone smoothened by decades and decades of wind and rain, and as soon as her body crossed the threshold, the wind stopped. The land settled. And Nieve felt her strength return in a hot, violent rush.

She sucked in her first deep breath of air in what seemed like an eternity, and took several gulps, tears falling from her eyes. She lifted her upper body up on her arms first, and her shoulders rose and fell as she calmed her thirst for air.

The animals did not abandon her. They remained, and more gathered as she collected herself. By the time she was able to stand on her own feet, the entire circle was surrounded by forest creatures. The cat, however, remained beside her. She used the cat to steady herself and turned to look at the trees which trembled in spite of there being no wind, nor shaking of the earth.

Her sprite had somehow extricated itself from its merged state with the trees and wove through the maze of legs and paws and hoofs toward her, tottering, tiny, and seemingly insignificant. Nieve knelt as he approached and lowered her hand, palm-up for the little thing to climb on. She then straightened just in time to see a large draft horse round the bend and hop with astonishing ease over the gaping gash that divided the pathway. On its back was Raynes, and behind him—slung behind the saddle like a heavy, droopy pack—was Tammin, who looked much like Nieve had only a few moments before. Waxen and weakened, his wild, dark, terrified eyes locked almost immediately upon her face.

Raynes rode his horse right through the barricade of living creatures. They parted to let the great stomping horse pass. He dismounted as soon as the horse came to a stop, and reached to help Tammin. Tammin batted away Raynes's hands and slid off the horse, trying to compose himself.

When he was suitably in order, he approached Nieve, and put his arms around her. She reciprocated the embrace, and buried her face into his chest.

28. The Wildening

"If I had known your illness would be dispelled by the stones, I'd have brought you here the moment we arrived home," Raynes told Nieve over Tammin's shoulder. She released Tammin and moved around him, capturing Raynes's hands.

"Thank you, Raynes, for bringing Tammin here."

She turned to look over her shoulder at her beloved who was gaping at the animals all around them. Raynes did not reply, but only gazed at her and smiled wanly. She could see the hurt and the loss in his eyes, and she felt sorry for it. But there was no time for lamentation. Not when the colossus she'd come to see that very first time with Tammin was no longer along the horizon. Only a bleak grey sky and, at the edge of the greenlands, a dark, dusty cloud.

"You have my gratitude, Raynes, but now you must go. Get to the bottom of the hill as quickly as you can."

Raynes dropped her hands, and turned reluctantly, giving Tammin a final glance before throwing himself up into the saddle and reining his horse around. They watched him pass through the phalanx of fauna, and disappear down the path at a clumsy canter. When he was well out of sight, Nieve turned to Tammin.

"I'm not sure what's required of us. But we are here, as we were needed," she said.

Tammin looked up at the tall stones, and then spun slowly, taking in the stark view, the greenery spreading out like a great coat across the rippled landscape, the steeples and gables and towers of buildings rising up over the trees, and the patchwork of farmed lands in the distance. The winds had returned, but now they were the natural kind uninfluenced by the magic of the Mennin.

Had they given up? Had the presence of a Fae in the sacred circle tamed them at last? What now? Nieve wondered.

Tammin moved to her side and took her hand. His fingers were warm and comforting. The skin, dry and a little rough, slid across hers and tightened around her hand. How she had missed him. She felt like she'd spent most of her life missing him. Even before she even knew him.

At that moment, it felt like there was only she and he in the whole world. She felt a rush of heat in her eyes, and the tears stung as they filled the brim of her eyelids and dolloped over onto her cheeks.

"Why are you weeping, my dearest Nieve?" Tammin asked. He turned to face her, placing his hands on each side of her face and using his thumbs to wipe away the tears.

"I don't know. I am just... tired. Tired of being parted from you. Tired of all the things that stood to keep us apart, and all the people who had somehow interfered. All I want is to be with you without intrusion or obstruction; without the legacy that burdens us."

Tammin took in her thick, tear-heavy lashes, her shining eyes, and wrinkled brow. How he loved this face. He could not help but bend down to kiss her, covering her delicate, rosy lips with his. When he withdrew she let out a little gasp, and that only made him want to kiss her more. He gripped her jaw and drew her in again, this time bearing down upon her with a kiss imbued with passion and desire. A little noise rose up in her throat and she leaned into him, her hands traveling up his sides to his shoulders and then his head, her fingers lacing through his dark, thick hair.

The winds had picked up again. The whispers returned in jubilation, and there was freshness in the air that smelled like spring and like lushness and like the unfurling of new life. All around them the wind and the voices roared in celebration. The animals that had accompanied Nieve raced out into the forest, and the trees swayed as if in happiness.

The couple scarce noticed. They were spellbound in their passion, the intense love of their embrace, and the deepening heat of their kiss. The veil reached out to them, wrapping them with its magic, and they were drawn into it, the circle, a protected space. The creatures danced all around them. The air became spiced with scents and sensations that only intensified their passion and made them forget where they were.

The voices intensified as their meeting did. Tammin's hands slid down her shoulders to the nape of her neck, and then they moved to the front, to the place underneath her bust, where he found himself unfastening the drawstring of her gown. They were no longer standing in the bare space of the standing stones, but in the veil's version of the place, where there grew a bower of leaves and flowers had sprouted up from between the stones and enclosed them. It was seething with movement from the tiny fairies and nymphs and sprites that populated it.

Forgetting themselves and everything else, Tammin and Nieve knelt down into the soft leafy bedding of this magical place, and submitted completely to the other.

Outside the veil, away from the circle of stones, where only but the faintest shimmer of a shadow of the couple could be seen, the world was changing. With every moment, the edges of the greenlands surged forward in pulses, like the beating of a heart. The vines and trees and sprouts threw themselves out against the onslaught of the desert and took root in the seething roils of the living sands.

Storm clouds gathered and rumbled, and electric charges spidered along the cloud-bottoms. Rain fell in thick drops, splattering the earth. The storm washed the sand dust from the leaves and the surfaces where the clouds had blown in from the incursion, and merged into rivulets along the ground, carrying it back out to the edgelands and into the rivers and lakes.

Powered by the veils themselves, , and the merging of Life and of the Earth, the vines arced out in great reaches, . The Fohomok and soldiers who were battling the encroaching sands stood in awe as the green lushness of the shrinking greenlands suddenly began to retake what had been stolen, and then expand even farther beyond the plateau in great explosions of growth.

The vines and tendrils plunged deeply into the living sand, invading it with growth and roots and moisture that slowed its movement, made it sluggish and heavy and eventually inert as the flora and the rain and runoff filled it, separated it, diluted it, and infused it with life. The people of the greenlands watched in astonishment as their sacred green, their consecrated Life, spread across the deserts faster than their horses could run, and surged through the sand settlements and washed around the sand-ships like a great wave, splashing over the buildings and covering the sand in a burgeoning of mosses and ferns. Seedling trees sprouted up, their trembling leaves reaching up to the sky as new ones swiftly unfurled on stems that grew with preternatural speed.

The land and the winds and the skies were beholden to life once again. The Wyldwaerd that had wished to destroy everything were rendered powerless in their private spaces. They roared in protest, but they were unheard over the jubilation of the life within the magical place. For the first time in centuries, a male and female of the Mennanfae had reunited and consummated their love, beginning the process of rendering the world back to the way it ought to be.

The Fae magic spurred the great Burgeoning. The fecund Fae living in the sands were now inside the spreading green, and the barriers that kept them from the center-lands, and from the men that they were fated to be with was gone. The curse was broken.

29. The Mennin

The sky was grey and bleak, and the clouds appeared heavy with rain. Nieve's suspicions were soon confirmed when a fat raindrop plopped onto her nose. She reached up to wipe it off, and Tammin took his umbrella and opened it, lofting it above her head. The sound of the raindrops pelting the taught fabric increased in cadence as they walked.

Around them, the city of Dufren bustled. Two coaches clattered by, one four-in-hand, the other with a pair of dexterous sand-dancers which looked too delicate and spindly to be pulling the tall curricle. The driver huddled underneath the calash, his passenger—a lovely dark-haired, olive-skinned desert beauty—laughed loudly at something he said, and he joined her in mirth. Around them, people walked along the sides of the broad street and crossed between coaches and riders, some jogging to dash between raindrops.

The tall, plain-faced, austere architecture of the buildings seemed off-putting against the greenery that burst from between very building and over the top of every roof. Trees that looked a hundred years old had only appeared a few months before. Now they swayed in the breeze, and the leaves trembled from the rainfall.

"It's so different," Nieve muttered, still struck into awe. "I spent two summers here, and it was as bleak and sandy and lifeless as Rethros was. And now it, too, is probably like this…" She could not believe she could hear birdsong here, nor did she ever imagine she'd catch the scent of petrichor on the street of this former desert city. She clung to Tammin's arm tightly, a whimsical smile on her face.

They'd chosen to tour the former desert countries for their honeymoon now that there was no more congress of selection to stop people from coming or going from the greenlands. It had expanded to such a point that it no longer required any control. And it continued to grow, once and again, and with increasing frequency as the daughters of the Mennanfae found themselves drawn to their male counterparts who were now traveling freely as well.

Every growth spurt that overtook the sands, now weakened and barely alive enough to fight, meant that another couple had united. And when it was accompanied by a storm, it meant they had united in *all* senses of the term. Nieve blushed at the thought and bowed her head, the red creeping up her neck and washing over her ears.

Tammin smirked as if he sensed Nieve's train of thought and raised a brow. "Perhaps we need to go back to the Inn? The edgelands could use a little expansion."

Nieve rolled her eyes and giggled. "Stop."

She hugged herself closer to him, and they walked on underneath the pummeling rain. They found Mr. and Mrs. Bellendean at the tea house where they said they would be. They were gathered around a small standing table where they were partaking in a cup of tea and a plate of freshly baked scones with thick lemon curd and vibrant red raspberry jam which the shopkeeper had apparently made from the newly grown berries that had come up in her formerly barren garden.

"*There* you are," Mrs. Bellendean exclaimed, reaching out her gloved hands for Nieve. The younger girl accepted them. "Is it raining again? How extraordinary it all is." Mrs. Bellendean giggled.

They'd met Mrs. Bellendean and her husband at the Inn at Booros, the first city they visited on their honeymoon tour. Mrs.

Bellendean by some great coincidence was a friend of a girl that Nieve had grown up with. That connection was all that was required to foment a firm friendship the moment they sat down for supper. They traveled together as they had a common destination: Nieve's home city. She wished to visit her family's former home.

"We took the liberty of ordering a service for you only a few moments ago," Mr. Bellendean explained as the couple joined them.

Tammin shook his new friend's hand and thanked him.

"How was your walk, dearest Nieve?" the fair-haired greendlander asked. She was lovely as a flower, her pale hair surrounding her face in perfectly shaped curls with a cap and bonnet over the back of her head. The bonnet was pale lavender and it framed her face so beautifully. She wore a rose-pink walking gown and gloves the color of wine. Her shawl was a pale wooly white draped over her left shoulder, and she carried a delicate, cane-length umbrella.

"Mind boggling," Nieve said with a sardonic smile. "It is a different world from what I recall."

"Oh, yes. I'm eager to see how Rethros has changed," Mrs. Bellendean agreed. "These sand-strong buildings just look strange as anything surrounded by wild growth. I don't think I'll ever get used to it."

"I will force myself to get used to it. If I don't see another grain of living sand for the rest of my life, I will be cheerful evermore," Nieve declared with a sweet smile. She leaned back so that a fresh steaming cup of tea could be placed before her on the table. She avoided Tammin's gaze, as the moment the words escaped her mouth, she saw a wry, slightly lascivious smirk forming on his lips.

"I don't see any sand in my foreseeable future," he mumbled, his brow rising up suggestively.

Nieve blushed a deep rosy red and avoided further eye-contact.

"Well, where shall we venture to today? Perhaps stop at Sableston? See what has become of the little oasis?" Mr. Bellendean suggested.

Everyone nodded emphatically at this idea, and they discussed their plans further as they finished up their tea.

The foursome took to the street towards the inn where their coaches awaited on the wide sandstone cobbles. All around them, even in the pelting rain, the people of the former desert countries were out and about, all smiles and pleasantness.

We started this, Nieve thought to herself. *We brought this glee to the world.*

The oasis of Sableston was now a broad, shimmering lake, which had unfortunately taken a few of the buildings along with it as its shores had grown by an untold amount in the Great Burgeoning. But the people of Sableston seemed quite unperturbed by the loss of a few houses and streets. Instead, there was already new construction activity taking place on the edges of the shoreline. And again, as they had seen as they had made their way over the former edgelands into the newly greened lands, the people of the sand country were elated and happy. There were new patches of farmland being tilled, bringing the scent of upturned soil.

The rain had abated and the sun was shining this fine afternoon. The two couples found a lovely guest house to occupy at the edge of the lake, and agreed to go on a brief walkabout in town to see the sights. As usual, Tammin and Nieve took their own path, and they left the Bellendeans to their own devices. They did this mostly because since the day of the Great Burgeoning, and their union at the top of Winden Hill, it happened that wherever Nieve went or lingered for even a moment, a little blossom of life would follow. Wherever there was wood, life would emerge from it. Wherever there was stone, a soft peach fuzz of moss would flock the surface. Wherever there was growth, tiny fairy creatures would appear, or flowers would bloom as if accelerated in time.

Tammin had a similar effect on the world, but his was somehow more inclined towards the animals, and they found that whenever he was out and about, there was some kind of wild creature nearby. Birds were especially present. Particularly, for some odd reason or other, the Oak Eagle, which with its shimmering blue-black plumage, could sometimes be startling when the massive bird would alight on a nearby tree, or fencepost, or land noisily on a window-ledge to peer inside at them wherever they were. His effect was not as apparent as Nieve's. Especially when they were anywhere for any length of time. Their rooms at Halenwood had become a bower in and of itself, teeming with little creatures.

They were no exception, however, as the weeks went on after the event. As new Mennanfaes' powers were awoken by the life around them, stories began to filter down to the couple about a young woman here or there who was leaving a path of lush, vibrant, beautiful life in her wake. Nieve had been agonizing over the whole idea of that happening during their wedding, but as the stories became more frequent, she grew slightly more comfortable with what she was, and who she was. She did not enjoy the attention it brought. She hoped, after time, and after more Saed appeared, she would become less of an attraction.

The Bellendeans took it in stride. What they witnessed of it. Mrs. Bellendean especially was quite adept at ignoring the tables growing sprouts and leaves, and the minuscule creatures crawling out of budding flowers and leaves and scampering or fluttering away. The only thing Mrs. Bellendean did acknowledge with aplomb was her desire and adoration of Nieve's hairpin. "Oh, it is simply precious. I do wish you would let me have it."

At Sableston, the blossomings were as they were, however it did attract attention that Nieve had dreaded from the moment she and Tammin and united. And that was the encounter with one of the ancient Wyldwaerd factionists. It was the first occasion where their enemy had been given a face. They would learn that they were not completely safe from encounters with the bitter, seethingly rageful old men that tried so hard to destroy not only the race of common humans, but also the entire world, and ultimately, their connection to their own counterparts, the Saed. The creatures of the veil protected the couple by whatever means they could. But when there was a Wyldwaerd, they could do little to stop him from facing their precious pair.

It happened in Sableston. But the encounter taught them how to put an easy end to these confrontations.

That day, at the lakeshore, they were walking together as they always did, Nieve's arm clutched around Tammin's. Nieve, who was already so beautiful, seemed to glow even more brightly since her full awakening, as did Tammin seem even more handsome if not still a slight bit brooding. They stopped to take in the prospect from a partially flooded road. As they stood there, the stone on the road began to exhibit a growth of mossy green and some tendrils of grassy plants began to push up between the joints of the wide sandstone pavers. An eagle emitted a piercing cry and appeared in the sky above them circling. It landed with a bit of a swish onto a branch that dipped and swayed under the weight of this massive bird.

They were so absorbed in the view, and their moment, that they did not see the older fellow appear along the road, scuttling towards them. As he neared them, something a little extraordinary happened. Their wings and horns—seen only once inside the veils while they danced what seemed like ages past—began to take shape and become visible to the naked eye. It was Tammin who noticed it first when Nieve's wing brushed his collar and left a moth-dusting of glowing flecks on his shoulder. He stepped away, and Nieve, peering up from beneath the brim of her bonnet, gasped in shock.

"Oh! You have horns again!" she exclaimed.

Tammin turned and pointed at her wings. Nieve, unable to see them round the edges of her bonnet, turned rather comically twice before glimpsing the tip of one of her long dragonfly wings. She covered her mouth and giggled. "What's this? We can't go anywhere like this!"

"How would you enter a doorway with that span?" Tammin replied laughingly.

Nieve lowered her wings to rest behind her, parallel to the length of her body, covering the back of her skirts with the glimmering dust.

It was then that Tammin witnessed the presence of a third person. It was a man of about sixty years of age or so. He wore a banyan rather than a frock coat, and he had a little pillbox hat on his head in the same garish, old-fashioned fabric. He looked as if he'd stepped right out of his sitting room to find them.

"You can't hide from the likes of me, you despicable traitors!" he shouted angrily.

He did not approach. He remained a good ten or twelve lengths away from them. It only took Nieve a moment or two to understand why. He feared that her presence would temper him. Nieve, feeling slightly irritated by this confrontation, taunted him by dropping her arms and advancing on him. He almost fell from scrambling back and away from her.

"Why would we need to hide?" Nieve asked, tilting her head and clasping her hands innocently. Her wings rose up again to their full width, and she smiled in the most pleasant fashion.

"You will allow the scourge to repopulate our precious world again and destroy everything!" he shouted.

"They are a form of life," she replied, stepping towards him once more. "They are our responsibility as much as everything else. We must protect them, as we were always meant to do. If they once took the world and the gifts we gave them for granted, then it rests upon us to ensure that doesn't happen again. Killing them, that is not the answer."

She advanced upon this older man slowly. Her bright eyes had captured his, and he was almost immediately beguiled by them. After a few steps, he stopped backing away. He remained rooted, his gaze locked onto hers. Nieve sauntered forward and lifted her hand. When it came to rest upon his shoulder he was fully subdued. He almost trembled at the sight of her. Her touch brought forth his hidden traits—his horns coiled into existence. The spiraled, heavy, gold-flecked cornicles were like those of an aged ram. His shoulders sagged and his head lowered as if he felt the weight of it all of a sudden.

A half-hour later, he was happily ensconced on Nieve's other arm, accompanying them to the inn where he insisted he would take tea with them. The parade of the three magical creatures—followed by the dense blossoming, the flurry of living creatures, insects and magical sprites, along with the flutter of wings, and the padding of wolven feet in their wake—was a sight to be seen. But the most significant thing taken from this brief encounter was that the time of the angry, vengeful Wyldwaerd was past. And the return of the Saed meant that the anger could be defused, and they could be made right again, undoing all the damage that had been done when they parted the first time.

It would be that soon, all the rageful remnants of the Wyldwaerd would be subdued by the presence of their true counterparts again. And the world would once more be in balance, with the presence of the common human amongst its now lush and thriving life.

30. *As it ought to be*

"Landie and your father will be meeting us at Redsands in two weeks as planned, and then will travel with us to Rethros," Nieve declared, her hands folding the latest correspondence from Halenwood. "She says that the little one has grown so, that we should scarce recognize her."

Tammin nodded, tilting his head to look at Nieve for a moment, lowering the book in his hands. He had committed to taking several examinations upon their spring return to the center-lands, in order to receive a diploma from his college. He spent most of his evenings with his nose in a book, or taking prolific notes. He had a trunk filled with his tomes, and the footmen clearly resented him him for it.

Outside, in a tree, a great flock of starlings chattered and chirped in the trees in front of the guest-house, settling in for the night.

"This is where she lives? Your grandmother?" Tammin asked.

Nieve nodded. "Indeed. She is most keen to see us. We had resigned ourselves to never seeing her again, after having been given our residency permits to the greenlands. This is an unexpected benefit of the Great Burgeoning, I suppose. We are able to see our relatives again. I do not remember her very much in truth."

"If she is anything like the family I am familiar with, she will be a delight," Tammin assured her. "And my family will be able to meet her too, as we are all to converge there."

Nieve nodded emphatically.

"I am shocked to be speaking these words, but I look forward to seeing my father." He chuffed through his nose at the irony of it. "Also your aunt. And my little sister too."

Nieve's eyes smiled at her new husband. Just as she did, a pair of Ravens landed on the windowsill outside and pecked at the glass.

"Shoo birds, shoo!" Nieve shouted, jumping to her feet and waving her hands at the window. When she stood to do so, she left behind a cushion of newly grown springy moss.

In Nieve's hair she felt a little tickle of movement from her hairpin. She reached up and brushed the smooth wood with her fingers, feeling the little thing almost trill with pleasure. With a pert little smile, she took her husband's arm, and they joined the throngs into the great opera house of Rethros, which on its walls still depicted the scenes of the sands that once surrounded the place.

As her eyes swept the soaring ceilings of the space, she caught movement. Her gaze stopped on a little leaf unfurling from the wooden truss that crossed the vaulted ceiling. As the leaf opened, a tiny fae—which was little more than an assemblage of flower petals, stamens and stems, with a tiny round face—unfolded itself from within the bud of the leaf and stood as it spread out beneath its feet. It peered down at her, and with a delighted smile on its miniscule face, it leapt gracefully off the leaf. From behind its back, in a smooth, liquid transition, a pair of butterfly wings in a bright sapphire blue edged in gold and crimson blossomed, catching the air. It glided away over the heads of the audience. A hand reached up from the throng, and a enchanted giggle ensued as the fairy alighted on a lady's finger.

Ahead of them, by only a few paces were Landie, her grandmother, the Viscount, who had the elderly lady on his arm, and was charming her delightfully with his handsome smile. They were all appointed in their finest for this performance of the The Wildening, a new opera just created by Rethros' most revered composer. Little did the composer know that the couple that he wrote the musical performance about was in attendance at its opening night.

There would be some clue of it, for the cavernous space was budding with little signs of life, and tiny creatures, sparkling and bright, were dropping from the growth and flying about above the heads of the audience as they filed in. It was so accepted now, that the people merely reveled in it.

This was the world that was meant to be, Nieve thought, her grasp on Tammin's arm tightening. She was beaming with contentment. She peered up at him. He too was enraptured by the little scene. He looked down at Nieve, a soft smile forming on his lips. Things were as they ought to be. That is what his expression said. He twisted his shoulders and planted a kiss on her lips and grinned at her. His beautiful eyes were unchanged from the first moment she met that fateful day at the lake. This ruffian in gentleman's clothes. Oh, how she loved him so. Her Tammin. Her beautiful Wyldwaerd.

The End

Miranda Mayer

About the Author

Miranda Mayer lives in the Mount Hood territory of Oregon. A polyglot, artist, avid historic costumer and lifelong equestrian; her interests are broad, and edge on geekery most of time. She is married with one child.

Miranda's stories range from Science Fiction to Urban Fantasy to Fantasy. She writes from her heart, imbues her writing with her quirky humour, and tries very hard to make her characters as real and three-dimensional as possible. Her unpredictable and rather Attention-Deficit-Disordered nature guarantees that her stories will take readers to unexpected places.

The Seed of Winden

Other titles by Miranda Mayer

The Trilogy of Tinna:

Tinna's Promise

Tinna's Might

Tinna's Reign

Red Slipper series:

The Wizard King

A Problem of Ghosts

The Beast with Silver Eyes

The Red Witch of Tirdonne

The Belletrist

Blackroot

With author Shéa MacLeod

Wolffe & Bane – Book 1: The Talisman Killer